BENGAL'S QUEST

Berkley titles by Lora Leigh

The Breeds

BENGAL'S QUEST	BENGAL'S HEART
RULE BREAKER	COYOTE'S MATE
STYGIAN'S HONOR	MERCURY'S WAR
LAWE'S JUSTICE	DAWN'S AWAKENING
NAVARRO'S PROMISE	TANNER'S SCHEME
STYX'S STORM	HARMONY'S WAY
LION'S HEAT	MEGAN'S MARK

The Nauti Boys

NAUTI ENCHANTRESS	NAUTI DREAMS
NAUTI TEMPTRESS	NAUTI NIGHTS
NAUTI DECEPTIONS	NAUTI BOY
NAUTI INTENTIONS	

Anthologies

OVERCOME
(includes novellas "The Breed Next Door," "In a Wolf's Embrace," and "A Jaguar's Kiss")

ENTHRALLED
(with Alyssa Day, Meljean Brook, and Lucy Monroe)

NAUTIER AND WILDER
(with Jaci Burton)

TIED WITH A BOW
(with Virginia Kantra, Eileen Wilks, and Kimberly Frost)

PRIMAL
(with Michelle Rowen, Jory Strong, and Ava Gray)

NAUTI AND WILD
(with Jaci Burton)

HOT FOR THE HOLIDAYS
(with Angela Knight, Anya Bast, and Allyson James)

THE MAGICAL CHRISTMAS CAT
(with Erin McCarthy, Nalini Singh, and Linda Winstead Jones)

SHIFTER
(with Angela Knight, Alyssa Day, and Virginia Kantra)

BEYOND THE DARK
(with Angela Knight, Emma Holly, and Diane Whiteside)

HOT SPELL
(with Emma Holly, Shiloh Walker, and Meljean Brook)

BENGAL'S
QUEST

L O R A   L E I G H

BERKLEY BOOKS, NEW YORK

BERKLEY

An imprint of Penguin Random House LLC
375 Hudson Street, New York, New York 10014

This book is an original publication of Penguin Random House LLC.

BENGAL'S QUEST

Library of Congress Cataloging-in-Publication Data

Leigh, Lora.
Bengal's quest / Lora Leigh. — First edition.
pages; cm
ISBN 978-0-425-26546-8
1. Paranormal romance stories.   I. Title.
PS3612.E357B46 2015
813'.6—dc23
2015007660

FIRST EDITION: June 2015

PRINTED IN THE UNITED STATES OF AMERICA

10   9   8   7   6   5   4   3   2   1

Cover illustration by S. Miroque.
Cover design by Rita Frangie.

Penguin
Random
House

Find your mountain and take the first step . . .
Climb it.
Find your song and take that first breath . . .
Sing it.
Find your story, pick up your pen . . .
Write it.
Find that perfect picture, camera in hand . . .
Take it.
Whatever your dream, wherever it exists, reach out for it . . .
Live it.

Climb your mountain. Sing your song.
Write that story. Take that picture.
Live that dream.
Do it now, before you realize the time for it has passed.

· T H E   W O R L D ·
⊙ F   T H E   B R E E D S

They're not shifters or werewolves.

They are experiments in genetic engineering. Created to be super soldiers and the advanced lab rats needed to research new drug therapies for the human population.

They weren't created to be free.

They weren't even created to live.

They existed to serve the men and women who created them, tortured them, filled them with rage and a hunger for freedom.

Now they're free, they're living and they're setting the world, and their mates, on fire.

———————

For a glossary of Breed terms, please flip to the back of the book.

✦ PROLOGUE ✦

BRANDENMORE RESEARCH
GENETICS RESEARCH UNDERGROUND FACILITY

Cat stared at the white wall of the cell she'd grown up in and she cried. She hadn't cried in a long time.

It hurt G when she cried, so she'd stopped crying when she was scared, when she was five. She was twelve now, and unless the therapies just hurt so bad she couldn't stand it anymore, she didn't cry.

This hurt worse than the therapies, though. This hurt worse than even when she'd begged G to let her die.

Because G was gone now.

At least all the alarms were quiet. It was the alarms that woke her and the only other occupant of the cell.

First Honor's momma and daddy had taken Honor home. Now they said G was gone, that he had run away. But G wasn't a kid and he wouldn't have run away without taking her and Judd with him. He wouldn't have. She knew he wouldn't.

And her teddy bear was gone too. G only let her have the teddy bear when she came back from their experiments and her whole body felt like it was being torn apart. Then he would let her cuddle it as he cuddled her.

"He took my teddy bear," she whispered. "He must have been very scared, Judd. He must have known the men in the black clothes were going to take him."

Judd was a Bengal Breed, like G was, but G said Judd's Bengal was asleep. Dr. Foster had said it was recessed. Sometimes G tried to explain things to her like she wasn't grown up. She was grown up. She knew lots of stuff. And she knew Judd was making his Bengal sleep. It wasn't awake because he wouldn't allow it to awaken.

Judd was cool, though. With soft black hair and really deep green eyes. He looked like he had a wonderful tan, but that was just his skin color. A soft dark earthy color that most Breeds shared.

He was as tall as G, though not as hard in his muscles. He watched everything all the time and sometimes G explained things to him, but Cat knew they were things Judd had already figured out.

"The men in the black clothes didn't take him, Cat." He lay on his own cot just staring at the ceiling like he always did.

He'd told her once that if he stared hard enough then his mind took him away to places where he ran free.

She had never been able to do that, mostly because G was always talking to her, telling her things he said she had to remember.

But she remembered everything she heard and everything she saw. G only had to tell her things once.

Things like, if the men in the black suits came for her, not to be scared. Don't fight them, just be calm, because he would save her before they put her to sleep. The men in the black clothes had taken all the other older people who had been taking the therapies over the years.

Dr. Foster became very sad when they left and she'd heard him tell G that at least they wouldn't hurt anymore.

"The men in the black clothes took him, Judd." She tightened her arms around her knees to keep herself from rocking back and forth. "My teddy is gone." And she needed her teddy bear when G wasn't there. She was so very scared. "G wouldn't do that unless he was scared."

"Gideon doesn't get scared, Cat," he reminded her.

He'd told her that many times over the years.

"He wouldn't leave us." She knew he wouldn't. G loved her, and he knew she loved Judd too. He would save Judd too because she would never be able to leave him behind to suffer.

"I want G," she whispered, her breath hitching, the fear that always threatened to overwhelm her dragging her under now. "They took him away from me, Judd. Why did they take him away from me? I need G."

Silent sobs shook her shoulders, she didn't dare let the scientists hear her crying. They would punish her for being loud. They would give her that horrible drug that trapped her inside her own mind and made her crazy with the pain they inflicted.

"Gideon ran away, Cat." Judd's voice was hollow, resigned. "You have to accept that. I don't know why he took the teddy bear but I know the soldiers didn't take him."

She needed G. He protected her. He made hell bearable and he gave her hope. And Judd was wrong. G wouldn't leave her. He just wouldn't do that. G knew she didn't have anyone else. She had no one but G . . .

FOUR MONTHS LATER

They had taken G, now they were taking her and Judd.

Cat watched the men in the black clothes as they moved up the hall to the cell. There was no one left in the research center now but her and Judd. They would take her for sure, she knew. She was the one they called a disappointment during the last therapy.

"Remember, Cat, don't fight. Stay calm," Judd murmured when he moved to stand beside her. "Don't say anything. Don't tell them anything."

But G wouldn't save them.

Judd thought he would, but how could he, when the men in the black suits had taken him and put him to sleep?

She wouldn't fight, though. She'd promised G she wouldn't fight in the center. She'd wait. She'd watch. If he didn't come for her, then first chance after they cleared the labs, she would run. He'd promised there would be a chance.

She would try to run, just like he'd taught her. She would run and hide and grow up and learn the rest of the fighting lessons. When she knew them all, then she would find out who gave the order to put G to sleep, and she would make them suffer.

Then what would she do? she wondered. Because she couldn't imagine life without G after that.

"You hear me, Cat?" His voice hardened, sounding almost like G's.

"I hear you." There wasn't enough time to say anything else.

The men in the black clothes were at the cell. Hard faced, their eyes so flat and cold, without mercy or compassion.

The metal door slid open soundlessly.

"Come on, you're in transfer," the tallest one announced as he moved to Judd. "Turn around."

Judd turned, not even flinching as they strapped the hard plastic cuffs around his wrists.

Turning, Cat put her hands behind her back as well.

Both men laughed. "Yeah, you're a real threat," the shorter one scoffed before slapping her against the head painfully and pushing her to the door. "I'm not wasting my restraints on you."

That was a mistake, but she wasn't going to tell them that.

She was tiny. She looked frail. But an animal lurked inside her. One they wouldn't expect and wouldn't be prepared for. One determined to live.

FOUR HOURS LATER
SOMEWHERE IN THE PENNSYLVANIA MOUNTAINS

Judd wondered if he should be in shock.

He stared at the guard who had gotten into the back of the van with them. He was sprawled out on the floor, the side of his neck ripped open as he stared up at the ceiling of the van sightlessly.

Cat hadn't been messy about it. She'd moved so fast, with such deadly precision and sharp little teeth and claws, that at first Judd was certain he'd imagined what he was seeing. Until she'd reached into the guard's belt, retrieved the releasing device and loosened the restraints on Judd's ankles and wrists.

She'd returned to the narrow bench, huddled in the corner and stared at the narrow window where the scenery passed by in a haze of midnight shadows.

"G said I had to be ready," she whispered. "We'll only have one chance to run."

She still believed Gideon had been taken from her. No one had been able to convince her that Gideon had escaped and left her and

Judd there alone until he could arrange for Dr. Bennett, the new director of the center, to have them transferred to the euthanasia facility.

What would she do when she realized Gideon was really alive?

"Cat, listen to me." Kneeling next to her, carefully Judd reached out, touched her dirty face and turned it to him.

Gideon was going to go ape shit. The lab techs hadn't allowed Cat to properly bathe since Gideon's escape. Her hair hung in dirty strings and dirt marred her face and hands.

"Gideon will be here . . ."

She shook her head fiercely. "He wouldn't leave me like that." Tiny fingers curled into fists. "He wouldn't leave me, Judd."

"To save you, he would have left you, Cat."

A feral snarl and snap of tiny incisors had him jerking his head back instinctively, staring back at her in shock.

"G wouldn't do that!" The pain in her face, in her eyes, broke his heart for her. "He wouldn't leave me alone. Never. And he wouldn't take my teddy from me even if he did."

But he would have, if he'd hidden dozens of nano flash chips in it that he'd filled with information he'd stolen over the years. Generations of experiments, genetic coding and Breed research had been hidden in that tattered little bear.

There was no time to explain all that, though.

He was out of time.

Gideon's warning shot sounded and lit the night sky like the fourth of July.

Throwing Cat to the floor, Judd covered her slight body with his own, remembering Gideon's warning clearly. If Cat received so much as a scratch, then he'd take it out of Judd's hide.

Judd would have preferred she receive the scratch than the disillusionment this kid had coming when she saw who was rescuing them.

◆　　◆　　◆

G.

He'd really escaped. He'd run away from her, and now, he was dying.

"He's lost too much blood, Judd." She was frantically trying to stem the flow from his chest and as he stared up at her, even the whites of his eyes turned that eerie jade-flecked amber. "We have to transfuse . . ."

"No . . ." The snarl in G's voice was a horrible sound.

She stared down at him in shock. He'd never been a reasonable Breed, but this was crazy.

Lifting her gaze to the Breed across from her, she begged him silently to ignore the command of the Breed they'd both freely accepted as their alpha years before.

"If he dies, I'll never forgive you," she sobbed as Judd dropped his head, ignoring her imploring gaze. "Do you hear me, Judd? I'll never forgive you."

"I'll kill you." G wheezed, the warmth of his blood still easing over her hands.

"Don't do this, Gideon." Judd stared back at him now, his jade green eyes flashing with an inner flame Cat had never seen there before. "Please don't make it like this."

"You know it can't happen." G coughed.

"G, please. You can't leave me alone," she begged him desperately, her tears mixing with his blood as she tried to make him understand.

"You lied to me, G. You left me once. Don't leave me like this. I can't live if you leave me like this."

The sobs were jerking through her body, shuddering through her as she made him look at her. She had to make him understand.

"They'll come after us. How can we fight without you? Please, G. I don't want to fight without you."

"My little cat." His voice was so weak it terrified her as his hand trembled, reaching up to touch the tears falling down her face. "You live, Cat. For me. You promised me."

She'd sworn to him she'd live. Sworn she would never give up on living.

"It doesn't count if you leave me," she screamed down at him. "It doesn't count, G."

"It counts . . ." An enraged snarl tore from his throat as he felt the pressure syringe Judd stuck to his neck. "No . . . you bastard!" G cursed him. His gaze turned to her, pure green fury lighting the depths. "I'll kill him, Cat. Do this and I'll kill him. I'll kill both of you."

She eased back, watching as his arm fell helplessly to the ground beside him.

Moving quickly to her feet, she rushed to the other side where Judd was laying out a small pallet of blankets from the supplies G had brought. A medical pack sat beside G's prone body, the transfusion supplies ready.

"No," G demanded again. "There's no serum, Judd. You know what that means."

She had no idea what the serum was and she didn't care. She knew her blood would help him heal, that was all that mattered.

"I told you, Foster was wrong," Judd was arguing as Cat lay down next to G and turned her arm up for the other Breed to apply the transfusion syringe into her vein. "Dammit Gideon."

"Cat." The growl had her turning her gaze to him, staring back at him and realizing far more than he knew. "Do this, Cat, and you'll die . . ." he snarled.

"I love you, G," she whispered. More than anything she loved G, she couldn't let him leave her forever, no matter how much he might hate her for it.

Staring back at him she felt the first-ever flash of fear for the Bengal she claimed as her G. Green fire filled his eyes, covering the amber, obliterating the black pupils and the whites of his eyes. It was terrifying.

"I never loved you," he sneered back at her as she felt the most agonizing pain of her life strike at her heart. "Why do you think I rescued you? You were an experiment. My experiment. That was all . . ."

"God, Gideon, shut the fuck up," Judd snarled.

Before Cat realized what he intended to do he'd given G more of the paralytic, effectively ensuring his alpha couldn't curse the smallest of their pack any further.

But it was too late, the words were already said, the damage was already done.

"I still love you anyway," she whispered, hurting so bad that the pain blocked her tears.

Turning from him, Cat stared up at the starry sky and forced herself away from there. Judd had told her how he forced himself from the horror of the labs, freeing his mind while his body was still trapped. Cat forced her mind back to better memories. Back to the sound of G's voice, gentle and tender when she hurt, easing her from that horrible pit she always felt awaiting her.

She forced herself back to the security and protection she'd felt when he was there. When she'd believed she belonged to someone.

Believed, she had. It had been a lie, just as everything else had been a lie.

Dr. Foster had said once that she was Gideon's experiment, and she hadn't known what he meant at the time. She knew now. She'd known since G left the labs that she had been an experiment all along, just to see if her body could be cured of the disease she was born with.

But she'd been another experiment as well.

She hadn't been born a Breed, she'd been made into a Breed through the experiments. The horrifying wracking pain, the agonies that lasted for days and days. She'd been turned from a regular girl into one with an animal hiding inside her.

Gideon's experiment, Dr. Foster had called her when she was younger. G worked with him all the time. He was smarter than anyone at those labs. Dr. Foster had said he was smarter than even himself. And Dr. Foster was a Breed maker.

G had put the animal inside her. He'd hurt her just as all the scientists had, just as Mr. Brandenmore had. She had just been his experiment . . .

◆　　◆　　◆

She wasn't surprised the next morning when she awoke and found him gone. Where he'd lain, a piece of paper was folded with her name.

Run, Judd, get her the hell away from here. Hide her. When I heal, and I will, I'll find you. And you'll die. Both of you will. I'll peel the flesh from your bones and make you wish you'd never infected me as you have.

The rest of the letter she left unread. Folding it, she handed it silently to Judd, rose to her feet and began gathering the supplies and blankets together and placing them back into the packs.

At least G had left them that much.

"You read this?" Judd asked behind her.

Cat nodded.

"You understand it, Cat?" The gentleness in his voice should have surprised her, but she didn't think she could be surprised right now.

She shrugged. "I'm not stupid. I'm smart, remember? G made sure of it."

He'd always told her that, how he was making sure she was smart, smarter than she would have ever been if she hadn't been sick when she was born.

"Yeah." He sighed. "G made sure of it."

He sounded so sad, almost as sad as she felt. Almost. Inside her heart she was so sad that all she wanted to do was just close her eyes and dream it hadn't ever happened. But she couldn't do that. They couldn't stay here. If G came back he would kill Judd, and he would kill her. G always kept his promises.

"Were you his experiment too, Judd?" She turned to him slowly, never really understanding the part he'd played in the research center.

A self-mocking smile curled the Breed's lips.

"I'm his brother, Cat," he finally said, sighing heavily. "But I'm damned if I know what I am to him anymore."

G's brother.

Even Judd had someone, even if it was G.

She had no one . . .

⋆ CHAPTER I ⋆

THIRTEEN YEARS LATER
WINDOW ROCK, ARIZONA

The world called her Claire.

Once, her legal name had been Fawn.

Neither was actually her true name.

Where it counted, to whom it counted, she was Cat, a carefully hidden, maturing, restless feline Breed ready to pounce. A tigress growing slowly impatient with those around her and the machinations being played against her.

She'd been growing tired of it for quite a while. The farce of living as a woman who had actually died as a young girl years before, of pretending to be quiet, studious, and without backbone, had worn her patience away.

She had backbone.

Once, a geneticist and a Bengal Breed named Gideon, one she had called G, had ensured it.

She had a backbone of steel and it was getting ready to lock into place.

"Claire should return to protective custody. With the proof that's come to light of her father's crimes against his family as well as the Breed community, she'll become a target." Jonas Wyatt, the director of the Bureau of Breed Affairs, addressed the group gathered in the conference room of the Navajo Suites Hotel just outside Window Rock.

He wasn't wrong, exactly. What he neglected to mention was the fact that she had been a target since the tender age of twelve. It was nothing new to her.

For some reason, this Lion Breed had decided she was his favorite project, though. Since learning that her father, Raymond Martinez, had been behind his own sister's abduction by the Genetics Council and later her death, the Breed was like a shadow she couldn't shake.

Not to mention the fact that she was the only bait he had to draw out a creature he still had yet to learn was far too dangerous to play with in such a way.

Jonas didn't address his concerns to her, though. They were addressed to Claire's family members.

His freaky silver eyes swirled with concern amid the expression of sincerity that creased his sun-bronzed face.

He was about as sincere as the German shepherd that pretended to smile at her each morning. That bastard would take a bite out of her hide at first opportunity if she dared allow it.

Not that Jonas wanted to see her harmed, unless it was for the greater good. He was just more concerned with that greater good.

"It would seem to me that decision should be Claire's." The new director of the Western Division of the Bureau of Breed Affairs—a hell of a mouthful there—Rule Breaker, the real Claire Martinez's uncle, spoke up at that point.

Claire had a Lion Breed for an uncle. Whoopee, wasn't she lucky?

Lifting her gaze from her hands where she'd folded them atop the table, she directed it to the black-haired, blue-eyed Rule and wondered how much he suspected, how much he knew.

Quite a bit, she was certain, though she doubted he'd been told everything.

"I agree." Her grandfather, Orrin, spoke up. "She's the one who would be confined for the period of time required. She should decide if this is what she wishes."

Oh, this was about to get really good.

Orrin never agreed with a woman making her own decisions about her protection. Not since his teenage daughter had disappeared over three decades before.

If she had needed confirmation that she was silently being pushed out of the Martinez family, then Grandfather Orrin had just given it.

The ache in her chest grew sharper, the heavy weight of grief sinking deeper inside her.

"I think Claire knows the risks," Jonas suggested as though he could read her mind.

Perhaps he could.

It was said he had some mad Breed powers going on. Who knew what he could actually do.

"And those risks would be?" The newcomer to the group, a Wolf Breed, Lobo Reever, asked the question with such arrogance she had to bite back a sneer. "Why don't you explain them before we're asked to lock a young woman away, a young woman who, it appears, has known nothing but restraint all her life, Director?"

This was so good, such a classic G—oh, excuse her, *Graeme*—maneuver, that she'd seen through it the moment Reever stepped into the meeting. As though she hadn't known where the Bengal was for months now. That he was working right beneath Jonas Wyatt's nose, posing as some Lion Breed security manager for Reever's estates.

Graeme Parker, her ass.

A Lion Breed? Really?

How the hell had he managed to pull that scent off? To mask his Bengal scent with that of a Lion's was such a stroke of biological and genetic genius that she could barely comprehend it. She'd always known he was too damned smart for his own good, but that one surpassed even her expectations of him.

Jonas wasn't happy with the objections. His expression went from concerned to blank so fast Cat wondered if she'd blinked.

"Claire? It would seem your opinion is required here." The subtle mockery in Jonas's drawl made the decision for her.

He expected her to just agree. To do as Claire had always done and agree with the decisions made for her protection.

He was certain Claire still lived . . . No, he knew she wasn't Claire. He'd known from the beginning and he'd simply been patronizing her, using her to draw out a Bengal he was determined to find.

She turned her gaze to the two men who had tried to protect her for the past thirteen years, Orrin and Terran. The men Claire had called Grandfather and Uncle. How she wished they were truly hers to claim.

How she wished someone, somewhere, was hers to claim.

The sensible thing to do, the smart thing to do, would be to agree with him. Breed protective custody wasn't so bad. It was simply incredibly boring and impossible to slip away from. It was confining to the point of being smothering.

"She's not a child, Jonas." Lobo spoke up, his wild green eyes narrowed on the director. "I'm certain she doesn't appreciate being spoken to as one either."

Jonas slid his gaze to Lobo, a slight smirk to his lips before turning back to Claire. The arrogant confidence on his face had her teeth clenching. He actually thought she would be so easy to control, that he could force the truth from her. She'd already decided her course here, he could force nothing.

"Not a child, Lobo, but I'd say definitely tired of being under her father's thumb." Confidence gleamed in his odd gaze, so certain she'd fall into line, his line, and do as he wanted her to do. He knew who she was, what she was, and he believed she was weak. She'd allowed him to believe she was weak, just as she had allowed others to believe it.

The time for that was past.

It was time to stop pretending she was Claire, and be the person, the Breed, she'd grown into.

It sucked. She hated it. And it was going to cause her more trouble than she wanted to deal with at the moment, but this farce had gone on too long as it was.

"I'm neither Raymond's puppet nor yours, Mr. Wyatt." Standing to her feet, she faced the men, *men*, who had come together to decide on *her* protection, as well as her future, for her. As though she didn't have the ability to do it for herself. She'd had enough of that before she'd turned eight.

And though the need for caution was uppermost, no doubt, her ability to feign submission no longer existed.

"I never imagined you were a puppet, but I think you and I are both aware of the fact that Raymond's association with the Genetics Council is more a threat to you than you're willing to admit." It was a reminder.

A reminder that her past was known by Raymond as well as Jonas, her real identity a weakness she couldn't escape. And one Raymond had no doubt already reported to those willing to supply him with the funds he believed would aid in exonerating him on the charges the Breeds had brought against him. The list was extensive.

"Child." Orrin rose as well, his wrinkled face, gray braids and frail body a reminder that age was taking him from so many who loved him. "You must do as your heart, as your spirit, guides you, not as those who love you would have you do. But the danger is not something you will face alone," he told her. His voice was gentle, but still, he was encouraging her to face this without the family she'd depended upon as Claire Martinez. "You will never face that life, or any danger that would find you, alone."

Another reminder, one he'd given her thirteen years before. There were those who watched out for her, who would never see her harmed if they could deflect the danger first. In all the years she'd been protected beneath his granddaughter's identity, she'd never asked them for help either.

"Orrin, respectfully, that's bullshit," Jonas objected sharply, anger snapping in his voice with such strength that he drew the attention of the entire room.

Silver eyes seemed shot with mercury as they obscured the black pupils, swirling with a primal, primitive rage that would have affected her if she hadn't been used to such a look long before she'd come to this desert land.

"Perhaps, Director, you are the one full of bullshit," Orrin suggested smoothly, by no means intimidated by the Lion Breed either. "This is her fate, not yours. The questions you claimed to have when you came here have been answered. You have what you assured us you were searching for, the answers to your daughter's health. You can leave now. The safety and protection of our own, we can handle."

Orrin's deliberately arrogant claim filled the air with anger. With Wyatt's anger.

"But she isn't yours, is she? No matter how much she claims to be. When do the lies stop?" His hands smacked on the table as he leaned forward, the sight of blood-tipped claws now protruding from the tips of his fingers an assurance that the primal genetics he possessed were rising hard and fast inside him. "Do you take me for a fool? Do you imagine I don't for a second know who and what you are?"

He stared at her, knowledge and demand burning his gaze. He was her genetic superior, that gaze seemed to remind her. She would submit. She would follow his lead. She would . . . tell him to go to hell if he kept trying to intimidate her in such a way.

"I take you for a bastard!"

Before she could restrain the urge, the tigress that resided inside, normally silent and well hidden, slipped its leash. Her own claws emerged before her hands slapped to the table as well. She could feel the markings at the sides of her face shadowing her flesh, feel the incisors at the sides of her mouth dropping lower, feel the animal infused in her genetics merging with the human.

Shock filled the room. Satisfaction filled Wyatt's gaze. Did he truly believe he'd maneuvered her so easily? That she hadn't considered the consequences to what she had just done.

"You are an unregistered Breed female," Jonas snarled, his voice a lash of icy dominance. "You will do as you're told by the only alpha claiming you."

The only alpha claiming her? He was as insane as he believed the Bengal he was chasing to be.

Thankfully, being claimed didn't count if she didn't want it to.

Lobo eased to his feet, though not in fear, not even wariness. Sharp interest definitely, and a hint of concern for her, not of her.

"You are no alpha of mine, Director," she assured him, her tone sharp, melodic, rather than rough as many males' voices were when their animals slipped free. "That scent of demand, that look of furious command, has no effect on me. My alpha marked me years ago and no other will usurp his place no matter how hard they may try."

She had accepted her alpha freely when the tigress inside her first showed itself. The mark of that acceptance, not just by her but by the animal inside her couldn't be wiped away, no matter how she'd already attempted to erase it.

"An alpha who wants you dead." The reminder was given with a baring of sharp incisors and a flash of fury.

Well, he really didn't have to throw that one in her face, now did he? Not that she believed Graeme wanted her dead, but it was the impression he'd given others searching for her. She didn't consider that nice of him either.

"Is that what you believe?" She let a low, amused hint of laughter free. "Trust me, Director, if my alpha wanted me dead, then dead I would have been the night he found me when he first got here. You roused the monster, Director, in your search for me and Honor. Now you've found us. But believe me, he found us first, and nothing you do, no plans you make, no matter how deep you bury me, will keep him from me."

She'd always known that, always accepted it. There was no hiding from the Breed that had, in essence, created her when he'd developed the genetic serum that saved her life.

"Do you think he intends to allow you to remain alive? Have you fooled yourself into believing he actually felt anything for you when you were a child?" He sneered back at her as she straightened, glanced at her claw-tipped fingers and slowly retracted the sharp extensions until her seemingly perfect manicure was in place once again.

Blood still dripped from the director's claws to the table. Two perfect scarlet teardrops.

Lifting her gaze to him, she clenched her teeth, forced her incisors back and with a low, deep breath, restrained the genetics that surged free at his demand.

It was an ability she was rather proud of. In past years she'd learned how to push that part of her so deep that even Breeds couldn't smell the mutation of her DNA or she could call it forward until the scent of the Bengal Tigress all but overwhelmed the scent of her humanity.

There wasn't a Breed in the room that could sense the Bengal female that had faced them moments before, it was so completely recessed now. Though, it was becoming harder and harder to achieve that little trick with each passing month.

Muttered curses met the phenomenon, though Jonas remained silent, glaring at her, the scent of strength and demand still trying to exert itself over her. Alphas were marked by their ability to lead and their strength. Those two qualities had a way of merging into a particular scent that could encourage other strong-willed Breeds to follow, or force those of lesser will to do so. Cat wasn't a Breed he could force until she wanted to allow him to believe such a thing.

She really wasn't in the mood to play that game though.

"I think it really doesn't matter," she assured him. "I'm not hiding any longer. I've suffered for the cure those bastards injected in my veins only days after my birth. I suffered, as did Honor, Judd and Gideon. I won't suffer further by trying to hide from my fate. One doesn't hide from Gideon, Director. That only pisses him off, didn't you know that?

You face him, spit in his face and pray you've amused him enough that he has mercy when he finally gets around to killing you."

"Can you get any more overdramatic?" he sneered, glaring at her. "You have no alpha. That places you under my protection as well as my command. You are unregistered, without the protection and registration an alpha or pride affords you. You do not have the choice of denying any alpha's claim."

She shook her head slowly. "I'm a Bengal tigress, Director. Even in the wild no lion would dare try to intimidate such a creature. I'm no submissive to your demands. I suggest we call this one a draw."

"A good idea," Lobo injected, obviously not in the least pleased with the director's attempts to force his will. "If the alpha mark even I sense within her isn't enough to encourage you to heed her wishes, Jonas, then I'll back it with my own standing as an alpha and that of my pack. She doesn't stand alone against her enemies, or your deliberate attempts to force her into accepting your arbitrary decisions."

Jonas's sneer only deepened as he shot the Wolf Breed a glare. "Your agreement with the Breed Tribunal and the Bureau of Breed Affairs doesn't extend to countermanding any decisions I make, Wolf," he informed Lobo with cold distain. "This isn't your fight."

"There's no fight involved," Cat injected, finished with the damned male posturing and the pissing contest in which the two Breeds were becoming involved. "I make my own decisions. I neither want nor need a man to back them, whether he be Breed, human or something in between." She shot both men an imperious look, determined to make her point clear. "I am fully capable of making decisions on my own, without all your manly, Breed arrogance if you don't mind."

Jonas turned back to her slowly, the look he turned on her one known to shrivel confidence in Breeds far stronger than she was.

Thankfully, the genetics that would have forced her compliance with such a look were so deeply buried that only a hint of trepidation spoiled the mocking arch of her brow in return.

"Think yourself my equal, do you, little cat?" he scoffed, the scent of his contempt, of his prejudice, so clear it nearly choked her. Prejudice. No different from that which the humans felt against the Breeds. She wasn't a Breed created before birth as other Breeds had been created. Yet he forgot, it seemed, she wasn't the only one.

She shook her head again. "You've always known who I was and what I was, Director. I knew that. Be careful how you handle this from here on out, though, because the day will come when your daughter may well draw conclusions you don't want in how you handle a female who was born human then made into a Breed, rather than simply created. I can smell your hatred of what I am. I hope she never has to feel it as well."

Turning, she stalked from the room before his shock could turn to rage and the animal genetics surging beneath his human skin slipped free.

He could decimate her and she knew it.

His training, his strength, was far superior to hers. She'd always known that and she'd remained in the shadows because of it. Remained there, hoping to protect one who didn't need her protection, and trying to deny the truth to herself.

G—Graeme now, rather—had deserted her years before. He'd left her and Judd to be run down like diseased dogs by the Genetics Council and their soldiers. Forced her to hide in a way that had only hurt her and in a way that left Judd completely alone.

Graeme was her alpha; he owed her his backing, his strength. Instead he'd abandoned her and was determined to destroy her. He'd left her to face maturing alone, without his guidance, to becoming a woman alone with no one to lean on, and he'd left her to face a life pretending she was someone she'd never been intended to be. She had fought alone for thirteen years, refusing to ask for help, and only one person realizing she sometimes needed help. The quiet shadow that slipped in and out of her room occasionally to deliver a healing salve, a splint for a broken bone, or a sweet treat when she'd felt lost amid the hatred she faced each day. He rarely spoke to her, she'd rarely known he was there until she awoke and found the gifts.

Dane Vanderale, Breed ally and supporter, the heir to a fortune that defied belief, an enigma, even to those he helped. Especially to Cat, because she'd never understood why he'd helped.

He'd done what her alpha should have done, what the Breed known as Graeme should have done. He'd been there when she needed help the most, and he'd helped rather than attempting to destroy her.

And that was exactly what Graeme was doing, destroying her. From the moment he'd found her, each move, each carefully calculated maneuver was to reveal who and what she was, to take every last vestige of protection she'd found over the years. To ensure she was as lost and as alone as she felt.

Once he'd learned through Jonas's search for her that she was still alive, the maddened creature he'd turned into had been on the hunt. As long as she'd been left alone, as long as she'd remained hidden, he'd been content.

But she hadn't remained hidden to everyone. The Genetics Council had begun the search for her, and they'd known the general area where she'd disappeared, but they'd never identified her, despite Raymond's threats. Those heading the Brandenmore research center, even after the owner's death, was hungry for her return, she knew that. Jonas Wyatt had done more than just focus on her last-known location though. He'd parked himself in Window Rock and began a concentrated search for a rabid Breed that he'd known wasn't there, one he knew would draw the Bengal Breed there though.

Jonas had known that directing any search related to the Bengal once known as Gideon, would draw the Breed there and no doubt he'd known both Cat's and Honor's identities would be revealed as well, forcing Gideon to reveal himself.

He hadn't revealed himself though. He'd found a way to hide in plain sight and then he'd begun stripping Cat of every defense she possessed.

He'd taken not just her protection though—he'd stolen her illusions, her belief in belonging, and in herself.

Her alpha may well want her dead. But at this point, she owed him the same coin. It was now just a matter of time before they likely destroyed each other.

◆　　◆　　◆

"You don't have to go." Terran Martinez stood at the open door of the bedroom that evening, watching her with somber, dark eyes, his expression heavy as she packed.

He'd played the part of her uncle, even protecting her from the man who had sworn to treat her as a daughter. For thirteen years she'd let herself pretend she had a family, a place to belong, only to realize she had no such thing.

Terran didn't ask her not to go. He didn't tell her it didn't matter that she wasn't Claire, he only said she didn't have to leave.

Once, she'd been a part of the extensive Martinez family. Her cousins, Isabelle and Chelsea, had visited often after she'd moved in with Terran several months before, after Raymond, Claire's father, was indicted on crimes against Breed Law.

Claire's mother, Maria; her father, Raymond; and her brother, Linc, whom Cat had been genuinely fond of, had turned their backs on her within days of the charges being officially brought by the Breeds and a date set for a hearing in front of the Breed Tribunal.

Maria and Raymond both had known she wasn't really Claire. They had been there the night she had taken their daughter's identity, had participated in the cover-up. Linc, though, she was never certain what he knew and what he didn't.

"I know, Terran," she answered quietly as she placed her clothes in the suitcases she'd bought after leaving the meeting with Jonas Wyatt. "It's better this way."

Not that Terran and Orrin both weren't aware of who she had been all along as well. Everyone knew. But no one had wanted to admit that the real Claire was gone, despite their knowledge.

Terran had lost his treasured younger sister to the Genetics Council when she was only sixteen. He and his father—and, he'd believed, his older brother, Raymond—had searched for thirty years for her, only to learn of the horrific death she'd suffered while still a young woman and, with her death, the disappearance of several of her Breed children. One of which had been a girl. And he'd lost his niece, Claire, at fifteen to drugs and a tragic car accident.

This family had already suffered so much.

"Better for who? For you?"

His question surprised her. She paused in placing her jeans in the suitcase and considered it before turning back to him.

"The cat's out of the bag, literally," she reminded him, the overwhelming sadness that she could no longer pretend to be the person they loved weighing at her heart. "I can't pretend anymore. I can't put my head down and be nice and quiet and sweet while raging inside. My maturing genetics just won't allow it."

The frown at his brow grew heavier. "We didn't demand that you take Claire's personality as well as her identity when the ritual failed."

The ritual. That otherworldly episode that had given her so much of who and what Claire Martinez was. Lying amid the steam and the scents of earth, dampened herbs and life itself, she'd felt the spirit of the dying girl whisper through her, determined to protect her with her own identity, with everything she was. Cat had felt herself drift then, into a sleep so deep, so dark, she'd immediately railed against it.

When she'd awakened from that sleep it was to find that spirit still there, watching over her, protecting her when other Breeds were there by effectively hiding any scent or realization to Breed senses of her true identity. For years Claire Martinez had protected her. Until Gideon's return. Now the awareness of the spirit that had watched over her was gone.

"Claire's gone. The change was too sudden." Frustration ate at her now, rising from a well of painful realizations that refused to be hidden. "I lost too much too fast and now I have to figure out where to go from here. I won't endanger the rest of you while I do that."

She wasn't Claire.

Her genetics would begin adapting now that the maturation of her Bengal genetics was beginning. The tigress that had merely lurked within her, only coming out when she called it, was now beginning to merge with her human genetics in a way she may not be able to hide for much longer.

"So you'll face it alone?" The scent of his anger began to fill the air. "And you expect us to simply accept that?"

She swallowed tightly, her fists clenching in the clothes she'd retrieved from the bed as she turned to him.

"I'm not Claire," she reminded him, desperate to hear him say it didn't matter. "I don't have the right to ask any more than that of you."

His lips thinned. Something bleak and filled with rage flashed in his gaze before it was gone as though it had never existed.

Rather than speaking the words she needed to hear, he shook his head, pushed his fingers through his graying black hair then turned and headed back to the front of the house.

Cat clapped her hand over her lips to hold back a cry, a shattered sound of disillusionment. She'd been so certain he'd tell her it didn't matter that she wasn't really Claire. That she was family anyway. She'd been his acknowledged niece for thirteen years, he'd been part of her protection for just as long. But he couldn't tell her it didn't matter.

Because it did matter.

She'd always known when push came to shove, that it did matter.

Shoving the pain to that place where she'd shoved the other broken promises and disillusioned realizations, she fought back her tears and finished packing. Three suitcases contained her life. Twenty-five years and so very little to show for it.

A small collection of knives she'd found each year on her birthday for the past years. Just as many small crystal dragons. They were her only keepsakes. Presents over the years had included gift cards and clothes. Terran had given her his older-model pickup when the one she'd bought last year had been repossessed within weeks of her losing her job as a receptionist at the tribal headquarters.

Raymond had ensured it was repossessed, she'd known that.

Lifting the largest suitcase in one hand, she slung the strap of the overnight bag on her opposite shoulder and picked up the smaller case.

Over the years she'd acquired a few things herself. Weapons she'd hidden, cash she could access. It wasn't much, but it was enough that she didn't have to worry about the fact that no one would hire her since she'd moved from Raymond's house.

Either employers were put off because of the charges brought against her supposed father or, if that wasn't it, they weren't hiring her because Raymond had specifically asked them not to. For whatever reason, the position she was left in was precarious at best.

She did seem to have a place to live, though.

Surprisingly, the voice text that had come through from Lobo Reever just after she left the meeting was an offer of a rental house he owned just outside his huge estate in the desert. A nice little place with a pool, adobe walls surrounding nearly an acre of property. It was private, easy to secure and, she hoped, safe.

She was certain Lobo hadn't been behind the offer alone, though. Graeme was quite good at getting the very influential Wolf Breed to do his bidding. She just hadn't figured out how he'd managed it yet.

She wasn't going to look a gift wolf in the mouth, though. It was a place to live. She didn't have to force herself on the Martinez family any longer, nor feel as though she were some orphan relation to the Breeds.

Jonas may pretend to want to be her new best friend but in the few seconds that her sense of smell had been at its peak, she'd scented the truth.

Contempt, distaste, arrogant superiority. They'd all filled him. He didn't see her as human nor as Breed but as some inferior in-between without worth.

Which didn't bode well for the daughter she knew he adored.

How a man, or a Breed, could hate one and love another of the same genetic mutation, she didn't understand.

29

She didn't intend to spend much time trying to make sense of it either. She had other problems, much larger problems. One in particular, a big, muscled Bengal Breed posing as a Lion and determined to destroy her.

If only she could make herself just as determined to destroy him.

◆   ◆   ◆

"I don't like allowing her to leave like this." Terran watched the pickup until it was out of sight.

The anger in his voice matched that of his scent, the tinge of regret and sorrow filling the early evening air.

"I know," Cullen assured him. "These are decisions she has to make alone, Terran, we've always known that."

"Not like this," the Navajo argued. "It doesn't matter if Claire still protects her or not. I accepted her as my niece the night she took Claire's identity. Whether or not Claire's spirit survives to shield her has nothing to do with it."

"Graeme and Orrin are the ones you should be arguing with," Cullen sighed, pushing his fingers through his hair as he blew out a hard breath. "They decided this was how it had to be, not me."

The old Navajo had guided Cat this far, Cullen could do nothing but trust in Orrin's visions now and pray Cat survived the coming realizations she had to face. As for Graeme, there were complications there that Cullen had no desire to consider at the moment.

"That brother of yours is a menace to Breeds and humans alike," Terran muttered. "And I don't trust him. He should have come to her, faced her . . ."

"There is nothing on the face of this earth that will stand between him and Cat." Cullen turned to face the other man fully now, staring at him intently, willing him to understand, to know, that Graeme would never tolerate it for an instant. "Do as Orrin instructed. Let Cat face what's to come. Encouraging her to hide from who and what she is now, could get her killed."

It could get all of them killed. And life might not be exactly what he'd envisioned sometimes, but he still had things to do, dying before he completed those tasks wasn't something he wanted to face.

"She's been deserted all her life, Cullen," Terran snapped, the scent of his anger growing. "Even by him. And by God following suit with everyone else in her damned life doesn't sit well with me."

Turning Terran stomped back into the house, leaving Cullen to turn and stare into the desert, the weight of Terran's words weighing on his shoulders. Because he was right. They'd all deserted her in one form or the other, to save her. But in ensuring her physical survival, what had they done to her heart?

· C H A P T E R 2 ·

"Your Cat is in the guesthouse and settling in, according to Khi." Lobo Reever stepped into the large cavern accessed by the steps leading from the estate house above and paused as Graeme lifted his head and stared back at him over the top of the computer monitor he'd been staring at. The Wolf Breed appeared just as supremely confident and detached as ever, but Graeme knew the façade for what it was now. Lobo Reever was anything but detached. Supremely confident, most certainly, that was a Breed trait if nothing else was. Excessively arrogant, he had that in spades, but once again, that too was a Breed trait. Hidden beneath the layers of carefully honed Breed instincts and strength was a storm brewing closer to the surface by the day though.

As for his stepdaughter, Khi, she was a catalyst that could end up destroying both Reever brothers. For now though, she was controlling her anger. Partially because Graeme kept her distracted by allowing her to participate in some of his less complicated little games. She seemed to enjoy them a little too much, but at least this way she had something to keep her far-too-quick little mind busy.

At the moment, the Reever family's eccentricities were the least of his worries. One little cat's safety and realizations were pretty much consuming his time.

"Martinez made contact with a high-level member of the Senate Breed Appropriations Committee several days ago," he informed Lobo. "I finally cracked the encryption on the number he was using and managed to identify his contact. I'd like to send one of your men to shadow him."

Lobo's brow lifted slowly. "A senator?" the Wolf Breed wasn't surprised, merely interested in the information.

Graeme nodded shortly. "His name hasn't been mentioned in relation to the Council, nor has he or his family been associated with any of the suspected members of the remaining organization. Until this, he was above suspicion. Within hours after the call several suspected Council commanders began moving though and rumors of an escaped experiment began filtering through targeted lines of communication. Martinez has revealed her identity."

The bastard would die. Graeme couldn't strike just yet, not while Martinez was being watched so closely by the Bureau of Breed Affairs enforcers, but they had to blink eventually. When they did, the bastard would pay for his betrayal.

"Send Rush." Lobo nodded "He's good in the shadows. Send Rath along as well, for backup. They work well together in these situations."

"That was my thought as well," Graeme assured him as he shut down the program he was working on and rose from his chair. "I'll notify them immediately so they can head out."

He was aware of Lobo watching him closely, the intense, dark green of his gaze somber and hinting at questions Graeme knew he was in no mood to answer.

"Do you know what you're doing, Graeme?" Lobo asked quietly then. "She could end up hating you."

No, she wouldn't hate him. Kill him, perhaps, rage for years most likely, but it wasn't possible for Cat to hate him. She was too much a part of him, just as he was too much a part of her. That didn't mean he didn't have doubts. Doubts the Wolf Breed didn't need to know about.

"Do you know what *you're* doing?" Graeme asked him rather than answering the question. The game the other Breed was involved in at the moment was every bit as complicated and dangerous as the one Graeme was in.

"Hell no," Lobo muttered almost immediately. "I don't have a clue at the moment what I'm doing, or how it's going to end. All I know is that I seem to be committed to it."

Graeme's lips quirked at the truth of that statement. "I'll give Cat a night or two to settle in before going to her. She needs the rest." And that was true enough. According to Cullen and Terran Martinez, Cat often paced the floors at night, if she didn't outright slip from Terran's house to wander the desert.

Graeme had tried to follow her several times, both furious and proud as hell each time she managed to lose him. He wouldn't allow her to continue to do so, but still, he was damned proud of her. And he was curious. Where did she go when she disappeared into the desert?

"I wish you luck," Lobo drawled. "I have a feeling that allowing her to catch up on her rest may not bode well for you though."

"No doubt." A rueful grin tugged at his lips at the observation. "I have to say though, I believe I'm looking forward to it."

"I envy you then." A flash of hidden fury gleamed in his gaze for just a moment. That storm, Graeme thought, the one that may well escape the Wolf's amazing control far sooner than anyone anticipated. "And on that note I wanted to let you know Tiberius will be arriving this evening. We'll meet here." He looked around the huge cavern, his expression brooding. "Hopefully, after Khi's retired for the night."

That situation was going to be the death of Lobo, Graeme thought, and perhaps his brother Tiberius as well. The two Wolf Breed brothers rarely saw eye to eye about Khi, especially since learning of her mother's involvement with the Genetics Council.

"Jessica's still eluding him?" Graeme questioned thoughtfully.

"As though she's disappeared off the face of the earth," the Wolf Breed sighed, shaking his head as his fists clenched momentarily at his side. "He hasn't found so much as a rumor of where she might be."

And Tiberius was one of the best trackers Graeme knew. Not as good as Graeme was, but still, he was good. Perhaps, Graeme thought, once this situation with Cat was dealt with, then he'd see if he could ferret out Jessica's location. The world might believe she had died in a riding accident over a year before, but Graeme, as well as the Reever brothers, knew better. She was still alive and making Lobo's life hell.

"I'll make certain the main cavern's ready for Tiberius and his men." Graeme nodded. "Will you need me present when they arrive?"

Lobo's sharp nod affirmed Graeme's suspicion that this wasn't a visit as much as an exchange of information too important to trust to any traceable means.

He'd be busy tonight, thankfully. Sitting in the silence of the caverns and watching Cat on the security monitors would play hell on his determination to allow her a few nights' rest. At least this way, he might manage to actually stay the hell away from her.

Cat sat beneath the shade of the table umbrella on the patio behind the guesthouse Lobo Reever had offered her use of and watched as his stepdaughter, Khileen, Khi to her friends, strode from the kitchen doorway toward her. She carried a pitcher of icy sweet tea, the only kind to drink, she'd assured Cat, and two glasses.

Her long, curling black hair was restrained in a braid, though stubborn tendrils and riotous curls had managed to sneak out here and there. Dressed in snug ripped denim shorts a shade shorter than Cat would have worn, and a snug white tank top, she displayed her tanned limbs without a sign of self-consciousness. Without a sign of it. Cat had caught several vague tinges of just that, though, as the other girl showed her the house and how to use the electronic controls for lights, temperature and entertainment.

Cat didn't know Khi well, she'd kept a distance between them rather than drawing Raymond's fury at any friendship that might develop.

Raymond had hated Lobo Reever enough that distracting him from any trouble he could have caused the Wolf Breed had been extremely difficult at times. Had she actually formed a friendship with Khi, it would have been impossible. His hatred hadn't been just for the Reever Wolf Breeds but for the stepdaughter as well. It now made sense why that hatred hadn't applied to the mother. Jessica Reever had been part of the Genetics Council as well, and no doubt one of Raymond's contacts.

"Here we go, the perfect cure for a hot day." Sitting the icy pitcher and glasses of ice on the table Khi slid into the chair across from Cat gracefully.

Waiting for Khi to pour the dark liquid into glasses of ice Cat used the silence to try to make sense of the emotions roiling beneath the other girl's surface. Unfortunately, they seemed so jumbled and chaotic that Cat doubted even Khi could make sense of them.

"Excuse the way I'm dressed." Khi finally sat back after taking a long sip of her tea and focused on Cat ruefully. "It pisses Lobo off, but I think I cut the shorts a little short this time." Her lips tugged into a self-mocking curve. "I wasn't trying to be rude."

At least it made sense now. Khi Langer had actually once graced the best-dressed lists among the elite social set in both America and Europe before her mother faked her own death, supposedly to escape Lobo Reever's justice for conspiring with the Genetics Council.

"I thought you got along with Lobo." Cat stared back at her thoughtfully.

"When I was younger perhaps." Khi shrugged, the somber pain that shadowed her gaze instantly covered beneath a quick roll of her eyes. "He's very arrogant, you know? Since Jessica rather rudely tried to kill us all for her Council bosses, he's become very overprotective."

Cat hadn't heard that piece of information. "Your mother tried to kill you?"

"Well, at least it's not common knowledge," Khi drawled with a hint of anger as her deep blue eyes flashed with the betrayal.

The scent of her pain was almost overwhelming for a moment then she seemed to restrain it, push it back until it was completely hidden. Cat had a feeling the other woman's restraint over that anger was rapidly becoming harder to maintain.

"Anyway, as far as the world is concerned she's dead." Khi shrugged then. "Killed in a riding accident." She sipped at the tea then met Cat's gaze coolly. "Tiberius is searching for her now. With any luck, she'll soon be as dead as everyone else believes she is."

The statement was delivered so matter-of-factly and with such ice that she ached for the little girl hiding beneath such a need for vengeance. How horrible it must be to face such betrayal. Perhaps, Cat thought, not having parents hurt far less in some ways.

"I'm sorry, Khi," Cat stated softly, aching for the pain such deliberate cruelty caused.

"Don't be." Khi waved the expression away. "It's far better to know how evil someone is than to be fooled by them forever. And I didn't come here to discuss the Council's bitch anyway." Her tight smile didn't come close to hiding the morass of emotions tangled inside her. "I'm glad you're here, Cat," she said sincerely. "I was worried when I heard what Raymond was capable of. I always knew he wasn't a nice person, but evil such as he carried inside him is always a shock when you learn it's someone you associate with often."

"He hated Lobo." Cat sighed heavily. "He hated having Breeds in Window Rock and the protections the Nation afforded them. It was always difficult to turn down your invitations, Khi, but it was better for us as well as Lobo that I did so. It kept him from focusing too much on the trouble he could have caused if he wanted to."

"Lobo would have decimated him." Khi gave a bitter little laugh. "He was always having to deal with Raymond's roadblocks and ignorance anyway. But I rather guessed why you refused them. No hard feelings."

And there weren't any, Cat sensed. She rather guessed Khi was too busy trying to navigate the internal hell she was going through herself. Whether or not Cat accepted an invitation probably hadn't kept her up at night.

The reality Khi had to face daily was one Cat guessed made sleep extremely difficult if the dark circles under the other girl's blue eyes were an indication. There was also the strange, very subtle scent that lingered around Khi, one Cat couldn't quite make sense of. A very elusive trace of a Wolf Breed, but not a mating scent. It was almost two distinct scents that made it impossible to identify.

"So, I understand you and Graeme have a bit of history." Khi wagged her brows as she broke the silence between them.

Leaning forward, the other girl shot her a teasing little wink. "Come on, dish up the details there, girl. What is it about you that makes that tough-assed Bengal get all gooey-eyed?"

Graeme? Gooey-eyed?

"You must be mistaking gooey eyes for that death stare he has," she guessed, though she had no idea how anyone could mistake it. "Trust me, Graeme doesn't get gooey eyes for anything or anyone."

The very thought of such a thing was laughable.

"Trust me, gooey-eyed," Khi assured her with a light laugh as she relaxed back into her chair and watched Cat curiously now. "I've known him for a year and every time your name's been mentioned he has this little pause, and whatever rage burns in his eyes seems to dim a bit."

Cat shook her head, denying any thought that Graeme had such tender feelings for her. Not anymore.

"I'm his own personal experiment," she revealed. Khi knew the truth of who and what she was, she'd announced that when Cat stepped into the house. "His intelligence, even in the research center was frightening. The geneticist that created him allowed him to design the therapy used to save my life from the disease I was born with. If he has any softer feelings for me, then it's no more than one a scientist has for a favorite lab rat."

Khi's crack of laughter was filled with disbelief. "Honey, you keep telling yourself," she stated, barely holding back more laughter. "Right until the minute that bad-assed feline is fucking you silly." The smile that filled Khi's expression was one of genuine amusement and when she spoke of Graeme, the scent of an almost sisterly fondness was clear. "I can't see him getting all hard and hungry for a lab rat, no matter how fond he might be of it." The laughter she was holding back nearly escaped once again. "Thanks for that little moment of amusement though, I needed that."

No doubt she did. Still, Cat narrowed her eyes on the still far too amused woman. "You're strange, Khi," she stated. "And you have some very strange ideas."

The other woman did give another light, clearly genuine laugh at that. "Naw, I'm complicated, there's a difference," she assured Cat with such satisfaction and pride in herself that Cat nearly laughed herself. "Ask anyone. I'm very complicated."

"And you enjoy encouraging that belief," Cat guessed with a smile.

"Of course I do." Widening her eyes with charming innocence Khi batted her lashes demurely. "What would be the point in beginning the rumor otherwise."

Shaking her head, Cat finished her tea then watched as Khi refilled both glasses. She didn't miss the subtle little addition Khi made to her own glass. The scent of the strong liquor wasn't in the least subtle. Cat didn't comment on it, rather she merely filed the information away to broach another day.

For now, she let Khi find what relief she could from the emotions Cat sensed were far too confusing for the young woman filled with them. Who was she to judge what solace another could find from their demons? She only wished she could find a bit of solace from her own. Because she could feel the confrontation with her own personal demon nearing, and she was terribly afraid there was no preparing herself for it.

◆　　◆　　◆

She was incredible.

His little cat.

Slipping into her bedroom through the open balcony door the next night, Graeme couldn't help but marvel at the young woman she'd become.

Twenty-five years before, when Phillip Brandenmore had laid her in his arms and informed him coldly that her survival was his responsibility, Graeme had never imagined the exceptional creation she would become—even the arrogant Brandenmore hadn't realized. Graeme had ensured it. Every therapy, every drug, every second in that godforsaken hellhole had created this wondrous creature.

Long, burnished gold and deep earth brown strands of silky hair spilled over her pillow and around her face, framing the dark cream flesh of her face perfectly. Her features were feline enough to give her expressions a shadow of mystery, the tilt of her eyes hinting at the exotic.

Her lips. They were sweetly curved, tempting, and made him want to taste.

The need, the hunger to taste her had tormented him since finding her. It haunted his dreams, his fantasies. It kept him aroused, iron hard and ready to mate.

There were days he hated her for that need to possess her, the certainty that once he had her, protecting her would become more hazardous than it had been in the past.

She was a weakness.

She was pure and certain destruction if he wasn't extremely careful.

No one had accused him of being careful in years, though, and he saw no reason to give them cause to do so now. He was what they had created. If they didn't like it, then they had only themselves to blame.

Breeds were created to be master manipulators, tacticians, guerrilla fighters and highly tactile lovers. Graeme was all those, yet, in his creation they'd somehow missed the fact that they'd created a Breed whose aptitude in their scientific deviations far exceeded their own. He'd taken what had been done in Brandenmore's research center, watched, manipulated the scientists and techs and, in the end, had almost run the labs himself.

Until Brandenmore had brought in a new head researcher and geneticist. One who had somehow sensed the hold one Bengal male had over everyone there.

Good ol' Dr. Bennett. Skinny-assed bastard.

Rubbing at his chest, he remembered the feel of Bennett's fingers wrapped around his beating heart as he gave the soldiers their orders to find "the girl."

The girl.

He focused his gaze on her once again.

She was the girl. The one who had forced her blood into his veins and allowed the madness to overtake him. That madness had then given birth to the monster as a scientist ordered her recapture with the express intention of lifting her beating heart from her chest as well.

Bennett hadn't held a beating heart for five years, even his own, and he never would again. Graeme had ripped that organ from Bennett's chest. Digging his claw-tipped fingers through flesh and cartilage, he'd gripped the pulsing flesh and, as the good doctor watched in helpless horror, ripped it from him.

That memory was one of the best he possessed, though the night it had occurred, when he'd gone through the labs on a killing spree that left few within them alive, was often hazy.

The monster he'd become that night had been a final, welcome relief. Because that creature had no mercy, no regrets or recriminations. He was pure superior intelligence and primal instinct.

When the monster retreated and the Breed found a measure of sanity, there she had been, the cat that had begun his downfall. And the knowledge that she would always be his downfall.

Gripping the sheet covering her, Graeme eased it slowly down her body, his lips quirking as the frown deepened at her brow.

She should have already awakened.

Were he a Council soldier or Breed, then she would have already been dead. Or raped. Possibly both. Probably both.

But then, no doubt she would have awakened before a threat made it to her bedroom. He'd watched her over the months and he knew her instincts were damned good. The Breed instincts maturing inside her kept her on her toes.

And apparently, trusted him far too well; otherwise she would be clawing rather than stretching sensually beneath his gaze as the sheet cleared her body.

She could have worn one of those sexy nightgowns she owned, he thought in regret at the sight of the loose, sleeveless top and snug cotton pants she slept in. She even wore socks.

A grimace pulled at his lips. He'd have much preferred the sexy nightie, dammit.

Easing back from the bed and moving to the chair she'd placed next to the open balcony doors, he slouched back in the comfortable seat and just stared at her. He let his gaze caress her from her delicate face along the slender column of her neck to the rise of her breasts beneath the thin top.

Nice breasts. A perfect handful and his fingers ached to cup them, stroke them.

The many ways he could amuse himself with those lush, peaked curves tempted the control he exerted over his lusts. He wasn't accustomed to restraining himself. Whether it be his need for sex or for blood, patience was used only when it made the game more exciting.

Restraining himself would definitely make this game more exciting. So far, maneuvering her into place, pulling the pieces into play and beginning this particular game had called upon more patience than even he had imagined he possessed. The question was, could he maintain it?

Focusing his gaze on her, he let his senses connect with the always alert part of her genetics that marked her as his and called her from sleep. Connecting with her inherent senses had always been particularly easy. Too easy.

◆   ◆   ◆

Cat didn't come awake slowly.

Her eyes snapped open, aware of the presence even before she'd awakened. Furious that her sleeping senses hadn't awakened her sooner. Could they have warned her first? Hell no. She had to wait until he commanded her to wake up.

"So the cat's awake." The growl came from the far corner of the bedroom, directly across from the large bed. Slouched in the chair she'd positioned there for him, just to the side of the opened balcony doors, he watched her like the very dangerous feline he was.

The asshole.

"You're late." Sitting up as she slid her legs over the side of the bed, Cat watched him carefully. "I expected you the last night."

White teeth flashed in the darkness of the room as he shot her a mocking smile.

"I was here." The shrug of his shoulders wasn't missed, nor was the latent confidence in it. He had to be related to Jonas Wyatt. The two were far too much alike.

"No doubt you were," she snorted. "You've turned into a stalker, G. I hadn't expected that of you."

The racing of her heart gave lie to the casual attitude she'd adopted, she knew, just as the scent of her wariness would be easily detected by him.

His amusement was frightening.

Icy, watchful, predatory.

She didn't like it.

"What did you expect of me then, little cat?" he drawled, shifting to lay his ankle on the opposite knee as he watched her with odd, amber-flecked green eyes.

Like Jonas Wyatt's silver eyes, there were no black pupils to separate the color. And when rage filled every molecule of the Breed, that color would bleed into the whites of his eyes as well.

"I didn't expect to wake up." The admission wasn't easy to make, but she had no illusions about her ability to fight the animal in front of her.

There would be no fight to it, it was that simple.

He only narrowed his gaze on her.

"You thought I would kill you in your sleep?" he asked with an arch of his brow. "I'd at least give you a chance to fight."

The superior mockery in his voice assured her that he was well aware there would be no risk involved in allowing her a chance to fight. Only a moment to laugh at her.

"Well, doesn't that make me lucky," she snorted. "That's really big of you, G, that you'd give me a chance to realize how helpless I really am. I appreciate the thought."

She hadn't expected that much, she realized. He could have easily sliced her throat in her sleep and that stupid heffer of a tigress inside her would have bowed down and let him without ever giving Cat a warning. Stupid Breed genetics.

"I assumed you would." The mocking drawl just grated on her nerves and had those Breed genetics she so often cursed rising to the fore. "See what a nice guy I really am?"

Yeah, he was just a helluva guy, wasn't he?

It would have been nice if the genetics she possessed could have risen when he first slipped into her room. At least given her a chance to run, maybe?

"Yeah, just a teddy bear," she murmured belligerently.

A teddy bear.

A flash of memory, a ragged teddy bear, one eye missing, just big enough for a small child to wrap her arms around.

What had he done with it when he stole it? she wondered. It had been the only possession she'd had in the research center. And one that would have been taken from her if anyone but her cellmates had realized she had it.

"I was surprised to find you here," he stated, dragging her thoughts back to him. "In this desert. I expected you and Judd to head for the jungles. For the hidden places where you could disappear easier."

That had been an idea, until Orrin Martinez had found them and convinced them otherwise.

"Could I have hid from you, G?" she asked, rather than explaining their choice. No doubt he already knew. "Do you think there's a single place in the world where you wouldn't have found me?"

There wouldn't have. She'd been so desperate to see him over the years that she'd stupidly tried to find him or contact him more than once. As she'd grown older that need had become a hollow, painful ache she'd never been able to fully understand.

Sharp incisors flashed in a cold smile. "I rather doubt it. Hiding from me wasn't an option, Cat. You know that."

Yes, she knew that now, just as she had known it then.

Hiding from him would have been impossible, just as depending on his protection had been a fool's dream.

"Then isn't it a very good thing that I didn't try to hide from you?" Rising to her feet, she turned her back on him and headed for the bedroom door. "Want a drink? I think I need one."

The growl that reverberated through the room had her pausing. Instinct rather than inclination stopped her in her tracks while the desire to give him the submission that sound demanded clashed with her determination not to.

"You're not my alpha any longer, G," she warned him softly. "No matter what you or my Breed genetics may want to believe."

The lie slipped out easily, but even she wasn't convinced, let alone the Breed, with such cool purpose.

"That's not what you told Jonas the other day," he reminded her, the mocking amusement in his tone grating on her nerves. "I believe your comment was that no other could usurp my place as your alpha. I think I liked the sound of that declaration. Repeat it. This time to me."

He was joking surely.

"That claim is nonexistent. Besides, everyone lies to Jonas," she informed him with an edge of disgust. "It's the only way to deal with him. Now, I want that drink whether you do or not."

She had to literally force her feet to move, her fingers to curl around the doorknob. She could still feel him behind her, staring at her, demanding she return to him.

Damned stupid Breed genetics. They could have slept just a little while longer.

Or at least given her a warning.

Because before she even realized he'd moved, he had her pressed against the door, the hard length of his body holding her in place. Sharp teeth nipped at her ear, shocking her with the heated sensation. Not quite pain. Definitely too much pleasure.

Pleasure?

No, G would never deliberately pleasure her, no matter how many times she'd fantasized about it in the past months. If he'd known he'd done so, he'd likely ensure she never made the mistake of believing he'd do so willingly again.

"G . . ."

"Graeme." The name was growled at her ear, the order emphasized by the rumbled warning in his voice. One her Breed genetics, as well as the human, recognized. "Too many in the research center knew you called me by my initial rather than my name. Don't make that mistake again, Cat. It could get us both killed. Surely you don't want to do that, do you? Wouldn't you cry a little bit if I died?"

Everything familiar was being taken from her, because of him, by him. She was already stripped bare, without friends or family. Hell, even her Breed genetics would betray her if she allowed them to. What more could he take from her but her life? Or his life. Could she bear to face the future without him in it in some way. Even as her enemy, her tormentor, was better than his death.

"Let me go, *Graeme*," she bit out, feeling the urge to release her claws, to fight, scratch despite the realization that he was still that important to her.

He wasn't her alpha, no matter the primal instinct that still existed inside her. Her alpha would not have deserted her. He wouldn't have threatened her or left her to fight alone.

He wouldn't have allowed her life to be stolen for all the years she had had to hide from the Genetics Council and their goons. Her alpha wouldn't have stripped her life down to nothing.

"I'll never let you go . . ." The guttural claim stripped her of control. The hell he wouldn't.

A hard twist, a turn, a slash of claws high on his thigh and, oh yes, he did release her.

Dropping to the floor to evade the quick grab he made for her, Cat rolled out of reach before jumping to her feet and facing him at a half crouch. Breathing hard, heart racing, she watched him with narrowed eyes.

He was amused. Too damned amused. As though she had done exactly as he expected her to do.

Then slowly, deliberately, his gaze dropped to his thigh, high, inside his thigh, no more than inches from a heavy, denim-covered bulge. There, the material was slashed in three long rows as blood spilled from the slices in his flesh to wet the fabric.

"Close," he murmured.

"The next time, I'll neuter you." The bravado was completely false.

Oh God, what had she done? The lacerations in his upper leg were spilling blood too fast. She'd sliced deep, the sharpened claws she possessed far more effective against his flesh than she'd ever believed they would be.

He chuckled at the threat. "I'd delay that one if I were you, little cat. As your mate, I'd be rather ineffective, wouldn't you agree?"

Before she could speak he was out the bedroom door, closing it behind him as Cat stared at him in denial and disbelief.

His what? That wasn't possible. She wouldn't allow it.

"Where the hell are you going?" Jumping to her feet and rushing to the door, she jerked it open, staring at the empty hallway in shock.

"Graeme?"

Dammit, she'd called him Graeme rather than G. She hated him. She hated her genetics. She hated anything Breed right now.

"Where the hell are you?" Stomping from the bedroom and along the open hallway to the stairs, she still didn't see him.

All but running down the curved staircase to the small foyer, she stared around the open living room, dining area and kitchen. And still no Graeme.

G, she reminded herself fiercely.

Damn Breed alpha bullshit. Pain-in-the-ass genetic encoding.

She hated it, she reminded herself.

Stalking through the house, room by room, she merely confirmed what she already knew: He was gone.

"Did the bad kitty have to go fix his boo-boo?" she sneered, stepping back into the silent kitchen. "Poor arrogant-assed Bengal. I hope it hurts."

Moving straight for the fridge and the wine she'd placed in there earlier, she poured a half glass. Rather than sipping at it, she simply threw it back like a shot of whiskey before refilling and promising herself she'd sip it.

She really didn't hope it hurt.

How had she done that? She hadn't meant to. She hadn't even meant to release her claws as she tried to escape his hold.

With everything between them, though, she hadn't expected him to claim to be her mate either. As though she was unaware what a mate was and what the claim meant. Just because she pretended not to be a Breed and got away with it, it didn't mean she hadn't witnessed that Breed-mating crap.

Why lie to her? Did he think she wouldn't know the difference?

"I know you were lying, Graeme," she snapped aloud.

Of course he'd have the house bugged. He was smart like that.

"I'm not stupid. I'm no mate of yours."

She'd not allow herself to be tied to someone she couldn't trust nor depend on. He'd proven both over the past ten years.

She had no doubt he'd been well aware of the area she was in before Jonas ever came looking for her, Honor and Judd. He might not have known exactly where she was, but there was a chance he had known that too. Graeme—damn him—he could be more frightening than Jonas.

Quiet, secretive, mysterious. His intelligence had never been rated, his genius in Breed physiology and biology had never been documented that she knew of. But while under the tutelage of Dr. Foster, the first head of genetic and biological research at Brandenmore's labs, he had excelled to the point that she'd wondered if even Dr. Foster feared him.

Then Dr. Foster had disappeared and a new research scientist had been brought in. It was then Cat had seen exactly how manipulating and calculating Graeme could be. For almost a year he'd maneuvered the scientist, played him, worked the information he'd gained . . . then he'd disappeared as well. One night he'd been there; the next morning alarms had awakened her and Judd and his cot had been empty.

He'd left them alone.

Honor had gone home just weeks before, finally cured of the illness that had brought her there. With Graeme's escape, she and Judd had been left alone.

Cat had been devastated.

She could still remember the shock, her utter rejection of the idea that he would leave her. She'd been convinced they'd killed him. That Dr. Bennett had ordered his death.

Until the night he'd jerked open the doors on the van taking her and Judd to be euthanized, she'd been certain he was dead, that there was no way her G would ever desert her.

But he had. He'd left them. The truth was there in the wild green eyes and Bengal stripes bisecting his face. And because he'd attempted to rescue them, he was dying.

The bullets he'd taken to his chest had created horrifying wounds. Judd had fought to stabilize him, then been forced to inject the weakened

Bengal with a small amount of the Council paralytic to still Graeme's struggles, which the guards carried in the event one of the breeds they were transporting became too violent.

He'd cursed them as Judd attached the crude lines between Cat's vein and Graeme's. He'd cursed them, threatened them, then, staring in her eyes, he'd assured her he'd kill her. He'd peel the meat from her bones if she didn't make it stop.

I love you, G. She'd whispered those words without crying, her twelve-year-old heart breaking at his fury. *I can't lose you.*

I never loved you. You were my experiment . . .

He'd sliced her soul open when he'd told her he didn't love her. Sliced it open and left it bleeding with an agony she hadn't been able to comprehend.

Yes, he'd proved he didn't love her, that he'd never loved her. The mark he'd left as her alpha had tormented her, the pain of her disobedience had weighed in her for years. Until she'd managed to convince herself that she'd managed to destroy it. A lie. She'd known all along that mark would linger as long as the breed mutations lived inside her.

When Cat had awakened the next morning and found, once again, G was gone, she'd given Judd her loyalty, but he'd already had that anyway. When he'd held his hand out to her silently, his gaze filled with such regret, she'd taken it and acknowledged to herself that she had no one . . . she couldn't even allow herself to depend upon Judd. Damned good thing, because months later an attack, the six shadowy warriors who rescued them, and a group of six Navajo spirit men, had changed the course of her life.

At least until now.

"You're right, you're not the one I knew as G," she whispered into the silence. "My G would never have left me so alone and frightened and in such danger. You always were Graeme. You should have told me then who you were. I'd have allowed you to die as you wished."

Turning out the kitchen light, she moved slowly through the large open room to the staircase, taking each step with such weariness that reaching the top seemed to take forever.

She left the bedroom door open, left the balcony door open and crawled into the bed. Dragging the blankets over her shoulders, she lay, staring into the darkness, dry-eyed, aching and wondering why it still hurt so damned bad.

After all, she hadn't been under any illusions, hadn't fooled herself into believing he'd felt any differently than he'd claimed to feel that night. So why did it hurt so damned bad now?

REEVER ESTATE

"My G would never have left me so alone and frightened and in such danger. You always were Graeme. You should have told me then who you were. I'd have allowed you to die as you wished."

But he wouldn't have died.

The wounds were bad, he gave them that, some of the worst he'd ever had. But Dr. Foster had created him, and just as they had perfected Cat's genetics, Foster had perfected his. And his brother's.

Those genetics, the DNA that created the Breed as a whole, had ensured any wound was immediately isolated and all the body's strengths and power went to healing it.

He would have healed, it just would have taken longer. And he would have retained his sanity. By giving him Cat's blood without the serum Dr. Foster created to counteract the newly emerging hormone in her blood, he'd been driven mad. She was a child, still a baby, and far too young for the mating hormone showing up in her system. Far too young to mark a fully adult Bengal Breed that wasn't quite sane to begin with. Nothing had mattered but stopping the transfusion. When he couldn't stop it, nothing had mattered but ensuring she never searched for him. He had to keep her away from him until she'd had time to become a woman, to allow both her human and Bengal genetics to mature.

Reviewing the surveillance video of the house as he perched on the steel cot in the middle of a small cavern beneath the Reever estate, Graeme paused in the careful stitching of his thigh to glance at the video.

He could see her face, so stark and pale, her eyes filled with such bitterness, and felt his chest clench at the knowledge of the pain he'd caused her.

She actually believed he'd left her alone and unprotected? That it was possible for him to ever do so? There was still a part of him that was amazed she hadn't laughed at him when he claimed he didn't love her. She'd always seemed to know and to understand him so well. Yet, she'd taken his words at face value and believed he'd left her alone.

Shaking his head he finished the old-fashioned stitches, spread a healing cream over the wounds then bandaged it carefully.

He'd heal quick enough, but the slices into his flesh had come far too close to the artery. He'd bled like a stuck pig before reaching the tunnel that ran from the main estate to the small house nearly a mile away. Thank God, he hadn't walked the distance that night. While the motorized buggy had made its way through the tunnel on auto, he'd managed to put pressure on the wounds to keep the loss of blood at a minimum until he reached the med room he'd created in one of the smaller caverns.

The tunnels and caverns ran for miles beneath the Reever estate. He doubted even Lobo knew where all the tunnels exited and exactly how many caverns existed beneath the large main house and its grounds.

Graeme knew, though, and he'd made excellent use of many of them. Electricity, stolen from the main grid running underground less than a mile from the estate's walls, now lit the tunnels he'd deemed most important as well as the caverns used for research, medical supplies and the store of medications he'd begun putting together.

Lobo had given him free access to the tunnels and caverns, and Graeme made use of them as he saw fit. He didn't trust the current climate of Breed-human relations, but hell, he didn't trust humans, period, in most cases. He'd learned the folly in that at a very young age. He could count on one hand the number of humans he trusted and not use all his fingers.

The monster he'd become during his last stay in Brandenmore's research center trusted no one. Never. To trust was to become weak, to chance a mistake that could be stopped, to risk what it had come into being to protect.

A growl rumbled deep and low in his chest, a snarl trembling on his lips. The monster was never far below the flesh, always waiting, taking no chances, ready to spring at a moment's notice to protect what it claimed.

Taping the bandage into place, he lifted his gaze once again and stared at the face in the monitor.

She was still awake, still staring into the dark, the bitterness and loss she felt still reflected in the deep, golden brown eyes.

He wanted to tell her he was sorry, while he'd been there, and hadn't been able to. He'd looked into her eyes and seen the child he'd betrayed with words when he'd severed her belief in his loyalty. He'd wanted to tell her he'd hurt himself far more than he'd ever imagined possible with the words that had flowed from his lips in his attempt to save them both. To save her the pain he could have caused her in accepting that transfusion.

She would want explanations, though, and he couldn't explain. To even broach why the rage had exploded inside him, why he'd rather have died than take her blood that night, was something he simply couldn't do. Even for himself. Even at the time he'd not been able to fully understand it.

He'd never been particularly sane, he admitted with a bit of morbid humor. Even at a young age he'd been called feral, untrainable, crazed. That night, the insanity had taken over, leaving him to exist on instinct alone for years.

Until the Council had recaptured him and returned him to the research center. Until the night Dr. Bennett had lifted Graeme's beating heart from his chest and given the order to find the reason for the odd properties in Graeme's blood that kept him fighting, that kept him alive.

That night, the monster had leapt forward and there was no ridding himself of it now. He could restrain it now. He could deal with it, live with it. But he'd never be free of it. And over the years, he'd realized he didn't want to be free of it. The monster had always been a part of him, it had always existed. It only needed the right reason to show itself.

He watched as Cat's lashes drifted over her eyes, closing slowly as sleep finally came over her.

A second later a single tear rolled from the corner of her eye along the silken flesh of her cheek. Glistening against moonlight-kissed skin, trailing slowly to her upper lip, where it was sleepily brushed away with a muttered little whimper.

A whimper.

Wiping his hand over his face, he forced himself to his feet, ignoring the twinge in his thigh and turning away from the sight of her.

If only fate hadn't decreed the necessity of Wyatt finding her. If only that bastard Raymond Martinez had known a sliver of loyalty, of honor. If only the Council hadn't learned she was indeed alive.

The suspected mate of the Bengal that had massacred a lab filled with scientists and soldiers less than twenty-four hours after his third vivisection. Oh yeah, they wanted her, and they wanted her bad. Bad enough that the monster that had slept for a while had awakened once again. And once again, it awoke hungry.

Hungry for blood.

But this time, there was another hunger as well, stronger and far less controllable than it had been when he'd first found her.

That hunger was only growing, while the need for the enemies' blood was becoming secondary.

The need for her . . .

It had never been secondary.

CHAPTER 4

She was no crazy-ass Bengal Breed's mate.

Cat still couldn't believe the insane statement Graeme had made the night before.

She knew what mates were, just as she knew her cousin Isabelle and her friend Honor, who had taken the identity of Liza Johnson twelve years ago, were both mates to Breeds. Isabelle to a quiet, too intense Coyote, and Liza to a huge, dark Wolf Breed. Both women were crazy about their "fiancés" and shared a bond with them that the tigress she was had quietly acknowledged.

The scent of the mating, the physical and emotional needs as well as the bond the couples shared was unmistakable to other Breeds. Some may not have a name to put to it, but the scent of it was a warning to Breeds of the opposite sex, as well as confirmation of a unique, enduring bond.

They loved as well. Even before the mating scent became stronger, deeper, the scent of their emotional bonds had been clear.

She and Graeme had no bonds. What might have grown from those early years, when he'd cared for her in the labs, he'd killed the night he'd vowed to kill her. The night he'd assured her that she'd been nothing but his own personal experiment.

The sheer insanity it had taken to make such a claim almost matched the madness behind the number of cameras he'd placed in the house Reever had offered for her use.

Upstairs, she'd found six, downstairs, so far, she'd found four and hadn't even made it to the kitchen yet. And she had no doubt there were cameras she hadn't yet found.

Dumping the ones she'd collected into the kitchen trash, she was just opening the first kitchen cabinet door when the doorbell rang.

Kneeling on the marble countertop, she threw a disgusted look toward the doorway.

Who the hell was insane enough to ring her doorbell? Didn't they know a crazy-ass Bengal Breed was lurking around somewhere? Hadn't Jonas announced it to the free fucking world yet?

Jumping down with a growl, she stalked through the house to the door, coming to a hard stop at the scent of the men on the other side.

She didn't need this. She didn't need to deal with this. Where the hell were all the other crazy-ass Breeds when you needed them?

Gripping the doorknob and jerking the door open, she faced the men with a hard frown.

"What the hell do you want?"

Raymond Martinez had his politician's face on. The somber, compassionate face that fooled damned near everyone he came in contact with. With the light touch of gray in the black hair at his temples, dark brown eyes and swarthy skin, he was still a reasonably presentable man, though the heaviness at his middle and under his skin was ruining any chance at attractiveness that he may have had.

His son, Lincoln Martinez, was another story. At thirty-two, Linc was in fine shape. On leave from the military, he was all muscle and a closed, brooding expression.

Linc had obviously managed to secure leave from the military far quicker than she'd expected. She hadn't expected him to arrive on her doorstep with his father though.

"Claire, please . . ." Linc began.

"Oh, give me a damned break," she snapped at Raymond, the use of his daughter's name infuriating her. He damned well knew what her name was, he'd been told the night his daughter's body had died and her spirit had remained to watch over Cat. "Haven't you told him I'm not his sister yet? You disappoint me, Raymond. I assumed you'd already blown that bridge to hell and back."

Raymond grimaced at the statement.

"Can we do this in the house, Cat?" Linc growled, glancing around the yard, with its stone and pebble ground cover and succulents growing in carefully arranged small gardens. Well, evidently Raymond had told him.

Or had he known? She'd always suspected Linc was part of the spirit warriors the Unknown, but if he'd become part of the secretive sect before or after his sister's death, she'd never been certain.

"Ah, I see you didn't disappoint me," she murmured, the sarcasm infusing her voice surprising even her as she glanced at the man who had once sworn to be part of a carefully coordinated circle of protection. "By all means, do come in."

Stepping back from the door, she waved them in. As they cleared the doorway she slammed the door hard enough that the resulting crack had Raymond jerking around in fear. Linc merely shook his head before rubbing at the side of his face and glancing at her in chastisement.

Her tight, unapologetic smile was accompanied by the crossing of her arms over her breasts and a curious tilt of her head as she looked between the two men and silently compared their looks.

"You know, Linc, I think you'll be happy when you're older that you've taken after Terran and Orrin rather than him." She flipped her fingers toward Raymond. "He's not aging well."

The dislike in Raymond's eyes now was closer to what she normally faced and much more comfortable than the patently false warmth he'd tried to display.

"You little bitch . . ." He sneered furiously.

"Enough!" Linc's voice was a lash of command that had Cat's brows lifting in surprise when Raymond immediately silenced the harsh words.

"Impressive," she murmured, actually impressed by the sharp tone and underlying strength of it.

"That goes for you as well," Linc informed her sharply, shooting her a brooding glare. "We're here to talk. I'm not in the mood to listen to insults between the two of you."

He wasn't her alpha either.

"Then I suggest you take him and leave," she informed the man she'd once called brother. "Because as far as I'm concerned, he's nothing but an insult to the human race. It's rather hard not to point that out at every chance."

Jerking the door open, she threw both men a hard look before stomping through the entryway to the kitchen at the back of the house. She'd already had enough of this particular discussion.

"Stay here, dammit," Linc ordered his father as he ignored the open door and gripped her wrist firmly. "I can't believe you've pissed her off like this. Where the hell was your mind? You were supposed to protect her, not antagonize her."

Cat inhaled sharply. Well, that answered one question. She'd always suspected Linc was part of the group called the Unknown, whose job it was to protect her from the Genetics Council should Raymond fail to adequately convince the world of her identity as his daughter. She had never been completely certain until that statement. Only a member of the Unknown or those present that night, would have known that information. Cat allowed him to pull her across the foyer, more interested in what he wanted than scratching Raymond's eyes out at the moment.

Turning, she faced him as he entered the kitchen. He was taller than his father, easily six two. His black hair was cut close, a midnight shadow over his scalp as his black eyes watched her with inscrutable mystery. A mystery she'd always seen in his eyes whenever he'd been around. Linc had been kind to her whenever he was home, but unlike others he hadn't pretended a love or a connection that wasn't there. She'd wondered if that was merely because he was years older than his sister, or if he had known the truth.

At least he hadn't lied to her as everyone else had. He hadn't led her along that gilded path that led to the belief that she might belong somewhere. "Why are you here?" she demanded the second he cleared the kitchen doorway. "After all these years you suddenly find an overwhelming need to play brother? Where were you when Claire needed you?"

When it had been Claire he faced within Cat's body. During that time that Cat had slept, protected by a spirit that walked and talked within her body.

Anger flashed in his dark gaze. "I'm not here to discuss Claire, Cat.

I refuse to discuss Claire." Something painful and dark filled his expression for a moment. "This is about my father. He may be an asshole, and he may not have always been kind . . ."

She had to laugh at that.

"Dammit, Cat, I won't let Wyatt railroad him. If he was as terrible as those charges claim, then he would never have helped you." Loyalty was something that dug sharp, merciless claws clear to the heart and soul of who Lincoln Martinez was as a man. Like his uncle and his grandfather, he was a man born to lead, one born to shelter others and it was evident Raymond had convinced him of his innocence.

Who would he believe, she wondered. His father, or the woman his sister had sacrificed so much to protect?

"It is inconceivable to me that you've allowed him to fool you," she bit out in disgust, infuriated that such a smart, intuitive man couldn't see the evil that infected his father. "Let Wyatt railroad him? Linc, if I could get away with it, I'd kill him myself. As a matter of fact, if I could have convinced several Breeds to let me, I would have murdered him, gladly, years ago."

Linc stared at her as though he couldn't believe what he was hearing. After several seconds his expression hardened, became emotionless.

"He wouldn't have betrayed his daughter nor his sister like that." The hard iciness in his voice was something to be wary of. It was dangerous, a warning of retribution if he felt it warranted. "I admit he wasn't always kind . . ."

"Kind?" she sneered in disbelief. "There wasn't a day that Claire didn't feel his hatred, and once I became aware once again, there wasn't a day that I didn't feel it."

Sometimes blood was thicker than water, it seemed. Funny, Linc had managed to surprise her. She'd expected him to at least be curious why she hated Raymond so deeply. Why she wanted to kill him, would have killed him, easily.

"Believe what you want to. Why are the two of you here?" Pushing her fingers through her hair, she reminded herself that she shouldn't have been surprised.

Linc might have pretended to be her brother when he was home on leave, but he wasn't her brother. She was nothing to him.

"Son of a bitch," he muttered, still staring at her too intently, a brooding frown pulling at his brow as he watched her. "I was hoping you'd come to the tribunal with us, present a family front. If for no other reason than to preserve your own precarious safety. He protected you. He deserves that much."

He'd protected her?

She blinked back at Linc before she had to laugh again, mocking amusement nearly choking her as she stared at him.

"Is that what he told you? That he protected me?" She questioned him in disgust as one hand went to her hip in challenge. "He really managed to push those words past his lips without choking?"

"Well, I'll be damned if anyone found you while you were under his roof," he claimed, frustration filling his voice. His gaze wasn't filled with frustration though, it was hard, cold and analyzing.

"Do you really believe that, Linc?" she asked, certain he had to at least suspect the truth. "They have proof that he contacted a known Genetics Council informant just after leaving the meeting where it was proven he not only sold his sister to them, but knew where she was all along. He let her die during one of the most horrifying acts anyone could endure."

Why had Terran and Orrin kept this from him? They knew the truth.

"The hell they did. Cat, he was accused, not proven." He was fighting the truth, she could smell it, sense it.

"He was lying," she snapped. "Everyone there knew he was lying."

She remembered the scent of Grandfather Orrin's horror and his slow acceptance that his eldest son had done something so horrible. He'd known Raymond had done just as he was accused of doing. He'd sold his sister and allowed her to suffer to death beneath a surgeon's scalpel.

"Breeds?" Linc questioned, his voice, his jaw tight with fury. "They smelled his lies? And I'm supposed to accept that?"

"*I* smelled his lies." Staring up at him, fists clenched to hold back the claws she wanted to bare, she silently begged him to call her a liar.

He blinked back at her, silent now, his face drawn so tight it could have been carved from marble.

He knew what she was, knew what she had been to his sister, and if he didn't know she had no reason to lie to him, then he'd learned nothing over the years since she'd come into his family.

"Then why help you?" He didn't want to believe it, didn't want to accept it, but at least he wasn't denying it completely any longer.

"Because he had no other choice," she pointed out. "His brother and father were part of it. You were part of it and he knew it. He was told it was the only way any part of Claire would survive and he had to preserve the illusion that he loved his daughter. He couldn't let any of you suspect how he truly felt. If he did, then he risked his secrets being suspected or even discovered. But don't fool yourself into thinking there was a day of my life in that house that he was ever kind. Unless you were there."

Linc wasn't a cruel man. He was a man driven by the need to fight for what was right, for justice. His belief in the Breeds' right to exist had filled the better part of his life. He'd become involved in that cause even before joining the military. Once joining, he'd been part of several missions not just to protect them, but to completely destroy the Genetics Council.

By essentially spying on Linc, Raymond had learned quite a bit about missions against the Council, which he'd dutifully reported to his masters. The calls had been logged on satellite phone intercepts, but the phone had remained covert until Cat had found it just after they'd learned what Raymond had done to his sister.

"If that's true, why didn't you report it?" The need to prove she was wrong was dwindling, she could see, though the need for loyalty lingered.

Raymond was his father. Admitting what the man was wouldn't come easily to Linc.

"Because he would have revealed who I was, and where I was at a time that I couldn't have defended myself, just as he often threatened," she told him softly. "Just as he did once I refused to obey him and back him when his crimes were first suspected." Bitterness ate at her. "Don't ever ask me to help him again unless it's helping him straight to hell where he belongs."

"Why didn't you tell me?" Fury flashed in his expression, in the low, grating sound of his voice. "Why didn't you come to me?"

She stared back at him, remembering how helpless she'd felt during those first years after she'd awakened to awareness and realized the life Claire lived.

"Why didn't Claire tell you?" She asked him sadly, watching the dark pain that flashed in his gaze. "There was no way for you to help, Linc. You were in the military. Any attempts to help would have only put you at odds there," she breathed out wearily. "If you don't want to believe me, then don't. Either way, get that bastard out of this house before he infects it with the evil inside him. He's a malignancy and I don't want him anywhere around me."

Linc flinched.

It was painful to see the sudden flash of indecision in his gaze, the glimmer of suspicion. He knew. He didn't want to admit it, but he knew the truth. What he decided to do was another matter.

His lips parted, but whatever he meant to say was disrupted by a sudden snarl and the sound of a man's squeak of terror.

Linc moved, fast. So fast that Cat found herself behind him as they rushed into the foyer and came to a sudden, stunned stop.

Pure fury filled Graeme's face. The stripes that would have revealed his true nature as well as his true identity weren't apparent, but she had a feeling they weren't far behind.

One hand was wrapped around Raymond's throat, the other the side of the door as he suddenly heaved the older man out of the entrance to the pebbled yard right on his ass. Then he swung around, clearly prepared to do the same to Linc.

Coming to a stop, Linc lifted his hands, his expression closed as he faced what he believed was an enraged Lion Breed.

"I'm just leaving, Graeme," he assured him. "I should have never listened when he begged to come with me. It's a mistake I won't make again."

The fact that he seemed to know Graeme was surprising. She hadn't expected that at all.

"You should have never brought him here," Graeme snarled. "It's a mistake I promise you'll regret."

Glancing through the door at Raymond as he lay on his back, groaning as though he'd been sliced open rather than just thrown out, Linc shook his head wearily.

"It's already one I regret," he said softly. "And one I apologize for."

With that, he moved from the house. This time, Cat flinched as Graeme slammed the door with violence that nearly rocked the small house.

"Well, that was really mature, wasn't it?" she sneered as she crossed her arms over her breasts for the second time that morning. "Think you impressed them with all that Breed strength in beating Lobo's door against the frame?"

The stripes suddenly shadowed his face. Jagged dark marks beneath his flesh, extending over one eye, across his arrogant nose and opposite cheek. A sharp point ended at the corner of the other eye. Others curled around the side of his neck.

Cat stepped back warily as the green of his eyes, normally amber flecked, became green-flecked amber, filling the whites of his eyes and obliterating the pupils.

"Now, Graeme, all this fury is just uncalled for," she informed him with far more bravado than she felt. "It would be a really good time to just chill out and calm down."

She didn't know this Breed. Even his scent was tinged with something different, something elusive and so wild it went far beyond primal.

"Calm down?" he snarled, the deeper, rougher growl causing her to wonder if perhaps she should have just remained quiet.

"Yes, calm down." In for a penny, in for a pound. Right? "I had all this completely under control and Linc would have never allowed him to attempt to do anything."

"'Linc'?" His gaze narrowed on her. The predatory look was almost scary. "Now, mate, what is that scent of affection I can smell coming from you?"

Oh, he really wasn't going there. And what business was it of his who she was fond of and who she wasn't fond of? As for this mate crap of his . . .

"'Mate'?" Propping her hands on her hips, she let anger override wariness. "Are you fucking crazy . . ."

"Fucking bet on it." He moved before she could anticipate it, before she could jump away from him.

She found her back against the wall, lifted from her feet, thighs spread and gripping his as the fully erect proof of his arousal that strained his jeans pressed into the sensitive flesh between her thighs.

Aroused?

"Does manhandling me really turn you on?" Fingers gripping his shoulders, she wondered why the hell she wasn't trying to rip him apart with the claws that emerged to hold to the hard flesh beneath his shirt.

Because he felt so good.

So hot and strong, his hands holding her hips, his muscular thighs parting hers, holding them open as his hips shifted to rub the denim-covered erection firmer against her.

"It really turns me on," he growled. "It makes my dick so hard I could fuck for hours."

Suddenly, she was aching. The sensitive folds between her thighs were moist, her clit throbbing, the depths of her vagina aching. She was becoming aroused where she never had before. Nerve endings were clamoring to get closer to him, parts of her body tingling that had never tingled before. Her breasts were becoming swollen, her nipples hard.

"Then get a life," she gasped. "Find someone else to get your jollies with." She'd kill him if he did.

"You are mine." The snap of incisors just in front of her nose had her blinking back at him in surprise. "Allow that bastard to so much as caress your cheek and I'll slice . . ."

"The meat from his bones?" One of these days she might learn to just keep her mouth shut. "That one's old, Graeme. You really need to learn some new material."

Her claws flexed at his shoulders, totally against her best judgment, but his hips shifted again, dragging the material of her jeans across the silk of her panties, which in turn rasped over her swollen clit. And it felt so damned good.

"How's this for new material? Let's see what it does for you," he bit out, but it wasn't in anger. The stripes were receding as his head lowered, his lips moving to the bare flesh revealed by the thin straps of her cami top.

He didn't kiss her flesh. He didn't bite it. He did something in between. Right over the heavy vein throbbing in her neck, his teeth gripped, raked over it just before his tongue lashed at the heated flesh.

"Oh my God. Just kill me now," she whimpered as lightning-fast trails of exquisite sensation raced from her neck to erogenous zones she hadn't known she possessed. All of them combining to create one hot ache between her thighs as she felt heated moisture spilling from her body.

This was a major problem. It was a problem of enormous magnitude, because it was a weakness, and Graeme always made use of any weakness he discovered.

"Kill you?" he growled, his lips moving along the column of her neck as she found herself helpless to do anything except tilt her head to the side and allow him access. "Killing you isn't on the agenda, little cat. Fucking you is."

Why did her womb clench in such sudden pleasure at the threat that it stole her breath?

There wasn't a damned thing romantic about his declaration. It was pure lust, pure hunger.

"Not a good idea," she panted, though her lashes drifted closed and she arched closer, the feel of his lips at her collarbone dragging an unbidden moan from her lips.

"Like hell." One hand moved to the back of her top and in the next breath it was a piece of torn material drifting to the floor.

He'd ripped her shirt off?

She stared back at him, uncertain if she was outraged or completely turned on.

His gaze dropped to her breasts, the amber color of his eyes darkening at the sight of the swollen curves, even contained as they were in the sensible cotton bra she wore.

"I saw lace and silk in your drawers." The glare he turned on her had her lips parting in surprise. "Why don't you wear it?"

"Ever try running or fighting in a lace bra?" she snapped back breathlessly. "It's not real durable."

"Wear the lace and I'll do the fighting for you," he rasped. "I'll kill for you to see you in it."

His hand lifted, a single claw extending before it slid beneath the material between her breasts and sliced it apart, brushing the cups aside to allow him to stare down at the bared flesh.

"Graeme, this is crazy," she whispered.

"As you said, I'm insane," he answered absently as he brushed his cheek against the side of one swollen curve. "Why would I pretend sanity at this late date?"

His breath wafted over her nipple, the slight caress of heated air nearly dragging a whimper from her.

"You'll regret it later," she assured him. "You know how angry you get when you regret things later."

She would definitely regret it. She already regretted it. Yet her head was falling back, her back arching and her fingers sliding into his hair to hold him to her as his lips covered the hard point of her nipple.

A cry tore from her when his lips surrounded the tender tip, pulling it into his mouth and suckling at it with firm draws of his mouth. His tongue lashed at it, laved it, licked at it. Sharp teeth gripped the tortured peak. Holding it there, he rubbed his tongue against it then flicked over it. The caresses set it afire with such pleasure she was arching against him, riding the hard ridge of his erection, desperate to ease the throbbing need growing between her thighs.

Dampness spilled from her vagina, coating the folds beyond and dampening the silk covering her sex. Each draw of his mouth, each lash of his tongue or rake of his teeth against her nipple sent such sharp spirals of sensation exploding between her thighs that she found herself helpless against them.

She'd never known pleasure like this. She'd never ached like this or found herself so helpless against a man.

And it was Graeme. Graeme who had destroyed her, who had taken everything she could have fooled herself into believing might actually be hers.

"Enough." Her voice was weak, faint. She'd had to force the protest past her lips.

She'd be damned if she would reward him for tearing her life apart.

"Stop, Graeme. Just stop . . ."

His head jerked up, his lips swollen and sexy as hell. And she hated herself for noticing it.

"I won't regret it," he suddenly snarled in answer to her earlier declaration. "But I have no doubt you will regret letting that nonsense that just passed your lips free."

Before she realized what he intended, he released her.

Holding her hips until she was standing on her own, he moved back, amber fire still filling his eyes as he stared at her, his breathing hard, erratic.

No doubt she would regret it. Hell, she already regretted it.

"You need to leave." She might never get her breathing back under control. The breathless sound of it was something she'd never heard from her own lips before.

Her claws were digging into the wall behind her, her bare breasts still holding his gaze, her nipples still tight and hard, as though begging him to ignore her words.

Her body was betraying her just as eagerly as Graeme had betrayed her years before.

"Of course I do," he snarled. "God forbid you might have second thoughts, right?"

"Exactly," she hissed back at him, the feline sound harsh and filled with her own inner conflict. "God forbid I should actually depend upon you to do anything but make my life hell, is more like it. Why should I reward you for that?"

"Reward me?" Amazement filled his voice as well as his expression. "Trust me, baby, you were the one about to get the reward."

"Really?" she all but purred as she slid away from the wall, her gaze sliding over him slowly as she passed him, knowing better; the scent of his lust was far stronger, far hungrier than her awakening senses and she knew it. "Then it won't bother you a bit to know how I've fantasized about having a lover." Fantasized about him while she slept, helpless against the images. "And all the ways I've imagined rewarding him for being the man I've ached to have."

The shadows of the primal Bengal pulsed beneath his flesh as a growl rumbled in his throat.

"Don't push me, Cat," he warned her, his tone guttural as she gripped the step railing and started up the stairs.

"How I wondered what it would be like to taste his flesh, to lick over hard, hot flesh like I would lick a favorite treat. Or to rise above him and lower myself . . ."

The snarl that left his lips sent her racing up the stairs, all thought of teasing him fleeing beneath the sound of a fully aroused, lust-filled Bengal Breed intent on one thing and one thing only. Pure mindless sex.

She slammed the bedroom door behind her, locked it and stepped back from it warily, wondering if he would dare to breach it.

"You like to play very dangerous games, mate," he called out through the door.

"Go mate yourself. I wouldn't have you on a bet," she informed him mutinously. "Sorry, asshole, go find someone who doesn't know you as well as I do."

A dark male chuckle met the dare. "Think you know me, little cat? Is that really what you think?"

"That's what I know." Retrieving another bra from the drawer, she hurriedly clipped it in place before reaching for a shirt to cover it.

Damn him, that was a new bra he'd destroyed too.

"Then you should be well aware of the fact that what I claim, I keep." The low, furious warning in his voice had a chill racing up her spine. "Don't test me on this. Let another touch you, let another spill the scent of his lust around you, and you'll see just why those stupid Council scientists whimper at the very thought of me."

"Because you're fucking crazy?" she suggested mockingly, glaring at the door. "Because they know the strain of rabies they coded into your defective genetics?"

He made her so mad it was all she could do to keep from jerking the door open and confronting him again. The problem was, she'd probably find herself begging him to touch her again instead.

"Because I have no problem reaching inside their chests and allowing them to watch as I rip their hearts out." Animalistic, so primal and rough, his voice had chills racing up her spine and filled her with a heavy sense of dread. "Remember that, my little cat, if that bastard Lincoln Martinez ever even thinks to touch you. Except I'll rip his dick off first and shove it down his throat."

She blinked at the threat, almost allowing the sudden spurt of humor she felt to slip free at the final threat.

And Jonas had called her overdramatic? He hadn't heard drama yet.

The slamming of the kitchen door assured her the enraged Bengal was gone. Thankfully.

Sweet Jesus, she was in trouble here.

Pressing her hand to her stomach, she inhaled deeply, frantically trying to figure out a way out of the mess she found herself in. And yes, it was a mess. Because he might have left, but the arousal he'd created inside her hadn't.

She was going to have to change panties, because she'd definitely soaked hers with the hot spill of moisture his touch created.

And she didn't consider that a good thing. It wasn't a good thing at all.

CHAPTER 5

She would be the death of him.

Graeme had always sworn she would be the death of him. From the moment she'd begun crawling, he'd known that woman was going to be more trouble than he would know how to deal with.

Moving quickly through the tunnels between the small rental and the Reever estate, Graeme remembered how tiny she had been even then, and how she seemed to find trouble no matter the effort made to ensure she was safe.

He'd been only eleven when Brandenmore had placed her in his arms, giving the responsibility of her care to him. Her survival was up to him; he'd known it in such a heartbeat of realization that it had been shocking.

Until that moment he'd never really known a point of time when he could designate that he'd felt his animal genetics in such a separate, fierce flow of energy. It had happened in that moment, though. The boy and the immature Bengal had stood side by side inside him. The boy staring at the child, bemused by how to care for such a sickly creature. In that moment, the feral displacement between Breed genetics and human had disappeared, the animal bonding with him completely to claim that child.

He'd known she was his. The animal, as immature as it had been, had claimed her instantly. At first he'd excused it as claiming her as part of the Pride he'd always sworn he'd have. Yet he'd known better.

Judd was his brother, his twin, and though the bond of twins was always there, his affection for Cat had still been different. She would belong to him once she reached maturity. In a blink, boy and animal had known that. It hadn't been a sexual knowledge, it had been instinct. He'd found his other half, if he could ensure her survival.

His intelligence even then had been far superior to anyone he'd come in contact with. The depth of knowledge he could amass had been driving him insane, tearing his mind apart as his humanity fought the animal merged with it.

Staring into her weak, pain-ridden eyes, the bonding of the often volatile parts of all he was happened in an instant. And very little of it was actually human.

His intelligence, both human and animal, would have torn him apart if it hadn't been for that moment. Cat had centered him, had given all those jagged pieces a place to fit.

A job to complete. Her survival.

Her survival meant not just curing the genetic malfunction in her body, which he'd immediately sensed, but also ensuring such a human frailty never weakened her again.

He and Dr. Foster had isolated the genetic function of the serum created before Dr. Foster was assigned to the project. The doctor and Graeme had known that part of it could never be revealed, and they'd fought to keep it hidden. It would cure Cat, just as it was curing Honor, but with Cat the genetic virus, isolated and for the most part taken from the serum, would be added back in once Foster coded in the Breed genetics needed to activate it.

Bengal genetics.

Entering the large main cavern beneath the estate, he strode to the desk and bank of computers set up in the nearest corner. She'd managed to find most of the cameras, but he'd known she would. There were still enough left to monitor her, to ensure her security.

The grounds were heavily covered with cameras, electronic sensors and alarms. He wouldn't take her safety for granted.

Checking each level of the security he'd installed, he was aware of the scent of the approaching distraction.

Lobo Reever rarely visited the caverns beneath his home that he'd turned over to Graeme. They were Graeme's domain, it had been agreed. And now, he was visiting twice in once week.

Stepping from the rough-hewn stone staircase, the Wolf Breed moved silently into the main cavern before striding to the security monitors located on the wall to Graeme's side. Those monitors, nearly two dozen in all, encompassed the estate as a whole. His gaze lingered on one displaying the pool area and the young woman stretched out beneath the rays of the sun with lazy abandon.

"Need something?" Graeme questioned, his attention on the monitor displaying the status of the various security measures on the rental.

"Jonas was here." Lobo's attention remained on the pool area, his gaze brooding as he answered the question. "He wanted to speak to you, but it seems you weren't in."

"I had something to take care of at the rental," Graeme informed him. "Sucks to be Jonas."

Lobo's mocking grunt was more an agreement than anything else.

"Aren't you curious what he wanted?" the Wolf Breed asked after several seconds.

Was he?

"Not really." He was more intent on isolating a particular anomaly that appeared in the security programming. "Jonas rarely concerns me and what he wants is never in line with what I seem to want at the time, so I normally don't worry about it."

Amusement flickered around the other Breed.

Lobo had an odd sense of humor, though. Graeme had learned to tolerate it. After all, the Wolf Breed tolerated his often bloody hobby of interrogating Council Coyotes, so they tried to agree to disagree on such subjects.

"He's insistent I allow two of his enforcers to watch the rental," Lobo revealed. "So insistent, actually, that he's making it a Bureau request. I do have an agreement with the Bureau, Graeme. One I'd prefer not to break."

The statement wasn't a request of any sort. He was informing Graeme that, in this case, the Bureau could take precedence over Graeme's disagreement.

An irritated growl slipped past his throat. "That Lion is going to push me too far," he murmured as he set the security program to isolate and eradicate the anomaly in the security protocols he was evaluating. "Keep him away from her."

"Graeme, as much as I rarely give a damn about your various little projects in my caverns, I must point out that I don't answer to you. The favor you've extended in giving Khi this small period of time to consider her options is greatly appreciated. But I won't go to war with the Bureau of Breed Affairs for it."

Graeme lifted his lashes, staring up at him for long moments.

"At least not easily." The Wolf Breed exhaled in frustration. "That woman will be the death of me."

"It would seem we face similar ends, then," Graeme pointed out in self-disgust before pushing back from the holo-board and deactivating it. "What's Jonas's argument?"

He'd rather just rip the Bureau director's throat out, but that might upset his daughter a bit and Graeme had become fond of the toddler over the months that he'd secretly given her the serum needed to save her life. Brandenmore had found a way to initially inject the infant in an attempt to force Jonas and the Breeds to find a cure for the destruction of his own body that the serum he'd injected himself with was creating. He'd convinced Jonas the same would happen to Amber.

Lobo lowered his gaze as Graeme slid his chair from the desk and tilted the back to rest against the wall behind him before propping his feet on top of the desk. Lacing his fingers behind his head, he watched the Wolf with narrowed eyes.

"Your level of disrespect astounds me," Lobo pointed out with lazy humor.

"Your level of supposed superiority often amuses me," Graeme assured him. "But I rarely hold it against you. So what does our esteemed director want?"

The Wolf almost let a mocking grin of acknowledgment curl at his lips but held it back at the last second.

"Besides your hide?" Lobo asked.

"Well, yes." Graeme nodded. "Besides that. I'm aware it rates fairly high on his list, though."

"I'd say it tops his list," Lobo grunted. "But other than that, he's demanding that I allow Bureau surveillance of the grounds surrounding the house.

He seems a bit put out that his satellites are having trouble zooming in on it. Seems there's some atmospheric or magnetic interference."

Graeme smiled, he couldn't help it. Satisfaction could be a wonderful thing.

"I'm quite pleased with the interference as well as its cloaking." The Wolf's gray eyes mirrored Graeme's own satisfaction. "I'm especially pleased that it's untraceable. So far."

"The algorithm only kicks in when satellite detection is intercepted and it's changing constantly." Graeme shrugged. There were also protocols that helped detect any attempts to trace it. It was one of his most ingenious programs yet. He loved it.

"I consider myself quite lucky to have acquired your loyalty for the time being." Lobo sighed. "But Wyatt has the potential to become a problem, Graeme. On-the-ground surveillance could also pinpoint the location of the satellite interference."

Graeme restrained the urge to roll his eyes.

"On-the-ground surveillance won't pinpoint the problem, Lobo," he assured him. "I told you that."

"But you haven't told me why." Ice coated his voice.

No, he hadn't told him why. He hadn't explained to either Lobo or his head of security how it worked, and he wasn't about to. But tracing it would be impossible where Jonas was concerned.

Dropping the chair to all four legs, Graeme rose to his feet and moved away from the monitors as he kept Lobo in sight.

"Why doesn't matter," he reminded the other Breed. "It works."

"It's not magic, therefore, it's vulnerable," Lobo argued.

"Is this becoming an issue, Reever?" Facing him fully, Graeme narrowed his eyes on the Wolf and waited.

Losing Reever's loyalty would be a problem, but it wasn't insurmountable.

"Not an issue." Lobo shook his head, not at all concerned by Graeme's stance. "Simply an observation. At the moment, my only issue is Wyatt. As I said, a war with the Bureau would be a problem at this time. I'd prefer to stay on the friendly side, if you don't mind. But I'd also prefer not to have enforcers lurking around my property."

In that, Graeme didn't blame him a bit.

"Tell them they can watch the house all they like from the property line," he suggested, unconcerned with the problem. "Your agreement with the Bureau does not arbitrarily allow for Bureau surveillance on the grounds itself."

"Graeme, they're already watching from the property line." Reever sighed, crossing his arms over his chest, likely wrinkling the pristine white silk shirt he wore.

Lobo didn't like wrinkles, Graeme remembered in amusement.

Damn. If he had to make this a personal favor, then he was going to lose one of the debts he'd gathered over the years. Likely several of them. He didn't like the thought of that.

"Doesn't the new division director of this area owe you a favor?" Graeme asked then, his eyes narrowing on the Wolf. "You allowed the use of this cavern to take care of a little problem he had not long ago."

The execution of the man who had betrayed Rule Breaker's mate wasn't exactly a nominal debt. Reever had given the use of the caverns, supposedly, as well as a promise to keep the location and Breaker's part in it secret.

"That's the only debt Breaker owes me," Lobo growled. "I'd prefer not to use it."

Graeme stared back at him in surprise. "You want me to use my brownie points?"

"You have far more than I do in this instance," Lobo drawled knowingly. "It seems only fair you use one from what appears to be an abundance of points rather than using the only one I've acquired with the new division director."

"I've an abundance because I don't spend them without thought or give them away like fucking candy, Reever," he growled, irritated at the thought of spending one of the precious debts he'd managed to acquire.

"I want this to go away, Graeme." Smooth, without command but definitely a warning, Lobo gave a brief inclination of his head as a farewell before turning and walking away.

"Yeah, well, and I want to let the freak loose, but I keep him contained," he muttered, striding furiously back to the computers and throwing himself back in his chair.

Dammit, he didn't have time for what Lobo wanted.

Glaring at the computer screen, his eyes narrowed at the program's response to his earlier command. The anomaly wasn't part of the programming, but neither was it identified or located.

Pulling up the holo-board he went back to work.

Jonas would have to wait until later.

◆ ◆ ◆

She'd been certain she could find at least some measure of peace at the small Reever guest estate, Cat thought as she opened her eyes the next afternoon and stared across the pool at Graeme. She'd sensed him watching her, known before she even opened her eyes that he was there.

Drifting lazily in the pool behind the house, dressed in nothing but a miniscule bikini, Cat admitted that the urge to enjoy the water might have been a mistake. The Bengal was watching her like an afternoon snack after missing breakfast.

"What do you want?" she muttered.

Pushing the inflatable lounger to the steps leading into the water, she slid from the float and stepped warily onto the rock patio.

Graeme was prowling closer, his gaze flickering over her body as water dripped down her tanned flesh. The look was so intent she wondered that she couldn't feel the touch of it like a physical caress.

"Stop undressing me with your eyes," she demanded as she moved to the umbrella-shaded table and the bottle of water resting in the ice bucket there.

"You're already undressed," he assured her, his voice smooth seduction. "I was merely enjoying the view."

"Then stop enjoying the view." Not that the retort fazed him.

His lips quirked in the beginnings of a far too appealing hint of humor. And was still watching her, still stroking her with his gaze, caressing her. And she found herself far too responsive to it.

She reached for the light robe she'd brought out with her.

"Please don't, Cat." It wasn't a demand.

Turning, she met his gaze, the hunger and need in it blistering, the demand clear, but his tone was gentle, requesting. He was asking her not to put the robe on, not demanding it. At least not demanding it vocally.

"Why?" She had to turn away from him, the need she glimpsed in his gaze weakened her, made her want to forget the past thirteen years, and she didn't dare forget.

"Because you're the most beautiful vision I've ever had." His voice was rough now, the sound of it flooding her senses and her body with the most incredible weakness. The pleasure that flooded her entire being shortened her breath while causing her heart to race in excitement.

How did he do this to her? Why had her entire life been consumed by this one Breed and all the conflicting, pain-filled emotions he inspired in her?

"Why are you doing this to me, Graeme? Why are you trying to destroy me?" He'd been her world then he'd destroyed it. She'd been a child. Nothing had mattered to her but him, and he'd destroyed her.

"Destroying you was never my intent." He moved behind her, stopping only when he was within a breath of touching her. Gently, firmly, his fingers curled around her hips as his head lowered to her bare shoulder. "Hurting you was never my intent, Cat."

"Then what was your intent?" Fists clenched, she fought the lure of his body, the memory of the incredible sensations his lips could create against her flesh. "Because for something you didn't intend, you're doing a damned good job of it."

He was destroying her senses, her determination to remain aloof, her promise to herself that she would never allow him to shred her heart again. Or what still remained of her heart.

Callused fingers clenched at her hips, holding her in place when she would have eased away from him.

She couldn't do this. If she continued to stand here, to let him hold her against him, then she would cave and she would beg him to take her, to continue ripping her apart. One hand slid from her hip to her stomach where it flattened against the clenched muscles of her lower abdomen. Her eyes closed, the sensual weakness building, making a mockery of her determination to withhold herself from him.

"I can smell your need, soft and heated," he whispered at her ear. "An addictive scent I find myself longing for at the oddest moments."

"I'm sure there's a twelve-step program for that somewhere. I bet Jonas Wyatt could point you in the right direction," she assured him, forcing the sarcasm into her voice rather than the breathless need she couldn't hide from him.

The feel of his teeth raking against her neck was followed by a low, warning growl in reply to the suggestion.

"Bad girl," he berated her. "I'm sure I don't need Jonas's help in any way."

"You need help period," she assured him before gasping and finding herself turned so quickly she barely registered the move.

One second she was staring away from him, in the next she was staring up at him, her breasts pressed into his cheek, his erection, restrained only by the denim he wore, pressed into her lower stomach.

"When I found you, I was completely maddened," he growled, staring down at her with a hungry demand that flickered in the gold flecks of jungle green eyes. "I was instinct and intellect only. No mercy, no compassion." One hand threaded into the back of her damp hair, clenching there as his gaze flickered over her face. "The last time I was in this desert searching for you, only the scent of Claire Martinez surrounded your body. There was no hint of my Cat, no matter how similar you were in looks, I was fooled. When I returned, there was no hint of Claire, only my Cat, and her pain. Her loneliness." His voice dropped, his head lowering as his lips brushed against the corner of hers. "All the madness that had driven me for so long eased away and the monster I'd been settled back. What little sanity remained snapped into place and I knew why the monster existed to begin with." He paused, his lips whispering over hers, but refusing to initiate the kiss she was suddenly hungry for. "Do you know why it existed, Cat?"

She shook her head, fighting to breathe, fighting not to take the kiss she needed.

"Why?" She forced the question out, wishing he'd just hurry and give her what she needed.

"For you," he breathed. "It lived for you, Cat. To protect you. To hold back the horror of the risk of Bennett finding you and dragging you back to the center. It existed, to ensure you lived."

The monster everyone spoke of in the past months had existed for blood . . . And each time it had taken blood it had been someone that threatened her, or those she cared for.

"You swore to kill me." It was all she could do to force the words past her lips. "To kill me and Judd. You knew what you were saying."

She remembered that clearly. Cold, deadly purpose had filled his eyes, his expression.

"I was a child, G," she whispered, remembered pain slicing at her heart again. "You were all I had to depend on. All I knew of love."

I never loved you . . . You were my experiment.

She pressed her forehead to his chest, wishing she could wipe the memory from her mind, from her heart.

"I needed you." The fingers gripping his shoulders curled into fists. "Years, Graeme. For years I worried, I cried, I searched for you." Shudders tore through her body as aching, furious rage tore through her. "I needed you." It was a snarl, a deep female rasp of overwhelming pain as she tore from him, memories and so many nights of unrelenting hunger to just see him. "Damn you, G. Damn you. I survived without you for the past thirteen years and I'll survive without you now. Get the hell away from me."

She felt as though she was going crazy now. Rage and hunger. The need to push him away, the need to hold to him so tight she was never without him ever again. The conflicting emotions were tearing her apart.

"You survived?" Catching her arm he swung her around again, his lips pulled back from his teeth in a grimace of anger. "Is that what you call it? Hiding? Pretending to be Claire Martinez? You took her personality as well as her identity and hid everything you were, every part of you, when you could have been who you were, who you were intended to be."

Mockery shot through her. "Who was I intended to be, Graeme?" she questioned with such false sweetness she nearly gagged on it. "It seems only you know that answer. What did you think you created when you shot that shit inside me with those therapies? Did you justify it each time I screamed and cried and then lay wasted for days begging you to let me die?" she screamed that question at him. A question she hadn't even known tormented her until that moment. "What was I supposed to be, G?"

Tears filled her eyes. She hated that. Hated the weakness and the emotions that tore her apart each time she remembered that she had been his experiment.

His *experiment.*

"You were supposed to live," he growled furiously, gripping her arms and hauling her back to his chest, glaring down at her as the pupils of his eyes became obliterated by the green. "You had to live and there was only one way to ensure that, with Breed DNA. There was no other way to wipe that fucking disease out of your body and I wasn't going to let you die. You were mine."

"I was your experiment," she cried out. "You said it yourself, you never loved me." A sob tore from her throat, knowing that wound had never healed. "Do you know what you did to me that night? Do you have any idea what you did when you told me that?"

"Do you have any idea what it did to me?" Before she could answer him, before she could do more than recognize the animalistic rasp of pain in his voice as his lips suddenly covered hers.

Hard. Possessive.

His tongue pushed past her lips, determined and hungry and spilling the most alluring hint of spice. That hint of taste captivated her, left her wanting more and had her lips closing around his tongue, some primal impulse demanding she draw on it, to pull more of that elusive taste into her senses. Moaning, clutching at his shoulders once again, Cat reveled in the pleasure, losing herself in it.

She should be fighting him and she knew it. She should be fighting this overwhelming need, and she couldn't, had no desire to now that she was being consumed by his kiss. All she could do was hold on to him, hold him to her and relish in the fact that he was here now. That the lost, agonized part of her soul found solace.

When his head jerked back, his lips pulling from hers, Cat could only stare up at him, dazed and uncertain. Blinking in shock at the abrupt withdrawal it took a moment to realize what had disturbed the chaotic hunger he'd unleashed on her. The Wolf Breed scent was vaguely familiar though she couldn't quite place it until he spoke.

"Sorry, Graeme," the Breed cleared his throat uncomfortably. "We have a situation at the estate. Alpha Reever asked that you be found immediately."

Cat moved to turn and face the Breed, uncomfortable with her back turned to him.

"Don't." Graeme held her still with a growl as his hand jerked out and returned with the robe discarded on the back of the patio chair.

Staring up at him she let him help her into it, remaining silent as she pulled the front edges together and belted them snugly.

The disturbance was for the best, she thought. No good could come of the trust she wanted so desperately to give him, or the emotions burning in her chest. He'd already betrayed her once, he would betray her again.

"This isn't over," he warned her as she stepped away from him. "Don't imagine it is."

Cat could only shake her head. "It was over a long time ago, you just refuse to accept it."

Without turning to face the Breed that came for Graeme, Cat escaped back into the house and the realization that nothing would ever be easy, or simple, where Graeme was concerned. And what was left of her heart had no escape from the destruction he'd wreak in it.

CHAPTER 6

Night was encroaching across the desert before Cat managed to get her emotions, let alone her hormones, under control. Confusion was still running rampant, though. The confusion part was probably harder to deal with.

Stepping to the patio outside the large family room, a glass of wine in hand, Cat couldn't help but marvel at the beauty of the landscape, the rich black velvet and diamond-drop brilliance of the sky above and the sweet scent of a land unmarred by the scents and sounds of the city.

For all of Window Rock's conveniences, at the moment she wouldn't trade a single sweet breath for all of them. How she'd longed to escape to the shadowed, seemingly barren land over the years. So many nights she'd wanted to run, to hunt, to slip away from the ever-present gloom the Martinez household seemed to possess.

The scent of booze-laden escape didn't exist here, neither did the putrid scent of guilt, suspicion and hatred. But there had been happy memories, though none had anything to do with Raymond or Maria Martinez.

Grandfather Orrin, with his dry sense of humor and unexpected calls to Raymond to send his "granddaughter" to him immediately. He would hustle her into his truck, wink at her, then sometimes, for days at a time, show her the desert he loved, or the memories he'd amassed in pictures.

Terran, Claire's uncle, would often take her on vacations with him and Isabelle and Chelsea. A week of lazy wallowing in the sun next to some tropical beach where drinks were delivered by barely dressed men and Raymond's cruelties didn't exist.

Where were Isabelle and Chelsea now? she wondered. She knew Isabelle and her new husband, or mate, were honeymooning in some secret location. Just as Honor and her husband-mate, Stygian, were doing.

Undisclosed locations. Yeah. They were hiding in Breed Secure desert homes in the area. They were close, but she hadn't seen them, hadn't heard from them.

Chelsea had visited once, but the revelation that her cousin was an imposter had made the visit a bit uncomfortable for the other woman. She'd been distracted, choosing her words carefully as they talked.

Linc was the only member of her former family that she'd seen, outside of Terran and Orrin, in the weeks since the charges against Raymond had been filed.

Charges Linc had clearly wanted to deny. Not that she blamed him. How horrible it must be to have to face what his father truly was. To admit he had come from such filth as Raymond Martinez.

Why hadn't she contacted him and told him how cruel Raymond was? Because she'd known he would have never stood by and allowed it. And her suspicion that he was part of the Unknown had kept her from contacting them as well. Informing anyone of Raymond's cruelties might have resulted in him actually contacting the Genetics Council sooner, though, and they would have moved her. What the Unknown hid, no one found. And she couldn't risk not being there when Graeme came for her as she had known he would. The Unknown would have ensured even he couldn't find her.

The shadowy group of warriors assigned to protect her while she'd posed as Claire Martinez had pulled back once she'd stepped away from the protection of Claire's identity, she'd been told.

She'd never needed them, but knowing they were near had always given her a measure of confidence in her security.

A security she didn't have confidence in now.

Hell, she didn't even trust Graeme's or Lobo Reever's security around the house and she couldn't pinpoint why.

No doubt she hadn't found all of Graeme's cameras, and he would have the house and grounds secured from every corner. Against everything and everyone but himself. The one thing she probably needed protection from thc most.

Was he truly as crazed as he seemed sometimes?

She almost smiled at the thought. Of course he was. He'd always been a little left of sane, but as a child, she'd loved him that much more for it.

I never loved you . . . you were my experiment . . .

She flinched at the memory of the pain that had ripped her apart that night. As if someone had reached inside her soul and torn it free of her body. It had destroyed years of trust, of security. It had destroyed her perceptions of who she was, and why he had forced her to live so many times.

Not because he needed her childish adoration. Not because she meant anything to him. Because she was his experiment. The Breed he had created from the scraps of a dying child.

He should have allowed her to die. Her childhood had been a series of experiments so excruciating she still had nightmares of it. Once escaping that, she'd been restrained once more and forced to watch life pass by as Claire Martinez in the hopes that by doing so, she'd be there when he came for her.

She'd ached to run, to hunt. To train and fight. The few times she managed to escape Raymond to do so had been so exhilarating it had been actually painful to return to that gloomy house. And each time she'd escaped into the night, she'd searched for her G, wondering if he'd finally found the clues she'd sent to reveal to him where she was and the identity she was using.

Now here she was, watching the night, enclosed by walls and being monitored by cameras once again. Damn. When would it end?

Finishing her wine and returning to the house, she locked up, checked the windows and doors one last time and moved upstairs to her bedroom. For the first time since moving there she closed the balcony doors and locked them.

She felt restless, on edge. The rapidly maturing Breed genetics were being a bitch. She couldn't seem to find a balance at all, especially since Linc and Raymond's little visit.

A long shower later she crawled into the overly large bed, one of the lacy little nighties Graeme had bitched over covering her body.

Bastard. She told herself the decision to wear the sexy little gown was to torture him. She was terribly afraid the truth was far more primal. He'd wanted her to wear it. And at one time nothing had mattered more than pleasing her G.

No doubt he was watching her.

Where else would he hide cameras that she hadn't thought to look? she wondered as she yawned and snuggled into the bed. She'd have to go through the house again tomorrow and see if she could find any other likely hiding places.

An instant, raging alarm clashed through her senses with such abrupt speed she was instantly awake. And it was too late. She sensed the breeze drifting past the balcony doors, but something else moved much faster, with far more deadly accuracy. The second the pressure syringe injected the drug into the vein at her neck, Cat knew the restlessness she had felt earlier for the warning it had been.

"No!" Her ragged snarl was one of rage as everything began shutting down, even as knowledge flashed through her mind.

That agonizing burn along her nerve endings—every nerve ending— a pain no Breed had ever been able to fully describe began shutting down her ability to move, to speak. To protect herself. Animal instincts honed to perfection surged forward, giving her just a moment to jump from the bed.

She nearly fell instead.

A fiery lash of agony began tracking through her body, spreading through her. The burn raced beneath her flesh, moving steadily to her brain.

No. This couldn't be happening.

The paralytic was fast acting, taking the ability to move, to speak . . . to scream.

She had to escape.

Dammit, she shouldn't have destroyed so many of the cameras. What if there were no more in the bedroom to alert Graeme of what was going on?

She was screwed. It was that simple.

She made it as far as the middle of her bedroom floor, only halfway to the door before she crumpled. Unable to cushion the fall, or the wrist she felt break as she went down. The pain would have been agonizing if she hadn't learned long ago what true agony was.

The burn was moving through her brain now, the rest of her body was sensitized, pain receptors heightened and awaiting the next lash of sensation.

Helpless. Far too vulnerable and with no defenses whatsoever.

How had her balcony been breached without the alarms going off? She hadn't touched the cameras or the security sensors there.

Unless it was Graeme.

Would he be so cruel as to inject her with the paralytic? To hurt her this way? No. Graeme would find a far more effective way to punish her. This wasn't something he would do.

The drug, created by Genetics Council monsters, was amazingly efficient. There was nothing she could do while under its effects. No Breed had ever been able to fight past it, no matter how strong their will.

A faint creek of the floor outside the bedroom had her fracturing senses pausing for a moment, waiting, feeling the danger coming.

Lying on her side as she was, she could see the bedroom door moving slowly, opening as though in slow motion, making her wait.

He thought all she knew was the shadow moving toward her through the entrance.

His scent reached her even before the door opened, filtering through the animal's senses.

It wasn't Graeme.

She watched as Raymond moved steadily closer, the scent of his malevolent hatred sickening. With the door opened, other scents reached her as well. She could smell the scent of the Jackal Breeds now. The few to have survived were used by the Genetics Council only when absolutely necessary. So few survived the creation process, but those that lived were vile, brutal soldiers with instincts that had amazed the trainers.

"Fucking animal." Raymond's curse was followed by a hard kick to her undefended ribs.

Agony erupted in the point where his boot met her body. She could do nothing to show her pain, nothing to escape it. It made the animal inside her crazed.

It made *her* crazed.

Her breath didn't even break as the pain of it focused at the contact point, exploding outward as far as flesh and bone would be affected. The paralytic kept her vital organs working properly while ensuring the pain was agonizing.

Nothing broke. She prayed Raymond didn't know that or he'd make certain it did.

She couldn't even turn her gaze up to him, couldn't force him to stare into her eyes as she glared her hatred at him. She could only stare straight ahead, unable to so much as blink.

There was no way to shield the agonizing pain gripping every cell of her body, though.

"Bitch," Raymond snarled. "You finally managed to turn Linc against me, didn't you? You've been nothing but trouble. Nothing but a blight on my family."

And here she thought he held that title. Damn. How wrong could a tigress be?

"Thought you could escape me, didn't you?" Raymond bent closer to her, the broad, sneering features filled with distaste. "Thought the Breeds could save you by hiding here. Intimidate me," he hissed. "I contacted the Council. They're here for you, you freak. They'll take you and cage you just as you should have stayed caged all along. As soon as I've finished with you they'll make damned sure you never open your mouth again and cause me so much as a moment's trouble."

But they hadn't meant to keep her caged.

They had meant to euthanize her.

She had escaped then, she would find a way to escape now. She hoped she found a way to escape . . .

Rising again Raymond aimed another blow to her ribs, connecting with her stomach instead.

She couldn't even throw up.

Cat's stomach pitched and roiled with the agony, bile gathered in her throat, but the paralytic refused to allow it to release.

"Let's see what they do with you then, fucking freak," he grated out at her with hate-filled fury. "I won't have to deal with you ever again. Will I?"

God, she had to find a way to stay alive. And she would, as soon as she could think, as soon as the pain eased just enough for her to pull her senses back in place and to figure out just what to do.

"They'll have fun with you before they take you out of here," Raymond snarled. "Lobo Reever's security bastard will find your blood, smell the scent of your rape, and we'll see how crazy he gets then. Son of a bitch. I'll kill him yet."

Kill Graeme? He may well kill her, but he'd never kill Graeme. And once Graeme realized what had happened here . . . *Oh, Raymond, how I would love to hear your screams.*

Right now, the only screams she could hear were the ones in her own head. The amplification of pain had agony resonating from her wrist. Her ribs were pounding and she was terrified one may be cracked. Her stomach was on fire from the kick to it, and fear was a vile taste in the back of her throat.

How long she lay there she wasn't certain. The pain radiating through her nerves had eased, but the broken wrist and bruised ribs had yet to stop screaming. That would take a while. She remembered that. She was barely four the first time the scientists had broken bones while she was under the obscene effect of that drug. Four years old and she had believed her G had deserted her, that he'd let them hurt her. Until she'd been returned to the cells to see the tears that streaked the savage, agonized expression on his face and the restraints that held him to his cot.

He hadn't deserted her then, but he had deserted her eight years later. He'd left, only to return for vengeance and blood. He'd probably gloat that she'd been caught so effectively after destroying the cameras. Or would he? He'd been enraged when he found Raymond and Linc there. Would he be angry instead?

With Graeme, it was anyone's guess.

No, it wasn't, she realized. Graeme would go insane if he saw her now. The maddened creature lurking inside him would emerge with such a need for vengeance that there would be no stopping it. He wouldn't rest until those responsible for her pain suffered a hundred times worse. When they died, it would be only after he'd inflicted all the torture possible to inflict. Jackals could take a lot of pain, they could withstand it for weeks. Raymond would take more finesse to keep him alive for the pain she knew Graeme would mete out.

She belonged to him. She always had. He had stood by stoically when the therapies had left her screaming, her body feeling as though it were being torn apart as they reshaped who and what she was. But the few experiments Brandenmore had ordered had left him crazed.

The door began opening again, slowly. There was no scent to herald this arrival. It wasn't Raymond, it wasn't a Jackal.

The shadow that entered the room was far different from Raymond's. Taller, more powerful.

Graeme.

He was the bogeyman, and the scent of icy merciless death radiated around him and filled her with an overwhelming fear that who she faced now may never allow the Graeme she knew to return.

"Now, what kind of trouble have you gotten yourself into this time?" he asked softly, the ice easing as just a hint of anger tinged his voice. "Would you like a bit of help, my little cat?"

• C H A P T E R 7 •

Like a bit of help?

He was kidding, right?

Damn him, she'd known he would gloat when the insanity took hold of him. He just had to show all that superior attitude before helping her off the damned floor and getting rid of the trash downstairs.

She'd call him an ass, but it didn't apply.

Graeme had moved past the ass phase at fourteen, surpassed prick before he was fifteen and made maniac look like a picnic by the time he was seventeen. Now, at thirty-six and in the grip of a rage that was far beyond primal, he was simply asinine. Insane and asinine

Cat wanted to scream at him. She needed to curse him. If she managed to get out of this she was going to . . . what?

It wouldn't exactly do her any good to tell Mommy on him, now, would it.

She didn't have one.

Dammit.

The bastard moved lower, practically lying down on the carpet beside her so he could stare into her eyes.

So she could stare into his eyes.

A hard amber flecked with jungle green glittering like fire and obliterating both the pupil and the whites of his eyes stared back at her. Black stripes bisected his bronzed flesh, primal stripes, they were called. A Bengal's primal marks would show up along his body from face to ankle. The sight of it would be completely sexy, she thought, irritated that she'd even considered such a thing.

He just stared at her for what seemed forever. He didn't smirk, didn't sneer, just stared back at her. She'd never known this part of him. She'd sensed it a few times at the research center, lurking beneath the killing rage, but it had never really emerged. And now that she was seeing it, she fully understood why his name could cause the Council's scientists to tremble in fear. What had Dr. Foster created when he created this creature.

Graeme shook his head then, his expression one of mocking disapproval. "I'm so disappointed. I trained you better, little cat. Much better. What the hell happened?"

Disappointed? He was disappointed?

A heavy breath left his lips when she didn't speak. But then, the asshole knew she couldn't speak.

She hated him! Right now, she simply hated him.

"Come on, baby, let's get you off the floor." He finally lifted himself to a crouch beside her, his arms sliding beneath her to lift her against him.

She was boneless. Unable to stiffen, to speak or even to scream as the weight of her hand began settling in her wrist.

The agony was indescribable.

Reality receded just a bit. Everything flashed and exploded around her as the pain detonated along her nervous system, amplified by the paralytic and exploding over and over again through her senses.

For a second, Graeme froze. Then carefully, very carefully, as agonized, silent howls of shattering pain reverberated through her head, he slid one arm beneath her wrist to support it.

His eyes were locked on hers as he lifted her, watching her, and she wondered if he could see the pain there. If he could sense not just her but the animal inside her screaming in agony.

Oh God, it hurts. Oh God, G . . . mindlessly she cried out for him as she always had in the labs.

As she often did in her nightmares.

A hard growl, rife with rage, rumbled from the chest she was held against.

They'll die for this, little cat, the words whispered through her mind, shocking her with his ability to connect with her there. *They will die painfully.*

He laid her on her bed, settling her head against her pillow, his gaze still connected to hers. Gently, almost reverently, he settled her arm to the bed last, ensuring her wrist was cushioned to ease the pain as much as possible.

"Poor little cat, my Cat." His tone grated with guttural fury. "That's okay, baby, they'll never have a chance to hurt you again."

Never have a chance to hurt her again?

What had he done?

Lifting his hand, he trailed his fingertips down her cheek, and even amid the pain there was the faintest sensation of pleasure.

He was going to drive her crazy, make her just as insane as he was.

"You're mine," he told her, his voice hardening as he stared into her eyes. "My little cat. No other is allowed to harm you in such a way without paying for it dearly. What I have done, what I will do, is my right as your mate."

No one but him, right?

He glared down at her. "I have never harmed you physically," he answered the thought. "Never, Cat, would I see you harmed. No matter your belief."

When this crazy drug wore off she was buying a ticket so far away from him that it would take him a lifetime to track her down. She should have done that at the first rumor that a crazy Bengal was tracking someone in the desert.

He grunted, the sound beastly. "After all your hard work to draw me to you?" He tsked. "I had already found you, you know."

She was going to kill him.

He simply chuckled as she strained against the drug holding her immobile.

"They're waiting for me, just as they left you waiting," he promised then. "Come on, now, let's see what damage has been inflicted so I can take care of the trash in the other room."

It was going to hurt.

She wanted to beg him to be careful. She wanted to scream as his touch neared her wrist. Just before the point where the explosive pain would rupture through her, he stopped.

"Broken wrist," he snarled, breathing in harshly and shaking his head. He moved his fingertip slowly, only barely whispering over the skin, to her fingers.

Moving to her other arm he checked it, then her legs. And still, he watched her eyes. Even when she couldn't see his, she knew he was watching hers.

Could she bear it if he hurt her further? She expected it. It could still come. He would be that diabolical. Trick her into believing he wouldn't push the barriers of sensory agony only to break them.

Such distrust, little cat. I am the monster the world will forever know should you be taken from it. You are all that holds what little sanity I can call my own in place. And you would distrust me so? The mockery in the thought was tinged was such a well of complete icy intellect, logic and merciless hunger for the enemies blood that terror skated through her.

He moved to her neck, collarbone.

She could see his eyes now.

Fury mixed with madness and some emotion she couldn't define.

His hand lifted, a single finger extending, and as she watched, a lethally sharp, strong claw extended from the tip, splitting the skin as it emerged and came into view.

Yeah, neat trick. She could do that too. Without the blood staining her nail.

His lips quirked as she felt him, she actually felt him, somehow merged with her, reading the pain-filled mockery and fear.

Lowering his hand, he sliced her gown straight down the middle.

Silk fell away from her, baring her breasts, the naked mound of her sex. She had never had curls between her thighs. As with all Breed females, body hair on her arms, armpits, legs and between her thighs was nonexistent.

She should be completely embarrassed. Cat knew she should be. She had never been able to bare her body to anyone, especially a man. She was still a virgin, though she doubted that state would remain long if her earlier response to him was any indication.

Bending closer to her, Graeme stared at the area just below her breasts. His fingertips whispered over it, tested the discoloration around it before lifting his gaze to hers once again.

"It's not broken," he promised.

Then his eyes, the gold in them burning, moved back to her breasts. From there, his eyes narrowed, looking lower, easing to her thighs as Cat watched him from her periphery, trying to hide her fear of what he would do from the connection he'd made while in the grip of the beast he'd become.

"Not while you're unable to fight," he snapped, furious with the moment of uncertainty she'd felt. "Dammit, Cat, as beautiful as you are, my only intent is to ensure you're not in need of medical attention before I take care of that vermin that dared do this."

His lips thinned in fury, the stripes crossing his face blacker than they were last time, as though they lightened or darkened according to the level of his anger.

He returned his gaze to her thighs and her mound, and she knew he'd found the faintest trace of the scars there.

A fingertip brushed over her upper mound, the sensation so different, so heated and extreme, that the fierce pleasure radiated over the echoing pain in her wrist and the areas Raymond had kicked.

"You'll tell me how this occurred," he whispered, the sound almost too low to hear. "No one marks what's mine and doesn't pay dearly for it."

They paid by my hand.

The Coyote she suspected Raymond had ordered to punish her years before had found his blood running from his neck as he awoke in the desert several nights later. She hadn't called the Unknown, she'd found him herself and exacted her vengeance. He looked at her one last time, regret flickering in his gaze.

"You've turned into a beautiful woman, little cat," he growled, reaching across her to draw the sheet over her body.

She could still see him as he moved, reaching for a pack she hadn't known he'd laid on the floor. It took only moments for him to show her the pressure syringe he held in one hand.

"It will ease the effects of the paralytic. Your ability to move will return far quicker and it'll ease the pain of the broken wrist." He placed it at the side of her neck and activated the injector. "And any Council bastard stupid enough to inject you again will find it has little effect on you. Consider it an immunization."

He'd always been all about the immunizations, she remembered.

Cat barely felt the burst of pressure that sent the drug into her vein.

Pulling back, he touched her cheek, his thumb hovering just above her lips before he paused glaring down at her. "I have matters to attend to downstairs now. Two Jackals and one Nation chief. They'll be able to scream for you. I always thought it rather cruel to paralyze the ability to scream, didn't you? I believe I've adjusted that nasty little drug to allow for the screams," he promised her.

He'd lost his mind.

And he was going to have who scream for her?

Raymond and those Jackals he'd secured?

He thought she wanted to hear that?

She had never tortured any of the Council Breeds she had been forced to kill. She had never wanted to hear their screams. Hell, the sight of blood even made her queasy. She couldn't stand to look at it for long.

She stared back at him as he watched her eyes, knowing his freaky ability to read her thoughts would allow him to sense her complete distaste of such a thing.

Another rumble of rage vibrated from him as a heavy frown jerked between his brows. "Fuck. Council's gotta be using defective genetics. I swear to God, where have all the bloodthirsty Breeds gone? The ones with balls? Breeds don't have balls anymore," he snarled down at her. "Is it too much to ask? Too much to expect a Breed to want blood? We were fucking created to crave the taste of blood. What the hell happened to you? I gave you all the right genetics. I know I did."

She had actually never craved such a repugnant thing.

Cat remembered this rant, though it had obviously strengthened over the years. Graeme had become discontent with the level of courage and fight in his enemies even before their escape from the lab.

"Don't want to hear their screams, do you, Cat?" He sounded disgusted now. "Of course you don't. Now, just what made me think any differently? The fact that they wanted to hear your screams, perhaps? How about all those years I taught you better than to have mercy for your enemy?" he snapped furiously. "By God, I know I did."

The stripes across Graeme's face seemed to flare and darken again as madness lit his gaze and the amber of his eyes glowed like golden fire.

"I can't believe this," he muttered, straightening, still glowering at her. "Cannot fucking believe you. I know I taught you better than this. I remember it . . ."

He seemed to be having quite the conversation with himself. She wondered if he ever needed anyone to participate other than himself.

Yes, he'd tried to teach her to show no mercy. He'd taught her how to kill, taught her to separate justice and vengeance. He'd taught her blood was necessary to survive. But he hadn't taught her to enjoy it, though she knew he seemed to.

He seemed to. Inside, though, deep, where he thought no one could sense it, Graeme regretted far more than even he suspected.

At least, he once had.

What had happened to him?

The need to reach up and touch the harsh line of his lips, to draw them to hers, was like a hunger she couldn't push aside. The need to push away the insane fury in his eyes destroyed her.

"Pity, Cat?" he sneered, flipping the sheet over her bare body. "Is that pity I can feel reaching out to me? For me?" Demonic amusement flashed in his eyes. "Save it. Those bastards downstairs need it far more than I do."

No, they were beyond pity, but it wasn't pity she felt. It wasn't compassion or sympathy. What it was, she wasn't certain, but it hurt to see the soul-deep fury raging in his eyes.

Where had it come from? Even in the labs it hadn't been rooted so deeply inside the essence of who and what he was.

"You don't want to know what let the monster free, little cat," the beast snarled. "But you will know the price your enemies will pay for striking out at you."

A savage growl rumbled in his chest as his lip lifted in a snarl. "And, I hope you can ignore what you don't want to hear, because I want to hear their fucking screams." He thumped his chest with one hand. "And by God, I was created with enough balls to make sure they scream loud and long."

Of course he was.

He was Graeme. Gideon. G. All the parts of the Breed she had adored with every fiber of her being. But she'd never been unaware of the strength and determined savagery inside him. It was the pure mercilessness she'd been unaware of.

Turning, he stomped—*Graeme stomped?*—back to the bedroom door and slammed it closed behind him.

Graeme stomped? Oh God, that couldn't be a good thing . . .

What, she wondered, would happen when he returned? Once he'd heard the screams, spilled their blood and rendered them lifeless?

Where would the madness go then? What would its focus be once he'd killed . . .

She couldn't allow it to happen, not here, not for her or like this.

Raymond Martinez needed to answer for his crimes, not escape them so easily. And the Bureau needed to know about the existence of the Jackals. Graeme needed to let Jonas take care of this, build a rapport with the Bureau that would protect him should suspicion of who he was ever come to light.

Dammit. When was that fucking drug going to ease so she could move?

So she could stop him. Because he damned sure wasn't listening to her anymore.

◆　　◆　　◆

Damn her.

Fucking damn her.

Those bastards were going to rape her in her own bed while she was paralyzed by that crazed Council drug and she didn't want to hear their screams?

Well, he did.

He wanted them to scream until their voices broke, until they were rabid with the fucking pain, insane from it. They were fucking Jackals, they might actually make it worthwhile to torture them.

Raymond Martinez would scream for a long time, he was sure. That bastard wanted to live. He wanted to live a long time. Long enough to spend that fucking case of cash and gold those Council misfits had given him as payment for Cat. And he knew. The son of a bitch fucking knew his daughter lived in Cat. That Claire Martinez's spirit was still a part of Cat. And he didn't care.

Moving back to the living room he crouched next to the two Jackals first.

Bastards.

He'd taped their lips to keep them from screaming and distracting him before he was ready to deal with them.

Damn her. Damn that woman . . .

He ripped the adhesive from their lips, smiling at their grunts of discomfort.

Even Jackals were weak-kneed little pussies after all.

"You think that's uncomfortable?" he muttered. "Discomfort is the first vivisection and you can't scream. It's feeling their fingers probing at your organs and innards and praying for death as you piss yourself."

Silent screams. Silent prayers.

The Jackals stared back at him with cold, hard purpose, watching, waiting, searching for a weakness.

He smiled slowly, satisfaction rumbling in his chest at the flicker of unease in the biggest one's pale yellow gaze.

"You know who I am, don't you?" he whispered. "Do they still call me the bogeyman?"

"They'll be pleased you're still alive," the Jackal rasped, barely able to speak. "As well as your mate."

The monster, the freak without mercy, compassion or any semblance of warmth, jumped further into his senses; the sound that left his throat was demonic.

"I have no mate," he growled. "I have only the obligation to protect those of my Pride, Jackal. My only purpose. My only reason for being." Because the mate would suffer without them.

And in a way it was true. When the monster was free, all bonds, all affection, all respect was obliterated. Only one purpose filled him. Protecting the mate only Graeme could claim.

And he was convincing. He could smell it on them.

"I've made the strongest Council Coyotes piss themselves within ten minutes," he observed then. "How long will the two of you last before the scent of your urine offends my senses?"

He'd give them at least fifteen minutes. These two looked pretty strong. And Jackals were tortured from childhood, their training a reign of terror designed to ensure only the most brutally strong survived. Before they reached age ten, only one littermate would still live. The only one strong enough to watch the others starve so he could eat. The one strong enough to murder all who stood in the way of his escape from the putrid, waste-packed cell they were locked into.

"She would have me know mercy," he growled, and hope flickered in their eyes.

Graeme smiled. A curve of his lips that dimmed hope and brought the knowledge of certain death instead.

"She doesn't know, they tore the mercy from me the day they tore my heart from my chest . . ."

The monster ached, craved, hell, it salivated for the sounds of their screams.

Narrowing his eyes on them, he watched them, drew their scents into his senses, broke the markers down, noted the various differences and, as he'd learned to do in the research center, tracked every fucking gene that made them what they were. That was a Jackal's weakness. Facing what he actually was, knowing his history and discovering that someone else knew it too.

"Do you know why they call me the bogeyman?" he asked softly, lazily, despite the sound of hell in his voice.

The strongest simply stared back at him. The weaker one, his gaze flickered for just a second. And Graeme knew why, just as the Jackal did. Because Graeme could sense far more than the Jackal wanted known.

He focused on that one. "Do you enjoy servicing your Council master?" he asked softly, the scent of the human's domination over the Jackal still lingering on the creature. "I can still smell his release on you, despite your attempt to clean it. Do you pretend to enjoy having his release fill you, rather than the other way around?" Jackals could be driven to a maddened death by attempting to dominate them. The scent of humiliation was thick on this Jackal.

A vicious snarl, enraged and exhibiting a loss of control, escaped the creature.

The other still stared back at the monster that would kill him and his partner. But what Graeme sensed there was something far different.

"When will you kill his rapist?" he asked the stronger of the two, delving straight to the Jackal's weak spot. "Do you enjoy sharing your lover?"

Jackals simply didn't share. Anything. Not food, not loyalty or compassion or lovers. It wasn't in their nature.

What they did do was form partnerships with their lovers. Strength and tactical advantage. And they formed lasting partnerships. The weaker Jackal was this one's partner in all ways.

The stronger had decidedly more control over his possessiveness, though. He simply stared back, saying nothing, feeling nothing.

"Doesn't matter," Graeme decided. "You'll both die here, so neither of you will have to face the Council's indignities again. Will you?"

"What do you know of their indignities?" the bigger one asked then, his tone rather curious. "The bogeyman was once the favored child of his creator. Would you have been favored had you starved your littermates to escape a cell packed with the waste and decay of the dead?"

Graeme's brow arched at the question. "Thankfully, I was created not simply to follow orders, as Jackals were, it seems."

"If I were simply following orders, then the woman would have already been taken and given to the scientists awaiting her." He shrugged. "I was in place long before she came here." He looked around the room to indicate the house. "His call to the Council and his demand to hear her screams first merely gave us the opportunity to achieve our own ends."

"I don't negotiate for freedom, Jackal," Graeme snarled, furious that the attempt was being made. "There's nothing you can say, nothing you have, that would convince me not to kill you and your partner. If I won't spare you for her"—he pointed toward the foyer and stairs leading to Cat's room—"then nothing will spare you."

"Your mate or your child," the Jackal grunted. "Either one is a weakness."

"An alpha's Pride is his children, his brothers, his sisters," he informed the creature with insulting disgust. "Something those of your ilk know nothing of."

Jackals may fight in groups for protection, but they fought independently of one another.

"Weaknesses," the Jackal repeated. "You are defined by them. Weakened by them. Your survival is limited, Gideon."

The monster filled him, darkening the stripes on his face and body, filling him with a primal intelligence and savagery that was like being on a high. Like a drug that opened all the senses, sharpened reflexes and knowledge. A possession of such power he reveled in as it filled him.

"Limited, Jackal?" The deepening of the grating tone wasn't lost on the Jackal. For the first time, what the Jackal sensed coming from the Breed they called the bogeyman filled him with fear. "My survival never concerns me. If tomorrow comes, it comes with visions of blood, of my heart beating in front of my face even as my body fights to survive. If it doesn't come, then it's peace. You deserve no peace, but I'm here to give it to you."

The Jackal was finally accepting there was no negotiating with a complete lack of sanity.

"She would have me kill you quickly." He watched the two with calculated interest. "Doesn't want to hear your fucking screams. Well, I want to hear your screams!"

Claws lengthened, razor sharp, strong, the slight curve perfect for ripping and shredding flesh from living body.

Glancing to his side he watched as Raymond Martinez looked on in horror, terror filling his expression, shock glazing his eyes.

"You're next," he promised the Nation chief. "Take notes." Graeme had perched him on the living room chair before going to his little cat in anticipation of letting her listen to the Jackals' screams.

Unintelligible mutters came from Raymond's taped lips as drool eased down his chin.

A chuckle rasped from Graeme's throat. The monster he became in any threat against his mate drew satisfaction and strength from his enemies' fear, from their pain. Anything, anyone, evil enough to strike against such perfection as his Cat deserved all the pain he could give them, and more besides.

"What are you?" the lead Jackal asked curiously, obviously fighting against the paralytic, trying to force his body to move.

He was growing desperate, though only the scent of that desperation was apparent. Desperate to save his partner.

Looking between the two, he growled low, a rumble of warning, of intent.

"The Council's worst nightmare," he rasped. "A monster they dragged from the depths of an agony no man or beast should ever know."

"Others will come." The warning was given freely. "They believe she's your mate, your weakness. They won't stop until they have her."

"And I won't stop until all of you are dead." Echoing with death, his voice was dragged from the pit of the monster's soul as he moved to the weaker Jackal. "This one is your weakness, Jackal. You can hear him scream . . ."

CHAPTER 8

"Gideon?" Her voice, sweet, a summer rain infused with innocence, caused the monstrous rage filling him to pause.

"Leave," he snapped without looking at her. "You have no stomach for it, so go now."

He could smell her pain, her certainty that she could call him back from the rage consuming him.

She didn't understand. It was her only protection. This merciless determination to do what must be done at all costs. His ability to retreat and allow the monster free. Without it, he would have never survived the insanity that had crawled through him over the years.

"Don't do this, Gideon," she whispered, stepping into the room as he turned to her. Her gaze locked with his, her voice low, calming. "Let Graeme and the Bureau handle this. I called Graeme. He'll be here soon."

His gaze narrowed. What the hell was she doing?

She was reaching into him, touching his soul as she pleaded with her eyes.

Forcing his gaze from hers he let it rake over her. She'd dressed in durable black pants similar to combat wear. A black short-sleeved T-shirt and a weapon strapped to her hips. For a moment pride and satisfaction filled him. The injection he'd given her wasn't just an antidote and immunization against the paralytic. With it, he'd added a unique healing agent that would work with the Breed genetics she possessed to aid in healing wounds, or mending bones. And it worked far faster on her than he'd anticipated.

She definitely looked ready to kill rather than initiate a game he would no doubt enjoy. If it didn't get both of them killed.

"Jonas doesn't have the balls for this," he growled, though there were a few times Jonas had shown amazing promise in that department.

"Graeme has cameras in here somewhere," she stated as though assuring him of it.

Of course this was being recorded. He kept records of everything.

"What they attempted, what Raymond attempted, can't be denied." Moving closer, she held him as nothing ever had. "Let Graeme handle this, Gideon. You have to leave before anyone else realizes you're here."

Rage pulsed through him, filling his blood, his senses, but it was easing. The insanity was locked on her, centering. The stripes would disappear.

Raymond and the Jackals would learn Graeme and Gideon were the same Breed unless he did as she implored him to.

It wouldn't matter if they knew the two identities were one, unless he did as she asked and turned them over to Jonas. If they learned he was Graeme as well, then he would have no choice but to kill them.

Either choice was tempting. The game or the kill?

His gaze turned back to the Jackals watching curiously, then to Raymond, whose dark eyes filled with calculated hope.

There would be no screams to soothe the maddened monster raging inside Graeme, no matter how it craved the sound of them.

A snarl ripped from him, vicious, one that hungered for blood.

"What did you do to my perfect little cat?" He snapped at the silent horror that refilled the Navajo's gaze. "Such weakness. She would have never allowed an enemy mercy had I been able to complete her training. She shouldn't have anyway." The snarl he flashed to his captive had him paling.

It did little to alleviate the disappointed disgust he could feel.

"I raised her for twelve years," he raged, staring into the deep brown, panic-filled eyes. "I tried my best, I swear I did, to instill the right values in her. To teach her the value of blood and when best to spill it. Where did I go wrong? Where did I teach that fucking girl mercy? I had none."

But he had. Gideon had. For one four-day-old babe he'd known the oddest mercy. The most peculiar affection. As he'd stared into her pale, ill little face and seen the shadow of death lurking in her gaze, he'd known mercy. The Bengal that paced and growled inside him had stilled, staring at the child almost as perplexed as he had been.

"I molded her to live and you have somehow showed her how to die instead." He sighed in exasperation. "For that alone I owe you hours of agony."

The fucker was muttering again. Begging for his life. Please. Please . . . yeah, he'd heard it all before. Thank God it wasn't quite words. He hated all that pleading and crying bullshit. It did nothing but feed the madness inside him.

"You lost control of her," the Jackal pointed out. "You let her go while she was young enough to learn weakness."

He hated it when the enemy was right. And he hated this particular Jackal. The fucker. He'd end up being trouble yet again, he was betting on it.

"You and *Graeme* will regret this," Graeme snapped, allowing her the game.

He knew he was going to regret it. He could feel it tightening through his senses, a primal premonition there was no escaping.

"Graeme can handle this." She had far too much confidence in what little sanity she believed he possessed. "Jonas will definitely handle it, and he'll enjoy doing it. Besides, Graeme could use the debt Jonas will owe him for these two." She flicked her fingers toward the Jackals.

No doubt Jonas would fucking come in his jeans when he learned the prize awaiting him.

"Leave, Gideon," she whispered. "Please. Before Graeme and Lobo arrive."

Because the separation she was creating between Graeme and the monster he harbored could also become his protection. And it could start here.

A low, enraged snarl left his lips, and before the inner chaos of killing rage eased he moved quickly for the hall and the back of the house.

She wanted Graeme, did she?

She may find Graeme had about as much mercy for those bastards as Gideon had.

◆　◆　◆

Cat restrained the sigh of relief that might have escaped otherwise and kept her attention focused on the two Jackals watching her intently.

Graeme might not have taught her mercy, but he had taught her quite well how to block her senses and how to ensure no Breed, no matter how perceptive, could read her if she didn't want to be read.

"I would have sworn you were his mate," the bigger Jackal mused softly.

She merely rolled her eyes before stepping back to the foyer entrance. There were Breeds parked outside the front entrance of the house. It would take very little to encourage them to storm over the walls.

Lifting the laser weapon from its holster, she smiled back at the Jackal as he watched her. The paralytic was wearing off; she could see the slow tensing of the muscles in his partner's hand.

Flipping the weapon to ammo rather than laser, she fired off three quick shots, holstered it then leaned against the door frame as she smiled back at the bigger Jackal.

"Your buddy isn't as good as you are at hiding the fact that the paralytic is wearing off. And I don't trust you."

Disgust filled his gaze.

"You would have made a worthy mate to that crazy-ass Gideon," he grunted. "Neither of you shows so much as an iota of logic."

"Logic is highly overrated," she assured him as the front door flew open and, rather than the two male enforcers she expected, she found herself face-to-face with two female Coyotes and their alpha instead.

Ashley and Emma Truing paired with Del Rey Delgado? This was really about to get interesting.

She turned back to the Jackals. "Oh boy, your ass is really in trou-ble now."

"Cat." Del Rey's weapon was held confidently at his side as he strode toward her warily, his greeting making it evident Jonas had made him aware of who she was. His nostrils flared as a grimace of distaste crossed his face. "Tell me that's not fucking Jackal I smell."

"And here I bathed just for this little gathering," the bigger Jackal muttered mockingly.

"It would appear so," she assured him as Ashley and Emma flanked their alpha more protectively now. "They were given a paralytic, but it appears to be wearing off. Chief Martinez's is still fully in effect, though."

The small group stepped to the doorway as both Graeme and Lobo, followed by a small Wolf Breed force, rushed from the kitchen entrance.

Thankfully, Graeme had quickly changed clothes. The stripes were gone from his face, the scent of Bengal rage no longer covering him like a coming storm. The Lion Breed scent was once again in place, the amber eyes were green once more and even his facial features seemed less savage, less sharply defined.

"Cat?" He stepped to her, drawing her quickly to him as he watched Del Rey narrowly.

"Graeme." Del Rey nodded, familiarity apparent in his greeting.

Did he know everyone?

How the hell did he manage it? She doubted Del Rey had been to Window Rock more than a few times.

"Alpha Delgado." Graeme nodded as the Breeds following him and Lobo entered the room to restrain Cat's "guests further." They were a bit nicer about it than Cat had expected as well.

"Jonas is on his way," Del Rey informed them. "I notified him when I heard the shots Cat fired." He glanced at her questioningly. "What were you firing at?"

"To get your attention." She shrugged. "I needed the trash taken out, and I didn't trust these two to do it effectively." Flicking her fingers at Lobo and Graeme, she gave both men a tight, hard smile. "I assumed you would contact Jonas that you were going in, though. Tell him he can thank me for the packages. I'll send him my bill soon. It wasn't easy."

Graeme made a funny, guttural sound, as though he were quietly strangling behind her. She hoped he was. She couldn't believe he'd actually been going to torture two Jackals and Raymond Martinez. All three were invaluable sources of information where the Council was concerned. Besides the fact that this evidence against Raymond was simply a godsend for the charges the Bureau of Breed Affairs was trying to prove to bring the chief before a Breed tribunal for crimes against Breed Law.

All that, and a favor Jonas would definitely owe her now. If Graeme had played nice to begin with, then she would have allowed him to take credit.

"Nicely done, Cat," Lobo murmured at her shoulder. "Not excessively wise, perhaps, but nicely done."

"And you can tell him Gideon made contact," she snapped to the Coyote alpha. "He captured them; I merely kept him from killing them. And Graeme has cameras here somewhere that recorded every second of it with full audio as well as video. He has them all nicely wrapped up and tied with a very pretty bow. If Jonas is nice, I'm certain Lobo will agree to send a copy of the security videos."

"And your bill will be in the mail," Del Rey snickered, his gaze as amused as the scent of his laughter when he turned to Lobo. "She's worth keeping, isn't she?"

Graeme's low growl earned him her elbow in his side while Lobo's chuckle hid the sound of the warning rumble.

"Only if she wants to be kept," Cat assured him with sharp sarcasm as she jerked from Graeme's hold and moved to the staircase. "Tell Jonas we'll talk later. It's late and I'm really not in the mood to deal with more arrogant, superior Breeds without sleep. I'll talk to all of you later."

"Cat?" Del Rey had her pausing and turning back to him. "Are you okay?"

Her brow lifted at the question. "I'm walking and talking, right?"

"A bit stiffly," he acknowledged with a hint of a grin. "Do we add assault to the Jackals list of charges?" It was evident he wanted to.

"Add it to Raymond's," she informed them shortly, preferring not to go into details. "Any damage done, he inflicted it."

"Brave little tigress, yes?" Ashley piped up, the Russian accent heavier as she held back her laughter.

"Brave?" her sister questioned. "I don't know if 'bravery' is the word for it."

Cat glanced back at the two Breed females, aware of more than a dozen pairs of male Breed eyes on her. Particularly one, the Bengal posing as a Lion.

"Bravery?" She let her gaze slide over the males. "Self-preservation, ladies. Self-preservation."

CHAPTER 9

Graeme watched as his delicate little mate moved unhurriedly up the stairs, her cute little ass bunching in the most delicious way.

Turning, he growled at the other males in the room watching as well, especially the two Jackals watching him with narrowed consideration.

The first spoke up. "She doesn't carry your scent, Lion. I sense the bond, but not the completion of it. Complete it, before your rival does."

The rumble of warning in his chest was one the Jackal took seriously. Shrugging as though it were none of his business, and ignoring the Wolf Breed at his side whose warning growl backed up the primal command, the stronger Jackal let a smile quirk his lips.

"Hey, Lion," he said, calling Graeme's attention back to him. "My name is Kiel, my partner Lowen. It would pay you to find a moment to speak to us before we meet Jonas's volcano. Which I'm certain we will sooner rather than later."

The rumor of Jonas's volcano was a truth many scoffed at. The volcano meant there was no evidence, no trace of the director's steps to ensure that certain types of evil were extinguished forever.

"Why would I want to do that?" Graeme sneered.

He'd learned all he needed to know, that when it came to Cat, he was far too susceptible to her desires.

Pale yellow eyes flashed with a moment—just the faintest heartbeat—of somber knowledge before a mocking smile crossed his lips. "Just for the hell of it perhaps."

Just for the hell of it.

"Bureau heli-jet is landing, alpha," Ashley called out to Del Rey as he stood watching the exchange. "The big bad director of Breed Affairs is on board."

Glancing at Lobo he could see the Wolf Breed preparing himself for this meeting. It wouldn't be quite as easy as it would have been had Cat not called Del Rey and his girls to witness the Jackals' capture before Lobo and Graeme arrived. And it sure as hell would have been easier had she not dropped the little bombshell about *Gideon* and that she was directly responsible for the packages being saved for the Bureau.

The little witch. She'd outmaneuvered him with such sweet deception that he could do nothing but admire her for it. That didn't mean he was going to allow her to get away with it. Because it was damned sure Lobo wasn't going to let him forget it.

Any debt Jonas owed for the first known capture of a Jackal team, as well as the proof the Bureau needed against Raymond Martinez, was now owed to Cat.

At least now perhaps Jonas would get off Lobo's back about sending enforcers onto the grounds to oversee Cat's protection.

"Well, gentlemen, what do we have here?" Jonas stepped into the foyer, followed by his assistant director, a tall Celtic Coyote Breed, Rhyzan Brannigan. The assistant director's gaze turned first to Raymond, a cold smile quirking one corner of his lips. When he glanced in Graeme's direction his amusement couldn't be missed.

Behind them, several Bureau Enforcers stood alert, their hard gazes locked on the prisoners as satisfaction filled Jonas's gaze.

"I hear she had another visitor tonight," Jonas announced, frowning back at Lobo. "I guess it's too much to ask that he's in custody as well?"

The son of a bitch. One of these days Gideon was going to kick his ass. That day was rapidly approaching as well.

"I would say that's asking for quite a bit tonight, all things considered," Lobo agreed, moving between Graeme and Jonas and pulling the director's attention to himself. "It would seem to me the night's catch was pretty damned good, though."

"Compliments of Gideon and his little ward?" Jonas's lips curled insultingly as he glared at the three prisoners. "Did I hear mention of a video of the attempt against Cat?"

"You'll have it as soon as we've reviewed it and made our own copies," Lobo assured him. "A matter of hours."

Neither of which was required. Graeme could have used his sat phone to send the command to the security center beneath the house and upload the file in a matter of seconds. Jonas didn't need to know that, though.

"I'd like to talk to Cat, if you don't mind." The order in his tone instantly had Graeme fighting to pull back the possessive, warning growl threatening to escape.

Ashley stepped forward. "Really, Director?" she exclaimed with lazy irritation. "It's late and I'm not feeling well. I believe you sent me out too soon." She batted charming gray eyes up at him with impish sweetness. "Talk to her tomorrow when I can enjoy the show."

Jonas turned to her slowly, the quicksilver of his gaze icing over as his expression tightened with a coming snap of disagreement.

"Jonas." Her alpha stepped forward, clearly not hesitating to defend the young woman Graeme knew was an intricate part of his pack. "Tomorrow."

"There's no rule that says Ashley must come along," Jonas drawled.

"Of course there is," Ashley pointed out imperiously. "I wish to be there. And we all know how you enjoy spoiling me for being such a good little Coyote warrior and surviving my wounds. Yes? Consider it an early birthday present."

"It's not your birthday yet, you little imp," he growled, but his fondness for her scented the air, as well as his concern.

"So it's an early present," she declared, one small hand going to her hip in an outrageous display of deliberate maneuvering.

"Six months early?" Jonas questioned smoothly. It was obvious he was well aware of her calculated effort to keep him away from Cat.

Ashley shrugged. "Six months, eight months, who really knows? All gifts are accepted with much appreciation at any time." A pout formed at her pretty lips. "This is my request. You are not allowed to deny me."

Jonas's nostrils flared as the silver gray of his eyes threatened to overtake the pupils. "Not allowed?" he drawled.

"It could cause a relapse." Her hand lifted until it lay over the area of her chest that the bullet had penetrated. "I could become depressed again, you know? Remember how you worried when I wasn't giving you heartburn with my antics?" Her eyes widened innocently. "Refusing this request could be detrimental to my health."

It was obvious Jonas was just barely holding back his laughter.

"Del Rey, she's a menace," Jonas informed her alpha.

Del Rey merely grinned at the accusation.

"Interesting," Kiel drawled at that point. "For all the rumors of calculated deception against this director, he treats the rest of you like favored family members." He chuckled at his own comment. "Hell, Director, and here I was concerned about the rumors of volcanoes, interrogations where enemies lost skin, and unspeakable tortures. While you're giving out birthday presents, mine's next week. I'd like to be released tonight as a present, if you don't mind."

The Jackal hit the floor a breath later, sprawled back, his arms out-spread, compliments of Jonas's fist as a snarl of fury filled the air.

Jonas motioned to the enforcers behind him to remove the uncon-scious body before turning his attention to the other Jackal.

"You have any requests?" he snapped.

That Jackal lifted a brow mockingly. "Not at the moment."

Both Jackals were dragged from the house, Kiel held by the back of his jacket, his head lolling to the side.

"First thing in the morning, Lobo," Jonas stated before following the enforcers from the house. "First thing."

The director and his little entourage of force were gone as quickly as they'd arrived, leaving the Coyote alpha, Ashley and Emma staring at the doorway broodingly.

"He's an acquired taste," Ashley drawled, her accent thickening. "Better in small doses rather than large ones." Then she gave a soft, charming little laugh at her own observation before tossing Graeme a bright smile. "He's quite funny when he gets all irritated like that, isn't he?"

And here, everyone said *he* was insane, Graeme thought in amaze-ment. Those who made the accusation had yet to see the various inner workings of Breed socialization. It was complete madness with a high quantity of pure insanity.

Good God, what was he getting himself into?

✦　　✦　　✦

Cat was still awake when the bedroom door pushed open forcefully to reveal a less than pleased Graeme as he stalked into the bedroom. Snapping it closed, he turned the lock, crossed his arms over his chest and glared at her.

Staring back at him, she was sitting on the bed, the black training suit she'd worn earlier exchanged for soft cotton shorts and T-shirt. She wasn't going to let Graeme's glare intimidate her.

"Before you even begin chastising me for whatever you have on your mind to chastise me for, I'd like to know how Raymond Martinez and two Jackals managed to get past security and into my room to inject me with that damned drug."

She should have heeded her own restless senses earlier in the evening, a mistake she wouldn't make again. But still, their ability to slip past security concerned her. The glare eased from his face as he reached to rub at the back of his neck.

"Martinez placed a nano-nit into the security system while he was here with his son." Disgust filled his voice. "The bastard. It was unfortunate for them that I found the anomaly in the surveillance feed that tipped me off to a problem. I caught the intrusion as it happened. Otherwise, Martinez would have never had a chance to kick you."

As he spoke, Graeme moved closer to the bed, his powerful body filled with a tension that seemed to tighten by the moment.

Staying in place, Cat watched him carefully, feeling her own body tighten, the tension that filled him affecting her as well.

"How's your wrist?" Settling next to her on the bed, he reached out and lifted her arm to stare at the location of the break.

"Skin splint?" His gaze narrowed on the ultrathin brace nearly impossible to detect. "I've only seen those once."

"Dane Vanderale," she said, answering the question she sensed in the comment. "When I was fifteen I broke my leg and refused to let anyone know. Dane was in the area at the time and must have seen me. That night he slipped into my room, left several skin splints, jars of salve for wounds and other supplies he thought I might need."

If it hadn't been for Dane, she didn't know what she would have done. The supplies he'd left had literally saved her ass several times.

Graeme slid his finger over the skin splint. "After my escape from the labs the second time, I developed an infection I hadn't expected. I was in some African jungle when I was found, and taken to the Vanderale's. Such a brace was used to stabilize several breaks I'd acquired."

He said it so simply, but she sensed far more behind the explanation.

"You did a very bad thing tonight, Cat," he stated before she could question him further as his fingertips trailed up her arm. "I'm not rational when I'm like that. You could have been hurt."

"You're just as inclined to hurt me now as you are at any other time." She tried to keep her breathing even, her heartbeat steady, but it was impossible.

His touch did something to her, it made her weaken, made her melt with the sensations that began building in her body and the pleasure that began spiraling through her senses.

"And later," he pointed out with a vein of humor. "Very cleverly stealing that debt from Jonas for yourself. I didn't see that coming. Lobo wasn't happy with it either."

"My heart breaks," she murmured. "Really, Graeme, not all the lessons you taught me were wasted."

"So it would seem." His fingers lifted, his arm outstretching as he leaned closer, bracketing her body as she leaned back into the pillows.

"What happened in the research center when they recaptured you, G," she whispered as his lips lowered to the curve of her shoulder. "What pulled that rage from the depths of your soul and created the Gideon I saw tonight?"

He stiffened against her. She had to know what happened to him. True, he'd never been completely sane, but he'd never let that part of himself free either. It had slept, lending him strength, adding to his intelligence, but always in the background.

"Nothing that need concern you." The arrogance in his voice astounded her, as did his refusal to answer her.

"And you expect me to trust you?" she all but begged him for answers. "I don't even know who you are anymore."

"I don't require your trust," he rasped. "I require your touch, and the freedom to touch you."

"Only the physical?" Bracing her hands against his chest she stared back at him, hating the weakness, the need to give in to him. Hating his arrogance and refusal to let her know him. It enraged her. He wanted all of her and wanted to give nothing in return.

Lifting her hand from his chest he gripped her fingers, moving them quickly to the heavy weight of the arousal contained behind the zipper of his jeans.

A gasp of shock, of arousal, left her lips as he curled her fingers around the evidence of his erection.

"That's physical," he snarled. "So fucking physical it's tormented the hell out of me for five years. When you gave me your blood without the serum needed with the transfusion, you began this, Cat. You set this in motion, though I warned you not to."

"You were dying." The memory of that night was another nightmare, another reason not to trust him.

"Death was preferable to the Mating Heat, damn you."

His hands gripped her shoulders, giving her a hard shake as he glared down at her. "You were fucking twelve. When I awoke I was crazed with pain and the knowledge that if I stayed with you, I could end up becoming more of a monster than those I helped you escape from."

Anger flashed through her. Lifting her head until they were nose to nose, she sneered back at him. "Then perhaps you should have been more careful in who you chose to become your own personal little experiment. Or chose the genetics you forced inside my body more wisely."

He had created her. If he didn't like who and what she was, then it was his own damned fault now, wasn't it?

His eyes narrowed on her, the amber flakes burning brighter in his gaze.

"Cat . . ." The warning growl only offended her further.

"Get off me." She pushed at his shoulders, determined to escape the pleasure, the warmth she felt at his touch. "Get off me now, Graeme. *No* means *no*, and I'm telling you now I don't want you."

He jumped away from her, the low, feral snarl that accompanied his action causing her to move quickly across the bed to jump from it and face him from the opposite side.

"You want me," he accused her furiously, his brows lowering heavily over the jade green glitter of his eyes. "I can smell the scent of your arousal and it deepens each time I touch you. You're my mate. Mine, Cat."

"I'm no mate of yours," she denied with a disgusted curl of her lip. "I may enjoy playing a few of your games, and I may be forced for the time being to accept your protection, but I don't owe you jack for it. You owe me, Graeme, and you owe me dearly."

She would never forget each instance that he owed her for either. They were burned in her brain. Lacerated into her soul with scars of such betrayal that at times, she'd hated him for each and every one of them.

"I owe you?" The dangerous rasp of his voice didn't affect her in the least. "And how do you imagine, my little tigress, that I owe you?"

"Think about it, Graeme," she bit out, her voice tight and filled with years' worth of resentment. "Why would a tigress renounce her alpha? And trust me, I renounced you years ago. Use those superior senses Dr. Foster claimed you had, big boy. Because that mark you left on me has been gone far longer than you can even imagine."

The mark he'd left on her was the same he'd left on Judd, Honor and, over the years, several other Bengal Breeds. It was a primal, mental mark, one he hadn't believed could be wiped away. Especially by his mate, by the tigress he'd ensured existed inside her.

But she was right. Allowing his Breed senses to reach out to her, to search for the bond he'd assumed was still there, he was shocked to realize there was only the faintest remnant of it left. A part of it he doubted she even knew was still there.

The knowledge rocked him to the core. He felt off balance, stunned by the weakness of a bond he'd been certain couldn't be destroyed.

"You destroyed that bond," she accused him then, her voice soft, the bitterness grating. "You destroyed what you created, Graeme. I might have had the potential to be your mate, but like the alpha bond, it doesn't exist now. Nothing exists now but my need to see the only part of you that I still feel some fondness for survive. Strangely enough, it's not the part of you that I know as Graeme that I even give a damn about. It's that part of you the world knows as Gideon that concerns me.

His survival is tied to yours, though, it seems, so I guess I'm stuck with that part as well. Stuck with it. Not mated to it. So why not leave me in peace to get what little sleep I can until I have to deal with a crazy Lion Breed as well in the morning."

Years of heartache, of nightmares that had tormented her vulnerable heart, and the loss of her only friend, had shattered her slowly over the years, over and over again. She'd never had a chance to heal, a chance even to catch her breath before she'd had to deal with another blow.

All she'd ever wanted was to belong somewhere, to someone. To be a part of something besides her own aching loneliness. And even now, he refused to share enough of himself to allow her to feel secure in belonging to him again.

"What are you waiting for?" she cried out painfully as he stood, eyes narrowed, simply staring at her. "Do you think glaring at me is going to replace that bond? That you can intimidate me into it?"

A mocking laugh fell from her lips. "You did come to find me because I was your mate. You came for vengeance and I was just stupid enough to lead the way, wasn't I?"

His arms crossed slowly over his chest, the powerful stance only enraging her further.

"You enjoy lying to yourself, don't you, Cat?" he suggested, the superior amusement he displayed insulting.

"Not nearly as much as you do," she retorted furiously. "Now, why don't you leave, please. I simply can't deal with you anymore. I refuse to deal with you. Get the hell out of here and don't come back before I leave myself."

She had few options. The only assurance she had of protection would also endanger the one person she had no intention of revealing to either Jonas or Graeme.

"I'll go for now." His arms dropped from his chest. "I'll be back in the morning when Jonas arrives. And we will finish this conversation then."

Turning, he left the room, the door closing behind him as Cat felt the strength drain out of her.

It was too much.

Too many upheavals, too many losses and revelations.

She wanted to escape. She needed to escape.

And she had no place to go, no way of surviving if she ran as she longed to run.

And God help her, but she longed to run.

· C H A P T E R I 0 ·

Dealing with Jonas was something she just couldn't do.

The next morning she was up, showered and out the back door by daybreak. The small pack she carried on her back held water, fruit, two peanut butter sandwiches and a weapon.

She strapped her knife to her thigh, over the black pants she'd hurriedly pulled on the night before to rush downstairs before Graeme could torture his enemies. The black shirt overlay a racer-back tank top while hiking boots covered her feet.

With any luck, she'd have an hour to run before Graeme caught up with her. She had no doubt he'd catch up with her, just as she had no doubt he was aware she was leaving the grounds.

She wasn't a prisoner. She hadn't allowed herself to be a prisoner since she had escaped the research center where she'd been raised. Where Graeme had turned her into the Breed with the potential to be his mate.

The bitterness that had spilled from her the night before had surprised her. As the pleasure of his touch had heated her, spreading through her senses and sending a sensual lethargy through her, she'd wanted nothing more than to lie back and to give herself to him.

In that moment, she'd felt him, felt that primal connection she hadn't felt with anyone since the night she'd renounced him as her alpha.

She'd been a child. Broken, betrayed one time too many, and lost within herself without the only person she'd depended upon all her life.

Her G.

It was different. What she felt now wasn't a child's love and adoration. What she'd felt the night before was a hunger she'd never felt before. Hunger for a man she could feel seeping inside her, becoming a part of her. No, he'd always been a part of her. But she could feel him taking more of her now, and she couldn't deal with that.

Running through the chill of the desert morning, the wind racing over her face, she tried to tell herself she could fight it, she could deny it. That the sensitivity of her flesh could be ignored, that the hunger for his touch could be denied. That she wasn't his mate.

She belonged to herself.

Didn't she?

As she ran, the need to escape the chaos her life was becoming rose inside her with a fury that left her at a loss for how to deal with it. For thirteen years she'd allowed her life to be dictated by the need to hide from those searching for her. Always aware that if she was captured, if she allowed that to happen, then Judd and even Honor were at risk as well. The weight of that responsibility had always been with her whenever she'd longed to escape the hatred and malevolence of the Martinez household.

How had Claire, the somber, far too serious young woman whose life she'd stepped into, borne it for the fifteen years she'd been raised in that house?

What had caused Claire to drive the car she'd stolen from her father that night over a cliff with her best friend beside her, resulting in a tragic, near fatal accident for both Claire and Liza, Cat had never really known. Even Claire hadn't remembered why she'd done so. Before she'd disappeared entirely, her essence absorbed completely into Cat as part of that ritual twelve years ago, Claire had remembered very little from her life before that wreck.

What Cat was certain of, was Raymond Martinez had something to do with it.

As the sun burned the chill from the morning, Cat watched from a vantage point at the base of one of the stone towers that rose from the desert floor as the Bureau's heli-jet landed outside the grounds of the house Lobo Reever had allowed her the use of.

Graeme would know she wasn't there. Thankfully, he hadn't followed her. Not that she knew of. She hadn't sensed him behind her, but that didn't mean anything. If he had followed her, he was leaving her alone for the moment at least.

He was the only one leaving her alone though. No more than minutes after sitting back to enjoy the view she sensed the advance of two Breeds. It wasn't their scent that alerted her first so much as the sense of invasion, and manipulation.

"Nice place." It didn't take long for them for step into view and to disturb the beauty of the morning. Jonas Wyatt and Rule Breaker. She just didn't need this right now.

"What the hell are you doing here?"

Dressed in dark silk slacks, a white silk shirt, sleeves rolled up and barely wrinkled, he didn't look as though he'd been carefully follow-ing her since she'd left the enclosed grounds of the guesthouse.

He was a fucking magician or something.

A smile quirked at his lips as he moved into the shelter created by the boulders before easing down to sit at the base of the tower. Leaning back against the cool stone he looked out between the boulders, obvi-ously enjoying the same view she'd claimed as her own.

"I knew you wouldn't be at the house this morning," he told her, snagging her pack before she could stop him.

Digging inside, he pulled out a bottle of water and one of her apples. Taking a bite of the crisp fruit, he glanced at her in appreciation before seeming to relax as he made his way through the fruit.

She waited.

She'd learned in the research center that pressing for explanations and answers made her seem weak. She wasn't begging him for a damned thing, and she didn't owe him a damned thing.

Finishing the apple and tossing the core outside the shelter for scav-engers, he opened the water, took a long drink then capped it. Holding it loosely between his fingers and bending one knee to rest his arm, his gaze narrowed on the desert below the boulders.

Cat just watched him.

Not enough people spent enough time watching this man's face and eyes, she thought. Not that he often gave anything away, but watch him long enough, pay enough attention, and sometimes hints of what he felt or knew would flash in his eyes or his expression. A time or two, she might have caught a scent of emotion, of regret.

"I don't feel superior to your genetics because of my creation versus your additions. What you sensed at that meeting is something difficult to explain, and your accusation of prejudice may not have been entirely unfounded. For that, I sincerely apologize," he said softly, still staring out at the desert. "I would like to mark it down as a moment of human weakness that has since been eradicated."

He turned his eyes back to her and the ice that normally filled them, that emotionally blank gaze he normally gave the world, was absent. Jonas had lowered his defenses, allowing the Breed and the man to be revealed to her uniquely strong sense of smell.

Regret, sincerity and perhaps even a hint of uncertainty. He couldn't predict whether she would accept his apology or not.

"Apology accepted." She shrugged, still watching him closely, aware of the emotions he tried to stem, or make sense of. He was a Breed that rarely allowed others close to, and trusted even less.

"Amber is as much my child as any Rachel will conceive from our union," he told her softly then. "She is flesh of my flesh, blood of my blood, and I want to know how Gideon made that happen."

Cat couldn't hide the flinch of shock at his words.

"What? What do you mean?" She shook her head, confusion filling her.

Jonas turned his gaze to her, the brooding intensity in it focusing on her completely.

"For six months, at the very least, he was slipping past every security protocol I used to alert me that he was there, and he was injecting my little girl, the child that came to me as a stepdaughter, with that evil that Brandenmore created. The files he left explained everything, but how Amber is slowly becoming a Lion Breed isn't explained. One with my genetic markers. And I want to know how he did it."

With Jonas's genetic markers? Graeme knew how to adjust the serum to mark the Breed genetics with familial coding and he hadn't marked hers in such a way? Was it something he'd learned only after leaving the labs? Or something he'd learned with his recapture?

"I don't know how he did it." She shook her head, staring back at him and allowing him to sense that inner part of her where truth or deception lay.

"I never imagined you knew how he did it," he acknowledged. "It's something I have to know, though. He'll return, Cat. He'll come back to you, he won't be able to help himself. You're his mate. You belong to him and we both know he'll never be far from you. That endangers you and it endangers him. The only protection either of you will have is me."

Oh, she could see where this was going now and the futility of what he wanted was almost amusing. Did he really think she would hand Graeme over to him so easily? Did he really believe he could control Graeme so easily?

"Jonas, you don't want to ever capture him." She sighed. "You don't want to ever attempt to force anything from him." The painful regret that filled her, she didn't even attempt to hide. "Don't you know by now, he'll give you whatever he can give. But you capture him and he will kill you. You and everyone who stands in the way of his escape."

Graeme would never allow himself to be imprisoned again. That creature that rose from all the inner rage amassed inside him would create a trail of blood unlike anything Jonas had ever seen before.

"He's not Superman, Cat," he informed her gently. "He can't leap tall buildings or deflect bullets. He's just a Breed, albeit a very intelligent Breed."

Cat shook her head and leaned forward slowly. "You are wrong, Jonas," she whispered painfully. "You are so very wrong. No, he's not Superman. He can't leap tall buildings. He can't deflect bullets. But he can sense what lies in wait in that building. He can sense the bullet being fired and avoid it. He can see past every mental shield you put up against him into the very spirit of who and what you are. And if you stand in his way, then he'll use every iota of information he has against you. Whatever Dr. Foster created when he created Gideon, the serum he was given in that research center amplified every human and Breed strength he possessed while wiping out any weakness you could possibly detect. And all that saves the world is that somehow, someway, he managed to retain enough compassion to keep the evil of humanity from overtaking him."

"Cat, do you really believe that bullshit?" Curious disbelief filled his expression. "Gideon is not a super-Breed."

"Leave him alone, Jonas." She would beg him for this if she had to, though it would do no good. "He left two Jackals living for you to interrogate and somehow convinced one to actually cooperate with you . . ."

"According to Kiel, it was you that did that," Jonas retorted. "You control the monster, he claims."

"Breed perception amazes me sometimes," she pointed out bitterly. "I don't control him. No one, nothing in this world, can control the creature he's become. But you can exist without capturing him. You can benefit from his freedom." She leaned forward imploringly, holding her hands out to him in supplication. "Jonas, the incredible, frightening intelligence he possesses can only aid the Breeds. Stop hunting him. For God's sake, give him some peace, if only for a short time."

If they pushed him, if they continued to come after her, be it Council or Jonas, then Graeme would never completely control whatever it was inside him that obliterated every vestige of mercy he might still possess.

"You fear him, Cat," he pointed out. "With good reason."

"I don't fear him. What do I have to fear? He may threaten to kill me. He may hate me with every fiber of his being, or love me to the bottom of his soul, who the hell knows. But he would never harm me. What I fear is what you'll do to him if you continue to push him."

"You saved the Jackals and Martinez last night. He would have murdered them . . ."

He simply didn't know the Breed he was dealing with, despite Graeme's attempts to show him.

"He would have executed them," she corrected him. "Like you execute those you consider past redemption in some remote volcano. Or like you put down an animal with rabies. He has never *murdered* anyone or anything."

Jonas nodded, but as he did so, the access he'd given her to his inner emotions slammed shut.

"Why did you follow me here, Jonas?" she asked him, this time with a genuine need to understand why he was there. "Did you really think I knew anything that would help you capture him? Or that I'd tell you if I did?"

Wry humor flashed briefly in his gaze. "Rachel felt that if I approached you without my 'normal arrogant attitude'"—he grimaced in distaste, pulling an unwilling little laugh from her—"perhaps you'd be willing to help rather than hinder my search for him. I'll have to be certain to tell her how well that worked." The mockery in his expression was more self-depreciating than confrontational.

"How horrible it must be to have the weight of so many lives resting on your shoulders," she said softly, drawing a surprised look from him. "To know every step you take, every decision you make, affects every Breed in the world, every unique and exceptional soul you fight to save. And with each Breed lost, I bet you feel as though you personally failed."

He looked away from her. She doubted Jonas rarely gave anyone a chance to see an unwilling emotion, let alone sense the depth of pain he felt at the thought of any failures.

"You and Gideon are the same," she whispered, sensing rather than seeing the tension that suddenly filled him. "The exception is that you perceive the intelligence he possesses as a failure of your own as well. If you can capture Gideon, then you could capture all the secrets he possesses and all the knowledge he has or will have."

Arrogance, confidence and denial filled the features that turned back to her.

"I see him as that rabid animal you spoke of earlier," he stated with cool detachment, rising to his feet to stare down at her. "One that has some value, though, when compared to the risk he poses, not enough to allow him to continue waging a war that could easily become a weapon used against the Breeds. The world wants justice, Cat, not vengeance."

"Nor protection? Or truth?" She shook her head firmly. "You're wrong, Jonas. Even as a child, long before I arrived in that research center, he was tortured. That serum nearly destroyed him. He survived because that intelligence enabled him to see how to use the serum to make him stronger, smarter, rather than killing him as it did so many others. And you want to lock him up for it?" She rose to her feet now, staring up at him fiercely. "No, that's not why you want to lock him up. You want to lock him up to use him. To steal that intelligence and strength." Now she was pointing one shaking finger at him. "You're no different from the Council in that regard and if I did know where he was, what he was doing or where he would strike next, I'd die before I told you or anyone else determined to carve another chasm into that Breed's soul."

It enraged her. It broke her heart.

"He'll never be at peace, Cat," he snapped. "He's fucking crazy."

"Maybe he should have just hid it better, like you do," she cried out hoarsely. "Like every other Breed in existence does. Because not a single damned one that I've met is completely sane. You want to use him, Jonas. At least be fucking honorable enough to admit it."

Jerking her pack from the sandy ground, she pulled it over her shoulders furiously. "I may have been done with his crazy ass the night he rescued me and Judd from being euthanized, as they called it, but I'll be damned, there's not many Breeds I haven't been done with at one time or another since. And I'm definitely done with you, Director. You should have stayed with the Council. At least they would have agreed with your asinine methods."

"Cat." The demand in his voice had her pausing to glance back at him. "Has he told you what happened when he was recaptured? What they did to him during the time Dr. Bennett held him?"

"Are you going to tell me?"

She'd wondered, she'd ached to ask, but she knew he wouldn't tell her. Just as he'd never told her what they did to him when Dr. Bennett had reinstated the gene therapy on him after Dr. Foster's disappearance.

"Ask him first," Jonas suggested. "If he won't tell you, then come find me. I'll tell you, with no strings attached, what created the monster you faced last night and why you can't trust him with your life any more than I can trust him with Amber's."

"More games?" She sneered in disgust. "You know, Jonas, I'd find you far more palatable if you would stop attempting to manipulate me and simply accept that getting what you want through me simply isn't going to happen."

With that, she launched herself from the protection of the boulders and began her return back to the house.

No matter how hard she tried, there was simply no peace to be found.

◆　　◆　　◆

"Well now, that went well." Rule moved from the side of the stone tower, thoughtful amusement creasing his expression as he too watched Cat run back to the house Lobo Reever was letting her use.

What did Reever owe Gideon that he was willing to risk breaking the agreement he had with the Bureau of Breed Affairs to protect him?

Jonas had no doubt he'd figure it out, just as he'd figure out exactly what Rule Breaker, his new division director and one of his closest friends, owed that insane bag of Bengal genetics as well.

"No, actually, that did not go well. But I had no delusions it would." He sighed, striving to be as honest with Rule as he'd always been.

After all, in the years they'd fought together this was the only instance he'd found where he couldn't entirely trust Rule. For some reason, whatever the Breed knew about Gideon or his whereabouts, he refused to divulge.

Jonas could understand that. There were a lot of secrets Rule and his brother would probably kill him for keeping if they were aware of it. It was an exchange, he thought wearily. Not an exchange he liked, but even if Rule revealed his knowledge, Jonas knew he'd never reveal his own secrets until he had no other choice.

"What now?" Rule questioned as though only curiosity was the reason for the question.

"I'll tell Rachel she was wrong." He shrugged. "That girl knows where Gideon's hiding. She knows far more than she'll willingly give anyone, even someone she trusts."

But she was still Gideon's weakness. Threaten Cat and he'd come out and play. It wasn't a move Jonas was willing to make quite yet, though. For now, there was information to collect.

For one, the role Reever played in all this. For another, the role Rule was taking in the intricate game playing out between Gideon and Jonas. And third, the fact that he knew Reever's stepdaughter was somehow involved as well. The list he'd acquired of Gideon's ties in the Breed community was surprising.

Gideon had a very well-hidden, though very powerful, group of individuals willing to help him, and Jonas wanted to know how one completely insane, violently vicious Breed had managed it. It was a trick Jonas needed to figure out in order to reveal everyone involved in this little conspiracy.

"Have you found the recessed Breed, Judd, yet?" Jonas asked as they moved around the tower to the Dragoon they'd driven out just before Cat left for her run.

"I don't even have a list of suspects, Jonas." Rule wasn't happy with that either. He was actually pretty frustrated over the fact, if his senses were correct, Jonas mused.

"I want a list of suspects by the week's end," Jonas ordered. "This can't continue."

"I'm not one of your enforcers," Rule batted back.

Jonas noted that the level of confidence the Breed had acquired had become a serious problem lately. Not that Jonas intended to do anything about it. Not that he could do anything if he tried. At least, not a lot.

"Then have one of your enforcers take care of it," Jonas snapped back at him. "This is a Western Division problem, Rule. You're the division director. So fucking take care of it. And take care of it by week's end."

Swinging into the Dragoon, he glared through the windshield, biting back a furious curse. Protecting Gideon was a laudable cause, and he would have helped at any other time. But protecting him wasn't an option now.

"Where to now? Back to her house?" Rule asked as he slid into the driver's seat.

Forcing himself to appear relaxed, he turned to Rule slowly.

"A hypothetical question," he stated. "In my place, what would you do if you knew one seemingly unique Breed wasn't so unique? That something had only triggered what you suspect other Breeds had been coded with? Breeds whose triggers could be far more sensitive?"

Rule stared back at him impassively for long moments before answering the question.

"The same thing humans do when they realize some psychopath's triggers are far more sensitive than others. Or some sociopaths are so intelligent that they may never be found," he finally said with a sigh. "We're not just Breeds, Jonas. We're part human, part animal and something in between that can't be defined. Each day we're free is a gift. When that gift is taken we may well need the monsters to ensure our survival."

"So we allow Gideon free rein?" he asked, knowing that wasn't possible.

"My take?" Rule asked. "Or is that a rhetorical question?"

Sometimes this Breed was far too smart for his own good as well. Of course, that was why Jonas had maneuvered him into the position of division director.

"Your take." Jonas nodded.

"None of us have free rein." Turning from him, Rule activated the Dragoon as Jonas narrowed his gaze on him, waiting. He knew more was coming.

"Free rein is the same fairy tale, where Gideon's concerned, as free will and freedom are mirages where the Breeds are concerned," Rule bit out, obviously not pleased with the conclusions he'd come to on the subject of freedom. "If I were in your place, I'd give him the mirage of freedom, though. The same fairy tale we give ourselves. It creates a debt, a favor owed. He's given the lie that he can live his life and make his own decisions, and he gives us the lie that we have his loyalty. Then when it all goes to hell and we find public opinion our enemy rather than our strength, we call in our favors and give the monsters the truth of free rein. It may be all that saves some of us at that point."

The Dragoon shot from parked to full speed in a matter of seconds, racing across the desert as the Breed behind the controls watched the terrain with a hard, almost bleak expression. One Jonas studied with narrowed eyes as he let the visions of all that surrounded this Breed filter through his senses.

The one that set his mind most at ease, though, was the Lion clothed in armor, claws tipped in steel, blue eyes savage and filled with death.

That creature would always be contained, always be controlled, until, as Rule said, the world went to hell where the Breeds were concerned.

It was the first time Jonas had sensed that part of this Breed, and he suspected it was that part of him that had convinced Rule to betray a decade of loyalty to Jonas, for one Breed's mirage of freedom.

Gideon had realized what lurked inside Rule.

The trigger, Jonas thought wearily. All it took was the right trigger, and that "something in between"—that part that Rule had identified that all Breeds had inside them—was the something Jonas feared the most.

Because he had a feeling the triggers were far more sensitive in many Breeds than anyone knew.

◆　　◆　　◆

Reporters. They were camped at the front gate like vultures perched and waiting for prey to die. Or to catch a glimpse of her.

She should have expected it—the minute news broke of Raymond's arrest and the charges being filed against him, one of which would have been attempted murder of the woman everyone believed was his daughter, Claire Martinez.

Would the truth come out that she wasn't Claire?

There weren't many who knew. Those who did wouldn't want the truth told any more than she wanted it told right now.

By the time she slipped back into the house and moved upstairs to check the property outside the walls, there were vans on each side of the grounds just outside the eight-foot walls.

Standing in the guest room and peeping through the lace curtains, she realized more than just reporters were out there. Across the narrow two-lane county road sat a familiar Dragoon. As she watched, a pretty, blond head popped up on the other side and Ashley was waving her hand madly, a teasing smile on her lips. No doubt she knew Cat was watching.

A second later the journalists had turned and were snapping pictures by the dozens as Ashley seemed to be actually posing for them. Until someone jerked her rather rudely back into the Dragoon.

What the hell . . .

Not even a heartbeat later, the encrypted sat phone Jonas had given her months before vibrated demandingly. Somehow, she pretty much knew who it was.

"Ashley, why didn't you just call me to begin with?" Cat answered the summons in amazement. "You didn't have to wait to catch my attention."

"Oh, I was waving at the paparazzi." The Russian drawl was pure lazy charm. "I bet they put my picture on the front pages again, Cat. See what a wonderful friend I make? Never fear, I'll save you from them."

Ashley was a nut.

For a while Cat had wondered if the Coyote female would ever bounce back from the bullet she'd taken to the chest and the near death experience that resulted. She'd died twice on the operating table. The second time the surgeons had nearly given up hope of bringing her back.

"I'm sure I appreciate it," Cat assured her. "But does your alpha?"

"Oh, Del Rey was called back to the hotel. He left Brim Stone to babysit. He's still spoiling me and allowing me to be a bad girl." Ashley drew the words out, her accent heavier, and Cat could practically see her winking before blowing Brim a kiss while she twirled her artificially highlighted blond tresses.

One of these days, Del Rey was going to lock her up for the sanity of the free world. She spread laughter and craziness wherever she went, if the potential for it existed.

"So, would you like my company for a minute?" Ashley asked brightly. "I thought I would saunter over to the very charming reporters, flash a little teeth—you know, my incisors were sharpened and polished to a wonderful sheen yesterday—then I could just hop over that little wall of yours and make them all feel like lazy little bums because they can't quite make that jump."

Oh, she so wanted to see that.

"Go ahead," Ashley suggested. "You want to dare me so bad, don't you, Cat?"

Never dare a Coyote. Cat almost laughed at the saying. Ashley begged to be dared. It was one of her favorite hobbies.

"Okay, Ashley, I dare you. But you can't hurt the reporters. Knee another one in the groin and you forfeit the hot chocolate I'm making."

"Ooh, I get hot chocolate, Brim," she told the alpha's second in command teasingly. "And she did dare me."

One day, Brim was going to put the pretty, flirtatious little Breed over his knee and paddle her ass.

"Fix my chocolate, Cat. I'm on my way."

Cat really wanted to watch the fun, but she was terrified of being called as a witness for Ashley again when she "accidently" maimed another reporter. No way in hell was she watching. What she didn't know, she didn't have to give a statement about.

She would make the chocolate and let Ashley tell her all about it.

Brim could give the statements.

No reporters were harmed in the spectacular display Ashley gave them.

Of course Cat couldn't help but turn back to watch the show. Ashley was simply far too entertaining.

As she said, a flash of her canines, God only knows what she said to them, then a lithe little jump and she was crouched on the edge of the adobe wall eight feet from the ground while cameras flashed. No doubt, she would definitely be on the front page of nearly every newspaper and website, in the nation.

"You're crazy, Ashley," she declared when the little blond Coyote female strolled into the kitchen, a pleased smile curving her lips as laughter lit her soft gray eyes.

Cat placed two cups of hot chocolate on the table set within an alcove surrounded by windows.

"I'm a Coyote," Ashley declared with a careless shrug.

Sliding into a chair, the Breed female propped one leather-clad foot on the upholstered chair seat, leaned back and eyed the steaming chocolate avariciously.

"Drink the chocolate," Cat laughed, taking a seat across from her. "And tell me what's going on."

A little pout pursed Ashley's lips. "I can't visit a friend?"

Cat lifted the cup of chocolate and sipped at it before setting it on the table once again and staring back at the other woman as she did the same.

A Breed's enjoyment of chocolate was simply astounding. The look on the Coyote Breed's face one of complete bliss. The sweet was to Breeds what some drugs were to humans.

Nothing more was said until the hot chocolate was consumed to the last drop, then Ashley sat back and stared at her, her expression more somber.

"Breeds are a strange lot, yes?" she asked softly, a hint of resignation touching her accented voice.

"I prefer the word 'unique.'" It sounded much better to Cat's ears.

"It is much the same." Ashley sighed. Leaning forward, she propped her chin on her palm and watched Cat with an intensity that was strangely disconcerting. "You have mated that crazy Bengal, have you not?" A quirky little grin touched her lips. "I knew he was no Lion." A little wrinkle of her nose followed the statement. "That scent was a little too perfect to suit me."

Cat merely stared back at her, refusing to comment either way.

"Now, Jonas," Ashley continued, "for all his intuitive powers, is so focused on one single-minded goal that he does not see what is right in front of his face. A Breed who is just as deceptive and just as intuitive as he is. They would make a frightening team, would they not?"

"Ashley, what the hell are you talking about?" Cat would be damned if she would allow this impish woman-child face Ashley put on to trick her into admitting anything.

She'd seen Ashley fool far too many people and silently acknowledged the young Coyote's ability to endear the trust of the most hardened Breed antagonists.

Ashley didn't even blink. "I know who Graeme Parker is, Cat. We both do. He is simply very lucky Jonas is too focused on Gideon to see what others, those who have gotten to know him so well, can see."

"And what do you think you see?" Cat scoffed.

"What you so obviously do not," Ashley countered. "A Breed tortured by things he refuses to talk about. One whose dedication to one surly Bengal female may well bring him to his knees. I would be displeased to find Graeme on his knees." Those gray eyes flashed with a warning, one most would find worrisome.

Cat didn't find it worrisome, she found it irritating.

"Graeme is very good at taking care of himself," she assured Ashley.

Rising to her feet and collecting the empty cups, Cat turned and carried them to the sink. When she turned back to the other girl, Ashley was merely watching her, studying her.

"He has made many friends while he has been here," Ashley pointed out. "Friends who would stand against even Jonas, as much as we would hate that. Or his mate, as much as he would hate that. Don't make enemies of the small group who have ensured his safety. We would not appreciate that."

Cat wanted to laugh but she was terribly afraid it would sound more like a sob.

"Why don't you leave, Ashley," she suggested softly. "This has been amusing, but I have things to do."

Graeme had been here a year, she had known Ashley for nearly five years, yet it was Cat receiving the warning rather than Graeme.

How ironic was that?

"You are very stubborn," Ashley observed then, her gaze once again compassionate.

"I'm stubborn?" She had to laugh at that one. "Maybe I'm not stubborn enough, because for years I've let myself care about people who couldn't give a damn about me either way, it seems."

She hated the ache that burned deep inside her chest, filled her senses and weakened the strength she was fighting so hard to find.

"We care for you, Cat, or I would not be here." Ashley sighed.

"You've known him a year." Her fists clenched at her sides, anger pouring through her. "A year, Ashley, but you stand here and tell me how displeased you would be if he were brought to his knees? How raw do you think my knees are because of him?"

She had cried for him.

For years, even after she'd been given Claire's identity, in those years when she should have been allowing someone else to face the world while she hid. Still, she'd awakened while Claire slept, just to cry. To sob into a pillow that wasn't hers, in a bed that wasn't hers, in a life that wasn't hers, for a Bengal who had turned his back on her.

"You think he has drawn such loyalty from only a year, Cat?" Ashley stared back at her in surprise. "When we first came to this desert, a crazed Bengal saved my and Emma's lives when a sniper would have buried his bullets in our heads. He brought us the sniper's rifle, snapped in two like a twig, and threw it at us. The stripes on his face were like scars of rage as he snarled at us in fury and ordered us back to the safe zone around Window Rock. We ran back like frightened pups. Not fear of the sniper, but the instinctive fear of a guardian's reprisal. Not six months later he saved our alpha, who we adore more than others adore a father or brother. He has saved friends, and done so without a price."

How little they knew that crazed Bengal. Like Jonas, nothing was free.

"He just hasn't informed you of that price yet," Cat snapped painfully. "Give him time."

"And we would gladly pay it, many times over." Ashley rose slowly to her feet. "You are a friend, Cat, and I do like you very much. But we owe him our lives and the lives of those we love. I, for one, would be very upset should Jonas learn who he was because his mate was not loyal to him."

Not loyal to him?

How little they knew her as well.

"He left me to die when I was twelve years old," she cried out furiously, the anger she kept locked inside her burning through her senses. "He left me alone when I knew nothing but his protection. Depended on nothing or no one but him," she sneered. "I was fucking twelve, and he was my world. So don't stand here and lecture me on the lives he's saved, because he destroyed my life. He destroyed me."

The bitterness, the years of loss and fear ravaged her now. Everything she'd kept locked inside her soul burst through the walls she'd placed around it.

"Cat . . ." The compassion in Ashley's gaze, in her voice, infuriated her.

Graeme had made certain Ashley had known he'd taken out the sniper, but Cat had never told the Breed female who had sliced the throats of two Council soldiers stalking them more than a year ago. She'd never told anyone the countless times she'd maneuvered their enemies into sight, ensuring they were revealed. Or ensuring they disappeared.

"Forget it. I don't need your pity." She was shaking, the strain of too many years of living a life of solitude and aching fear rising inside her.

And why had she done it? Why had she lived as someone she wasn't? Not for her own damned protection, that was for sure. She'd done it for him. Because she knew to the last reaches of her soul if she was taken then he would come for her. And that when he did, the chances of his destruction, of his death, were too high.

"Pity isn't a bad thing." Ashley sighed. "To feel compassion for one who sees only her own anger . . ."

"Give me a fucking break," Cat cried out, amazed fury pulsing through her. "You're damned right I only see my own anger, and you're not helping it in the least. You don't know what you're talking about, Ashley, or who you're talking to, so don't presume you do. And don't make the mistake of coming back here to insult me again with your precious advice, because I don't need it."

"You will need more than advice if you are the cause of Jonas learning who he is," Ashley snapped. "You will need a miracle to remain living should that happen."

Cat flinched, but not from what Ashley said or how she said it. Pain sliced across her senses, raged through her soul. Because she would give her own life to protect him from Jonas or anyone else.

"Sorry, Ashley, but there's really not enough of me left to give a damn." The bitterness was like a corrosive eating through her soul. "I gave my life for him thirteen years ago. Every breath I drew, every beat of my heart, every particle of my being was sacrificed for him when I remained as Claire Martinez rather than escaping the hell I found myself in here. There hasn't been anything left of me in a long time. And I don't think you or anyone else, especially Graeme Parker, has the right to ask anything more of me."

Yet they continued to ask for more and nothing, not even friendship or loyalty, was offered in return and the isolation facing her only enraged her.

"You blame Graeme for what saved you?" Ashley questioned her in disbelief. The conclusion the Breed female drew from the agony lancing through Cat's soul shouldn't have been a surprise.

It wasn't a surprise, she assured herself.

Lifting her hand to rub at her temple and the headache brewing there, she tried to tell herself it didn't matter. The Martinez household had been far better than the research center, but then, homelessness would have been better than that hell.

She'd stayed, though, because she knew Raymond would carry out the threat to contact the Genetics Council and tell them exactly where she was and who she was. If she'd been taken, then Honor and Judd would have been found and captured as well. Gideon would have come for her. And the Council would have been waiting for him. She couldn't bear the thought of it.

"I blame Graeme for a lot of things, Ashley," she admitted painfully. "Things that are none of your business. Don't worry—unfortunately for me, I'm just as stupid as the rest of you, it seems, because I'd protect his identity with my last breath. But I don't have to like it, and I don't have to deal with his *friends* while I'm doing it."

Turning, she all but ran from the kitchen. She didn't care if Ashley stayed or if she left. It didn't matter. Years of searching for him, of waiting for him, of silently spilling blood to save those who would turn on her now gouged another jagged scar on her soul.

And here, she hadn't thought there was room for more scars. Or more pain. She'd believed she'd hurt as much as she could ever hurt for the losses she'd suffered.

She was wrong. And she realized she was more alone than she'd ever imagined she could be.

· C H A P T E R   1 2 ·

Intuition. The mating bond.

Graeme wasn't sure what had caused the sudden certainty that Cat needed him. It was strong enough, though, to make him abruptly leave the meeting with Jonas and Lobo and race to her. He arrived just in time to hear, to feel, the blinding pain and betrayal ripping through her as she informed Ashley of the life she'd lived to protect him.

Stepping silently into the kitchen as she raced from it, he faced Ashley and the regret that filled her. A regret she hadn't allowed to stand in her way.

This little Coyote female was about as easy to predict as Cat, because he hadn't anticipated whatever had happened here.

She turned slowly to face him as he stood in the arched entrance to the dining room. Crossing his arms, he leaned against the door frame, watching her silently, forcing back the furious growls that threatened to rumble from his chest.

Brushing back the multihued strands of blond hair that escaped her braid, she sighed heavily, her gaze resigned as she faced him.

"She's upset with me now." That was a bit of an understatement.

"What did you do, Ashley?" The warning in his voice was one he didn't attempt to hold back.

Perfectly arched brows snapped into a frown. "Jonas is convinced she's the way to learning your location. I only informed her how displeased your friends would be to learn that was true."

"Son of a bitch. Ashley . . . !" Straightening from the door frame, Graeme bit off a vicious growl. "You're supposed to be her friend as well."

"I am her friend." Defiance waged in her expression and her stance as her hands went to her hips and her chin lifted as her gray eyes darkened and narrowed. "Only a friend would test her anger in such a way and force her to see how that anger colors her life."

The Russian accent thickened and, despite her declaration, he saw the flash of indecision in her eyes.

"Maybe you should think about that definition of friendship." Stemming the hard rumble of his displeasure was impossible.

"Why should I think about it? Her anger is nearly hatred, Graeme. Should Jonas learn who you are . . ."

"There's no doubt that will happen, Ashley," he snarled back. Hell, maybe he was keeping too many secrets from too many people, especially where Jonas we concerned. It could be time for a meeting. "And it will be none of her doing, it will be mine. Stay out of this fight."

"I hate felines," she snapped furiously, glaring at him. "All of you are far too stubborn and you make no damned sense. Just as she makes no sense." She growled then. "She does not even yell. She just closes herself up inside. How does she think she will ever survive mating with one like you?" One hand flipped out toward him as a feminine sneer of disgust curled at her lips. "I would have shot you by now."

Graeme didn't bother arguing with her or defending himself. A snap of his teeth and a hard rumble of command had her turning tail and vacating the house quickly, though. And why that worked he still wasn't certain. Because she knew damned good and well he would never risk the combined forces of feline, Wolf and Coyote Breeds should he dare to actually turn her over his knee and tan her little ass. Something her alpha should have already taken care of to curb her recklessness.

Moving quickly through the house to Cat's bedroom, he found her standing at the wide balcony doors, arms crossed over her breasts, as she stared out past the walled property.

"And how did I know you would be here?" The anger that filled her voice was a cover. Graeme could sense the pain that roiled like a gathering storm through her small body. "Why don't you leave too? I don't want you here."

But she did. What she wanted and what she needed were so twisted inside her, though, that tugging at either emotion only reminded her of what she'd suffered in feeling them.

And she had suffered. He knew that.

Healing that pain may be impossible, but he was helpless in the desire to do just that. Unfortunately, he knew what Ashley sensed. Facing this emerging feline Breed with soft emotion and gentle understanding would never resolve the conflicts inside her.

"Such a pretty little liar," he growled, giving the door a hard push to close it. "Do you think I don't know better, Cat? Do you think I don't know *you* better than that?"

So much anger and hurt. God knew he'd never meant to cause it.

The need to protect her had been far greater than any consideration where hurting her was concerned, though.

And now, it wasn't just her protection that concerned him.

"No, Graeme, I don't think you know me better than that," she retorted as she turned to him, glaring with all the flame and fury of an enraged Bengal female. "It's been a lot of years since you've been a part of my life. I'm not twelve any longer. And I sure as hell don't worship the ground you walk on now."

But she wanted to. The aching need to trust and to love him freely battled inside her, just as he battled with a past he couldn't change.

He could feel her, her need to step away from that anger like a flame reaching out to him. The scent of it intoxicated him, pulling him into the sensual hunger and emotional storm that raged in him as well. Subtle, a hint of spice and alluring sweetness, her scent infused his senses and spiked the already dark sexuality he possessed.

◆   ◆   ◆

The scent of male lust had been building in the room since the second he'd stepped inside it. A scent she'd been attempting to ignore.

Just as she fought her own need and the memory of his touch. It wasn't supposed to be like this, she thought painfully. The inability to remain completely aloof from him, to make herself remember how much it had hurt when he'd betrayed her.

How much it had changed her. And it had changed her. Once, she'd known she could trust that he'd always be there, watching over her. Accepting that she had no one to watch over her but herself had been a hard, bitter lesson to learn.

"Stop." The order was a hoarse growl, the anger in it flashing in his jungle green eyes.

"Stop what?" Her fists clenched, unclenched, the restlessness she couldn't ease like an itch beneath her flesh.

"Stop remembering," he ordered, his voice stark, dark with whatever emotion flashed in his gaze.

Cat felt that heavy thud of her heart, the pulse of adrenaline that hit her bloodstream and the breathlessness that always seemed to afflict her whenever she saw the somberness in his gaze as she did now.

"Stop remembering," she repeated softly with a shake of her head.

Clenching her teeth against the anger that tore at her, she had to glance away. She had to stop looking at him, stop weakening.

"Is that easy for you to do, Graeme? Is it easy for you to just push back what you don't want to affect the moment or the mission? How do you just not remember?" Was it so easy to just forget her?

Of course it was. She was just a child when he'd deserted her.

Twelve years of work he didn't want to see destroyed. And now she was a potential biological match that had his Breed genetics in an uproar.

Just another form of an experiment, nothing more.

He was on her before she could move. The jungle green of his eyes obliterated the whites, the primal instincts of his extraordinary genetics making themselves known in the fierce, furious glitter of amber pinpoints of light amid the dark green. "We're not going back. The past is just that, and it can't be undone." Savage anger filled his voice as well as his face. "There are too many things I can't explain, too many I can't revisit without risking the control I've gained over the months, Cat. That doesn't mean you're not more important to me than you ever were. Nothing means to me what you mean."

No explanations. Now, wasn't that just like Graeme?

"Not going back?" She tried to jerk away from him, only to find herself pulled against the hard, muscular frame of his body. "Graeme, I never moved forward. My life was stolen before I was able to live it, and my safety came in the form of living another girl's life and suffering the hell no one knew she lived in." Her hands flattened against his chest, claws emerging to prick the shirt he wore. "To save you. Because no matter how much you hated me, you would have come for me if they took me. No one would be allowed to own the experiment you created but you," she cried painfully, staring up into the harsh features above her. "That's all I am to you or anyone else. A fucking experiment. A means to an end. And I hate it."

Her claws dug into his chest, all the anger and pain she'd been forced to hold in over the years rising inside her like a storm she couldn't avoid.

Hard hands gripped her wrists, pulled her around and pushed her against the wall, her hands pulled above her head, body arched into him.

The feel of his erection, hard, heavy, pressed into her lower belly and set off a heated response she wanted no part of. She couldn't want it, but her body did.

"I won't give you explanations," he bit out, his voice low and hoarse. "Believe what you need to about the past, Cat, I won't fight it. But you damned well better believe this about your present and your future. You are mine. And not because of the genetics included in that fucking therapy either."

The declaration of ownership was a growl of primal intent that had her eyes widening and her senses sharpening.

He did that. He made the genetics she fought to keep under control rise inside her with a strength she'd never felt until he'd touched her the first time.

"I was your experiment," she cried furiously. "Just your experiment."

"My mate. Mine." His free hand moved to the back of her head, strong fingers pulling the pin free that held her braid secure. Then he was raking through the heavy strands, gripping them and pulling her head back as he stared down at her.

Swiping her tongue over her dry lips, she raked it against her teeth as she pulled it back, the slight itch beneath it as irritating now as it had been for the past year.

"I'll never belong to you like that, Graeme," she swore fiercely despite the need to give in, to be just that. Anything, everything he needed her to be. "Not now and not ever."

His eyes narrowed on her lips.

"Your tongue itches," he whispered, tightening his grip on her wrists as she struggled against him. "When I touch you, your flesh aches for more but you want my kiss first, don't you, little cat? You want my lips covering yours, my tongue touching yours . . ."

Her dreams were filled with that hunger. Since she'd come into her sexuality just after her eighteenth birthday her dreams, her sexual dreams, had always featured Graeme.

But how did he know? How did he know her tongue itched, that she ached, hungered for his kiss?

"I can smell the sweet scent of your need." Head lowering, his lips brushed against the lobe of her ear. "It becomes sweeter, more intoxicating, each time I see you. Each time I touch you."

"You need to run a diagnostic on that smeller of yours, Graeme. I think it's malfunctioning." Her lips lifted in a sneer.

She hated it that her body betrayed her anger for pleasure. Hated memories she couldn't forget and the pain she couldn't release.

"Do I, Cat?" The suggestive whisper was followed by a lick along the side of her neck. Slightly rough, a rasp of pure pleasure that had her biting her lip to hold back a cry of pleasure. "Or do I need to reach beneath your skirt and see how damp the silk of your panties is? Feel the moist heat preparing you for me?" His teeth raked against the bend of her neck as her breathing became harder, her need for him sharper.

"Do you know what's going to happen when I kiss you?" His lips drifted to her jaw. "I could kiss your breasts and only make them more sensitive. I could taste the swollen bud of your clit, draw it in my mouth or push my tongue into the aching flesh between your thighs, and you could still bear the added sensitivity you'd feel." Sharp teeth nipped at the side of her neck. "But if I kiss you again, if I rub my tongue against yours, then it will be far more than sensitivity, little cat. For both of us. It will become a necessity . . ." His lips brushed over hers, just the faintest caress that had them parting, pulling a moan from her lips that she couldn't hold back. "A fucking drug we can't bear living without."

"I don't trust you. No bond is strong enough to reach past that, Graeme. Nothing can change it," she protested even as she tried to get closer to him, forced herself not to beg him for everything he'd just described.

"Are you sure?" His breathing was harder now, his voice deeper, rougher. "Your body trusts me. It aches for me. Doesn't it? Would your body be so hungry for me if there was no trust, Cat?"

"It's called lust," she protested breathlessly, her head falling back against the wall as his hand lowered and he began dragging her blouse from the band of the skirt she'd changed into along with a cami top just before Ashley entered the house.

"Just lust?" His hand, broad and callused and so warm, cupped her side beneath the material. "Are you sure of that?"

His lips brushed against hers again, teasing her as her lips parted, a helpless moan falling from them.

"I ache with the need to kiss you. Burn with it," he growled as he released the catch at the side of her skirt, eased the zipper down and let the material fall to her feet. "I burn for you, Cat."

A second later her top and his shirt followed, leaving her clad in only the lacy white bra and matching panties that barely covered any flesh at all.

She was helpless. She couldn't fight him, couldn't fight the need, the hunger, or the emotions for him that were so tangled in the pain of betrayal.

How was she supposed to defend herself against the man who'd protected her, seen to her safety as a child and become the fantasy that followed her into womanhood? How was she supposed to protect herself against the man she had loved in one way or another for all her life?

"Gideon," she whispered, her voice breaking as his body pressed hard and tight against her own.

"No, Cat," he growled, the sound dangerous, warning. "What's my name? Say it."

"Now, or when you're sane?" She whispered the question, arching against the wide, muscular warmth of his bare chest.

All he wore were the tan pants the Reever Breeds wore, with matching shirts, as uniforms.

Her nails flexed against his fingers as he continued to hold her to the wall, then, staring back at him, she gave in to the rush of wild, adrenaline-laced genetics rising inside her.

She was primal as well, but in a far different way. She controlled the primal impulses, she controlled what she showed and the power she fed to it. The base animal DNA that infused her, that ensured her survival and marked her as one of the most least predictable breeds, a Bengal, was becoming stronger by the day.

For far too long she'd been forced to hide who she was. First, she'd had to sleep, to hide, remember that there were others besides her at risk if she allowed herself to awaken. Then, once again, she'd had to pretend, to make everyone, even Raymond and Maria, believe she was Claire.

She didn't have to pretend with Graeme. She didn't have to submit, she refused to submit.

Why should she submit beneath him or bury the confidence she'd built over the past thirteen years? she asked herself as the primal awareness, that primal power, filled her.

He had created what she had become. He had worked with the lead scientist, he had dictated the genetic typing placed within her.

Now he could deal with it.

She would never stand behind him, she would stand beside him. And he might own her sexuality, but she would own his as well. And she'd make damned sure no other woman could claim it.

No other would ever have a right to touch him, to belong to him, but her.

Her incisors lengthened. She could feel them, top and bottom, pushing to their natural length. The need to bite, to mark him, was growing inside her. To rake the hard column of his neck, to lick away any hurt the bite might have left.

Sensuality and her emerging sexuality rushed through her. The need to fight who she was, what she was, didn't exist here. Here, she could be the woman she had been forced to hide, the Breed she'd been forced to deny.

There was no fighting whatever bond the heat reinforced inside her; she knew it on a level so deep, so primal, that she didn't even try to fight it. Just as there was no fighting the hunger that only rose by the day.

She didn't have to trust him to own him. Mating Heat went both ways. He may own her body, but she would own his as well. Trust wasn't required.

This Bengal was hers.

The sound that escaped her throat wasn't helpless longing this time. The tigress was awake. Determined, fierce, she would mark this Breed as hers, just as he'd marked her.

Where it counted.

· CHAPTER 13 ·

Ahh, there she was, the tigress she kept hidden, kept locked away so deep, so tight, that even the scent of her was often impossible to detect.

That primal, perfect tigress that a monster had come to life to protect.

The growl that fell from her lips was one of sensual daring, the look in her hammered gold eyes a challenge he intended to accept. And right there, along the side of her face, two shadowed marks just beneath the skin darkening with a golden hue. They weren't black as his were, but a rich, Bengal gold, gleaming with wild promise.

The sight of them made him harder, sent the erotic hunger digging into his already taut testicles.

"How perfect." His voice was deeper than he liked, evidence that his own animal instincts were raging out of control.

Lifting his hand, he smoothed the pad of his thumb over one subtle stripe.

She was absolutely perfect, but he'd always known she would be.

"Kiss me or kill me, but do one or the other immediately," she snapped up at him, her gaze gleaming with the challenge in her voice. "You're wasting my time."

Wasting her time, was he?

He'd warned her what would happen if he dared to kiss her. There would be no turning back.

"Foreplay?" he drawled.

"Foreplay? For a kiss? Get real, Bengal. And make up your mind, I don't have all day." Her gaze was on his lips, the scent of her arousal filling his brain, making him high on the unique scent, the evidence that she hungered just as he did.

Sliding his hand to the back of her neck, his fingers cupping the fragile stem, he didn't stop to think. Burying his hand in her hair and clenching the strands, he pulled her head back, his lips lowering, his control shot.

The taste of her exploded in his senses. Honeyed female, sweet soft need and innocence.

Parting her lips for him, she met him, lip to lip, her tongue rubbing against his as it penetrated her lips, her body arching, reaching for him.

Silken flesh pressed against him, hard-tipped nipples and swollen breasts separated from his flesh by fragile lace.

Before he could stop himself, he sliced through the back of the bra with sharp claws, pulling it from her and tossing the remnants to the floor.

Churning, white-hot need shot through his senses. Slanting his lips over hers, he took the kiss, controlled it, his tongue teasing hers until she clamped on it with her lips, her tongue stroking over it, her mouth suckling it.

His cock jerked in demand. Pressing against the zipper of his pants, fully engorged and throbbing with the blood rushing through it, it flexed with the furious need to bury itself inside her. Releasing the material and shedding his pants was torture. He couldn't get them off fast enough.

An unbidden growl rumbled in his chest as he finally kicked free of both his boots and the denim, allowing him to lift her to him, before turning and carrying her to the bed.

Never had he ached like this. Never had the need for sex taken him by the balls so quickly and with such disastrous loss of control.

A sweet, wicked heat lashed at his chest as he dropped her to the bed. Looking down, a smile tugged at his lips at the sight of the three thin scratches she'd raked into the middle of his chest.

Running two fingers over the blood welling on his chest, he lifted them before lowering them to her lips to smear the scarlet dampness over the swollen curves. As they touched the kiss-swollen flesh her tongue flicked over them instead.

The feel of damp warmth licking over his fingertips sent a surge of lust-filled pleasure arrowing straight to his balls. They clenched, need exploding through his senses and stealing more of his control.

Pure wild hunger was overwhelming him, but just behind those animal urges he knew what waited.

"Am I still wasting your time?" Gripping her ankles and pulling them apart, his gaze centered between her thighs with aching hunger.

A heavy layer of slick damp heat covered the bare curves. Peeking from between the plump folds her clit gleamed wetly, swollen with her need. Tempting him to taste it.

"You're not doing anything," she whispered. "Do you need help? A few suggestions, perhaps? I'm sure I have some books with pictures if you need ideas."

She didn't wait for his permission, didn't wait for suggestions. But then, his little cat had never been one to be guided easily. Sitting up abruptly, with one delicate, claw-tipped hand she gripped the base of his cock, and a second later her tongue swiped over the engorged, throbbing crest in one long, slow lick.

Gripping the hair at the back of her head again and clenching, he held her in place, her lips within a breath of flesh far too sensitive as he stared down at her.

Innocence gleamed in her eyes, in the flush on her face, but hunger was quickly overshadowing it.

"Taking something else from me?" she asked, her eyes narrowing, some inner anger he'd sensed before shadowing her scent.

His hold tightened, teeth clenching, he pushed her head forward and gave her what she was evidently determined to have.

Take it from her? He'd wanted to ease her into this, not force anything from her or allow his genetics to control her. But he could sense her, the animal fully merged with her, demanding and determined.

His Breed.

She was more than he'd ever imagined she would be.

And she was his.

"Giving you all of it," he snarled. "All of me, Cat. Let's see if you can handle it."

Penetrating the lush heat of her mouth, watching her lips close around him with obvious hunger nearly stole reason. So many nights he'd awakened, sweat drenching his body, from the erotic dreams of her and she was here now.

Tentative at first, tasting him, testing her hunger, the sweet heat of her mouth began drawing on him. Sucking delicately, then with erotic confidence. As the reins holding back his lust began to fray, she sucked at the flesh stretching her lips and filling her mouth.

Restraining the shallow thrusts between her lips, Graeme couldn't help but allow himself to revel in this intimate acceptance.

Sweet, wet heat surrounded the brutal sensitivity of the crest, working over it as hungry flicks of her tongue lashed at it. Pleasure tightened through his system, drawing his testicles tighter, his cock throbbing with the rising need for release.

Every second he watched her, her lashes lowered with drowsy eroticism over her hammered gold eyes, her lips drawing on him, tongue flicking against the underside of his cock, pushed him closer. Pushed him toward that edge of oblivion—

"Enough." Forcing her head back, her lips from the engorged flesh filling it, nearly killed him.

Perhaps he'd be amused later at the threatening little growl that fell from her lips, the sharp little nails that pricked at his thighs. But right now, it wasn't amusement driving him. It was pure, unbridled hunger for his mate.

Securing her hands quickly once again and drawing them from him, Graeme pushed her back to the bed, holding her wrists to the mattress as he lay over her.

Years of madness, due to the separation from his mate and the animal genetics' insistence that he remedy the situation. Years of crazed determination to find her, to shield her from the danger of the Genetics Council. And so many years of regret, guilt, and the loss of the only person he'd ever allowed himself to care for.

The bond created here, the need that would be created, the hunger that would never die, would ensure he never lost her again. She could never walk away from him and she would come to trust that he could never walk away from her either.

"Look how beautiful you are," he whispered, still amazed at the perfection of her.

Her eyes were like hammered gold now, gleaming between her lashes as she stared up at him, seductive and demanding.

"How slow you are." Slender thighs parted, knees bending as her feet braced against the mattress.

Pushing between the silken limbs, unable, unwilling to wait any longer, he used his free hand to grip the heavy weight of his erection and pressed it between the heated, swollen folds of her sex.

He had to clench his teeth to hold back his snarl of pure, primitive pleasure.

This was unlike anything he'd ever known before, unlike anything he'd imagined possessing her would be like.

◆   ◆   ◆

Pleasure was racing through her, tearing at the determined shield she'd placed between her and the remnants of a bond she'd believed no longer existed.

The warming heat moving through her body threatened that shield.

As Graeme moved between her thighs, his hard, muscular body coming over her, she knew she'd made a grave error. The width of his cock parted the folds between her thighs, stroking over slick flesh as it began pressing inside her.

The need for this was unlike anything she'd ever known or imagined. Her fingers curled, the little sharp claws that tipped them burying in the quilt beneath her as she felt the entrance to her vagina begin stretching, burning as the width of his cock began penetrating her.

Shards of pulsing, desperate need for each sensation overwhelmed her, and an overriding hunger for another of those deep, spice-infused kisses only added to the needs rising with sharp, desperate force through her body.

"Kiss me." She couldn't bear the hunger for it.

Staring up at him, she was restrained by the powerful fingers holding her wrists above her head as the heavy crest of his erection began impaling her with a pleasure-pain that tore past the fierce hold she had on her senses.

A groan, part growl, was a harsh sound of male pleasure and need as his lips covered hers. His tongue pressed between her lips, that elusive taste of spice filling her, mixing with the heated hint of cinnamon she'd already tasted and combining to create a desperate hunger she feared was closer to an addiction.

The warmth of his body shielded her, the heat of his erection worked slowly inside her, stretching her, stoking the most incredible sensations through her inner flesh and sensitized bud of her clit.

The swollen bundle of nerves at the apex of intimate flesh throbbed and pulsed with a need she hadn't expected. With each advance of the thick length of hard flesh pressing inside her, each blistering stretch of the narrow channel he was taking, sizzling bands of sensual tension tightened around the aching bud.

She couldn't bear it. The pleasure and the pain, the heated sensuality of his lips moving against hers, his tongue tasting her as she tasted him. And she needed so much more.

Blistering waves of ecstatic pleasure rushed through her, increasing the sensual hunger she was helpless against.

Tearing his lips from hers with a growl, Graeme buried his lips at her neck, his breathing harsh and heavy as he gripped her hip with his free hand and paused. The blunt crest of his cock throbbed inside her, the heavy pulse stroking nerve endings that had never felt the intimate invasion she was experiencing now.

Releasing her hands, he seemed to have no complaints when she gripped his shoulders, the hardened, sharpened nails that tipped her fingers pricking his flesh. A rumble of pleasure vibrated against her breasts, the sound sending a hard strike of pleasure to bury at her womb, the sharp sensation jerking her against him.

"Hold on, little cat," he groaned, his hand tightening on her hip. "Just hold on to me."

Her only warning was the tightening of his hips and the hard thighs she gripped with her knees. A heartbeat later he drew back, the heavy crest stroking sensitive flesh until it paused at the entrance. Before she could draw a breath or prepare herself, a strong thrust of his hips buried the iron-hard length of his cock partway inside her. The thin barrier of sexual innocence gave way, her inner flesh clasping the fierce heat desperately before he drew back once again.

Each heavy thrust of his hips buried his throbbing erection deeper inside her, stoked the flames whipping through her senses and licking over her flesh.

Turning her lips to the hard column of his neck as she clung to him, Cat let the pleasure have her. There was no fighting it, no denying the hunger that had built over the years for this touch, for this Breed.

For this.

The heavy weight of iron-hard male flesh was buried to the hilt inside her, overfilling the intimate channel and electrifying sensitive nerve endings already overly stimulated.

Graeme didn't stop with just the possession. Nipping at her shoulder, he began moving, retreating before forging inside her once again.

Oh God, the pleasure . . . she had to get closer, had to have more. Involuntary ripples of reaction tightened her vagina on the invading length as chaotic flashes of sensation tore through her body.

Like electricity. It sizzled over her skin, the friction of his body against her, one hand stroking up her side to her breast, his thumb and finger finding the hard tip and creating such brutal lashes of sensation that the last fragile hold she had on any emotional defense against him disintegrated.

With each thrust of his cock inside her, each growl of pleasure at her neck, ecstasy tightened through her. Just the touch of his skin against hers was pure, undiluted pleasure. His lips at her neck, the taste of his flesh as her lips parted at his hard shoulder . . . She was burning around him, her senses were flying higher by the second, the lashing intensity of each hard thrust of cock stoking a conflagration building in her senses.

"That's it, little cat," he snarled at her shoulder, sharp teeth raking against her flesh, adding to the brutal chaos throwing her into rapture. "Tighten on me like that. Ah hell, Cat, fucking you is so good. So damned good."

She was lifting to him involuntarily, so desperate for more sensation, for added friction, for that boundary between reality and ecstasy to disintegrate and send her flying into the maelstrom awaiting her.

She could feel it swirling around her, coming closer, increasing the tension tightening through her body. Pulsing static flared out in front of the building storm, electrifying her nerve endings, dragging a shocking cry from her lips as his thrusts increased.

His flesh was stretching hers, pounding into her with increasingly quickened lunges that stoked the building storm, stroked over rapidly sensitizing flesh, burying to the hilt harder, faster. His fingers plumped her nipple, tightened on it, rasped over it. His teeth raked her neck as each impalement pounding inside her rasped her clit, stroked it, harder, faster . . .

The storm of sensation gathered, tightened . . .

The explosion tore through her with unexpected power and destruction.

She felt his teeth pierce the skin at her shoulder, a harsh snarl sounding at his chest, as hers pierced his shoulder, drawing blood as she held on tight, her tongue licking and stroking around the bite as whimpering, muffled cries were torn from her by the brutal, breath-stealing detonations of pure ecstasy that continued to tear through her body.

Graeme's release was only seconds behind hers, as was the most shocking, impossibly deeper orgasm that resulted from it.

She felt the additional erection as it extended from beneath the head of his cock and locked into a shallow crevice just behind her clitoris. The thumb-sized extension filled that hidden place inside her, found nerve endings so sensitive that the resulting force of the orgasm that gripped her locked her vagina around his cock as tiny spasms of reaction rippled through it.

She felt his release then. An eruption of heat jetting from the blunt crest as well as a sudden, burning pulse of sensation behind her clit.

It was impossible to process what was happening, what her body was experiencing or what his was doing. She was aware of his teeth gripping her shoulder, but hers were locked in his tough flesh as well. She was aware of the whimpers falling from her lips, her claws digging into the hard muscles of his back, her knees gripping his hips as her hips jerked against him with the violent shock of each striking flash of ecstasy.

He claimed her, but she claimed him as well.

A primal, instinctive part of her Breed senses opened. A part of her genetics that she hadn't known existed, a part of the tigress she hadn't anticipated.

She may be his mate, but she belonged to no one, especially the Breed male claiming her. She belonged to herself, and he would soon learn there was no turning back, no hiding the strength or the depth of the Breed DNA he'd placed inside her.

And he would learn there was no dominating her either, until she decided when she was ready for that dominance. When she decided he was worthy of dominating her.

And he hadn't quite attained that distinction.

She was betting he never would.

◆ ◆ ◆

Evening was gathering when Graeme dragged himself from the bed and called to the kitchens to arrange for dinner to be brought to the house. Thankfully, the little inventions that allowed Lobo his privacy as well as a secure information network made him far more than simply a member of the pack. Devril Black was Lobo's head of security, but Graeme was security manager, entitling him to preferred treatment. Normally, he enjoyed the perks.

His customary argument with the chef was halfhearted at best this time though. His agreement that he was antisocial and not worthy of refined company had Reever's burly Breed chef clearing his throat and promising to get dinner there as quickly as possible.

Hell.

He could still feel the effects of taking her.

Not the physical result of his release, but something that went far deeper. Something he couldn't quite explain just yet.

Pulling his pants on, he was pulling the zipper into place when Cat's eyes opened slowly, the boneless satiation of moments before dispelling as she turned her head to stare at him.

He watched as she pulled the sheet over her breasts. Her need to hide her nakedness from him made his chest feel heavy, made every instinct he possessed rise in objection.

He'd known about the barb that would lock him to her at the moment of his release. Just as he'd heard of the extreme tightening and milking motions of the female feline Breeds' vaginas once the barb extended.

The physical pleasure and extreme intensity of each physical reaction, he'd expected.

There were things he hadn't expected, though.

"So." She exhaled carefully before sitting up and propping the pillows behind her before leaning back and watching him suspiciously. "I'll assume you knew that was going to happen when you came?"

The distance in her voice was accompanied by the cool consideration in her gaze.

"Rumors." He shrugged. "There's a ban on discussing the true nature of the mating among those who haven't experienced it yet. There were instances of it in several labs, though, noted by the scientists who discovered the mates."

No one had mentioned that moment when two mates could see into each other's souls, though. That moment when their senses merged so completely that hiding exactly who and what one was, would be impossible.

Thankfully, Cat hadn't expected it either. She'd been too busy trying to slam that door shut to peek into the opened soul of the Breed in that second that he'd been laid bare before her.

"Makes sense." She nodded. "It could be difficult to explain it if the paparazzi got hold of this information. The vultures would really go crazy then, wouldn't they?"

Looking down at her nails, she smoothed her fingers over one, and her appearance might be one of discomfort, but he knew the truth was far different. She wasn't uncomfortable, she was turned within herself, repairing the break in a shield he hadn't even known she'd placed between them.

It would do her no good. She might have overlooked that glimpse into his soul, but he hadn't overlooked the one his senses sank into for precious seconds.

If he'd been amazed by the woman, the tigress, she was, then to say he was shocked now was an understatement.

"So, what do we do now?" The hammered gold had faded away; her eyes were now the soft golden brown they normally were.

His brow lifted at her question. "What do you want to do?"

"Leave." She didn't even blink when she answered him.

Damn her. She'd turned into a little smart-ass. No, she'd been a smart ass as a child when the situation warranted it. It just wasn't something she'd ever turned on him.

"Leave," he suggested softly. "You have about an hour, maybe two before the physical need for my touch, my kiss, begins to build. According to how stubborn you are, you might make it four to six hours before you find yourself unable to resist returning."

She nodded slowly.

Damn. Maybe he should have softened the reply. Then he thought of what he'd glimpsed when he saw inside her and he steeled himself against the thought. There was nothing he could say, no explanations he could make at the moment, that was going to soften the scars she carried.

Not even the explanations she was so hungry for would ease the pain she was carrying. That would take more than words.

Turning her gaze back to him, the speculative gleam in her eyes was all the warning he had before she spoke again.

"And you? How long can you stay away?"

Graeme snorted at the question. "If I make it five seconds once it starts, then we'll both be lucky."

And that was the damned truth. Now that he'd had her, now that he'd experienced the white-hot fusion of pure pleasure, there was no going back. Hell, he didn't want to go back. He was kicking his ass for waiting as long as he had.

"Nice of you to warn me," she said mockingly, the look in her eyes causing him to stare back at her thoughtfully. "And I have no doubt you knew what was coming, didn't you, Graeme? I guess I should have known to be on guard for the punch line, so to speak." Her eyes narrowed on him for one long moment. "I'll have to see what I can do to even the score now."

Even at twelve, Cat had been known to strike with swift, accurate results when exacting revenge for a perceived slight.

"Cat . . ."

"But then, warning me never was one of your strong suits, was it?" she pointed out as she lifted her knees and wrapped her arms around them while watching him knowingly.

"Cat . . ." He injected a note of warning in his tone, one she ignored. He hadn't really expected her to pay attention, he had just hoped she would.

"You stole that little bear from me when you left the labs," she said then, surprising him. "What did you do with it?"

The bear? What the hell did that bear matter to her now? It had been thirteen years and she wasn't a child anymore. Besides, it was his now, the last reminder he had of the trust she once gave him.

"Why?" Watching her warily, he wondered what she was going to come up with next.

"Because it was mine." Her voice was laced with steel but for a second a flash of something lost and lonely gleamed in her dark eyes. "It was something I loved. You threw it away, didn't you, Graeme? Just like you threw me and Judd away when you were done with us."

The brutal snarl that snapped from his lips wasn't an accident. The alpha command was one she would of course ignore. She might deny his place as her alpha but she didn't want to push it, especially right now.

Bitter cynicism curled at her lips. "I don't acknowledge you as my alpha. I barely acknowledge that mating bullshit. But then, you have only yourself to blame if I don't show the respect you so obviously want." Flipping the sheet back and rising naked from the bed, she threw a hard look over her shoulder. "You made me what I am, remember, Graeme? Your experiment." Her expression hardened but he sensed the pain burning inside her, sensed the anger and the grief. The grief he hadn't sensed until this moment. "Now you can live with it."

Turning her back on him, she took her clothes and strolled with no apparent haste to the bathroom, where she closed the door softly behind her. He heard the smothered whimper that escaped behind the closed panel, though, scented the emotions she fought so desperately.

Fury slashed at the control he was struggling to keep and, for the first time since the monster had made an appearance, it wasn't someone else it was lashing out at in defense of her.

It was Graeme.

Her pain had always destroyed him. The sight and scent of it had never been bearable.

There was so much she didn't understand, so much she didn't know and so much he couldn't tell her yet.

If she thought she hurt now, then the truth she hated him for not giving her would only hurt her more. He knew his Cat and he knew the sense of guilt she would feel if she learned why the monster existed. If she knew the unreasoned hell he'd experienced, it would destroy her. He didn't want her to come to him, to trust him, out of guilt. It had to be out of love, or the tigress he was determined to fully set free inside her would never have a chance to emerge as it should. Cat was holding parts of who and what she was restrained, and he couldn't bear it.

· C H A P T E R 1 4 ·

Two days.

So far, she'd made it two days, Cat assured herself as she paced her bedroom, all but growling in irritation. Because she wasn't going to make it much longer.

There wasn't a chance in hell she'd make it three days, and with the damned reporters camped across the road from the gates, escaping the grounds for any reason was out of the question.

They were like vultures. Scavengers. They were the worst of the lot. The tabloid reporters who wrote more lies than truth in their race for sensationalism.

A written statement, supposedly from her, had been sent to the press, causing many of them to pull up stakes and head to Window Rock in an attempt to catch sight of Raymond, Maria or Linc instead.

She wished them luck. The Breeds had Raymond locked in an

undisclosed location, while Maria was confined to the Martinez mansion until the inquiry into Raymond's crimes was completed and his sentence set.

Linc was keeping the reporters busy moving around, though. His "no comments" only had them hungering for more.

And Cat was watching it all on the television whenever she turned it on. She'd grown bored with it in the first few hours, though. Now she was also growing bored with the house, the grounds and the enforced isolation.

Escape was a thought, after she took care of the burn heating her from the inside out.

Damned Bengal. She was also convinced he'd done this to her deliberately. She just hadn't come up with a reason yet.

"It would appear your Bengal has finally set his mark upon you fully. Does this mean you've forgiven him?"

"Keenan."

Swinging around to the sound of the voice, she really didn't expect to see the leader of the small sect of winged Breeds that hid in the jagged cliffs of the nearby mountains.

"What are you doing here?" The anxious hiss as he stepped into the bedroom from the balcony doors was followed by an anxious look toward the bedroom door.

Wild brown and gold eyes filled with amusement as the feathers on those huge wings ruffled with a restless sound.

Keenan stood over six feet tall himself, but those wings were even taller. Rising at least a foot above his head before curving down and trailing a good foot behind him like a living cape in myriad dark colors, the power—and sheer beauty—of the wings he'd been created to bear was exceptional.

"There are no cameras in the bedroom now." He shrugged as he crossed his arms over his powerful chest and stared down at her thoughtfully. "For some reason he deactivated them just after the Jackals were captured. Beware, though, we detected many more throughout the house."

We.

There were very few of the winged Breeds. Six males, she believed, and a single female they'd discovered near death several months before.

"I'm surprised there aren't a few dozen in the bedroom," she muttered as she moved to the door and locked it securely. Just in case.

Turning back, she felt like squirming beneath the knowing amusement in his gaze.

"I warned you destiny could not be avoided," he reminded her.

She watched as he moved to the sitting area to the side of the bed. His wings lifted, parted and spread out of the back of the seat as he sat down and leaned back comfortably.

"And I warned you I'm damned good at avoidance," she snorted, moving closer to lean against the side of a nearby chair. "I assume you're here with an update on our project rather than to gloat?"

Their project.

She'd made a promise to herself the night she'd entered Claire Martinez's life. A promise that one day she'd reunite Honor with the momma and daddy she'd cried for before she too had stepped into another girl's life.

Honor had been finding more of herself by the day before she and her mate, Stygian, had moved to the small Breed Secure ranch just outside Window Rock. Unlike what had happened with Cat, Honor Roberts hadn't surfaced in Liza Johnson's consciousness until recently. How much she remembered now, Cat wasn't certain, but before she'd entered the secure grounds of the ranch, she'd remembered enough to begin checking on her parents.

The promise Cat had made hadn't been forgotten either.

"I am here with an update," he acknowledged. "But is this still the best time to begin the reunion? Perhaps after you've settled into this new life you are beginning . . ."

Cat shook her head, determination tightening through her.

"No, it has to be now," she insisted. "It's time, Keenan. It can't wait any longer."

If she waited, she might not be there to see it through.

He nodded slowly, his gaze still far too intent to suit her.

"Have you made contact with General Roberts yet?" she asked rather than giving him time to ask her whatever the hell it was he had on his mind.

"I have," he said. "The meeting is in two nights' time at midnight. I will collect you from here and fly you to the meeting site, then return you."

"Cool, I get to fly again." She grinned, though the excitement she'd once felt for the experience was no longer there.

The quirk of Keenan's lips left the suspicion that he knew she'd somehow lost the anticipation that had once risen inside her.

"Have I told you, Cat, that your aid has been invaluable to me and those I protect?" he asked, his voice gentle. "Should you ever have need of our protection, you have only to ask it of us."

Pushing her hands into the pockets of the jeans she wore, Cat shook her head slowly. "You don't need my problems, Keenan. Besides"—she rolled her eyes mockingly—"it's not as if Graeme would physically hurt me."

"Sometimes the scars that are hidden are far more painful than those the world can see," he said softly. "He is your fate, we both know this. But should you need time to consider the truth of fate and destiny, then I would provide you what time I could."

"You don't know Graeme, he'd freak . . ."

"Ah, but I know Gideon well," he said then, shocking her to silence. "But that does not affect my knowledge of you or my gratitude for all you have done. A debt to one does not cancel a debt to the other."

"How do you, Graeme, Jonas—all you sneaky male Breeds—always seem to know things that you shouldn't know?" Placing her hands on her hips, she faced him in amazement. "You know about Ashley's visit, don't you?"

"Of course!" He actually laughed at her amazement. "The reason sneaky Breeds know so much that they should not is because they have friends just as sneaky. Remember that, Cat. Whether by debt or by loyalty, power is gained from those willing to follow one and to reveal secrets others are unaware they've learned."

She shook her head slowly. "I hate Breeds."

"You love the drama as well as the excitement each day brings now that you can join the often chaotic, but always surprising world of those who stand between worlds," he told her, refuting her claim as he rose to his feet. "You are Breed, Cat, no matter how you were born. And when Wyatt calls Graeme's identity into question when he can no longer cloak his Bengal scent merely reminds the director of the anomalies of Mating Heat and that the strength of your Breed scent is increasing with the emergence of your genetics. The dominant mate's scent cloaks the other, and both change for it. Normally the male's scent cloaks the female's, but perhaps in this case, your rather fierce Bengal instinct is aware of the danger to your mate. That would explain why the Bengal scent would cloak a Lion's. After all, it's never happened before. Who is to refute it?"

As he strode to the door he slowly disappeared. Whatever the hell that black synthetic leather uniform he wore was created with, it completely shielded him, making even the huge spread of his wings invisible while flying.

A rush of breeze blew over her, indicating he'd lifted from the balcony in a surge of power to return to wherever he and his small group of winged Breeds hid.

She'd seen them fly once, deep within a hidden canyon where no eyes could see them other than those they allowed. She'd watched them train in aerial combat and had marveled at the grace and agility of such a huge wingspan. It had been incredible, a sight she'd marveled at for weeks.

With the rising conflict between Breeds and Raymond Martinez, though, those little outings had come to an end and only the most important meetings conducted face-to-face.

Such as this one.

In two nights' time she would meet with Honor's parents, give them the information she'd selected and the pictures that would lead them to their daughter. Honor deserved her parents.

Once, long ago, Cat had wondered why she hadn't deserved parents. Her mother had died from a disease she'd refused to treat, one she'd passed on to her newborn daughter because of her refusal to acknowledge it.

There had been no father listed on her birth record. Her mother had been without any known family. Cat had been born alone in the world and would have died had Phillip Brandenmore not claimed her and brought her to the research center to test his new gene therapy.

It sometimes seemed she was just as alone now as she had been when she'd been born. Without family, but not totally without friends, it appeared. Hell, Keenan was a damned good friend to have too, not to mention a rather cool one.

A grin touched her lips.

"Take that, Ashley," she murmured. "Bet you don't have an Eagle for a buddy. All you have is Graeme."

It might have been said defiantly, but the ache, the hurt that hadn't abated, reminded her just how much she wished so many things had been different.

As that thought drifted through her mind, the distant scent of enraged Bengal drifted to her senses and it was coming closer. Fast.

Jumping for the bedroom door, she unlocked it quickly and, opening it, came face-to-face with a furious Graeme.

It wasn't the maddened fury that brought out the Bengal to mark his eyes and his flesh. This was the Breed, the mate, who had somehow sensed more than he should have been able to sense.

"What the hell is your problem?" Stepping back, she allowed him to stalk into the room, watching his nostrils flare, wondering if he could detect Keenan's scent even when she couldn't.

Glaring at him, she crossed her arms over her breasts, waiting. He prowled around the room, a growl rumbling in his chest as she blinked at him in amazement.

"You're starting to worry me," she informed him with a glare. "What the hell is wrong with you?"

"Motion sensors on the balcony picked up movement, and it wasn't you." The growl in his voice was one that demanded not just answers, but the truth.

"Really?" Moving slowly to the balcony, she looked outside the open doors before turning back to him with an arch of her brows. "Well, it wasn't me, but how would you know?"

"Who was it?" The snap in his voice caused her eyes to widen in surprise.

"Check your damned cameras, Graeme," she snapped back at him. "Who the hell could get to my bedroom without you knowing about it now?"

Lying to him wasn't preferred for some reason, she didn't know why. No doubt he lied to her every chance he got. He was created to lie. He was a lie.

She could almost hear his teeth grinding at her question.

"No one should be able to get to your bedroom without detection," he admitted, not in the least pleased to do so.

"Maybe you should check your electronics," she suggested slowly, as though wary of his mood.

Screw his mood.

She was in a mood of her own.

"I checked my electronics." Facing her fully, arms braced on his hips, he confronted her with a heavy frown. "What are you up to, Cat?"

He said it so seriously that she had to laugh.

"What am I up to? Really, Graeme? I think I should be asking you that question. You're the master of games, not me."

Dropping her arms, she moved to the bedroom door and held it in preparation to slam it behind him. "Why don't you go check your electronics again, wild man, because I don't have time for your moodiness right now."

The change in him was instant, but then it only began to coincide with hers.

Mating Heat.

She'd been burning for him for two days. The need for his touch was growing like an addict's need for a fix.

She wondered if she could find a twelve-step program to fix it.

She doubted it. Her luck simply wasn't that good.

Surely to God there was a cure rather than just some stupid hormonal treatment to aid in the symptoms. Because she had news for him, she simply wasn't in the market to try another therapy.

She'd had enough of those as a child.

"My moodiness?" he asked carefully, his expression tightening, his eyes narrowing on her warningly.

She couldn't help rolling her eyes. "Haven't you figured out that expression and that tone of voice really don't work on me? The days of blind obedience are over, Graeme. They'll never return."

"You're no longer a child, Cat," he scoffed. "Blind obedience was never what I wanted. Yet you seem determined to keep us in the past, where every act, every response, is either black or white, when you know damned good and well our lives never existed on such a plane."

"You mean a plane where I could trust you?" she asked archly, her grip tightening on the door. "You're right there. We never existed in that place, I just thought we did."

"For someone with exceptional photographic memory and an aptitude for logic, you can be amazingly nearsighted and surprisingly illogical," he accused her as his expression pulled into lines of disapproval. "I taught you better than this, Cat. Why don't you use some of those incredible gifts I know you possess for something other than hating me?"

The slam of the door wasn't a shock. Even as her muscles bunched and the hiss of fury left her lips she threw it against the door frame with a powerful flip of her wrist.

"Because you're so deserving of my hatred?" she retorted, knowing it wasn't hate she felt.

She'd known that all along. She'd never hated him, not for a single moment. How much easier her life might have been if she could.

"In the eyes of a child, perhaps," he agreed. "But you aren't a child, Cat. Even at twelve you were no child, any more than Judd and I had the option of claiming such innocence. You knew when I disappeared that I hadn't been taken by that death squad, just as you knew a transfusion of your blood would have dire results. You ignored what you knew."

"You were dying!" she screamed, overwhelmed by the lash of remembered fear at the sight of his wounds and the blood he had lost. "I couldn't lose you."

But she had lost him.

He stood there, just staring at her, his gaze heavy and somber. And knowing.

She had known the transfusion would enrage him. She'd overheard Dr. Foster telling him never to risk it without taking precautions. She hadn't known what the precautions were, but she'd seen the injection he'd received before getting a transfusion from her after an experiment Dr. Bennett had performed had gone wrong.

"To you, it was worth the risk," he guessed, his voice incredibly sad. "That risk exploded out of my control."

"Because I infected you?" she sneered.

Stalking to the other side of the room, she rubbed at her arms, the ache for his touch nearly unbearable now.

"I won't fight with you over things you refuse to see." He breathed out, the sound fraught with weariness, or sadness. "I can understand your anger, Cat. I can even understand hatred. Your refusal to acknowledge what you knew then and now, I refuse to accept."

He refused to accept it?

He'd done everything possible to isolate her, to strip her of friends and loyalties, and he thought she should just accept it? Acknowledge what he thought she should know?

"I'll never trust you," she whispered painfully. "Never."

Moving toward her, he shook his head with slow, even movements.

"You already trust me, baby, you just don't want to accept it yet."

"You've lost your mind." Disbelief warred with the hunger rising inside her as he came closer.

"Yeah, I did, a long time ago," he agreed, his arm curving around her waist to drag her against him. "Then I found it in a lonely desert as I watched a tigress hunt and realized all I dreamed of had been right beneath my nose as I searched for her."

Surprise parted her lips and she would have demanded an explanation. But his kiss stole the words as well as the need for them. Sealing them together as the taste of the mating hormone spilling from both of them mixed, exploding through her senses and her emotions.

Wrapping her arms around his neck, her fingers spearing into his hair to hold him to her as a broken moan escaped her throat, Cat knew she couldn't have survived much longer without him.

She'd searched for him. She knew that. She'd drawn him back to the desert, gave him the clues needed to find her and refused to tell him who his contact had been. She'd waited for him, night after night, searched the night and the desert for him, and she'd told herself she hated him. She'd told herself she was simply tired of waiting for him to find her and kill her.

What he was doing was more painful, though.

Yet, she was cooperating, wasn't she?

A strangled cry of need and knowledge filled their kiss.

Tightening his arms around her, Graeme swung her from her feet and carried her to the bed. With his lips still covering hers, their tongues licking, tasting each other's kiss and their hunger, he moved over her. His body covered hers, his hands exploring, removing the clothing separating them and blocking access to naked flesh as she tore at his with sharpened claws until they fell away.

His rougher, tough skin stroked against her softer flesh as his lips tore from the kiss to slide across her jaw to the vulnerable line of her neck.

"You just shredded my clothes." He nipped at her neck as though in retaliation but the sharp pleasure had her tilting her head to give him greater access.

"I'm sure I'm so sorry. I'll do better next time," she whispered breathlessly, stroking her hands down his back, marveling at the hard muscle flexing beneath his skin.

"Make sure you do." Lifting his head, he stared down at her, catching her gaze and holding it.

It was as though he was seeing into her.

Did he see the nights she'd searched the desert for him, so hungry for the sight of him that she'd made damned certain he knew where she was? That he found out who she was? Did he see the fear she'd fought to hide as a child, the hunger she'd felt as she became a woman?

"My Cat," he whispered, brushing his fingers over her cheek before lowering his head to lay his cheek against hers. "Let me hold you, baby, just for now, be my Cat."

Just for now.

Hunger raged through her, a hunger that went far beyond the sexual into a realm of broken dreams, a broken heart and a scarred soul. But the need to be held by him had followed her through all of it.

The need to be his, in whatever capacity he would allow her to belong to him, had always been a part of her. Whether coded in by him, or matched by nature, did it really matter? Because the need for it far outweighed anything science could have created.

Closing her eyes, Cat gave in to the need, the hunger and the overwhelming emotion she restrained with such force that at times she feared it would strangle her.

She let herself be what she had been born to be.

His Cat.

She'd dreamed of his touch.

Lying beneath him, Cat wondered if she would ever regain her emotional distance now.

Callused palms stroked along her sides to her hips, the warmth and friction exploding against her sensitive flesh in flash points of pleasure. As she tightened her fingers in the blankets beneath her, the moan trapped in her throat escaped. The whimpering sound surprised her, the aching need it contained shocked her.

Her breath caught when one hand stroked up her side once again, his fingertips caressing, dragging with exquisite heat until they curled around the swollen curve of her breast. His lips smoothed from her neck to her collarbone, a little nip causing her to jerk her hands from the bed to grip his shoulders.

She needed to hold on to him, needed to steady her senses as his thumb brushed over her nipple and his lips moved over the rapidly rising flesh to the hard, aching tip.

"Graeme." Whispering his name didn't help her find that center.

His lips surrounded the tight bundle of nerves, his teeth raking over it before he sucked it into his mouth with firm, destructive pressure.

Cat ground her head against the bed, dizziness washing over her as pleasure crashed through her, forked fingers of sizzling sensation striking straight to her womb.

"Graeme." She cried out his name.

Arching against him, Cat gasped at the pleasure, the heated pressure devastating her control as pleasure raced from her nipple to the aching bundle of nerves between her thighs.

Electric pulses of tiny explosions raced through her body, dragging her deeper into the morass of chaotic needs, physical and emotional, that churned through her. As his mouth drew first on one nipple, then the other, before moving to the other again, Cat fought to drag her senses back under control.

It wasn't happening.

The pleasure was destructive. It tore down defenses she'd spent years building and replaced them with such burning need she wondered if she'd ever be the same again.

Wondered? No, she knew she would never be the same again.

She'd fought the knowledge that there was a part of her that would always belong to him, but here, in this moment, there was no fighting it. There was no denying it.

"I love the taste of you," he whispered, his lips smoothing over her nipple before he began spreading blistering kisses lower.

His lips moved over her midriff, smoothing over delicate flesh, trailing lower. Stroking his fingers down her sides once again, over her hips to her thighs, where he spread her legs slowly. He eased his kisses closer to the throbbing bud of her clitoris.

She couldn't bear it.

Her senses were swirling, caught in a whirlpool of nearing ecstasy that she was certain she would never survive.

"Just let yourself go, Cat, I have you," he whispered, the warmth of his breath wafting over the tight bud throbbing for his attention. "I have this, baby."

Trust him to hold her through this? He had this?

"Graeme . . . oh God . . ." Her hands slapped to the bed, claws extending into the blankets as her hips arched in reflex to the astounding pleasure that tore through her.

His tongue licked through the swollen, saturated folds between her thighs. A slow, sensual swipe of raw sensation rushing through her and obliterating any chance of saving her control.

It was gone.

Control wasn't even a thought. Nothing mattered but each luxuriant caress of his wicked tongue as it moved through the sensitive flesh before swirling around the tight bundle of nerves throbbing for release.

She arched, her thighs parted further. Each licking caress, each swipe of erotic sensation tightening in her clit dragged her deeper into the storm building inside her. She was racing toward the center of it, reaching for it, strangled moans tearing from her throat.

It was so good.

The intensity of each sensation, the turbulent rush of pleasure surging through her system only added to the euphoric haze filling her dazed senses.

Each pulse of blood racing through her veins carried the pleasure-laced adrenaline to infuse her senses, locking her in the sensual maelstrom Graeme was creating.

Graeme.

Her Graeme.

Whatever name he used, whatever persona he took, he was hers. He'd always been hers.

Just as she had always belonged to him.

Each path they had taken in life, each battle, each night that she had searched the darkness had been part of the journey leading to this.

To this pleasure.

A growl rumbled against the swollen bud of her clit as his lips surrounded it, drawing on the delicate flesh as his tongue rubbed against it, stroked it . . .

Oh God . . . the pleasure was indescribable. Each lick sent electric pulses rushing through her, building, burning along nerve endings so sensitive that each touch, each caress had the power to draw her deeper into a hunger she hadn't expected.

It swirled, building with each breathless moan, each touch.

Blinding, searing sensation rocked her senses. Muscles drew tight, her body arched and in a rush of pure, burning ecstasy her orgasm exploded through her.

Breathless, strangled cries escaped her throat. Shudders tore through her, each explosive rush of ecstasy jerking her against Graeme's body as he slid up over her.

She was certain the pleasure couldn't be any better. That the storm erupting inside her couldn't become more chaotic.

Until the broad, iron-hard length of his erection surged inside the flexing, tightening depths of her vagina.

"Sweet Cat." The primal sound of his voice at her neck was followed by the feel of incisors raking against the delicate flesh.

Cat wrapped her arms around his shoulders and turned her lips to his neck as well, her own incisors gripping the hard muscle of his shoulder where it curved away from his neck.

Pushing into each fierce thrust of his hips between her thighs, the feel of his erection surging inside her, stretching her with burning pleasure, pushed her toward a precipice she wondered if she'd survive.

Survival or not, the need to meet the flaming ecstasy he was pushing her toward became a desperate, driving race to her own destruction.

Each powerful thrust of his hips, the feel of his body covering hers, one hand gripping her hip, the other buried in her hair, fingers tightening in the strands to hold her head in place, assured her he was racing for that same blinding edge of rapture.

Her thighs tightened on his hips, her teeth grazed his neck and, in a moment of complete, blinding instinct, she bit into his flesh as the violence of her orgasm threw her over that edge with such power, such explosive sensation, that nothing else existed but the ecstasy and the man joining her in it.

She felt his release as it jetted from him. Hard, heated pulses of semen that triggered the primal erection of the male barb. It locked into place, holding him inside her as he jerked against her, his incisors piercing her shoulder and a deep, guttural growl vibrating against her shoulder.

And it was never ending.

The ecstasy continued to explode, over and over again. The jagged bolts of fiery rapture overwhelmed her senses, overtook them. And just as he'd promised her, he held her through it. Secured against him, shuddering, defenseless, she felt herself lose something to him. Something she knew she'd regret later. Something she knew would give him the power to destroy her as he hadn't in the past.

But he was holding her now, just as he'd promised he would.

She could feel his heart beating against her breasts, his battle to breathe as difficult as her own. Locked within her, his senses as overwhelmed as her own, his pleasure just as wild and untethered as hers.

At this moment he was hers just as much as she belonged to him. For this moment.

✦   ✦   ✦

Midnight was edging across the sky, the cool desert breeze drifting through the open balcony doors as Graeme laying staring into the night beyond.

Curled against his side, boneless in sleep, Cat and the gentle rhythm of her breathing seemed to soothe the restlessness that normally plagued his nights. Holding her, replete after hours of loving, had dulled that razor edge of fury that seemed to follow him closer than his own shadow, and replaced it with drowsy satisfaction.

His mate.

Stroking the heavy strands of hair that drifted over her pillow, he couldn't help but marvel at the fact that he even had a mate, especially this exquisite creature. When he'd first programmed the genetic serum for her he'd never imagined that connection he'd felt to her could be something so complex as what he felt now.

Hell, he'd been eleven years old, his mind filled with so many formulas and so much knowledge that insanity had already set in. No child, even a Breed child, should have such a capacity for decoding something so complex as the human and animal genome being researched in Brandenmore's labs.

He'd known not just how to decode it, though; he'd known how to code it as well. The complexity of identifying and mapping the unique DNA strands was something researchers who had studied it all their adult lives still didn't understand. Even Dr. Foster, one of the most renowned geneticists in his field, had been unable see what Graeme saw in each DNA strand under research. And even Graeme had known that 90 percent of what he knew, he'd never be able to reveal.

That knowledge had enabled him to guide Dr. Foster in the direction he needed to go for Cat's therapies, though. As painful as they were, as agonizing as they had become, it was all that would save her life.

The genetic abnormality she had been born with would have killed her within days. She'd been missing a gene vital to hormonal and immunity development. One he'd been able to replace with the Bengal Breed genetics.

By the time she was eight, he'd known that getting her out of the research center was imperative. Like Judd's, her development would progress in ways science, as it stood, would never be able to understand.

He'd planned everything with such precise detail. Everything but the bullets ricocheting off a boulder and slamming into his chest, thigh and abdomen. He hadn't planned for that, nor had he planned for the transfusion forced on him.

His Breed instincts had been unable to process the strength of the forced bond that began snapping into place. And he'd known Cat as he knew no other. The only way to force her away from him was to make her hate him.

There had been so much left to do to ensure her safety.

Then fate had stepped in once again and the Genetics Council soldiers had recaptured him and returned him to the research center.

Forcing back those memories, he glared beyond the opened doors, forcing back the volatile rage that filled him whenever he allowed himself to revisit that particular hell.

Cat shifted next to him, rolling to her side before sitting up on the edge of the bed.

Frowning, he watched as she rose from the bed, dragging the sheet along with her and wrapping it around her nakedness almost protectively. Inhaling slowly, he felt his Breed senses suddenly rioting, the insanity that was never more than a breath away blinking awake in sudden, furious awareness.

Graeme was out of the bed instantly, striding to her as she reached the balcony doors. Gripping her shoulders and turning her to him, he stared into eyes filled with bleak bitterness as he realized the scent of his mate was no longer present.

This wasn't his mate.

"Claire?" Where had she come from? He hadn't scented her in months, had begun to suspect she no longer existed.

She existed, though.

Cat's scent was so subtle, so diluted by the awareness of the protective spirit that existed within her, that she almost wasn't there.

"Aren't you so handsome," she said wistfully, staring up at him with a curiosity so lacking in anything sexual that he could only ache for the life she'd never had. "But I knew from Cat's memories of you that you would be. She's very lucky."

"Why are you here?" The deepening of his voice, the rage building in his senses, was the only warning he ever had of the monster he could become beginning to make itself known.

Somehow, she sensed that creature and the threat it could be.

"Don't hurt me." Fear flashed across her face. "Please. I'm here for Cat, I promise."

The stripes were beginning to shadow his face, his neck.

Releasing her abruptly, Graeme stalked to the other side of the room, desperate now to push back that part of him that could rise with merciless intent to destroy anything, anyone, that stood between him and Cat.

He wouldn't last long. His instincts were rioting and yet he knew that releasing that rage would terrify this timid shadow of a child that should have been allowed to pass when her body could no longer sustain life.

The stripes eased away. The grip on his control became firmer before he turned back to her.

"Cat's mine." He fought to keep his voice gentle, unthreatening. "She has to return."

"She's only asleep." The scent of Claire's fear was like a cloak surrounding her. "She doesn't know I'm here. She can't know. Promise me. I swear, I'm here for her."

A sharp nod was all he managed. At the moment his voice would terrify her.

"I had to warn you," she whispered, still holding the sheet to her. "I just wanted to see the night for a moment first." She glanced toward the balcony doors, the haunting sadness that was so much a part of her doing little to ease the instinctive need to force her back into hiding.

When he didn't speak, she gave a small sigh before meeting his gaze warily. "Breeds can smell a lie. I wouldn't lie to you. I'll just be here for a few moments. Is that really so bad? I just wanted to see the night before warning you . . ." She frowned, obviously fighting to choose her words.

"What's Cat up to?" He knew his Cat, and he had sensed her secrets. He was willing to wait, to gain her trust, but he had to do whatever it took to satisfy the young woman who had protected Cat for more than a decade. If she didn't leave quickly they would both regret it.

"If I betray her, then I'll be like everyone else, in her eyes," she said softly. "I can't tell you her secrets, but she's taught me there are other ways to say what must be said."

"Say it, child." He forced back the guttural tone filled with rage long enough to warn her that she didn't have much time.

"The past isn't over," she whispered quickly. "There are threads that she's sought. The danger isn't to her, it's to the fragile remnants of trust that allowed that bond she had with you to remain. But these secrets could destroy it. Beware of flight. If she takes wing, then you may well lose her forever." With that she stepped back to the bed and, unwrapping the sheet, lay back and stared up at him with such regret that guilt seared him to his soul. "I just wanted to see the night again. I've missed it so . . ."

Her eyes closed and as quickly as the spirit had shown herself, she was gone once more. The scent of his Cat filled the room, the mating bond, the mark he'd left on her, once again filling the room.

Graeme couldn't take his gaze off her.

There had been no warning that Claire would make an appearance. No warning that the spirit that had slept within Cat would awaken.

The eeriness of the presence threatened the sanity he'd found with his Cat, and the knowledge that Claire still existed within her was unsettling.

The ritual performed by the Six Chiefs of the Navajo over a decade before, to hide Cat from the Council forces determined to recapture her, had been designed to place Cat's spirit in a sleeping state while the spirit of Claire faced the world in Cat's body.

It had changed even Cat's genetic makeup during the time Claire had been "awake." Graeme knew Claire had slept more often than she'd been awake, though, and Cat had faced the petty cruelties and hatred she found in the Martinez household.

Once the need for that protection was over, Claire should have found that path to her eternal sleep or to whatever came after death.

There were times Graeme wasn't certain what to believe about the afterlife part, but he knew now that Claire hadn't found it.

Fuck.

This wasn't tolerable. He wouldn't allow it to continue. Cat had lost enough of her life. She deserved to face life without the danger of another awakening inside her and taking her place.

He deserved more than to have her taken from him so easily in such a way. When he'd faced Claire, nothing but the most subtle scent of Cat remained. So subtle that identifying her would have been impossible if he weren't her mate, though even the mating no longer existed when this woman faced the world.

A silent snarl curled at his lips.

She was his. He'd died for her more than once. He'd lived for her. He'd lost his sanity for her. He'd be damned if he'd allow anyone to take her from him now.

Not the Genetics Council, not Jonas Wyatt, and not that poor, sad little creature that had wanted to see the night so desperately.

Claire deserved her rest if she deserved nothing else in this world.

But even more, he and Cat deserved to face life without the knowledge that when Cat slept, the other spirit could awaken so easily without Cat's knowledge.

It was time to break the fragile truce he had with a certain chief and bring this to an end.

CHAPTER 16

The next night, Graeme moved carefully to the location where he knew the chief would be awaiting him. Even at a young age Graeme had inspired fear. He hadn't always understood it, though he often appreciated the ability. One man who had never looked at him with fear or even trepidation was Orrin Martinez, the highest of the Six Chiefs of the Navajo, the spirit men of the tribes of the Nation.

And he'd never managed to surprise Orrin either. Even at that first visit so many years ago, he'd found the Navajo chief waiting for him in the same place he was waiting for him now.

In a year of intense rains, runoffs and flash floods had carved out the land in many places and revealed surprising gorges as well as caverns once hidden behind thin stone walls and packed desert sands.

It was one of these caverns that he stepped into, aware that Orrin didn't wait alone. With him were four of the Unknown, Navajo warriors selected to protect the secrets the chiefs oversaw.

One of those warriors, Lincoln Martinez, stood silently, his features, marked by warrior's paint, nearly obscured by the design they used.

"I'd love to know how you figure out when we need to talk." Graeme shook his head as he took a seat at the small fire Orrin had prepared.

Orrin watched him closely, the solemn wisdom reflected in his gaze just as deep and just as knowing as it had been so long ago.

"The winds whisper to those willing to listen," Orrin stated quietly. "Many just prefer not to hear."

It was his standard answer when Graeme asked how he knew whatever he knew at the time.

The winds whispered the secrets to him.

"Does Claire hear the whispers when she's awake?" he asked the old Navajo, not in the least surprised when Orrin sighed heavily at the question.

"If so, she did not tell me, nor did the whispers that drift by me," he said softly. "My granddaughter, even at a young age, was well versed in keeping her secrets."

"She loved the night, didn't she?" Graeme asked then, wondering how much the chief did know where Claire was concerned.

Orrin's head lifted, his gaze staring beyond Graeme's shoulder before he turned to the warriors and nodded to the cavern opening. All but one left the natural enclosure. Lincoln moved from where he stood, though, and took a seat next to Orrin.

The Navajo hiding in the small crevice leading to another cavern came forward then, his saddened features and bitter gaze attesting to the fact that none of the Martinez family had escaped the repercussions of one son's actions.

Terran moved to Orrin's other side, sat and stared back at Graeme silently.

"You spoke to Claire?" Orrin asked then.

"Last night." Graeme nodded. "You told me once Cat awoke that Claire would find her rest, Orrin."

He hadn't known of the ritual until he'd scented Cat in the same body that he'd known carried a different scent years before. It was then that Orrin had come to him in the desert and explained the actions the chiefs had taken to save Cat and Honor, as well as Judd.

"The ritual was to place your Cat in a sleep so deep none could find her," he said softly, a small, rueful smile tugging at his lips. "Perhaps the winds did not tell me how determined that little Breed was to rule her fate, no matter who others believed she was."

"Plastic surgery was performed after the ritual?" Graeme wasn't pleased over that. He'd liked Cat's looks fine when she was a child.

But Orrin nodded. "The surgery was required to alter her facial features to more closely match those of Claire's." His voice hoarsened with emotion then. "Barely six months after the ritual Cat awoke and Claire went away for such a long period of time I feared she would not return. Then the Breeds began arriving, and Claire would return when they were near. She was your Cat's protector when needed, but otherwise, she slept so deeply that even I, with all my knowledge of the intricacies of that ritual, could not find her."

Yes, his Cat was determined, Graeme agreed silently. He had no doubt she'd come awake with a vengeance, but he doubted Claire had slept as much as Orrin suspected.

Graeme knew how desperately Cat had ached for a friend who couldn't be taken from her as everyone had been taken in the research center. She would have kept Claire awake every second possible.

"What happened the night Claire died?" Graeme asked. "What sent a fifteen-year-old racing into the desert with her father's vehicle into a canyon guaranteed to kill not just herself but also the girl she claimed as her best friend?"

Orrin merely shook his head, lowering it silently as though he didn't know.

He knew something.

Growling, Graeme glanced to Terran, who did the same, then to Lincoln.

"Are you going to lie to me as well, warrior?" He freely released a portion of the madness just waiting to leap free and do whatever necessary to protect his mate.

His body heated where the stripes emerged, his vision became so clear no detail was missed and those extrasensory abilities he'd acquired when giving himself to the pulsing fury became so much sharper he could almost hear the thoughts of the brother who himself ached to know why.

"She called Grandfather that night," Lincoln revealed as his grandfather expelled a hard puff of air. "You could hear the whine of the car's motor in the background and Liza's frantic cries that they wouldn't make it. Claire was crying." Lincoln swallowed tightly. "She told him . . ." He shook his head, turning away from Graeme.

"'Tell Lincoln . . .'" Orrin whispered Claire's words. "'Tell him, Grandfather, I'll miss climbing in the canyons with him. I love you all.'" A tear fell from the corner of the old man's eye. "Then she and Liza were screaming until the sounds ended in the crash."

"Your granddaughter was murdered," Graeme snarled. "And all these years you've called it suicide."

Orrin shook his head as his hands tightened on his knees. Gnarled and swollen with arthritis now, they whitened with the desperate pain pouring from him.

"Raymond found drugs in her room. The pills were known to produce hallucinations. Claire had been caught smoking, drinking . . . He was her father." Bitter anger resonated in his aged voice. "She seemed to love him. She never told me of any problems in her life, and Lincoln knew of none. Until the past days, the explanation seemed to make sense."

"Whatever happened that night I knew it wasn't drugs," Lincoln bit out furiously. "But he and Mom were broken that night." His jaw tightened. "Or they seemed to be broken. But any man who loved his daughter would be desperate to keep alive the young woman protecting her spirit within her own body."

Orrin, Terran and Lincoln, three men Graeme knew had loved Claire before her death, and each was immersed in the guilt of ignorance.

"What did my granddaughter say to you?" Orrin asked then, desperate for news of his granddaughter. "Did she have need of us?"

The hope he expressed was one Graeme almost hated to dash.

"She came to me with a warning that Cat would try to run, to escape." That much he would reveal. "And she said she wanted to see the night. She'd missed it."

"She loved the night," Lincoln whispered wearily. "She always said the night called to her."

"Why is she awakening?" Graeme focused his attention on Orrin. "She's been sleeping . . ."

"Not always," Orrin informed him with a hint of pleased pride in his granddaughter. "She and Cat, they were sometimes both awake at the same time. They would play within the world together, gaining knowledge and strength. If she came with a warning, then it's because whatever Cat has planned will endanger her. She is Cat's protector, Bengal. She is no danger to your mate, she will not replace your mate. She protects her. Until the time comes . . ." Orrin inhaled roughly. "On the night of the ritual, the winds whispered that with the awakening came death. I fear for both Cat and my granddaughter now. For I know the awakening nears. That time when the protection is no longer needed, and one spirit must pass on, nears. And I fear we will lose them both with it. I sensed years before that they had claimed each other as sisters. They now protect each other, a very dangerous development when the Awakening comes."

The hell they would.

A vicious snarl tore from Graeme's throat as he came to his feet, the monster he was inside moving swiftly through his senses.

"Listen close, old man"—primal, guttural, his voice echoed with the promise of death—"if she dies, then none involved will live. Hear that. What will be unleashed upon this desert is something you do not want."

Compassion filled the chief's expression, that and immeasurable sadness.

"So the winds have whispered," Orrin agreed. "The beast will stalk the night and blood will run in rivers." He shook his head in regret. "Go. Be with the mate that calms the monster you would be. And if the monster is set loose upon this land when the awakening comes, then it is what fate has decreed, and what the spirits have called."

A roar shattered the night. The ferocity of the sound brought the warriors standing beyond the cavern racing inside as Terran and Lincoln moved quickly to their feet as though to protect the old chief staring up at him sadly.

There was nothing more to say. Merciless, intent, the creature facing them now had no compassion, no regret. It knew no right or wrong but that of vengeance and blood.

The monster had come into being to protect what Graeme lived for, for the mate that held the last remnants of the Breed's soul.

Turning, he moved quickly from the cavern, the race to return to Cat suddenly desperate, filled with a certainty that a reckoning was rapidly moving closer.

The roar he released as the open desert surrounded him was a warning to anyone who dared to take her, to risk her, or to aid any willing to. It echoed through the chilly night, calling out to man and beast and those in between.

The monster wasn't chained, it only waited for anyone so oblivious to hell that he would face it. Because the monster knew well how to bring hell.

✦   ✦   ✦

Lincoln stared at his grandfather as his uncle helped the old man to his feet, his own knowledge, his own awakening abilities to hear the whispers in the winds assuring him that his grandfather knew much more than he was telling.

"Grandfather . . ." He would have demanded answers.

Orrin's hand shot up in a demand for silence, the strength and purpose in his dark eyes as brilliant now as it had been for as long as Lincoln had known him.

"A price will be paid," Orrin snapped. "That we cannot stop. What that price will be, I do not know. I know only that death will come, and that Cat will face a past that will bring that death. Claire was not fated to die, Lincoln," he ground out, his conviction in that belief without doubt. "I saw her fate at her birth, and it was not death. The winds whispered her path would be one no other would want to walk, and her heart would know scars others could not comprehend. But she is to fly from the flames and become a voice all will hear. Death is not her fate."

But even Orrin, who understood the whispers that drifted through the breeze of the desert better than any other, completely believed his granddaughter would never truly live. Lincoln saw it in his eyes, heard it in his voice.

Claire had lost her life but she'd been unable to find her peace. She protected a young woman who would have died soon after, had his sister not died. Her spirit protected that young woman now. Protected her in ways Linc had fought to understand for years.

He'd failed Claire; he'd been determined he wouldn't fail in protecting Cat. But he had. He hadn't realized the evil his father was in time, and Claire had suffered again alongside Cat.

He would kill Raymond if he ever faced him again, Linc feared. No man should ever face that within himself. But if he ever faced Raymond again, then the bastard would suffer . . .

◆　◆　◆

The tiger's roar shattered the silence of the night, jerking Cat from the diagram Keenan had laid on the patio table just outside the kitchen.

"That's one pissed-off tiger." The reflection in his voice, not to mention the understatement, was almost amusing.

"It won't take him long to get here." She sighed. "He's incredibly fast when he gives in to the full primal abilities he possesses."

Keenan gathered up the papers, folded them and shoved them in the leather vest he wore. "Did you see enough of the plans?"

She'd seen all of them. The maps and diagrams as well as the locations of the Reever security details. All she'd needed was one look, a glance at best, to imprint them on her memory.

"I saw enough," she assured him. "We won't have long before Graeme realizes I'm gone and manages to track me down. Let General Roberts know we'll have to stick strictly to the plan. Any deviations and I'm out of there. For both our sakes."

"I'll inform him of this." He nodded in assurance, those wild Eagle eyes watching her far too closely. "Will you weather the storm your mate brings with him, though?"

"Weather the storm," what a very apt phrase. Graeme was definitely a storm no matter his mood. Enraged Gideon or the slightly mad Graeme, whichever face he showed at the moment, he was still like a tornado sweeping through her life.

"Graeme's storms are well known to me," she promised, a small smile curling at her lips. "Weathering them is always an adventure, but not in the least dangerous."

"To you," he pointed out. "It seems the beast does have a leash, no matter what others believe."

"Well then, let's just keep that between ourselves," she suggested. "Go now, Keenan, before he's close enough to realize you've been here. When the beast is loose his senses are far too adept."

With a nod, he phased from sight and a moment later a hard push of wind signaled his departure.

Turning, she watched the back wall Graeme had disappeared over hours before, knowing he'd return the same way. Where he'd gone she had no idea. He'd slipped from her, believing she slept, thinking he could sneak away from her so easily.

As curious as she had been over where he was going, who he was meeting with, because she knew he was meeting with someone, still she'd taken the opportunity to meet with Keenan rather than follow him. This meeting with Honor's parents had been years in the making.

Their desperation to finally see the daughter they'd released, rather than chance losing forever, was like a hunger ravaging their lives.

Cat had contacted them years before, giving them periodic reports on the child they feared they'd never see again. Now it was time to instigate a meeting that would fully awaken Honor.

What would happen to Liza, though, she wondered, and Claire? They had sacrificed the peace they had deserved to find to protect Cat and Honor over the years.

The meeting was tomorrow night. She knew Graeme and Lobo had some meeting planned at the main estate and that would be the only chance she would have to slip from him. With any luck she would be back before he returned. She doubted that much luck was running around loose in her life, but she could hope, right?

At that thought, the sight of a shadow bounding over the eight-foot wall had her brows lifting in surprise. He'd made much better time than she'd anticipated.

She waited for him, knowing he would come to her. She'd heard the roar and the warning it carried. It dared anyone, anything, to face him in his rage.

Except his mate.

Except the woman still fighting to trust the man she was bound to.

"Where were you?" she asked as he prowled closer, his head lowered, amber eyes glittering beneath his lashes as the stripes shadowing his face highlighted the golden color.

"I didn't go far . . ."

"Don't play word games with me, Graeme," she warned him.

Crossing her arms over the loose shirt she'd donned with a pair of snug shorts after he'd left house, she watched him closely.

"I had a meeting." The snap of his teeth signified his battle to control the rage fueling him like gasoline on flames. "I was near. I won't leave you unprotected."

"I'm capable of protecting myself against most things." She shrugged. "I don't need a babysitter."

"Until it comes to that damned paralytic?" he grunted. "You won't be as susceptible to it again, though. The injection I gave you that night actually helps immunize against it."

Her brows lifted. Now, that was some interesting information.

"Jonas aware you have that?" she asked, understanding more by the day the advances Graeme had made in so many areas of Breed genetics.

"He's unaware, but that doesn't mean he hasn't been immunized." The grin that tugged at the corners of his lips was pure amusement.

Within seconds the stripes disappeared from his face and the amber color of his eyes eased, returning to the wild, jungle green she so loved.

Loved.

Inhaling deeply, she shook her head at him. "You're sneaky, Graeme."

Broad shoulders lifted negligently. "What was it you said, everyone lies to Jonas?"

Lowering her arms to prop one on her hip, she rolled her eyes at the comment. "He's like those overprotective fathers on television. The Breeds around him are terrified of his machinations and constantly on guard to ensure he doesn't interfere in their lives. They call him the Mate Matcher behind his back because he's always scheming to pair mates together."

"It's part of his genetics," he stated then, the amusement of moments before easing away. "Where the combinations of genetic material used to alter the sperm and ova that created me shifted to advanced biology and genetic engineering, Jonas's was deliberately programmed to create a Breed with the ability to lead many, with a demeanor to ensure their loyalty. That of a father. Unfortunately for the scientists, the twist in those genetics created a calculating and domineering personality that often can't see the trees for the forest."

"He gets lost in the bigger picture." She nodded, turning back to the house.

"Cat." Firm, gentle fingers gripped her arm before she took that first step. "Will you run from me?"

The wary somberness in his tone had her frowning as she turned back to stare up at him.

For once, he wasn't hiding from her.

Cat swallowed tightly, her heart beginning to beat heavier as her breath caught in her breast.

"What?"

Reaching up, his fingertips caressed slowly along the line of her jaw.

"Graeme . . ."

"You've always been mine," he whispered, his voice a breath of sound. "You believe I deserted you, that I left you undefended. I was at your back until the night the Unknown took you from that hotel while I kept Council soldiers at bay. I was half-mad, still healing, the need to ensure your safety like a sickness inside me. I lost you that night, when they took you to Orrin. I searched for months and couldn't find you. I believed you were safe and I left to finish what had to be done to ensure your safety. But I didn't desert you. I couldn't desert you, you were all that made my life worthy. Not my experiment, Cat. You were and are, the reason for my existence. And nothing but you mattered. Nothing but you has mattered since the day Brandenmore laid a four-day-old infant in the arms of an eleven-year-old creature spiraling into a long, dark tunnel filled with abject insanity. You saved me. You have always saved me."

Who was this Breed?

It was Graeme, she knew it was, but the Graeme she knew would have never opened himself so completely to her or to anyone else.

"Graeme . . ."

"If I lose you, my sanity will be lost forever," he whispered, his head lowering to her lips, brushing against them, caressing them with such tenderness, such hunger, that a cry nearly escaped her. "You *are* my sanity, Cat. From that first moment you looked up at me with a newborn's trust until I take my last breath. You are my sanity."

⋆ C H A P T E R   I 7 ⋆

Was he simply telling her what she wanted to hear?

Staring up at him, Cat remembered how easily he once manipulated the soldiers, scientists and techs in those labs.

The same ones he'd killed before escaping when they'd retaken him.

He had a way of looking inside a person, knowing their greatest desire and making them believe they could acquire it. That only with his help could they acquire it.

And he knew her. He knew her so well.

She had no doubt he'd quickly learned exactly what she ached for, what she'd needed most from him in the years she'd spent away from him. It wouldn't be all that hard to figure out. She'd idolized him as a child, weaved fantasies of how they would escape and travel the world. Then she'd shared them with him. When her pain had been so great she'd begged to die, he'd reshared those fantasies with her and added to them. He'd painted pictures of great adventures and how she would never be alone. Because he'd always be a part of her life.

But he hadn't been.

He'd left her alone with nothing but those fantasies and a love for him that had continued to grow despite her bitterness and the losses she'd faced. A love that had grown as she had grown, and as she had grown, it had only entrenched itself deeper inside her.

But that didn't mean she had to reveal it to him. It didn't mean he'd realized it existed. That part of herself she kept hidden in the deepest reaches of her soul. In a place that never saw the light of day, and rarely saw her own realizations.

"I know I've always been important to you, Graeme," she whispered, her heart beating with a heavy, sluggish pace as that emotion threatened to escape and swamp her. "You made me yours when you made me your experiment . . ."

Fury burned in his eyes as a sharp, commanding growl silenced her. Some commands she could ignore. That one, even she hesitated to ignore.

"That is not all you are to me now or then," he snarled, the abrupt shift from gentleness to frustration threatening to give her mental whiplash.

A vicious growl rumbled in his chest as he turned from her, raking both hands through his hair before whirling back to her just as quickly.

"You think what I feel, my dedication to you and to your safety, has been because of that fucking research?" The fury pulsing in his tone had her brow lifting, one hand moving to her hip and her eyes narrowing as she watched him.

"I think there's a very good chance you identified something genetic where the mating's concerned and you ensured it," she admitted, a sense of sadness overwhelming her. "We were without any sense of security or bonds in that place. I think you needed a bond to hold back that spiraling insanity you spoke of. You were alone, until you created something that would ensure you had something, someone, to hold on to."

If she hadn't had him, if she hadn't thought she was connected to him, that she had someone in that place, then she would have died herself long before any chance came to escape.

"You infuriate me." The declaration was followed by a slight shadowing of those stripes across his face.

Here was the Bengal she knew. He might call himself Graeme now, but this was the creature she had known and loved for so long.

Loved.

She wanted to smack herself for that thought.

"I infuriate you?" Her temper flared at the very thought of it. "Sorry there, big boy, but I passed infuriation several years ago when I all but laid out a red carpet to lead you to me and you bypassed it as though it didn't exist."

Something about his stance, about the air of heavy intent he directed her way, had her almost pausing.

"What the hell are you talking about?" he asked as though sincerely confused at the information.

She stepped closer, her hand dropping from her hip to form a fist at her side.

"Two years ago, just before Diane Broen began tracking you, *Graeme*," she hissed, "I contacted the email account you set up before we ever left the labs. I contacted you and I asked you to come for me." Her breath caught, the memory of that email slicing through her. "I told you where to find me and you didn't come."

God, how she'd needed him. She'd needed him so desperately she'd been willing to face the fury he'd felt for her, to see him, if only for a moment.

"I was here." The frustration evident in his tone would have been amusing if it hadn't hurt so bad at the time. "I've been here, Cat, watching over you since before that fucking email."

"You might have been here, but you didn't come to me." Her fist pressed hard between her breasts, the emotions that tore through her razing her senses. "You didn't come to me, Graeme. You didn't let me see you. You didn't hold me . . ." She whirled away from him, the betrayal she'd felt then almost as bad as that she'd felt when she was twelve. "You created me to long for you, to love you . . ."

"The hell I did. If I'd had such knowledge, I'd have created you to fucking obey me," he snapped back furiously. "I'd have created that code before creating anything else."

The bitterness in the laugh that escaped her might have surprised her if she wasn't so furious. "Perhaps you simply miscalculated there."

His head jerked up with such a look of superiority she rolled her eyes in amazement.

"I do not miscalculate." The very arrogance in that statement was a testament to the power and confidence that had only grown in him over the years.

Had she expected anything else? Really?

"So you thought it was enough to simply be here?" She spread her arms for a second before dropping them to her sides. "To just be wandering around playing your games when I asked you to come to me? What did you think that meant, Graeme? I asked you to come to me, not to camp your fucking ass out in the desert and watch me."

"I was so fucking primal you wanted no part of me," he snarled then, his incisors flashing in the darkness. "You called me to you when I was nothing but pure instinct. An animal, enraged and covered in blood, but I came when you called, Cat. I might have been unable to hold you, but by God I was here. I was here and I watched over you every night from the moment I arrived."

"Really, Graeme . . ."

"Do you think I didn't hear your sobs? Smell your tears?" The deepening of his voice, the primal rasp in it, had her watching him curiously now. "Do you think I wanted to touch you while I looked like this?"

He stepped into the small amount of light spilling from the house, and the sight of him had her breath catching.

"Gideon . . ." She whispered his name, the joy that flooded her reaching into a part of her being she hadn't known existed.

This was who she had longed for.

Graeme was his safety, it was the face he showed the world. This was the Breed that belonged to her, though. The one she belonged to . . .

Reaching up, she touched the dark gold and black stripes along his neck with the tips of her fingers and stared into eyes of hammered gold streaked with a wild, jungle green.

The animal pulsed just beneath the man's flesh, the wildness of the creature let free for her to see.

And she loved him.

She'd loved him as a child and dreamed of him as a woman. And when he'd come to her as Graeme, she'd feared he was lost forever.

"Damn you, mate." The hiss was filled with exasperation rather than anger. "You see the nightmare that plagues men's fears and sigh as though he were a long-lost friend."

Clawed fingers gripped her hips, pulling her to him with a gentleness she had only barely remembered him using when she was a child, screaming out in pain.

"I missed you." Her breath caught as emotion swamped her. "I didn't mean to make you so angry." A sob tore at her voice. "I couldn't lose you. I couldn't . . ."

She'd had no one else to call her own, then suddenly, she hadn't had him either.

"You left me . . ."

"I never left you." The tormented whisper at her ear sent a rush of pleasure racing down her spine. Of course, the feel of those claws scraping up her back in a sensuous caress might have had something to do with it as well. "Until they took me again, Cat, I never left you. I was always watching over you. Even after Orrin managed to hide you, even from me."

"But I didn't know . . ." A gasp ended the protest as the feel of his incisors raking over her shoulder sent a shaft of pure pleasure and longing racing through her.

Weakness flooded her entire being.

"You knew," he growled. "You want to deny it. You want to absolve yourself, to hold on to the anger and the pain that's so much a part of you. You sacrificed yourself for your vision of protecting me, Judd, even Claire, and when I learned of that, I wanted to kill everyone involved." His hold tightened on her, the scent of his frustrated rage surrounding her. "Sacrifice yourself again in such a manner, even risk yourself for another, and I promise you, if I survive the terror of it, I will make certain you never do so again."

She almost smiled when she should have taken the warning to

heart. But this was Gideon. It wasn't Graeme or any other name he'd used over the years to evade capture or detection. It was Gideon.

Her Gideon.

Her fingers moved to the buttons of his shirt.

"Do the stripes still cover your body?" She breathed out, anticipation like a sizzle of electricity racing through her senses.

Leaning back in his hold, she watched, releasing each button and smoothing the parted material to the sides until she reached the snug band of his pants. Once there, she didn't hesitate. She didn't bother with just pulling the shirt from the band, but released the button and slid the zipper of the dark-colored denim open.

Freeing the last button, she smoothed her hands to his shoulders to push the material over them and down his arms.

Her breath caught at the sight of him.

He'd taken her, sent her to heights of pleasure she'd never imagined could be reached, but she hadn't really looked at the body capable of loving her for hours at a time.

In his primal state the stripes covering him weren't black. They were a mix of black and tiger gold. Curling over his shoulders to his collarbone, over hard biceps, around his waist, across the tight, bunched muscles of his abs, they marked his body with animalistic beauty.

"I've dreamed of you coming to me like this," she revealed softly as he stood tense and waiting before her. "This was all I knew. The beauty of the man and the beast. When I recognized you as Graeme, I nearly cried for the loss of who I'd known."

As he'd grown older, even in the labs, the primal markings had eased until they'd disappeared entirely. The last year he'd been with them they'd gone entirely.

"There's no sanity in who I am here, Cat," he said, and the sound of his voice, the hard, deep rasp of it, stroked over her senses, drawing her into a place where only they existed, along with the hunger building between them.

"There's no sanity in the world we have to face as others," she corrected him softly. "Be my Gideon now, just for a little while? And I'll be the Cat I've wanted to be for you for so long. Just for this moment? Let me have my Gideon."

◆　　◆　　◆

Jonas listened to Cat's plea across the lines established by the communications nano-nit he'd managed to get in place. Staring at the holo-board controlling the almost microscopic device, he slowing reached out and deactivated it.

Damn, he should feel a measure of satisfaction. He'd suspected Graeme was Gideon for months and hadn't been able to prove it. There were nights it had nearly driven him crazy, that uncertainty, the need to know.

Now, it was regret he felt.

"She loves him, Jonas," Rachel stated softly from where she stood behind him while he was testing the nit. "And he loves her."

Hell, he hadn't expected it to work. Everything he'd had placed in Graeme's vicinity seemed to malfunction.

Until now.

"They're mates," she pointed out when he said nothing. "Cassie will blow you out of the water if you attempt to bring him in after mating."

Yeah, Cassie would have quite a bit to say to him if he attempted to arrest anyone's mate, especially Cat's. That didn't mean he wouldn't do it if he had to. But that all depended on Graeme.

"Jonas?" Rachel lowered her head until it rested at his shoulder. "What are you going to do?"

Glancing at her from the corner of his eye, he let a smile quirk at his lips.

"What I always do."

She groaned, dropping her forehead to his shoulder now as her slender hands gripped his shoulders. "I love you, Jonas, but one day, a Breed is going to kill you for interfering in their lives the way you do."

Yes, she loved him. She balanced him and often helped shape his plans as well as his views at any given moment.

"I only interfere now when I have no other choice," he promised her. "That Breed is possibly the most intelligent and most dangerous Breed ever created. The things he knows about Breed creation and physiology could terrify Genetics Council biogenetic engineers for centuries to come. He'll never be free, Rachel. Even his concept of freedom is flawed."

"Is it, Jonas?" she asked softly. "Is it flawed? Or is it in opposition to your concept of his freedom?"

✦   ✦   ✦

Let her have her Gideon?

The maddened creature that became a monster?

God, she had no idea what she was asking of him.

"Cat, this isn't what you want." It couldn't be. The blood that stained his hands concerned even him at times.

His shirt dropped to the patio floor as her fingertips trailed down his arms to his wrists.

"Would you accept me as less than who and what I am?" she asked, the caress of those fingers moving to his sides, his abdomen. "Would you want less than who and what I am?"

He couldn't bear it.

"Each time we're together the pleasure is astounding, always better than before. But each time, I know something's missing. A part of you is missing. I need all of you."

Would having all of him change anything?

He couldn't predict her answer to that question. He might have asked if she hadn't chosen that moment to go to her knees.

"Cat . . ."

"You're wearing your boots."

Nimble fingers worked at the laces, loosening them in what amounted to only a few heartbeats before looking up at him. Holding the leather footwear, she waited as he pulled first one foot, then the other, free.

Reaching up, her fingers gripped his pants and tugged, pulling the fabric down his legs where he stepped from them.

"Now what?" The growl in his voice was a natural rasp of his primal state.

"They cover your whole body," she whispered, touching one of the gold-hued stripes along his thigh.

Fists clenched, claws digging into his palms, Graeme fought the impulse to pull her up, push her over the small table next to them and just mount her.

That animalistic urge was growing like fire in his gut.

Fully engorged and spearing out from his body, his cock throbbed with the harsh beat of his heart while his testicles were drawn so damned tight they ached. The need to take her, to spill inside her, was becoming more imperative by the moment.

"Cat . . ." The warning in his voice should have been enough to assure her that time was becoming of the essence.

A light sigh of laughter brushed across his thigh as she rose sinuously to her feet, gripped the hem of her shirt and pulled it free of her body. It dropped to the patio alongside his, her shorts quickly following.

Fuck.

What he saw was not nearly as prominent as his own markings, nor the stripes as wide, but her soft flesh was just faintly shadowed with a hint of gold in a pattern of Bengal stripes that amazed him.

"You didn't tell me." Cupping her breast, he ran the pad of his thumb over one softly colored stripe arcing over the swollen curve and pointing toward her nipple.

"You didn't ask." The mild retort was followed by a sensual little gasp when he caught the hard tip between his thumb and forefinger, applying just enough pressure to send pleasure streaking through her.

The scent of that pleasure, of her hunger, had every muscle in his body tightening while his cock throbbed faster, the stiff length becoming further engorged.

"You don't have to wait for me to ask." Sliding his other hand in the hair at the back of her head to hold her still, his lips lowered. "Volunteer the information."

"When you do . . ."

He didn't want to hear more.

Covering her lips with his, Graeme gave her what she asked for, the mate that haunted both of them.

Holding her firmly to him, he took her parted lips with a rising need made sharper for the little moan that turned more to a purr as his tongue flicked across hers.

The taste of her was a sensual delight he'd become addicted to with the first kiss. Full of life, enriched with fight and the very nature of her stubborn independence. It was the essence of the most exquisite elixir and he ached for more. Ached for more of her.

Tilting her head back, he took more even as she fought to share in the control of their kiss. Her very nature refused to submit, but her submission wasn't what he hungered for. Not her submission and not just the fiery pleasure of finding release inside her.

What he longed for in the deepest reaches of his maddened soul was her heart. A heart that even now, he knew he didn't fully possess.

✦ CHAPTER 18 ✦

Cat tried to fight the pleasure, to hold back some part of herself, even though she knew there was no part Graeme hadn't already marked.

His kiss dominated her, fed into the hungers the Mating Heat was only strengthening and burned through her body like wildfire. One broad, callused palm cupped the swollen curve of a breast while the other smoothed down her side, her hip, before flattening against her lower stomach and pushing between her thighs.

Long, talented fingers slid through the excess moisture that gathered between the folds there, sliding over her clit, curving and finding the entrance to the depths of her aching sheath. And once there he didn't hesitate. As his palm cupped her mound, his finger slid inside her, parting the sensitive tissue as Cat went to her tiptoes with a gasp of pure delight.

Curling his finger once inside, he found that ache deep inside, the one that only the barb had found when he released inside her. Now the tip of his finger found it, rubbed it, caressed it, stoking the rising need gathering inside her until she didn't think she could survive if he made her wait much longer to climax.

The pad of his palm rubbed against her clit, stimulating it further, increasing each sensation gathering inside her pussy until she was on the verge of begging him to take her. She needed him to take her, ached for it, would have screamed for it if his lips and tongue hadn't trapped the sound inside her.

Each firm caress of his finger against that bundle of inner nerve endings pushed her further, pushed her deeper into the rising waves of sensual destruction. One arm slid around her back, holding her close, keeping her against him when her knees weakened. His finger continued to torment her, delight her, driving her wild inside with the need to orgasm. The unruly hunger pulsing inside her had her hips rising and falling against the penetration, riding his finger as she began to gasp, desperate to find that touch, that one caress that would send her exploding into release.

Graeme tore his lips from hers, moving his mouth to her ear to nip at the lobe as he eased a second finger in beside the first. The additional penetration had pleasure and pain riding side by side. Stretching heat sizzled through the intimate passage, building by the second as he filled her. Reaching inside her, both fingertips found that spot, stroked and rubbed, creating a storm of such sensation she became lost in the spiraling force of it.

"You're so fucking hot," he whispered, nipping at her ear again. "So sweet. That's it, baby, take it. Ride my fingers just like you're going to ride my cock. That's it, my little cat. Give it to me, let me feel you coming around me."

As though all she needed was his demand, her senses erupted.

Spasms of repeated rapture rippled through the flesh hugging his fingers, tightening on him, holding him inside her as a wail of tortured pleasure filled the air around them.

She could feel the rush of moisture as it spilled from around his fingers to her thighs, ripples of agonizing ecstasy racing from the tightening flesh of passage as pleasure exploded there to encompass her clit, where it detonated once again.

She was jerking in his arms, perspiration dampening her flesh and his as he held her through the storm, groaning in hunger as he gave her release while holding his own back. She didn't have to think about his pleasure, didn't have to think about anything but the explosions tearing through her and sending waves of brutal pleasure throughout her body.

The storm didn't abate, though. Even as the cascading arcs of release tore through her she could still feel the fire burning inside her, the need for more rising rapidly. The hunger inside her for this Breed was like a fever she couldn't escape. Even when she was certain she could contain it, still it slipped out of her control, rocked her senses and left her far too vulnerable, too weak to the need they shared.

"That's it, baby," he crooned at her ear as the shudders began to ease and the grip she had on his fingers loosened. "Now you can ride my cock."

Before she could do more than catch her breath at his sudden move, he was lying back on a padded lounger and drawing her over him.

"Ride me, Cat. Come on, baby, destroy me with your love."

With her love?

Oh God, she loved him.

She hated him and she loved him. Ached for him, and ached because of him. And she couldn't refuse either of them this shocking pleasure.

Straddling his powerful hips, her knees settled into the cushions at each side of him as she leaned forward, bracing her hands on his chest. With her eyes locked on his, Cat shifted back with her hips, fighting to breathe as his jutting erection began to part the slick, swollen folds guarding her sheath.

The gold of his eyes shifted to that wild jungle green, the stripes along his face slowly fading away. His hands gripped her hips, leading her gently, teaching her how to move against him, how to ride him with a steadily increasing pace.

"What do you do to me?" It was a plea, a sob, an inability to understand why she succumbed so easily to him and to his touch.

"I didn't create you, Cat," he whispered, the hoarse rasp of his voice multiplying the ache growing inside her. "You were created for me, to hold back the madness. You are my sanity."

Thrusting inside her with a surge of power, parting her snug sheath and burying to the hilt.

"Oh God . . . Graeme," she cried out, only barely aware that she hadn't called him G, and she hadn't called him Gideon.

"Ride me, Cat," he rasped, moving beneath her as the chaotic pleasure of moments before began to spiral inside her once again.

Each forceful, burning penetration of his iron-hard flesh had a whimper parting her lips. The pleasure was brutal. Locked in his gaze, moving above him, lifting and falling into the heavy thrusts between her thighs, Cat became lost in him. Her lashes drifted nearly closed, the sensual weakness building even as the scorching pleasure burned out of control.

"That's it, Cat, take me," he growled, his expression tightening, hands gripping her hips tighter as he pushed so deep inside her she swore he penetrated her soul. "Give to me, baby. Give me all of you."

He had all of her.

"All of me . . ." The cry was torn from her as his thrusts became harder, faster, driving inside her in jackhammer strokes that pushed her over the edge of reason, of reality, and had her exploding in a kaleidoscope of flaming, overwhelming ecstasy.

Beneath her, she felt Graeme tightening, a hoarse growl surrounding her as the blinding heat of his release jetting inside her sent her racing into another explosion of blinding pleasure. It was never ending, a rapturous pleasure she could never anticipate, found impossible to believe could be so incredible in the cold light of day.

A pleasure that locked them together as the barb emerged and spilled a secondary release as it pushed her past yet another rocking orgasm. Her sheath tightened on him, locking around the engorged shaft, rippling over it, ensuring nothing, no one could tear him from her.

For this moment he was here with her and he belonged to her alone. Not the madness, science or Jonas could tear her from him as long as she held him so deep inside her that she didn't know where he ended and she began.

Collapsing, Cat found herself sheltered against his chest, held by his powerful arms against the heat of his body and protected, for the moment, by the sheer strength he exuded.

❖   ❖   ❖

Cat hadn't expected to dream.

She'd learned years before how to block from her mind the horrors she'd experienced as a child, so nightmares had been rare. Not that she hadn't experienced many of them in the first few years after coming into the Martinez household. But never like this.

She'd never been taken back to the research center she'd been raised in, where she'd experienced such pain she'd begged Gideon to let her die. She'd pleaded with him to just let her go.

"He would have never survived if you had died, Cat."

She jerked around, her eyes widening at the image of the fragile woman-child whose life she'd been given. Claire Martinez could have been her twin, even before the minor plastic surgery that had ensured she was never suspected to be anyone else.

She'd talked to Claire many times in the past years since her spirit had been bound to Claire's through that ancient ritual the night of the girl's wreck. But never like this. Never in a dream, and definitely never in this place.

"What are we doing here, Claire?" she asked, staring around the enclosing cage warily.

That was all it was, really. A cage. One wall was glaring white, the other three were steel bars reinforced with an electric charge. The only privacy had been a tiny toilet room. There hadn't even been a shower. Just a toilet and a tiny sink to wash their hands and brush their teeth. Showers were under strict supervision.

"You never left here, Cat," Claire sighed, staring around the small area as she sat on the cot across from her. "You've always been trapped here."

Cat stared back at her, forcing her heartbeat to remain calm and steady.

"So the past years have been a delusion of some sort?" She didn't think so. No hallucination could be that messed up.

Tucking a strand of long, caramel-colored hair behind her ear, Claire looked around sadly.

"Where you are physically hasn't made much of a difference," she finally answered with somber reflection. "What's important is that no matter where you went, no matter the enemies you faced, you were still *locked in this cell, alone. You never left it after you realized Gideon had voluntarily left you here."*

She wasn't going to argue with a spirit, she rather doubted there was much point to it.

Claire smiled a bit wearily. "You'll deny it to your last breath, though, won't you, Cat?"

"I'd have to know what I'm denying first," Cat informed her, shrugging. "Why don't you take us out of here to somewhere nice. I don't like talking here."

It was a dream, she knew it was.

"It's no dream," Claire snapped, surprising her. She couldn't remember a time when Claire had ever snapped at her. She'd always been far too timid.

"Fine, it's no dream." She watched the girl with narrowed eyes now. "Does that mean when I wake up I won't be at the Reever house sleeping with Graeme?"

She almost smirked back at Claire, but being cruel to the girl just didn't seem right.

"Don't play games, Cat, both our lives are riding on this," Claire demanded firmly. Not angrily or fiercely, simply with a firmness Cat had never sensed in her.

"Our lives are riding on what, Claire?" Cat demanded. "On me admitting that we're in the research center? Fine, here we are." She spread her arms out to indicate the cell they sat within. "According to you I never left it. What now?"

Claire rose slowly to her feet. Her image was clad in the jeans and the loose tank top she'd died in. They were dusty, torn; her feet were bare. She looked like the waif Cat knew those who had loved her had seen her as. Frail. Far too gentle for the life she'd been born into.

"You can't see that a part of you is still locked in this cage, all alone, can you?" Claire whispered.

"Judd was here." He hadn't left. She'd always wondered why he hadn't left, though. He was strong enough, smart enough that he had to have known when Graeme escaped that night. Yet, he'd stayed.

"Why do you think Judd stayed?" Claire turned back to her slowly. "If he could have escaped this hell as well, why didn't he leave with Gideon?"

"Graeme," Cat corrected her almost absently, her own thoughts lost in that question for long moments before she finally shrugged. "Judd was as secretive as Graeme. He never told me."

"And you never asked?" Claire tipped her head to the side as she watched her inquisitively. "That doesn't seem like you, Cat. You're so damned nosy nothing ever gets past you. Why would you let Judd get by with not explaining that? I know you would have wondered."

"I thought Graeme was dead." She wanted to jump from the cot, wanted to throw herself out of it, desperate to escape the dream, yet she seemed locked in place as she watched Claire. "I guess I just assumed the soldiers assigned to the euthanasia team hadn't been ordered to take Judd."

What the hell was going on? What did Claire want from her that required them to be here?

Claire shook her head. "Until you realize you never left this place, until you ask yourself why and answer that question honestly, then you're risking not just your life, but also Graeme's." She sighed. "I always thought I was the coward, Cat, but I'm starting to believe, in ways, you're just as much a coward as I am."

"Don't piss me off, Claire," Cat warned her, narrowing her eyes on her. "I can still kick your ass. Dream or not."

Claire smirked. "You can't come off that cot, Cat. You can't kick anyone's ass in this dream. You're locked there, just as you were the *morning those alarms woke you. Alarms that you knew meant an attempted or successful escape."*

Cat shook her own head at this point. *"I thought the scientists were trying to trick us . . ."*

"Why?" Claire laughed derisively. *"Why would they do that, Cat? He was gone. You were smarter than that. Gideon made certain you were smarter than that."*

"Graeme. His fucking name is Graeme," Cat corrected her, growing angry now. *"Stop this, Claire. If you want to talk to me, then do it as you always have. We talk much better when I'm awake."*

Leaning against the steel bars, Claire watched her with such intent somberness that Cat almost feared the other girl would keep her within that dreamscape forever.

"You can leave anytime you want to, Cat," Claire whispered, her expression never changing. *"It's up to you to wake up, just as it's up to you to realize it doesn't matter if you wake up, you'll still be here."* She waved her arm slowly, encompassing the cells, the life Cat had once lived. *"Realize that before it's too late for both of us."*

She could wake whenever she wanted to? Well, she wanted to wake up now. Right now.

Closing her eyes tight for several seconds, she willed herself awake, willed herself away from the sad, waifish vision that showed far more backbone in hell than she'd shown in life.

"Hell?" Claire whispered. *"This isn't hell, Cat. This is what shaped you. This is where he saved you. Where he realized what you were to him . . . Before you took the first therapy, that enraged animal realized it and quieted, calming the maddened boy and allowing him to learn far more than any young mind should be able to learn. But he learned. For you."*

She would open her eyes and she would be awake. She'd be lying in

Graeme's arms, naked, his body warm against hers, his arrogant superiority infuriating her. All she had to do was open her eyes.

"Yes," *Claire whispered, sounding strangely distant now.* "All you have to do is open your eyes, Cat. But even open, they're closed. Poor Graeme, he'll always be Gideon in your eyes, no matter how much he's changed, no matter how much he loves . . ."

She didn't want to hear any more. She couldn't bear it. She would wake up now!

Opening her eyes quickly, she found herself staring up at Graeme, the gold swirling in those dark green Bengal eyes of his. The fires of fury, she thought. The madness. That part of himself he called the monster.

A low, warning growl sounded in his throat. "That presence will cause me to become violent." The low, vicious snarl was one she'd never heard from him. Even when he'd warned her that the monstrous part of himself was roused, still he hadn't sounded so powerful, so enraged.

"A dream . . ." she whispered desperately. It had to have been just a dream.

"Mine." Moving over her, his legs parting hers with dominant strength as he came over her.

There were no preliminaries, but she didn't need any. Her body answered his hunger, his need, just that quickly.

"Graeme . . ." Her gasp was followed by a low moan as his hands caught her wrists. Securing them to the bed next to her shoulders, he pushed inside her with a hard thrust.

"Oh God. Graeme!" Crying out his name, she was shocked at the sudden, answering slickness that filled her inner flesh, that met him, aiding the penetrating of his swollen cock.

"My mate," he snarled, bending his head to her ear, nipping at the lobe with his teeth. "Fucking mine."

Securing her wrists above her head with one hand, he moved the other to one thigh, dragging her knee to his hip as he began pounding inside her. Each fierce push inside the clamping heat of her pussy sent striking flames of response rushing through her. Her fingers curled against his hold, desperate for something to hold on to. Desperate to hold on to him as he moved inside her like a man possessed by arousal, by possessive lust. He was determined to somehow mark her more than he already had.

His hips slammed between her thighs repeatedly, driving himself to the hilt inside her, pushing to her cervix, rasping over flesh so sensitive that each penetration rode the boundary between pleasure and pain and drove her wild with the complete eroticism of his loss of control.

The feel of his lips moving down her neck sent a rush of dizzying pleasure surging through her, making her pliant, driving a rush of sensation through her already sensitized body.

Down her neck, nipping at her collarbone, his head bending, his lips covered the tight peak of her breast, sucking it into his mouth and drawing on it with hungry pulls of his mouth as his tongue lashed at it, pushing her higher.

Pleasure whipped through her with hurricane force. It drove through her senses, arching her body closer; each thrust inside her tightening channel was met with an answering arch of her hips. She took him deeper, harder. Strangled cries tore from her lips until the rush of complete rapture exploded through her. The violence of the pleasure stole her breath. Her hips arched, her thighs tight around his hips, she held on to him, held on to reality the only way she knew how. By holding on to him the only way she could.

CHAPTER 19

Graeme waited until they had completed breakfast before considering bringing up the night before with Cat. She would no doubt be expecting it, which would make it harder to breach her defenses.

Leaning back in the metal chair that matched the metal and glass breakfast table sitting in the little alcove just off the kitchen, he watched her curiously. She drank her coffee as she went over the news pages she read each day on her e-pad. Cat was curious as hell, not just about everything surrounding her, but about the world itself. And it wasn't likely she'd forget so much as a word that she saw, let alone read.

The information she retained with that unique memory of hers had never failed to amaze him, even in the research center. She might not understand exactly what she took in sometimes, but she could quote it word for word.

Understanding science hadn't been her strong suit. She'd been confused by it in the center even though she'd managed to retain everything he'd shown her. Cat's strong suit was people, strangely enough, though Cat detested crowds and rarely made friends as he understood it.

"Why did you give me Bengal DNA?" The question had him blinking back at her in surprise as her eyes lifted from the e-pad in asking it.

So much for quizzing her first.

"You read Dr. Foster's reports." Lifting his coffee, he sipped at the decaffeinated brew thoughtfully as he watched her, seeing her mind work despite her closed expression.

"Your reasons for it weren't in the report," she pointed out, her tone a little too calm. "I want to know what you were thinking when you decided to use Bengal DNA in my therapy. Were you looking for a sister, or had you already decided I was your mate?"

What was he thinking? He had no other thought at that time beyond saving her life. The missing genes in her makeup would have killed her within weeks of the base injection used to keep her alive until Dr. Foster could come up with a therapy. Graeme hadn't consciously made the decision to mark her with his genetics, but he had no doubt his animal instincts had.

"I'm Bengal," he finally answered, deciding on the truth rather than sugarcoating it as he felt she so often needed. "Brandenmore gave you to me. I felt that made you mine. I was eleven, Cat, why would I have considered any other DNA to introduce into the therapy of a child given to me for safekeeping?"

It was as simple as that, yet also far more complicated and he felt she knew it.

"You were never eleven," she snorted knowingly. "Even Dr. Foster said you were born far older than your years."

His brows lifted at that information. "He never told me that. But if it was true, then it was no more than he programmed into me. I know while the surrogate carried me, he ordered her to listen to a variety of scientific theories that had been given over many generations in genetic manipulation. He knew what he wanted when he created me, and he ensured he got what he wanted."

There was no resentment. Far from it. If he saw anyone as a "father" figure, then it was Benjamin Foster.

"He got far more than he bargained for, though, didn't he?" she guessed. "When did he realize your intelligence was off any scale invented to rate it?"

Graeme almost smiled at that question. He'd always been far more intelligent than Benjamin Foster had guessed.

"I rather doubt he ever knew just how far I'd exceeded even the genetic manipulations he was trying for," he finally answered her. "Man can manipulate all he wants, but the introduction of animal genetics is far more of a wild card than they ever imagine. Or want to acknowledge. And it will become more so in successive generations. If my suspicions are true, then once the children born of original matings reach maturity, they'll surpass even the original Breeds."

She paused for a moment, but evidently decided to allow that speculation to pass.

"So because I was given to you, you used the Bengal genetics in my therapy?" Cat pressed once more. "You chose Honor's genetics as well— why not use Bengal with her therapies too? Didn't you consider her worthy? Part of the Pride you claimed in the center?"

Oh yes, his little cat was far too intelligent herself. And she'd obviously been considering these questions for quite some time.

"Honor wasn't given to me. And the leukemia she suffered from had the potential to become far more deadly with the introduction of any feline genetics. It could have mutated into a form of feline leukemia far stronger than the incurable human leukemia she already suffered from." He finished his coffee and set the cup on the table before bracing his arms on it and leaning forward. "We were studying wolf genetics at the time she was brought in. Dr. Foster created her therapy himself based on his friendship with her father. I had no such ties where you were concerned, and you were mine."

He wouldn't deny that fact. The moment she was placed in his arms his animal instincts had instantly claimed her. Not as a mate, but as belonging solely to him.

"You knew I was your mate then?" Her mind was working, her need to understand her life and the choices made for her finally coming forth. He'd wondered when that would happen.

"I was eleven," he repeated gently. "I was maddened, nearing insanity and euthanasia. I was only weeks away from being taken to the kill center, despite Dr. Foster's best efforts to save me, when Phillip Brandenmore gave you to me. No, I didn't look at you and instantly decide you were my mate. I looked at you, saw the will to live and realized the mistake Brandenmore had made. He'd given me something worth fighting for."

He barely remembered life before Cat. He knew that, before the moment he'd held her in his arms, his brain had actually hurt from all the information he was trying to process. Headaches that surpassed even the pain from the experiments up to that time. Madness had been a constant companion, so much so that he'd felt himself slipping along a darkened tunnel that led only to a complete loss of any semblance of reality.

"So I was worth fighting for, but your brother wasn't?" There was an edge of anger to her voice that caught his attention. "Judd is your twin. Why wasn't he worth fighting for?"

"I didn't say he wasn't worth fighting for," he corrected her. "Both he and Honor were worth fighting for, and I'd hung on through those years for them. But I knew Brandenmore would have me killed soon. My sanity was questionable. I couldn't always control the animal genetics and the rage was eating me alive. The information amassing in my brain was far more than I could process. Perhaps those animal genetics recognized you as my mate, because those instincts instantly eased, the rage dissipated and I found the calm I needed to survive and to process more information than ever before. Whatever the reason, Cat, it changes nothing."

"Nothing is ever that simple with you, Graeme," she bit out, confusion and anger warring inside her. "I knew you then and I know you now. You were born to manipulate and deceive as well as to heal. I have no doubt in my mind your ability to manipulate far surpasses Jonas Wyatt's abilities. You were my world and you deliberately ensured I felt that way. Then I don't see you for thirteen years, no matter that, over and over, I did everything but take out an ad with the news agencies to have you contact me. If I belonged to you, then why didn't you come to me once you were sane enough to realize that something had been taken from you?"

He could see the pain in her face, the haunted need and search for answers. It was a need he couldn't ease for her. One he refused to ease.

Instead, he leaned closer until his face was only inches from hers.

"I always knew you were mine, Cat. Even when the monster raged unabated I knew and I watched over you as closely as I dared. Trust me, you did not want me to come to you then. Even my instincts refused to come near you. Nothing mattered during that time but blood. And I spilled enough of it that sometimes I feared I could drown in it."

Her eyes widened as he spoke, surprise gleaming in the golden brown depths for a second before her spine straightened.

He knew the moment she decided she could push him, that she could dare him.

"And you felt that was something you should and would handle alone. Without your *mate*," she stated. "Yet now that you've decided to claim what you feel is yours you believe you can oversee my every breath?"

There was no anger, no fire. The independence and sheer stubborn will he glimpsed in her were terrifying.

"They nearly took you," he reminded her icily. "They drugged you, incapacitated you and would have taken you, Cat, had I not been close enough to stop them."

"And you ensured I can't be incapacitated in such a way again," she reminded him, still calm, despite the emotions he could feel roiling beneath the façade. "Perhaps you should have taken care of that sooner, Graeme." Rising to her feet, she stared down at him, the hurt in her gaze nearly more than he could stand to stare into. "But then, there are a lot of things you should have taken care of sooner, aren't there?"

He was out of his seat just that fast.

Damn her. She had no idea what she was talking about, no idea the hell he'd endured to ensure she was never found, no matter what. No matter her anger that she didn't have the answers, he'd be damned if he'd allow her to continue to feel this way.

"This vendetta you have against me will stop, Cat," he ordered, the demand in the low, harsh growl impossible for her to miss.

Surprise flared in her gaze then. "Vendetta, Graeme?" she whispered. "You believe my need for answers is a vendetta? Some attempt to avenge whatever slight I might feel?"

"Isn't that exactly what it is?" What more could it be? He'd walked away from her; he understood her anger for that at the time. She was an adult now, she should understand that the need for her protection meant far more than her hurt feelings.

"You trained me to fight at your side," she reminded him with bleak knowledge. "You trained Judd and me both to ensure we were able to aid you in our own protection." Tears gleamed in her eyes now. "That wasn't what happened, though, was it? I'm sorry, Graeme, I don't know how Judd feels, but I feel as though both of you threw me away and I don't know if I can make myself forget it."

◆　　◆　　◆

Cat stalked from the kitchen, rather surprised that Graeme allowed her to go.

The dream, or whatever the hell it had been the night before, had left her unsettled. She couldn't get it out of her mind nor could she forget the accusation that she had never left the research center.

She wasn't stupid, she understood what Claire what saying, but merely rejected the idea of it, Cat assured herself as she moved to the small library/office off the foyer of the house. She didn't have time for this. She didn't have time for the second-guessing and soul-searching that each day with Graeme seemed to bring.

She loved him so desperately, but it wasn't the research center she couldn't escape. It was the knowledge that he had left her there. For months she had believed he was dead. That he had been so frightened that he had stolen the teddy bear she had been so attached to because he was frightened. Only to learn that he had left her and he had taken the only other comfort she'd had in her young life, that damned teddy bear.

Where are you, Claire? she snapped furiously, throwing herself into the large leather chair behind the desk. *Come out and play now, dammit, while I'm awake.*

There was no answer and she was growing used to the fact that the one friend she had believed she could depend upon was gone. And one day, she would be completely gone, Cat knew. Whenever the prophecy from that ritual came due, it was possible both of them would lose their lives.

The awakening would bring death. The words Orrin Martinez had whispered just after the ritual when he believed both Cat and Claire to be held in a deep sleep, had never been forgotten by Cat.

But she'd been awake for the better part of the thirteen years since she'd been given Claire's life and she hadn't died yet. But neither had she revealed herself until now. She didn't want to die, but she couldn't live as Claire Martinez any longer either. Especially if it meant allowing Raymond to continue to destroy the women of the Nation that the Council deemed experiment-worthy, such as Raymond's sister, Morningstar.

The bastards. They would burn in hell, every damned one of them, for the destruction they'd wrought in the past. What would happen to Raymond and the Jackals who'd been taken into custody by Jonas she wasn't certain, but she knew it wouldn't be pleasant.

Tonight, after she'd met with Honor's parents, following through with one of the promises she'd made to herself the night of that ritual, she and Graeme would have to fight this out. If she had to give him an ultimatum, then she would do it. He would come up with answers or she would leave.

Where had he been for the four months before he'd arranged for her and Judd's transfer, and what had happened to him when he'd been returned to the research center several years later? She knew why he'd lashed out at her as he did. She would have never stopped searching for him if he hadn't hurt her so deeply. Nothing Judd had said or done would have convinced her to leave without searching for Graeme the next morning if she hadn't believed she was hated by the Breed that meant so much to her.

Perhaps she'd known that then as well.

Moving from the desk to the glass door that opened to a private patio, she stood in the entrance and inhaled the scents of the desert around her.

She hadn't offered to give General Roberts the location of his daughter for free. She'd demanded all information on the two Breeds confined with her and Honor during the time they'd been at the research center, as well as the complete file on the reacquisition of the Bengal Breed Gideon.

She hadn't dared ask Jonas for it, but General Roberts was another story. His connections while his daughter had been in the research center had been strong. Afterward, she knew he'd stayed in contact with one of the few lead research techs Graeme had left alive after his rampage. That tech remained alive because he'd been in Washington delivering evidence against the center to the Bureau of Breed Affairs. Jonas still had him in hiding for fear *Gideon* would strike out at him.

"You know Graeme's completely pouting again." Khi Langer, Lobo's stepdaughter, stepped around the side of the house, her vivid blue eyes not nearly as amused as she would have had Cat believe.

Dressed in riding pants and a snug sleeveless white silk shirt and knee-high black boots, she looked as though she would be more at home on an English estate than at the Reevers' desert home.

"I wondered how long it would take you to visit." Cat sighed. "Ashley's already given her warning, I don't need another from you."

She'd known Khi was Graeme's little sidekick for months.

The bastard. He'd allowed this woman to aid him, yet he'd never given Cat that option, even now. She knew of his little midnight sorties into the desert each night as he patrolled for Council soldiers in the area. But had he invited her to patrol at his side?

Hell no, he hadn't.

"Ashley's been a little intense since she tried to stop that bullet with her heart," she snorted with a slight edge of anger. "Not that she was ever less than intense, she's just more so now."

Strolling along the short walk from the pool area to the little shaded, brick-lined patio off the office, Khi kept her eyes on Cat. What was she searching for? Cat wondered curiously.

"I'm not here to warn you, anyway," the other woman assured her when Cat remained silent. "I wanted to make certain you didn't need anything. A shoulder to cry on, perhaps, or a willing ear to listen to you curse that arrogant mate of yours. Of course, we could sit and diss men in general." Smiling, Khi plopped into one of the overstuffed chairs placed beneath the covered pergola. "I always enjoy that."

She wasn't lying, Cat observed silently, but there was an air of secrets that surrounded Khi that had always made her wary.

"If I start, I might not stop," Cat admitted with a shrug.

She remained at the entrance to the office, though she leaned against the door frame, one hand propped on her hip, the other relaxed at her side, rather than taking the other chair across from Khi.

"Yeah, I know that one," Khi admitted as she flicked something from the knee of her pants, her gaze remaining on that area for long moments before she lifted her head again and flashed Cat another of her bright smiles. A smile that didn't reach her eyes.

"Why are you here, Khi?" Tilting her head, a small frown pulled at her brow. "Does Graeme know you're visiting?"

Khi gave a light laugh at the question. "I don't ask Graeme Parker's permission to go anywhere on the Reever property." She gave a little roll of her eyes. "I don't even extend that courtesy to Lobo."

Cat lifted her brows at the statement. "Quite an accomplishment. I envy you," she snorted. "I imagine Lobo's arrogance more than matches Graeme's. And he seems just as domineering."

"Just as much an ass, you mean?" This time, Khi's smile was a bit tight. "I imagine he can be. I try to stay out of the way of his arrogance and he avoids my bitchiness. It works for us."

Interesting. At one time, Khi had been rumored to be quite close to her stepfather. Of course, that was before her mother tried to kill him.

Not many were aware of the fact that Jessica Reever had been one of the Genetics Council's spies. Her first husband had died attempting to help liberate an Irish Council research lab. She'd even appeared to mourn him for several years.

Breathing slow and easy, Cat drew in the other girl's scent, the subtle differences in it confusing. There was a hint of something that reminded her of Mating Heat, yet wasn't, as well as the odd scents of a Wolf Breed and fierce anger. Whatever Khi Langer was bottling inside herself was building to an explosion. She wasn't normally so mocking or caustic, Cat knew.

Cat didn't know the other girl well. Raymond's dislike of Lobo Reever, as well as his wealth, had ensured he did his best to make certain Cat's path didn't cross with Khi's.

"So, why am I here?" Placing her hands on her upper leg, Khi leaned forward and flicked Cat a quick look. "Because it's completely boring at the house: Lobo has the estate on lockdown, and everyone I really know from the area is in hiding, it appears." She rose gracefully to her feet. "How about a drink? I'm sure it's five o'clock somewhere."

"Why don't you return to the main house, and when Graeme asks you why you didn't see your babysitting duties through, you can inform him I asked you to leave," Cat suggested coolly.

It hadn't really taken long to figure out why Khi was there. Graeme was due to leave soon for some meeting with Lobo that would last well into the night, she knew.

"I'll do that." Khi nodded. "But let's have that drink first and give him time to leave for that meeting. You really don't want him sending Lobo's guards out instead. They're really assholes. Come on." As Khi brushed past her into the house, the scent of overwhelming weariness had Cat hiding an impatient sigh.

She had her own things to do.

"Tea?" she suggested rather than asking the other girl to leave now.

"Only the alcoholic kind," Khi demanded. "If you want to do virgin, it's your choice. Personally, virginity doesn't really appeal to me. It's been a hell of a morning."

And it looked like Cat was in for a hell of an afternoon.

She was going to kill Graeme. A babysitter? Really? For what?

What did he think Khi could do but tell on her if she attempted to leave the house? Khi wasn't protection, she was there as a tattletale and nothing more.

She had a few hours, Cat decided. If Khi wanted a drink, then she could have a drink. Come dusk, Cat thought, she'd just pretend to take a little nap. It wasn't as though Keenan and his men came through the front door. Not that Khi would see them if they did.

She wanted one of those damned suits they wore so bad she couldn't stand it. Unfortunately, Keenan was not all about sharing the technology. And not even the best nano-nit Cat had created had managed to get past the electronic firewalls built into the electronics either. Damned winged Breeds were like Graeme, too smart for their own damned good.

Following Khi through the office, Cat retrieved the e-pad to ensure she didn't miss any messages sent by Keenan or his second in command, Teal. Keenan had given her the device to ensure all communications between them was untraceable. If only there was a program for the babysitters Graeme chose.

✦   ✦   ✦

Graeme watched the monitor as Khi strode to the bar in the guesthouse and poured herself a drink.

She was drinking too much too often, he thought, concerned. He'd grown fond of her over the past year, respected her intelligence, the loyalty that went far too deep, as well as her determination, but that kid's heart was torn into two raw chunks and she had no idea how to deal with it.

Mated to one brother and in love with the other, unable to give in to either of them. It was a hell of a position to be in and he didn't envy her in the least. Still, he was going to have to discuss the drinking with her. They had a deal, and if he let her renege on her part, then she could slip down an emotional tunnel from which she might not return.

At the moment, Khi wasn't the concern, though—Cat was. Claire's warning and the knowledge that the protective spirit had roused again the night before as Cat slept had his instincts going haywire. There was something he was missing, he could feel it. Add that to his meeting with Orrin Martinez and Graeme was determined to find out what the hell was going on with Cat.

He'd be damned if he would lose her. He'd dedicated his life to ensuring her safety and his peace; he wouldn't let her down now, not when he'd already let her down as he had.

She'd been right, he'd trained her to fight at his side. Both Judd and Cat had been taught to fight. Cat was especially adept at it because her small stature and apparently fragile build managed to fool people, even those who should know better, into believing she would be easy to defeat. But Gideon had taught her to strike first and deal with her conscience later. She went for the jugular, literally, just as she had done the night the guards had attempted to transfer her and Judd to the kill facility.

The thought of that night brought with it the memory of the betrayal in her eyes when he'd thrown open the doors on the van. She hadn't been allowed to bathe or wash her hair often, he'd noted that instantly. Her nails were stained with dirt and blood, her face streaked with dust. The scent of such grief and pain that it filled every part of her struck him first. Then betrayal. Her entire being had flooded with a sense of betrayal as he stared back at her.

She'd just stared at him, so silent, almost in disbelief. But he'd seen that first slow fall into the distrust she now felt for him.

He would deal with that, he assured himself. Turning to the bank of computers in the underground cavern he used for security monitoring, Graeme told himself he would deal with that, just as soon as he dealt with Jonas and the interrogation of the Jackals that Lobo had managed to include them in on.

No one had broken the bastards yet and they still insisted on speaking to him alone if they were going to release any information. He had no doubt they had plenty of information to release; for that reason alone Jonas had agreed to bring them to Lobo's estate, and the small secure building the Wolf Breed kept at the back of the main estate house, for the interrogation.

Unfortunately the audio setup had yet to be extended out to there. Completing it before Jonas arrived was paramount.

Hopefully, Cat would talk to Khi and perhaps in that conversation Graeme could glean a hint of what was going on with his mate. Because he had no doubt she was up to something, and when Cat plotted, Graeme knew, life could become very dangerous indeed.

CHAPTER 20

Cat didn't think Khi would ever leave. She lingered for hours, chit-chatting, talking about life in Ireland versus on the Reever estate and how she'd once missed the country of her birth but it seemed foreign now. She talked about everything and everyone but Graeme. The few questions Cat asked about him she neatly sidestepped, though it was expected. Khi's loyalty to Graeme had never been in question—Cat had already suspected the other woman all but idolized Graeme.

The thought sent a wave of jealousy washing through her that had to be quickly tamped down. She couldn't afford to get into a confrontation with the reigning princess of the Reever estate. And she didn't really want to. Hell, the other girl had enough problems with the Reever brothers, she didn't need any from anyone else.

Finally, as the sun rose to its highest point, baking the already dry desert landscape further, the other girl rose from the chair she'd curled into on the patio and set her empty glass aside.

"I guess you've had enough of me now," Khi drawled. "And it looks as though that wily mate of yours is making an appearance."

Turning her head, Cat watched as Graeme strode from inside the house, the black pants and T-shirt he wore giving him a dark, dangerous appearance.

"I'm just leaving," Khi assured him as she flashed him a mocking grin. "I believe I might have time to dress for dinner with Lobo. He's been bitching about that lately." She shrugged carelessly. "I found the cutest pair of ripped jeans and a T-shirt with tanning oil stains on it. I thought I'd try it out."

Graeme actually winced. "He's going to ship you off to a convent, Khi."

She only snorted at that. "In his dreams." Throwing Cat a careless wave, she moved with unhurried grace around the side of the house and disappeared. Within moments a low, quiet hum indicated she'd left via one of the small, personal gliders Lobo often used around the huge desert estate.

"Interesting friend you have there." Cat remained in the lounger where she'd stretched out to listen to Khi's chatter. "And she's so quiet. How do you bear it?"

He hadn't been one to tolerate useless chatter when they'd been younger. Of course, the research center hadn't exactly encouraged chatter of any type.

"Stop being a smart aleck," he chastised, though there was a glint of amusement, affection and concern in his gaze. "She's a conflicted child at the moment."

Cat rolled her eyes. "Conflicted, huh? I guess that's as good a word for it as any."

Stopping next to the lounger, he stared down at her, the latent hunger and heated lust in his gaze instantly spurring the Mating Heat, which was making itself known by stronger degrees by the day.

Even her flesh was sensitive, aching with a need for his touch that she found distinctly unsettling. As she stared up at him, the image of him thirteen years before flashed through her mind. He hadn't been as muscle hard, but he'd been powerful, even then. His features were more defined now, more savage, and lacked the very slight softening of compassion he'd had so long ago.

Now there were the smallest lines at the corners of his eyes that had nothing to do with age or the sun. His features weren't lined, but the sharp definition hinted at the brutality of the life he'd lived for so long.

He'd changed so much. Over the course of the past weeks she'd learned that those changes went far deeper than she might guess as well. The changes weren't just physical either. He wasn't harder just on the outside, but on the inside as well, except where it came to her. He still treated her with a gentleness she knew was completely alien to him.

And he belonged to her on a level she'd never questioned, even as a child. As an adult, so many things made more sense, and yet others were so much more complicated. And there was one question she had to have the answer to.

"Did you ever love me?" she whispered, remembering his claim that he never had. "Or have you always just claimed me?"

If his features could have hardened further, they did, and she knew that flash of uncertainty she thought gleamed for a moment in his gaze had to be an illusion. Graeme was never uncertain.

"You're mine," he stated and there was no uncertainty at all, not in his voice or in his gaze. "And I would suggest you never forget that."

He claimed her.

She rose slowly from the chair.

"I would have thought you loved me," she said softly, the pain that sliced at her more than she would have expected.

"What do I know of love, Cat?" he asked her then, drawing her gaze back to his as he watched her with a hint of confusion. "What the world calls love, I highly discount. There's no loyalty in it, no drive to hold on to what they claim once that haze of lust dissipates. If that's love, then why would you want it?"

"That isn't love." She had to force the words out. "No more than possession is love, Graeme. No more than Mating Heat is love. Without real love, what separates possession from obsession, and Mating Heat from biological rape? Mating Heat can begin without love, but like lust, it won't bind mates without love."

"And what makes you a fucking expert on love, Cat?" he bit out, pushing his fingers through his hair in frustration. "When did Webster contact you for the definition?"

"When you decided I was your mate," she snapped back, one hand going to her hip as the dominance he displayed had her shoulders straightening and determination hardening her tone. "I'm far more an expert on it than you evidently, Graeme, because at least I recognize it when I feel it."

"And just who did you recognize it with?" Pure fury lit his eyes.

First that wild green spread across his eyes, obliterating the whites, then within a heartbeat later the tiny flecks of amber gold began to fill it as shadowed stripes began marring his face and neck.

"With you," she all but yelled. "Unfortunately loving you now does me about as much good as it did when I was twelve. And you include me in about as much of your life now as you did then." Stepping closer, glaring up at him, she could feel the tips of her claws flexing, aching to emerge. "When I was twelve you pushed me aside to fight alone and left my protection to others, and now, other than when you need to fuck, you push me aside to fight with Khi or Lobo or Rule or whoever else you decide is strong enough to stand at your side. When will you consider me your partner rather than your damned fuck toy?"

"When I'm not in danger of losing my fucking sanity at the thought of a scratch on your soft skin," he snarled back at her, head lowering until they were snarling at each other, nose to nose. "I taught you to fight to aid in your protection. Not to aid in my battles."

"If I can't fight with you, then I don't want to fuck with you," she sneered up at him. "Go on to your little meeting, Bengal boy." She waved toward the main estate with a curl of her lip. "Go have fun with the big dogs. See how much good they do you when that hard cock of yours needs attention, because I won't give you the satisfaction of taking care of it."

Swinging around to stomp away from him, she found herself pulled up short by firm fingers snagging her wrist, manacling it and pulling her around to face him once more.

"You are my mate," he reminded her, the gleaming brilliance of that fierce green swirling with glints of amber fury. "You can claim you'll deny me all you want, but the heat will always bring you back to me, Cat."

"Will it?" she asked tightly, her breathing harsh, anger and need and far too much love for such an arrogant beast raging inside her. "We both know exactly how stubborn I can be, don't we, Graeme. Let's see which is stronger. My determination or some biological lust that lacks any basis in emotion. Which one will win, Graeme?"

"Don't turn our mating into a battle, Cat," he warned her, his voice deepening to a guttural growl.

"No, you're turning it into a battle, not me. Even worse, Graeme, you want to weaken me, you want to destroy what you made when you created the therapy to save me. And I'll be damned if I'll stand for it. I've spent too many years waiting for my chance to be free. I will not put my head down and pretend to be weak ever again. Not for you. Never for you." She couldn't bear it. The very attempt would kill her.

Jerking her wrist from his hold, she all but ran into the house and up to her room.

He had to go to his precious meeting, well, she had a meeting of her own to attend. She'd worked too hard for this day, when she could keep the promise she'd made to the girl who'd shared those cells with her. The promise that one day her parents would find her. Jonas refused to allow it and Honor's mating with a Wolf Breed placed her under certain constraints where the Bureau of Breed Affairs was concerned.

Cat wasn't ruled by the Bureau, by Jonas nor by Graeme.

Honor still hadn't fully awakened and the protective spirit of Liza Johnson that ensured Honor's identity was hidden was still far too protective. Only one thing would ever force Honor to break through that dark labyrinth within her own mind to take control of her life once again. The parents who loved her enough to send her away rather than see her returned to the research center. Parents Jonas had yet to contact, and Honor had yet to awaken enough to remember fully.

Cat had never had parents. No mother who loved her and cried for her, no father who searched tirelessly for her or watched the faces of every female her age, hoping to see the child he'd lost.

This meeting, like all the battles she'd fought in the past years, she would do without Graeme. He couldn't include her in even the plans or meetings regarding her protection or her life? What could even make her imagine he'd help her with this? He wouldn't.

And if he did, the one thing she'd bargained with General Roberts for, she would never see. The files Dr. Bennett had submitted on Gideon's recapture and the tests performed while he was there. Something had changed him. Changed him so drastically that, as he said, sometimes he felt he would drown in blood.

To understand her mate, to know why he'd become so much harder, she had to know what had happened when he was returned to the research center. What created the monster that had raged for years after his escape, and what had enabled him to regain his sanity?

She knew everything else. Every move he'd made since he'd disappeared the night he'd rescued her and Judd from the soldiers escorting them to the kill facility. Every move made in the past year, she knew about. But what had happened in the center for the year Dr. Bennett had held him, she had no idea. Jonas wouldn't tell her. If Orrin had known, he wouldn't tell her. But General Roberts could acquire that information. And she had something he wanted bad enough to ensure he brought it to her. The daughter he and his wife had never stopped waiting for.

The woman the world knew as Liza Johnson was the child Honor Roberts, the friend Cat had lost forever in a Navajo ritual that had stolen her memories, her very identity, for years—so many years, that who she was as a child perhaps no longer even existed. But who she had been to her parents, who her parents had been to her, would never be lost, Cat suspected. And possibly it was all that would enable Honor to step back into her own life and take her place, fully, with her own mate.

Cat only hoped that perhaps, at some point in the future, she could take her own place. That maybe Graeme would soften enough to realize that Mating Heat *was* love. Without one, the other could not exist.

◆　◆　◆

The Six Chiefs of the Navajo moved into the sweat lodge behind two of the Unknown. Each of the warriors carried the still, silent body of a young Breed female—both females so unique, and so important to the Breeds as well as the Navajo, that the very land itself called out for their preservation.

As the procession moved into the steamy room, the herbs and potent medicines used to awaken and to guide the spirits began to scent the moist air.

In the center of the lodge two large flat stones sat between six mounds of steaming rocks. The damp heat from the steaming rocks wafted over the hard stone bed that one young woman was placed upon. Orrin Martinez stepped back and stared sadly down at the unique creatures the chiefs had been called to aid.

Graceful gold, creamy white and russet wings arced above the head of the first and framed a small body before ending far below her small, booted feet. Fragile, small boned, the young woman could have passed for a child were it not for the shapely woman's curves beneath the leather pants and vest she wore.

Long, light brown hair touched with russet highlights spilled along the side of her face and over her breasts in lush ringlets and Orrin knew when her eyes opened he'd see the fierce eagle hues of brown, green and a hint of black. Creamy flesh unmarred by her battles was now pale, the luster of life quickly dimming.

On the narrow stone next to her lay another young female Breed, this one having only just passed her twentieth year. This one Orrin ached for the most. The little Lion Breed female had known only a few years of freedom. She'd had no time to build dreams or the life Breeds had been promised.

As small and fragile as the winged Breed, the little Lion Breed female lay just as still and silent. There all resemblance ended, though. The Lion Breed female's hair was short, framing a curiously inquisitive little face with a pert nose. Wide eyes were framed by a line of dark color as though nature had applied liner around the slightly tilted curve of her lashes.

She wasn't dressed in leathers, but rather in the long white gown she'd been dressed in after being brought to the Breeds. There were no wounds on her body; the injuries had been internal but had healed. Her fragile spirit could no longer endure the life she was born into. Years of confinement and cruelty had worn her down. Her escape had given her only a few years to acclimate to freedom before she'd been forced to witness yet more atrocities in an attack against her and two other female Breeds.

The wound to her head was healing nicely, yet her spirit continued to seek escape. Life was bleeding from her with each shallow breath she took.

These spirits fought to escape while two others fought to linger. The awakening of Cat and Honor was completed, yet Claire and Liza had yet to walk the path to the afterlife. Orrin had been concerned by this until the winds had begun whispering the will of the land and the fate of two weary souls that would leave bodies strong enough to endure the ritual of placement.

Stepping back from the stone beds, his five fellow chiefs gazed at him silently.

"We are in agreement?" he asked them softly. "The winds have called us to this place prepared by the Unknown. In the breath of the land we heard the request to awaken and to prepare for death and to prepare for placement. The Unknown have been sent to bring to us the awakened. Should they seek life, these bodies will be theirs. Should they seek their rest, then the lands will show them the way."

"So the winds have whispered to us," the five agreed.

Orrin turned to the two Unknown who had brought the females to them. "To the Unknown have the lands called to take your brothers to the awakened and bring them to this place?"

"So the Unknown have been called," they agreed.

"Then we prepare," Orrin announced. "Tonight the awakened will be freed and placement shall begin."

The rituals were ancient and ones only the chiefs and the Unknown knew the intricacies of. The rituals were far older than the Nation, and their mysteries originated, it was told, as long ago as time had begun in the stars themselves.

They were the People, given to the Earth for safekeeping, given guardianship of the secrets of the lands by the Great Spirit and the winds themselves. For as long as the Navajo had drawn breath, their bodies filled with the air given by the winds, those winds had whispered vast knowledge and the secrets of rituals unlike any others could imagine.

They were the Six Chiefs. Always, there had been six chiefs. Always, there had been twelve of the Unknown. And from the Unknown, the chiefs that would carry the next generation would be chosen by the winds. So it had begun and so it would continue.

But with each ritual of awakening, there was the passing. With each life given, one was taken. The spirits of these fragile young women could endure no more. The horrors of their lives, of the cruelties of man, had been far more than they could endure. Their losses had sapped their will to continue in this life they were given.

The prophecy had been whispered to him the night his granddaughter's body had expired from its wounds and she had become the protector of the young Breed female known as Cat. The winds had whispered that with the awakening, death would come. He had known since Claire's birth that her destiny was to be one of heartbreak and fear in her youth, but one of freedom and greatness once payment was made.

No gifts were given without the battle to receive them, he knew. The Earth knew what many parents did not understand: Its children must work for the gifts given and only with sacrifice could they appreciate the happiness that came with those gifts.

His granddaughter Claire had sacrificed everything for future happiness. Though if the happiness did not come, perhaps at some point she might find contentment in finding a new life. Which of these exceptional young women's bodies she would be accepted into he did not know. The spirits of the young women had seen all they could see, fought all they could fight; their weariness was apparent in the dimness of their life force.

The Earth, the Great Spirit that guided them all, had other plans for their bodies and he only prayed those plans would see to the eventual happiness of the child he ached for, the granddaughter he feared he'd already lost.

If she were going to run, it would be tonight.

Focusing his attention on the display of the security feed from her bedroom on the secured e-pad lying in the dirt before him, Graeme reminded himself of that fact once again. Confronting her about it would do no good. To give answers, she would first demand answers, and revealing the horrors he'd experienced when he was recaptured was something he couldn't bring himself to do. Instead, he was here. The interrogation of the Jackals had been delayed, though a brief meeting with Jonas hadn't been. Even as he watched her shift on the bed and tuck back a stray strand of hair into the snug braid she'd bound the rest into, he couldn't push away the certainty that she was going to run.

Tonight would be her best chance if that were her intention. She believed him distracted by the interrogation of the Jackals with Jonas Wyatt. She was certain he was unsuspecting of her intent to leave. Had

Claire not warned him of Cat's intentions, then he might have questioned his certainty that something was wrong.

And something was definitely wrong. He could feel it. Even as he lifted his gaze from the security feed to stare at her open balcony doors, his instincts were raging. He hated her habit of leaving those doors open, it was a security risk that made his skin crawl after the attack by the Jackals and Raymond Martinez. But, like Claire, she enjoyed the night and the cool breeze that drifted into the bedroom. Personally, Graeme thought it was the sense of freedom the act gave her that she enjoyed.

Not that there seemed to be a risk tonight. The breeze was soft, cool but not yet cold. And for all the eyes on the small rental estate, there was nothing restless or dangerous that seemed to drift on the wind.

The six-man team of enforcers from the Bureau of Breed Affairs had fanned out around the walled property at perfect vantage points to watch the area. They thought they were hidden from Graeme's detection, but he'd found them instantly as he scanned the area.

The fact that Jonas's warning instincts were roused as well had the primal force inside him itching to emerge. Just beyond the gates of the property Brim Stone, along with Ashley, Emma, Rule Breaker and his mate, Gypsy McQuade, watched the front of the house in plain sight. The two human soldiers the Council had sent were in the shadowed rise of boulders about a half mile from the property, believing themselves hidden. Graeme had known the second they passed Lobo's borders the night before, though. There was no way for his Cat to be taken or to run without being seen. So why he was so certain her safety was in imminent peril he couldn't explain.

Beside him, stretched out on the rocky peak of the rise behind the house, Lobo waited as well. The Wolf was so still, so silent, Graeme could barely detect his heartbeat. Lobo was far more than others suspected and took extreme advantage of that fact. And like Graeme, he could be the perfect killing machine. They'd been in place since darkness had fallen and not once had the other Breed questioned Graeme's instincts. In the year since they'd formed their unusual partnership Lobo had given him what seemed to be unquestioned faith. If only Cat would extend a small measure of such trust.

"She's good," Lobo murmured as his gaze remained focused on the security feed. "Cool as ice. Whatever her plans, she's not giving anything away. You trained her well, Graeme."

Unfortunately, that was far too accurate.

"Perhaps at some things I trained her far too well." Graeme sighed, his voice barely a breath of sound.

Lobo gave a small, amused grunt.

"As a trainer your instincts are excellent. Even my own force has benefited from them immensely. Despite their dislike of felines." The wry comment had a grin tugging at Graeme's lips.

"They learn well despite my dislike of wolves."

The world believed the Breeds—feline, Wolf and Coyote—struggled with a perceived, instinctive dislike toward and prejudice against one another. The truth was, only those who had sided with their creators harbored such prejudices. For those born with the instincts more closely related to their animal genetics, there was no such dislike. It hadn't been in their training either.

"She's too patient," Lobo pointed out.

"Her patience has always seemed immeasurable. And it's vast. But it has a limit. When that limit's been reached she's already perfected a deadly plan of attack or retribution. She's incredible." He was in awe of her and she had no idea how he felt.

At twelve she'd done what neither he nor Judd had expected. When the transport agents had arrived to take her to the kill center they had deemed her without threat and hadn't restrained her. Not that their restraints would have locked properly around her tiny wrists.

She'd waited, seemingly drawn within herself, until she'd somehow sensed the perfect moment to launch herself on the agent guarding her and tear his throat out. Judd hadn't expected such a move and it had been accomplished before he could react. The silent accuracy and cold determination Judd had described had Graeme doubting him. In the time he'd watched her, though, seen her few desert hunts, he'd lost that doubt.

"And when she loses her patience with you?" Lobo asked in an amused murmur. "Will you survive?"

Graeme wasn't so certain he would.

"She'll shred me," he admitted. "Without mercy and without death, she'll fucking take me apart. But when she does she'll be the mate I know lurks beneath the calm."

Breaking that calm had been impossible so far. She was too calm. Too much of the protective Claire still influenced her instincts as well as the Breed genetics struggling within her.

"She's rising," Lobo alerted him.

Moving his attention to the e-pad, Graeme watched as she tossed the electronic device aside and rose from the bed. Striding to the dresser, she collected a short, filmy gown from a drawer and moved into the bathroom.

Dammit, he should have replaced the security equipment she'd removed from the room. Waiting, nerves on edge, he knew the sound of the shower long minutes later should have had him relaxing. But it didn't. There was nothing to indicate danger, no reason to suspect she was doing anything but preparing for bed, but he could feel the monster rousing. Some instinctive knowledge pulled it to the surface despite Graeme's attempts to push it back.

"Brim, take Ashley and Emma in to check the master shower," Lobo ordered through the communication link he wore. Graeme had been unaware that link had been programmed to connect to the Coyote Breeds.

Brim didn't answer but Graeme detected a hint of movement as the Breeds exited the Dragoon and scaled the fence at the front.

Graeme waited, watching carefully as security showed Brim, another Coyote and the two females entering the front door and proceeding upstairs cautiously.

"Something's not right." His voice was deeper, harsh, an indication he was losing his grip on the maddened force he harbored inside. "Damn her. She's flown . . ."

Flown. Claire had said she would fly, not run.

Swinging his head to Lobo, he pierced the Breed with a furious stare. "Are the winged Breeds in this desert?"

Lobo stared at him in surprise. "They're in South America."

"Like hell they are," the monster growled. "They're here and they have her."

The monster was free. Power flooded his body, shaped it, poured through his senses and sharpened each detail, each sight and scent that filled the night. And then, the smell of them, so subtle, barely there, reached him.

The winged Breeds had taken his mate.

A savage, enraged roar filled the night.

He'd kill every damned one of them.

◆　◆　◆

The thrill of flying with the winged Breeds would never grow old, Cat thought as Keenan landed with her on the desert floor next to a Limo series Desert Dragoon. The larger, expanded Dragoon with its luxury appointments inside and additional armor and weapons on the outside was quickly becoming adopted as the perfect defense vehicle in the Southwest.

Around the vehicle were four other winged Breeds with one inside the vehicle with the human couple. Reaching forward, Keenan opened the passenger-side back door and allowed Cat to slide inside.

The lighted interior had been hidden by the dark windows, but when she faced the couple, she could clearly identify where Honor had gotten many of her features. The general's hair was graying now, as was his wife's, but the attractive, almost aristocratic features made them look years younger.

They stared at her in shock, both the general and his slender wife silent, their gazes wide as they watched her. She flashed them both a grin as she pulled a leather-bound sheath of papers from the deep pocket on the thigh of her snug black pants.

"What were you expecting?" she asked, amused at the looks. "You knew the winged Breeds were flying me in."

"I wasn't expecting you," the general almost whispered. "Sweet God, Catarina, we thought you were dead."

She kept her expression amused, didn't deviate an iota from how she watched them, though inside she stilled at the name. Catarina? Who the fuck was Catarina?

"That was the idea," she answered. "If knowledge that I was still alive reached the Genetics Council, then I wouldn't have been alive long."

General Roberts shook his head. "So many years. You contacted us but not your parents? They still grieve terribly, despite the fact that they believe you died as a baby."

Everything in Cat was freezing. She was amazed she was still breathing. She had been told she had no parents. That her mother had died from her refusal to treat the AIDS she'd contracted and had passed the disease to her daughter. She'd been told that the woman had sold her child to Brandenmore for enough money to ensure she was buried properly rather than cremated as hospital property.

And Graeme had never told her any different.

Yet, she knew General Roberts wouldn't lie, and he would never speak of something he wasn't certain of.

"Tell me about them." She finally managed to force words past her lips. "I never learned who they were."

General Roberts shook his head as his wife's eyes filled with tears.

"They are our dearest friends," Annette Roberts whispered, tears filling her eyes as she stared at Cat in amazement. "Your mother, Helena, has been my closest friend since I was three. My God, you're the image of her, though I can see your father's stubborn jawline." A trembling smile pulled at her pale lips. "Helena still cries for you each year on your birthday and Kenneth still adds a single piece of furniture to the dollhouse he made for you before you were born."

Oh God.

They were killing her. Cat could feel her soul being shredded as it never had been before. It was being ripped from her one small piece at a time. She had parents? She belonged? And Graeme had never told her?

"How could you not know who they were?" the general asked then. "The Breed that came to us earlier this year, Graeme, gathering information on them, told us he intended to inform you of the lie Brandenmore had told of your birth."

"And you knew Brandenmore lied about it?" Cat asked, fighting to understand such deliberate cruelty. "The years Honor was at the center and you never told me?"

Regret and grief filled his expression as he reached out for her, sighing when she jerked back from his touch.

"How could I tell you?" he asked gently. "They held my child's life in their hands. Brandenmore could have killed Honor as easily as he cured her. I didn't dare let any of them suspect I was less than the good little Genetics Council follower. Then, just when I thought I could keep her safe, and could go to your parents, I was told you'd died in the labs when one of the Breeds there escaped. I couldn't find any proof otherwise and didn't dare add to your mother's pain."

"She never had more children?" Cat asked numbly.

"The genetic defect you were born with had something to do with an incompatibility between her and Kenneth's genetics," the general told her. "They didn't dare risk it. Losing another child would have killed Helena."

She was dying inside. Agonizing bursts of emotion were exploding inside her, ripping her apart with the force of them.

"And you say Graeme knew?" she asked.

The general nodded. "The Bengal boy that cared for you, Gideon I believe his name was, he knew as well. Once the genetic abnormality was being treated, Dr. Foster demanded to know who your parents were in case he needed further genetic information. The boy was there and I questioned his presence, though the doctor assured me he would never speak of it. I guess he didn't." He shook his graying head with sadness. "Damn, that kid loved you, though. There wasn't a guard or doctor there who didn't sweat whenever the therapies were given to you. Even Brandenmore walked cautiously around him where you were concerned. What they did to him later . . ." He drew in a hard breath as the scent of horrific disbelief wafted around him. "If they hadn't threatened to reacquire you, he would have died during that last vivisection." Horror flashed in his eyes and in Cat's soul. "There were three. During the last one, Bennett gave the order to acquire you at all costs to see if you could survive the same experiments. God knew he deserved the peace after what Bennett did. I hope he finally found some measure of it."

Three vivisections? They'd cut into him as he lived, exposed organs and inner flesh in an act that no other Breed was known to have survived? And they had threatened to do the same to her. There was no way he would have allowed that. Because of it, the monster that lurked inside him had risen like a demon of death to destroy anyone that dared threaten her.

This was what he'd hid from her, because it had been her fault. That transfusion placed her blood inside him, marked him with her mating hormone, and because of it Dr. Bennett would have been beside himself with glee at the thought of experimenting on a living, mated Breed.

"You brought the information?" The files detailing what had been done to him, why it had been done, and the birth of the monster they unleashed. That had been her price, she'd warned him, though she would have given him the information to find his daughter regardless.

"Had I known it was you, Catarina," he whispered, "I would have tried to dissuade you from asking that price."

From seeing what had happened to Graeme rather than briefly being told? What difference would it make, she knew now what Graeme had been trying to protect her from.

All the lies, his deliberate silence, his refusal to reveal she had parents, all of it had been his attempt to protect her, to ensure no one could harm her. The means was questionable, but the intent pure. That moment of insight broke what was left of her heart. She'd refused to trust him, even though she'd known, known in the deepest reaches of her soul that the man she'd known as a child would do nothing to intentionally harm her. "Graeme, the Breed that came to us some months back, said he knew where Honor was being hidden. He had yet to learn her identity, though." Gray eyes hardened on her. "We haven't heard back from him. We didn't tell him we were already in contact with someone giving us reports on her." Gratitude flashed in his eyes. "For that, we thank you. Living without her . . ." Moisture gleamed in his eyes as a tear slipped from his wife's. "So many years lost."

He handed over the flash chip to her. The information she'd bargained for was hers now, for what? To learn how far he would go to ensure her safety?

Cat in turn handed over the leather-protected sheath of papers, pictures and various flash chips she'd made of Honor's life over the years.

"Is Honor happy?" Annette whispered then, a thread of fear, that her daughter might not need her in her life now, hidden in the hope.

"She's with a Breed who loves her more than his own life," Cat told her softly. "But she still misses a mother to confide in and a father to lean on. The couple that claimed her as a daughter are wonderful people, but she never became close to them." Honor had never awakened as Cat had. At least, if she had, she'd never let anyone, especially Cat, know. "Take the information you have to Jonas Wyatt. He's at the Window Rock offices of the Bureau of Breed Affairs. Make certain the director of that office, Rule Breaker, is present during your meeting. Confront him, demand to see her, and Rule will make certain it happens. Otherwise, Jonas will have the Breed she's in love with move her."

"She's in danger?" the general guessed.

"For the moment," Cat affirmed, still trying to hold in her shattered emotions. "Letting her see her parents won't affect the situation, though. It may even help it."

"Catarina." Annette sat forward as Cat reached for the door to leave the Dragoon. "Whatever pain haunts your eyes could be soothed with a mother's love. Go to your parents, please. Because I don't know if I can watch her pain another year and not reveal the truth. And trust me, when I do, your father will go ballistic. He'll raze through the Breed forces with every favor he's amassed in his life and his father's, and God only knows the destruction he'll cause to find you."

"The Bureau didn't know about me. They didn't hide me, nor did they know where I was hidden. If they had, I would have died long ago. Trust me, Mrs. Roberts, those who hid me—no one can find them unless they want to be found."

"It won't change anything, my dear," the general warned her gently. "Kenneth won't allow it to. Once he learns you're alive, he'll tear the world apart to find you."

Cat stared through the window, watching as Keenan and his winged Breeds stood protectively around the Dragoon. Her world was no place for parents who had loved their daughter.

"I'm not the child they lost anymore," she whispered, refusing to look back at them. "They're better off not knowing."

"Cat—" Whatever the general had been about to say was cut off by a vicious roar, nowhere resembling sane, that split the night and had the winged Breeds reaching for their weapons.

"Go." Pushing the door open and diving out, she yelled the order to the driver. "Get them the hell out of here."

The winged Breed jumped into the driver's seat and was accelerating before Cat finished the order.

"Let's fly," she demanded, racing to Keenan.

The Eagle looked down at her with quiet contemplation as he shook his head.

"Better to face the beast here than to have him tracking us." He sighed. "Hopefully I'll still have some feathers attached when this is finished."

"No." She grabbed his arm, suddenly terrified as the roar sounded again, this time much closer. "I'll deal with him. Let's go."

"Fly, bastard!" Enraged, guttural, the demand came as a shadow bounded from the darkness, crouched, maddened rage gleaming in hammered gold eyes. "While you have feathers to do so."

Cat swung around to face . . . she wasn't even certain who he was. Whatever Graeme had become, it wasn't Gideon, and it wasn't the face he wore before the world now. He seemed taller, broader, so powerful it was frightening.

"Are you fucking insane?" She'd be damned if he was going to intimidate her or harm one of the few true friends she had.

The smile he gave her was frightening; the incisors gleaming with challenge were sharper, longer than before.

The look that accompanied it was one of such male satisfaction it made her claws emerge and flex in warning.

"I would imagine I am." The rumble of danger in his growl sent a chill racing down her spine. "Now, stand aside so I can convince your friends of it."

Her eyes narrowed. "Yes, they're friends, and you aren't touching them."

His roar shattered the night again. The only reason she didn't flinch was because she was too shocked by it. Shocked and well aware of the danger surrounding the winged Breeds now. If Keenan stood and fought as he intended to, then they might all die.

"They took you." This roar, and there was no other word for it, was filled with furious affront. "They called this free. They can deal with it."

"And how exactly did they call it free?" she snapped caustically.

She was scared to fucking death for Keenan and his men, but not herself. What Graeme had become was terrifying in the sheer power and primal force he displayed. But he was no threat to her. Unfortunately for him, the same couldn't be said of her.

"They took what was mine." He paced forward, his gaze locked on Keenan. "Come on, bird man. Come from behind the pretty girl."

"I'm not the crazy one," Keenan stated calmly. "I don't mind a bit letting her stand between us. I like my feathers."

Graeme sneered back at him. "Coward."

"'Sane' is more the word, I believe."

"You should have used that sanity and refused to fly her from me, then." The growl was mixed with such a wealth of frustration that it couldn't be missed.

As long as she stood between them, he wouldn't attack. At least not while she wasn't in danger. He'd have to calm down eventually, wouldn't he?

"I owe her, Bengal," Keenan stated then, his tone matter-of-fact. "More than I owe you. And as you're aware, my debt to you is large."

He owed her? It was the first time she'd ever known Keenan to outright lie. She didn't think he knew how.

He didn't owe her a damned thing. He'd come to her out of the darkness one night while she hunted and informed her that two Council Coyotes were sneaking up on her. He'd disappeared just as quickly.

She owed him.

But what did he owe Graeme?

"Repossession is in your future," Graeme snapped and though the rage still pulsed around him, it didn't seem as intense. "Count on it."

"That's when you'll get your fight." Keenan sighed heavily. "There is no repossession."

She was going to be asking questions, Cat decided, because she had no idea what the hell they were talking about.

"Graeme . . ." Suddenly, he was in front of her, his back to her, roaring out in challenge as he felt Keenan and his men moving to shield her between them, ready for battle.

From the shadows four figures emerged. Tall, dressed in warriors' leathers, as silent as death they moved toward them.

The Unknown.

"No. You'll not have her," Graeme warned, the monstrous sound of his voice terrifying once again.

Their gazes centered on her, finding her as she stared over Graeme's shoulder.

Faces painted, eyes gleaming darker than night, they moved forward slowly as even the breeze seemed to move with them. They were the earth, the darkness, the secrets of the land and the protectors of all its secrets.

Cat felt a sob fighting to escape her throat as electric pinpoints of energy began to whip through her body.

"Gideon!" She called out to him in fear as he whipped around and the winged Breeds moved back slowly, away from them, no longer defending, but heeding the sudden breeze pushing at them.

"No . . ." he snarled, catching her as Cat felt the strength leave her body.

She could feel herself being torn apart from the inside out. Her heart fought to beat, yet she could feel it slowing. The blood pounded in her head, trying to push through her veins, yet slowed. Terror sent adrenaline surging into her bloodstream, yet it had little effect.

The awakening. The prophecy said it would come with death. With her death.

She stared into her mate's eyes. Gideon, Graeme, whichever face he showed to the world, he was hers. His one drive for as long as she could remember had been her protection. Nothing, no one else had ever mattered but her. She'd always longed for a place to belong, but as she stared up at him, she realized she'd never had to fight for such a thing. She'd always belonged, because she had always been his life.

"I didn't know," she gasped, trying to hold on to him as an animal's scream of rage seemed to echo around her. "I didn't understand . . ."

Oh God, she couldn't breathe.

"I love you," she whispered, gasping, feeling her spirit being ripped from its mooring. "Hold me, G. Hold me . . ."

Darkness wrapped around her.

No. Not yet. She needed him one more time. She needed to tell him she was sorry for taking so long to understand. She needed to tear his ass for not telling her so many things. She needed to love him.

She didn't want to leave him.

But she was being taken. She could feel it, feel that all-encompassing weight coming over her, sucking the life from her and stealing her from all she had ever known . . .

Stealing her from the dream of holding the man she'd always known belonged to her. Heart and soul.

Her G.

Graeme stared into the sunlit landscape from the balcony of the bedroom, the heat of the day barely registering any more than the presence of those standing with him registered.

Jonas Wyatt, Rule Breaker and his brother, Lawe Justice. Lobo Reever and three of his Wolf Breed alphas and the one female, Cassie Sinclair. Where the hell Cassie had come from he hadn't even questioned. She'd been there, watching him sadly when he'd returned to the house, her face pale, tears standing in her eyes as he moved past her up to the bedroom.

Cat's bedroom.

The scent of her filled it, surrounded him. For hours he just sat on the bed, letting her scent seep into him, remind him of what he'd held. She smelled of summer in the mountains, high above the chaos of the world. That innocence and truth a man found only when confronted with the Earth as it should be. Natural. Free of artifice. That was his Cat.

They'd taken her from him and he'd been helpless . . . he, who commanded a creature unlike any he'd heard of, a primal base instinct that came alive to protect his mate, and he'd been helpless.

The winds had locked him in place, ignoring his roars, his struggles, and they'd taken her from his arms as he'd felt the life lifting from her. He'd screamed out to her, he'd begged her not to leave him.

And they had taken her.

The moment he'd lost sight of her the winds had released him, but there was no finding her. And the fight had just gone out of him. The monster had retreated, sulking in silence and waiting. Oh, it was waiting. His mate was taken, and the monster would have vengeance. Graeme would find them, he would tear apart every rock, every speck of dust in that desert and he'd find them, as soon as he could accept that they'd taken a lifeless Cat from his arms.

Lifeless.

He'd felt her spirit being torn from her body, torn from him. When he'd looked up he'd been alone. Even the winged Breeds had disappeared into the night, and he'd been left kneeling in the dust, silent, staring down at where Cat had been, unable to believe what he knew.

"We had no idea Keenan and his men were in the area," Jonas stated, his voice low as he stood braced by the railing of the balcony. "There wasn't so much as a whisper they were here."

"There were rumors they were hiding in South America again after hearing of surviving winged females," Rule interjected. "We sent messages to them, offering to help, but never heard anything back."

He would have helped them, Graeme thought. He had helped them. The technology they possessed to remain invisible to even Breed senses, he had given them. The armor in their leather clothing, he'd given them, just as he'd created the therapy that strengthened the muscles of their wings, allowing them to add more muscle to their bodies and still fly.

He'd helped them, yet they had taken her from him and allowed her life to be stolen.

His mate. His mate had been taken from his arms and he hadn't been able to do a damned thing to stop it.

He'd find them, those winged bastards, he'd kill Keenan. The others he'd make watch. He'd make that bastard scream for days before allowing him to die. Then one by one, he'd take out the Unknown and their leaders, the Six Chiefs. The Navajo spirit warriors did nothing without the chiefs knowing. And he'd start with Orrin Martinez. Old, weak, he wouldn't last long, but Gideon would leave the proof of the hell a Breed could bring when his mate was taken.

"Graeme . . ."

"I am Gideon," he stated softly in response when Jonas spoke. "I am retribution."

He heard a small sigh from Jonas.

"Our enforcers are searching for Orrin Martinez," Rule said. "Neither he nor the other chiefs have been found yet, but they will be."

He'd start with Lincoln Martinez, Graeme decided. When he made it to the Unknown, he'd go for Lincoln first. Claire's brother had been there. He'd been the one to take Cat from his arms, staring back at Graeme in regret.

"I'll bring her back," Lincoln had whispered. "Once the passing's complete, I'll bring her to you."

"Please . . ." he'd begged, unable to stop the warrior from taking her. "No . . ."

Still, Lincoln had taken her. Holding her gently in his arms, he'd walked away without looking back.

Blood.

He would take blood for this. The thirst for it was already building in his senses, the monster, cunning and brutal, plotting the best course of action. As soon as Graeme could make himself believe.

"Jonas, understand now I'll fight you if you try to pull Breed Law and take him," Lobo stated from where he stood at Graeme's side. "Our agreement gives me complete autonomy within my lands. Don't try it."

"Reever, if I'd wanted him, I'd have taken him when he and Rule were taking care of Rule's little problem months ago," Jonas snorted. "Don't insult me. I retaliate in ways you don't even want to experience."

Graeme had known Jonas was aware of who he was, Jonas just been unable to prove it.

"Then why the hell have you been pretending to hunt him down?" Lobo snapped. "The search you've conducted for him has drawn on every Genetics Council soldier, Breed and scientist in existence."

And that was exactly the point.

"That was our plan," Graeme stated absently. "We met after Amber's last dose of the therapy. I couldn't leave him and Rachel tormented with questions regarding her changes. Cat would have been angry with me if she learned Rachel was crying in fear for her child. Before that, we communicated often, though he rarely trusted my claims and refused to cooperate. Still, the intensity of the search was never what it was perceived to be."

He'd taken a risk and he'd known then he had. But the mother's tears had reminded him far too much of the tears Cat's mother had shed when talking about the loss of her daughter, Catarina.

His Cat.

Helena believed Cat had died in her arms at three days old from the genetic anomaly she'd been born with. And she still cried to speak of it.

"Son of a bitch, you two should have been twins," Rule cursed in disbelief. "One of these days, Jonas, your games will get you killed."

"Learn from it." Jonas didn't sound at all understanding. "If you want to take my place at some point, then you better learn how to do it."

Yes, Jonas was grooming Rule and several others. They were natural gamesmen, the Breeds Jonas was slowly attempting to bring into his world. Too slowly, Graeme had often mused.

He'd planned to help the director to teach his chosen directors how to manipulate the world around them and the information that came in. It would be incredibly easy for them once they pushed past their opinion of Jonas's machinations. That wouldn't happen now. There was simply no will to continue.

No will.

This was why he was not combing the desert for vengeance now. Why the monster had retreated into silence. There would be no vengeance because there was no will to fight. His Cat was gone.

"What was the point in all the deception, Jonas?" Lawe asked then. "The supposed search for an insane Breed you were conspiring with?"

But it wasn't Jonas who answered.

"Lines of communication between spies," Lobo answered for him. "Distracting the enemy into searching for what they thought Jonas was desperate to find while Jonas was slipping beneath the radar to acquire information himself. Identifying moles and rogues and those he could trust so he could begin strengthening Breed ties to communities, politics and infrastructures."

In a nutshell.

"If we're going to survive, we have to look past distaste for manipulations and games to ensure we strengthen the ties the Breeds have in the areas that will ensure we can't be wiped away easily," Jonas agreed. "Right now, our position is tenuous as hell. The world could turn against us as easily as they backed us. Unless we want to find ourselves hunted, then we have no choice but to be smarter, more cunning and deceptive than those who believe they created us. And the choices in doing so are limited."

To survive, those Breeds with the clarity to see beyond just survival had to make the hard choices. Graeme had once been one of those Breeds.

He couldn't be any longer. Without Cat, there was nothing to fight for.

There were a few loose ends to tie up, a call to make to Benjamin Foster to tell him good-bye. The man he'd called father would grieve, but Graeme could find no regret for it. The information he'd amassed since he was a child Graeme would have to pull together and ensure it went to the proper caretaker. Someone who would use it wisely. Jonas was the obvious answer, but Graeme had already chosen another whose strength and ability to see beyond games would serve the Breeds far more where such vast knowledge was concerned.

"Graeme?" Judd stepped to the balcony.

No, he wasn't Judd any longer. He was Cullen. Graeme hadn't expected his brother to arrive. The need to maintain the secrecy of his identity had been far too important.

"You shouldn't be here." Graeme sighed, wiping a hand across his face, shocked to feel the dampness there.

There was no way to hide who he was while standing at Graeme's side. They were twins, born of the same mother, split from the same egg, identical in nearly all things.

"Where else would I be?" Cullen asked, his voice weary. "My men are scouring the desert . . ."

"As one of the Unknown, you should know where they are," Rule snapped, the knowledge he possessed no longer deemed a secret. "Where are they, Cullen?"

"I'm not one of the true Unknown," Cullen informed the Breed, his voice tight. "I'm a member of their inner circle, called the Unknown, but not privy to their secrets, Rule. Especially this one. If I'd known, I'd have killed every one of them to stop it."

"Enough." Graeme turned his gaze back to the desert beyond. "It doesn't matter now."

Few things mattered.

Make the calls. Gather the information and make certain Cullen had everything in place to secure it properly. Then he would drift . . .

Something soft dropped into his lap. Looking down, he saw the tattered brown teddy bear he'd asked Khi for. Cat's teddy bear. He kept it in his workroom sitting at his desk. So many nights that one-eyed piece of stuffed cloth had kept the insanity from ripping his mind to shreds.

"She loved this damned teddy bear," he whispered as he reached out and touched one threadbare ear. "Cuddled it like it was a baby when she was little."

There was still the faintest trace of blood on it from when he'd killed a guard who was attempting to take it. He should have died for the transgression, but he'd been far too important to kill. Brandenmore had considered him the key to all the research he'd been conducting. The bastard had never known Graeme had already figured it all out. He'd let Brandenmore die a horrific death for the countless lives the bastard had taken needlessly.

"I shouldn't have taken it from her." He sighed, glancing up at Cullen. "I should have found a way to get both of you out when I escaped."

There had been no way to do it, though. He'd planned for years and hadn't been able to find a way to take even his Cat with him. And God knew he'd tried. Tried desperately.

"She's gone," he said softly, shaking his head as he rose tiredly from the chair. "Leave," he ordered all of them. "Just fucking leave."

He needed silence. He needed to lie in the bed he'd shared with her and wrap himself in her scent for just a little while and forget he'd failed her. Forget how he'd failed her.

"Graeme, Cat wouldn't want this for you," Khi whispered, her voice strangled, filled with tears. "She loved you. She wouldn't want you to give up."

"She's not here to make that decision," he snarled. "She's gone, Khi. They took her. She doesn't get to give her opinion."

"At least not until she's done kicking your ass."

Graeme swung around, blocking the doorway from the others as he stared into the room, certain he hadn't heard her. It couldn't be her.

Standing in the middle of her room, dressed as she'd been the night before in her snug black mission suit. It was dusty, smeared with a hint of mud and smelling of the earth wrapped in smoky secrets.

He could smell her as he never had. The mating scent was like a wildfire burning around her, calling to him, infusing him with such hungry lust he growled at the strength of it. That same dust streaked her face, layered her mussed hair as it strayed from the braid and lingered at the soft curve of her neck.

One hand was propped on her hip as she watched him with narrowed eyes, but, for all her bravado and challenge, the scent of her lust and the emotions roiling through her, he could sense exhaustion as well.

"About time. Come on, everyone, let's give them some peace." Cassie pushed past him with a gentle shove and strolled into the bedroom to grin at Cat. "I didn't know if he was going to drink someone's blood or put a bullet in his brain. Thankfully, he intended to wait to do either, so I thought we were safe waiting for you to return."

"You knew she wasn't dead?" Jonas sounded outraged, Graeme was certain he would be outraged as well, later.

"'Knew' is a rather strong word," Cassie informed them all. "She didn't feel dead, so I was hoping . . ."

Compassion vied with amusement as she left the bedroom, followed by the others, their expressions amazed as they kept their eyes on Cat for as long as possible.

"You were lucky, brother." Cullen stopped at his side, his hand pressing Graeme's back momentarily. "Don't fuck it up."

The grief in his brother's voice was subtle, reminding Graeme that Cullen had lost his wife several years before.

The door closed behind his brother seconds later, leaving Graeme to assure himself his mate was truly there.

"Cat?" he whispered, stepping closer, his throat tightening, emotion swamping him. "Baby? You're really here?"

She took the last steps to him, her hand reaching up to touch his face, her expression softening as the scent of love . . . it was love, wrapped around him.

"I love you, G." Tears fell from her eyes. "I'm going to kick your ass, I really am. But I want you to know, I love you so much. And I'm so sorry." A sob hitched her voice. "I'm so sorry."

She smelled of love. Indescribable, pure and invincible.

Love. He'd doubted love when she'd spoken of it, but in the many hours since he'd felt her die in his arms, he'd fully realized what he felt was love, but far more as well.

"'Sorry'?" he whispered, reaching out to touch her, to believe she was there, to prove to himself it wasn't some crazed hallucination brought on by his desperation to hold her, to touch her, once again. "Why should you be sorry, Cat?"

"For not understanding," she whispered, staring up at him with tear-filled eyes. "For not understanding your need to protect me, no matter the cost to yourself."

He shook his head, his hand lifting to touch her damp face, only to realize his hand was shaking, his fingers trembling so desperately he couldn't still them. And he had to touch her. Her lips, parted for him, soft as silk and so very tempting.

"We'll talk later." Later. He had to kiss her, had to hold her, show her his love for her. "Talk later."

Swiftly lowering his head his lips covered hers, his swollen, aching tongue piercing her lips to sweep inside.

The taste of honey, sweet, innocent and filled with life, met his kiss. The taste exploded through his senses, through his soul. The mating hormone, once barely present in her system exploded against his taste buds and filled his senses now like a spark exploding into a brilliant, consuming flame burning through his senses.

She lived, here in his arms, his heart, the soul of who and what he was, and nothing else mattered.

She lived.

The pleasure was stronger, hotter. The taste of spicy heat in his kiss sank into her senses with such power that she couldn't get enough, couldn't sate the overwhelming need for that taste spilling to her senses.

His tongue rubbed against hers, teased her into closing her lips on it and drawing the rich potency from the glands beneath his tongue. Then he'd draw back, tempting her tongue to follow his to allow him to do the same. The passionate duel became a dance of give and take as they tore the clothes from each other's body, determined to meet skin to skin.

Bootlaces were shredded, the leather kicked aside. Sharp claws ripped the formfitting black pants from her hips as Cat's claws snapped the band of the denim covering his before tearing the material down the legs, allowing him to kick free of them. Shirts were nothing but strips of material littering the floor, in no way resembling what they once were.

Naked, bodies burning, adrenaline infused with mating hormones, far too powerful now to deny the bond hidden by forces out of their control for so long that the hunger for it overrode any finesse or thought of foreplay.

Cupping her rear with clawed fingers Graeme lifted her to him, feeling her thighs lift to his hips, the slickness of her juices spilling from her, meeting the head of his cock as he pushed past silken folds to thrust inside the brutal ache centered in her vagina.

"G, oh God, it's so good," she cried out, claws pricking the tough skin of his shoulders as her lips buried at his neck as he thrust again, harder, going deeper as sharp ecstasy echoed through her senses with each penetration inside her sheath.

Each savage thrust buried him further inside her, parting flesh clamped with fierce determination to hold on to each inch forcing its way inside her. The instinctive female Breed response to her mate ensured the male battled for possession, while the ecstatic pain of each thrust heightened her pleasure as well as her mate's.

The savagery of their possession of each other might shock them later, for now, each pushed for supremacy, Breed genetics fueling a sensual, sexual battle ensuring the mating to the very depths of their souls. Nothing worth having came without a battle of determined forces pushing in opposition, and that primal instinct was such a part of Breed mating that each day became an adventure in both the sensual as well as the bonding of all they were.

A snarl left Graeme's chest as she fought each thrust, inner muscles clamping on his erection even as ultraslick fiery heat spilled from the depths of her vagina and the desperate need to have him filling her only tightened her channel further. The pleasure was indescribable. A lash of pleasure-pain with each thrust that dragged a cry from her throat, spilled more of her slick juices and only intensified the ache.

"Mine." His snarl was the only warning she had before she felt him retreat, lifting her and turning her before pushing her to her knees on the bed and mounting her with dominant strength. Pushing her shoulders to the bed with one hand while holding her hips in place with the other he thrust into her from behind, pushing deeper with each impaling drive of his hips until he was buried to the hilt and moving with furious strokes that ensured her inability to tighten the grip of those intimate muscles fully.

Spreading her thighs further apart with his knees Graeme came over her, his teeth locking in the delicate flesh between neck and shoulder, biting just hard enough to send flash-fire sensations erupting from the spot his teeth gripped her flesh to merge with the fiery brilliance of sensation exploding through her senses with each thrust of his cock into her body.

The ecstatic slash of pleasure and pain whipping through her body tightened the spiraling sensations building through her senses. She was overwhelmed with the desperation for more, for harder, deeper, for the blinding chaotic ride to that point where their souls merged in explosion of pure rapture and melding ecstasy.

The feel of his erection thrusting savagely inside her, burying to the hilt with each stroke, burning past nerve endings so sensitive to each touch that it only fueled that wildfire burning out of control inside her, only pushed her higher, faster. She was flying on the savage pleasure, female growls matching the male snarls of extreme pleasure vibrating against her back until her claws were shredding the sheets beneath her, her hips churning beneath him. A rush of sensation stormed through her body, pulsing through her swollen clit and the desperate grip flexing around each intrusion. It flamed through her mind, exploded through her senses and detonated in the depths of the center of her body with a power and ecstasy so powerful and savage she felt herself thrown into the blinding, fiery heat of release.

Immediately her muscles clamped on the erection burying full length inside her, rippling over it, sucking at it as he stiffened behind her and exploded with a low, drawn-out snarl of intense, male pleasure.

In that second, their senses collided once again, opening to each other, a part of each other, intensifying each surging wave of blinding sensation until they were locked in each other's souls. The barb located beneath the wide crest of his cock became erect, extending into the hidden, nerve-rich area just beneath her clit. The pressure of the throbbing extension spilling its own release exploded in the swollen bud, sending another violent wave of pleasure shuddering through her body as animal instincts surged closer to those of the male behind her, locking them inside each other's soul for an eternal heartbeat of time. They felt the other's unconditioned love, the fierceness of each other's needs, his to protect her, hers to fight beside him. They felt the acceptance of strengths, of weaknesses, and knew the battles they'd face. They each felt the eternal bonds of love that ignited Mating Heat and fueled the pleasure as well as the primitive responses it caused.

In the blinding seconds of release, they were so much a part of each other that there was no hiding, no covering each facet of who and what they were as well as the vision each had of the other. The beauty of the world they found for those fragile seconds within the soul of the other erased past hurts, secrets and fears.

If death came tomorrow, one wouldn't go without the other. There was no existing without a chance to find such beauty again. No existing without the love, shelter and peace they found in finding each other.

As the last pulse of brutal pleasure shuddered through their senses and that moment in time passed, they collapsed against the bed, exhaustion swamping them and pulling them into a sleep so deep, so filled with healing comfort that the scars of the past, of nightmares and fears slowly began to ease.

As they slept, the monster that had awakened years before to protect the mate eased from sleep and kept watch. Ever vigilant, ever searching for enemies, cunning and far too primal to ever exist alone, it ensured survival by ensuring the safety of the mate.

The boy might not have known what he held when Brandenmore gave him the babe, the animal may not have sensed it, but the instinct that created the monster had known, just as it had known that the babe's survival depended on ensuring all the facets of what made the Breed Gideon, became one hardened being rather than human and animal struggling for balance. It melded the two, infused them with the savagery of its primal strength and ensured the babe would live, mature, and become a mate strong enough to soothe the often volatile strength and intelligence of the breed whose soul she would possess.

The monster had known, just as it had known other monsters existed as well. Some slept, some waited, a few battled, but all existed for one purpose: the mate it was sworn to protect.

· C H A P T E R   2 3 ·

Cat came awake slowly, her lashes lifting as she turned her head to stare at the mate sleeping next to her. He slept, deep, but a part of him never slept, she knew that, had sensed it before with a vague trepidation, and accepted it now with thankfulness. Whatever that primal, fiercely intelligent part of Graeme that existed actually was, she wasn't certain. But she knew without a doubt that it would ensure Graeme's survival, as well as her own.

As Graeme slept deep beside her, that part of him was intensely vigilant, focused on her for the moment, watching, waiting to see her response to the primal awareness she now sensed.

When she did nothing more than allow a small smile to tip her lips as recognizing what she was certain Graeme was unaware of it, she could almost feel the focus shift from her to ensure once again that no threats were present.

Perhaps it was an instinct all breeds had to some point. That extra sensory perception that awakened them when danger neared, or warned them of danger. The subconscious, though in Graeme it seemed highly adept.

Whatever it was, monster as he called it, instinct as she thought of it, it had come awake with a vengeance at a time when Graeme would have certainly died otherwise.

That thought sobered her and reminded her of the past night and events that were still far too hazy in her mind while other sensations and knowledge were finally clear.

She'd fought, she'd endured another woman's life, endured the unquenched need for freedom for this, for the need to hold the man, the Breed she knew she belonged to. The one she knew belonged to her.

That moment of realization had come at the very second she'd felt her spirit being torn from her body, in that striking heartbeat between life and death. Drifting, alone, aware and yet disconnected, Cat had seen her life, her past in such vivid detail. Even her photographic memory couldn't have processed the information her soul had stored and released in that blinding moment.

The moments of connection with Graeme, those seconds where the animal senses they possessed met and merged, she'd blocked all she'd seen inside him, all she could have known about the Breed she loved with her entire being.

He hadn't deliberately marked her as his mate, he'd marked her with Bengal DNA because of the unique strength and wildness of both body and spirit that those creatures possessed. DNA he'd believed was superior to any other and better fitted to ensure her life.

She saw the moment Brandenmore laid her in the arms of the boy Graeme had been, felt the spirit of the creature known as Gideon fighting for freedom, enraged with the confinement he endured. There was nothing to fight for, no chance of escape or of life within the cages he'd known all his life. Until a four-day-old infant was placed in his arms. The animal inside him stilled, the savage impulses quieting and pure cunning overtook him.

Brandenmore had given the young creature he subconsciously feared the key to destroying him. The child the animal inside him recognized as intrinsic to his survival. There was no thought of mating, no sexual impulses, just a knowledge that she was his now and she was too helpless, too sick and frail to fight for herself. The savage nature, the monster strengthening inside him knew she had to live though. For the boy to live, the child must live.

Cunning intelligence, far more advanced than even his creator guessed, became stealthy, manipulative and deceitful. The emerging creature he called his monster stepped back and allowed the human and animal to meld completely within his senses and the intelligence he possessed only multiplied, amplified.

The creature Dr. Foster had envisioned had far surpassed his dreams, she realized. At any time after that moment Gideon could have escaped. He could have slipped from the research center and disappeared entirely, but to do so, he would have had to leave Cat behind. His brother was strong enough to follow him, but his Cat wasn't. And later, once Bennett arrived and sensed the threat the Bengal alpha could be, he ensured there was no way Gideon could escape without the chance of weapons discharging. Graeme had refused to chance Cat's survival in a firefight.

Once he'd managed her release and escape, she and Judd had forced the transfusion to save him, to ensure a survival that would have occurred far more slowly, possibly ensuring his recapture much quicker, his animal senses as well as human responses rioted. The mating hormone had already been found in her system, though not in Graeme's despite the tests that affirmed their match. Once her blood met his though, Dr. Foster had feared it would take hold of Graeme and create needs and desires Cat was far too young to face, and Graeme was far too honorable to tolerate. It would destroy him.

Repulsed by such visions of what his future could be he'd lashed out at her, intending to make her hate him, to drive her from him and ensure she never came searching for him, never tempted what he feared could happen until he returned to her once she'd reached an age he believed allowed her the maturity to deal with it.

He'd wanted her to have a life first. To be free. That need he'd had for her had been clear, so much a part of him she wondered how she could have not sensed it before that moment her soul had met his.

Through the years after she'd escaped to New Mexico, believing she was living that life of freedom, Graeme had begun a game of such masterful cunning that it amazed her. His animal instincts, the mating hormone in his system, and the animal's push to find Cat when Graeme still felt she was too young had distracted him at a time when the soldiers the Genetics Council had sent out for the research center, were too close though.

That recapture, what she felt and saw with the knowledge she'd blocked from those moments she'd been a part of him, showed her the Breed she'd refused to see. He'd endured death, three times. Surviving Bennett's cruelty would have been impossible if the monster he harbored inside him hadn't pushed forward with superhuman strength. That will to live, to survive and to ensure *her* safety and survival had been all that saved him. And it had remained contained until the research scientist had ordered a renewed search for the woman possessing the hormonal influences he believed were the key to Gideon's ability to survive each of the living dissections.

In that moment, Gideon had ceased to exist. The monster had surged forward, overtaking him, filling him with the strength, the ability to heal, to hunt, to kill, unlike anything man or beast had ever known.

His life after that moment was hazy, even to him. Years of cunning intelligence and instinctive calculation was all he remembered. The strength of the hold the monster had on him had been brutally determined to see to an ultimate goal. Ensuring Cat's safety. He'd collected debts for Gideon to eventually cash on. He'd searched out those Breeds and humans he sensed would mark her world and ensured they owed the Bengal in ways that ensured he would never be revealed to those that could be a danger.

Years of blood, savagery, plotting and the execution of goals that reached years into a future he'd instinctively sensed would evolve. He'd lived, a prison himself of such primal instinct that who and what he was became all but obliterated. Until she sent the email begging him to come to her. And he had come to her as she slept. Kneeling at her bed, the stripes easing, the savage neon amber of his eyes becoming a wild green once again, the pupils returning, the whites of his eyes once more present. Only in that moment had Gideon returned.

Thirteen years of hell that they'd both endured to bring them to that moment. To the second her eyes had opened, the animal she kept caged within her rising as she slept to stare up at him, to lift claw-tipped fingers to touch his face, a little purr rumbling in her chest.

"I'm scared, G," she whispered, her voice trembling and filled with pain.

Even she hadn't realized the fears that haunted her until she felt them, smelled them through his memories.

"I'm here, my little cat," he whispered to her. "Be strong for me, just a little while longer. Hold on for me.

Because he'd known what she hadn't. The animal's rage at Claire's presence and the inability to meld both human and animal senses completely without destroying the spirit that protected Cat's identity.

He'd known the battle being waged inside her spirit, one even she hadn't sensed.

"Hold on for me . . ." His hand lifted to hold her palm to his face, then to his lips as he pressed a kiss to it. "As I've held on for you."

"Hurry, G," she'd ordered, her expression tightening stubbornly. "I'm tired of waiting for you. Do it, now."

And he'd smiled. "You'll be angry with me."

"That never stopped you before. Wait much longer and I'll give up on you. I'm giving up on you, G. I'm giving up . . ." As her eyes had closed once again the monster had surged forward, amber filling his eyes, a growl rumbling in his chest.

He'd be damned if she would give up. She wanted him to hurry, she'd demanded he hurry, she could accept the consequences later.

Except she hadn't accepted them. She'd fought him, raged at him, nearly hated him for not revealing truths that he feared would over-shadow love with pity. He would have her love, he would have the mate he'd sensed the night he knelt by her bed, realizing in one blinding second what Cat had always known. She belonged to him, totally. His life, his heart, his mate.

And once again, her determination to have him in her life had dis-tracted him from other goals. This time, plans he'd had to ensure not just her future safety, but her happiness. She clearly saw how he planned to bring her parents back into her life in a way that would ensure Cat didn't suffer any doubts on her parents' part. He'd wanted to wait, to tell her of those years he was lost inside the monster. He'd wanted to do it at a time that she was secure in her love for him, at a time when pity wouldn't influence her emotions.

He'd wanted everything safe and secure for her, no matter the cost to himself.

"Sometimes, you see too much," he murmured at her side, eyes still closed, though his voice was resigned. "Stop thinking so hard, Cat, you'll give yourself a headache. Then you'll give me a headache."

She gazed at him thoughtfully for long moments.

"How long have you been able to read my thoughts, Graeme?" she asked softly, reminding herself to kick his ass.

One eye opened, peered at her for a moment with male irritation then closed once more.

"Not long," he finally sighed. "The night you were injected with that paralytic you were in so much pain it was easier to read you. The Breed mind is far harder to sense than a human mind, and even with humans, some of their blocks are incredibly strong."

"But you're reading me now," she pointed out suspiciously.

He grunted at that. "It doesn't work like that, sweetheart. The telepathy is more a highly developed impression. I can sense you saw far more than I'm comfortable with during the mating. I knew when I felt that merging you would know me, inside and out. And I've always known when you're thinking too hard. My head tightens in warning." The amusement in his voice earned him a moment's glare.

"That's not nice, Graeme," she sighed. "I was really looking forward to kicking your ass for hiding so many things from me. Now I can't, because you were right, throwing any of that information at me would have been too much considering everything else I was dealing with."

"Separating you from Orrin and Terran and the cousins was the hardest part," he said regretfully. "You love them, and they love you, separate from Claire. Claire drew strength from them."

She swallowed tightly at the mention of Claire.

"She's gone," she whispered then, feeling his arms surround her as he pulled her tighter against his chest. "Completely gone."

His hand stroked over her hair as his lips pressed against her forehead. "I'm sorry, sweetheart." And that sorrow was there in his voice.

Cat sat up slowly, feeling him follow her, the power he carried so effortlessly reaching out to her.

"What happened, Cat?" he finally asked as his arms pulled her to him once again, holding her close. "I felt you die." The agony of that sensation filled his voice. "I felt it. How are you here now?"

Cat swallowed tightly before pushing away from him enough to turn to him, to allow him to hold her gaze. "I don't know." And she didn't.

Frowning, she fought to remember more than the vague impressions she'd awakened with.

"I felt my spirit leave my body, but I wasn't dead." She shook her head, shaking her head tightly. "Claire didn't want to go, she was certain it wasn't time. It was like being half asleep, not certain if you're dreaming or not, words didn't penetrate wherever I went, just the certainty after a while that everything was going to be okay. When I woke, I was in a sweat lodge similar to the one where the first ritual was performed when I was twelve. Orrin and Terran were there, and Honor." Her eyes widened. "Honor was there and it was just Honor. Liza wasn't part of her any longer. Four of the Unknown helped us up and led us to another building, where we were given water and some kind of soup they said would help us regain our strength."

"I don't believe I can see Terran, Orrin or Lincoln without killing them," he warned her gently. "Forgiveness will be a long time coming, Cat."

"Orrin said you would feel that way." She nodded, still fighting the fog that filled those memories. "I felt something else there, Graeme." She stared back at him, that sense of knowledge so strong she grew frustrated with her inability to remember. "I don't know what it was, but something else was there."

"Cat, whatever it was, it will come to you once your senses have worked it out," he promised her. "You've spent too many years with your Breed senses trapped in a way, unable to fully stretch out and learn to process information correctly that it will take time for them to strengthen. Once they do, those impressions will strengthen."

Maybe he was right. Settling closer against his chest, one hand over his heart, she forced herself to let the inability to remember what had happened ease.

"There's so many things to talk about, and so much I want to do," she said then. "Honor's parents will be facing Jonas and Rule, most likely today. But Honor was desperate to contact Stygian and then her parents." The question of her own parents she held back, uncertain what to say.

"Helena and Kenneth are scheduled to arrive in Window Rock next week," he told her, holding her in place when she would have turned to face him once again. "Dr. Foster has been in hiding as well since he left the research center, just before Bennett arrived. But he went to the Graymores, your parents, because they were familiar with him when you were born, and he's explained what happened and why it was necessary to hide you. They're very anxious to see the daughter they never forgot."

Her parents. She was suddenly so frightened of seeing them that she instantly rejected a meeting so soon.

"We should wait . . ."

His arms tightened around her. "Cat, they love you. They will see nothing but beauty and light when they see you, because it shines from you like an inner flame. Never doubt that."

She doubted it, highly. But she knew Graeme. He'd made the meeting, it would take more than her objections to sway him now.

"Let them love you, Cat," he whispered then, turning her to face him, staring at her with wild green eyes and such love it immediately warmed every part of her. "No one can love you as deeply as I do, nor belong to you in the ways I belong to you, but parents center a female, even I know that. It's a center no man or mate can give to his woman when she's loved by those who gave her birth. Let yourself get to know them, to love them. They're good people, I promise you that."

Tears filled her eyes. "I should have trusted you more . . ."

Two hard fingers pressed to her lips as a rakish grin tilted his lips. "That goes without saying. I'll remind you of it in the future, I'm certain. Trust me now, Cat, you have nothing to fear in your parents. I promise you this. If you believe nothing else, believe in that."

"I believe in you," she whispered as his lips slid away and she let her lips touch his. "I always believed in you, G." Even when she wouldn't admit it to herself, she knew, she'd always believed in him, always loved him.

He was her G. Her love and her life. With him, all things were possible . . .

She had to remind herself of that, many times, a week later as she and Graeme flew into Window Rock, courtesy of the Bureau of Breed Affairs secured heli-jet.

Security was still a concern, as were the journalists as Raymond's tribunal hearing neared and news had been leaked that his daughter Claire Martinez had actually died years before, and a Breed female had been given her identity in a desperate act to save the escaped feline female. The Bureau's head of public relations had released the information along with Raymond's crimes and his many threats against Cat over the years to reveal her identity, culminating in his attempt to torture her before turning her over to the Genetics Council's Jackal team the night he was taken into custody.

The revelations had prompted a firestorm of media coverage and the renewed awareness of the atrocities still being inflicted on those Breeds rumored to still be held and experimented upon. The strengthened awareness of the Breed plight, weakened the arguments protesting groups waged against Breed freedoms and rights, with several new laws in Breed protections passing quickly by lawmakers eager to gain political points with what appeared to be a steadily growing movement still in favor of the mutated humans, as they were now being called.

The furor had been ignored by Cat in favor of Mating Heat and learning as much as possible about the parents she was about to meet.

Helena and Kenneth Graymore were strongly in favor of Breed awareness and rights. Kenneth, CEO and majority shareholder in a company deemed a family legacy spanning generations of Graymores, was not just a heavy contributor to the Breeds but also one of their biggest clients. The Breeds' reputation for providing reliable, loyal protection and security personnel was unsurpassed and highly depended upon in the Graymore businesses.

Helena Graymore had stepped into fighting for the rights of Breed children and the Breed community's refusal to subject the few offspring and living Breed children freed from the labs from further research or experiments labeled as evaluations. She'd recently taken her fight to Europe, where Breeds were denied visas to travel and forced to submit to "evaluations" periodically, which were rumored to be as invasive as the research done before they were freed from the labs.

In past years the growing tensions between America and its allies over America's laws of providing unquestioned Breed asylum had been growing slowly and stories of the steadily increasing cruelties in the evaluations were strengthening. Helena Graymore had even been accused of providing such Breeds safe transportation from those European countries and secreting them into America.

Those accusations were vehemently denied, but Graeme assured Cat they were indeed true.

Now landing atop the temporary offices of the Western Division of the Bureau of Breed Affairs, Cat had to tell herself once again, that Graeme knew what he was doing. Her parents couldn't help but love her, he'd sworn.

♦ ♦ ♦

She'd prayed that was true, because in learning she had parents, she already loved them. It would be devastating to learn she was a disappointment to them in any way.

♦ ♦ ♦

Kenneth Graymore wanted to pace the office that Director Breaker had shown him and his wife to. The richly appointed room was more of a large sitting room. A comfortable sofa and two wing-backed chairs sat facing a radiant fireplace that would give a real wood fire a run for its money in ambiance and warmth. To one side of the sitting area was a dark wood dining area and food-warming station. To the other side a pool table as well as several video game stations.

Soft, thick carpeting covered the area and heavy specially developed curtains one of the Graymore companies had produced to protect against electronic intrusion were pulled firmly over the large windows that looked out over the desert behind the third floor of the renovated warehouse.

Sitting with his wife on the sofa, his arm curled firmly around her shoulders he stared at the picture she held of the young woman they were about to meet.

Helena had cried and raged for weeks after Foster had come to them, a friend they had believed dead for over a decade, to tell them the story of the child they believed died and the experiments that ultimately saved her life and endangered it further.

She looked like her mother. Catarina and Helena could have been sisters, nearly twins, they looked so much alike. She was the mini-me Helena had laughingly called the baby before her birth. The horrifying truth that their pediatrician had known of the genetic defect their baby carried and hadn't treated it as it could have been treated in vitro, enraged him. That particular problem could be cured before birth if caught in time, but not after birth. To enable Phillip Brandenmore to acquire a child with such a problem and experiment upon it, the defect had been covered up in the fetal tests and hidden as though it hadn't been detected.

Dr. Foster hadn't hid the truth from them when he came to them. He'd given them the files, answered their questions directly and his own tears had fallen when Helena had collapsed into horrified cries at the knowledge of the pain their baby had suffered. Had it not been for the two Wolf Breed bodyguards that accompanied, one he claimed was his wife, Kenneth would have killed him with his bare hands.

Benjamin Foster hadn't been a friend, more an acquaintance, but he too had conspired with Brandenmore, albeit by force, but still, he'd never warned them or in any way tried to let them know their child was alive and suffering.

"She's all grown up," Helena whispered, not for the first time. "They changed her, Ken, made her a Breed. What if she doesn't like us now? What if she thinks we're weak?"

Their pride in her and her ability to survive knew no bounds. That baby that had stared at him so imploringly in those first days of her life, so weak and ill, in pain and looking to him to fix it, would have to fault him now for the horrors she'd faced. They had accepted the news that she had died. They had taken a lifeless babe whose face had been covered with a likeness of their own baby, and buried it as their own. They hadn't questioned it. They had trusted their doctors, trusted their own senses when their baby supposedly died in their arms.

"We love her anyway, Helena." He knew they did, they always would, no matter what she felt for them. The grief would be unbearable. The weight of it would be crushing, but they loved her, no matter what she might think of them.

"She's suffered so much," Helena said then, once again, not for the first time. "We didn't protect her. She would have to blame us for not protecting her." The sob that escaped her and the tears that fell down her face broke her heart.

"Helena, all we can do is love her," he repeated his answer, just as he had for the past week. "She's still our daughter, a part of us, and we love her more for her incredible strength and will to love. She has every right to blame *me*, protecting her was my responsibility, not yours. A daughter always loves her mother though. She'll love you, sweetheart. She won't be able to help herself." He kept his tone encouraging and confident, filled with that inner strength he knew she responded to. This woman was his rock, she always had been. Without her, he would be completely lost within the world.

How Catarina would feel about him, he wasn't so certain. She had every right to hate him, to blame him for not seeing the truth. There had to have been signs. Something he had missed that he should have seen, simply because she was she was his and Helena's child, a part of his heart and soul. When they had lost her a light that could never be replaced in their lives had been extinguished.

"Oh, Ken." Helena turned to his chest, one arm circling his waist to hold him closer. "None of this was your fault, and no one has the right to blame you. It's just been so long, and she doesn't know either of us, she believed she had no parents at all. And now she's so strong, a part of history in a way. I think I fear she won't see us worthy somehow. Won't see me worthy."

She was the most worthy person he knew besides their daughter.

"She's our daughter," he said softly. "With your compassion and pureness of heart, and I'm sure a bit of my pure bullheaded stubbornness. And she needs a mother, Helena. Every girl, no matter her age, needs her mother."

"And her father." The voice had them jumping to their feet and turning to the door, the pure sweetness of it, so reminiscent of her mother's, shocking them both.

"Catarina," Helena whispered, awed, so filled with hope and love.

"What of a father?" Catarina asked again as he held to the hand of the Breed that had arranged the meeting. "Don't they need their fathers as well?"

His throat was tight was joy, with tears, fury against the forces that took her and amazement that she stood before them now.

He cleared his throat, fighting to make it work.

"I don't know," he said, his tone hoarse, sounding almost broken. "But fathers need their little girls, no matter their age. No matter the years that separate them. We need our daughter," he affirmed then. "They took the light when they stole you. We need it back, baby." His voice broke, choked, and a single tear slipped past his control. "We need you back."

◆　　◆　　◆

They needed her. Not wanted her. Not just accepted her.

They needed her.

She took the first step toward them and they rushed to her. The scent and feel of their love surrounded her, behind her the awareness of her mate and their bond strengthened her.

She had always belonged, she just hadn't realized it. And now she belonged as she'd never imagined possible.

Catarina Graymore, Breed, mate, daughter.

Loved . . .

And complete.

+   +   +

Beyond the meeting room Cullen Maverick stood behind the open door, propped against the wall, arms crossed, his gaze on the abstract pattern of the composite cement floor.

He was a Bengal Breed, but he couldn't smell the emotions and bonds, connections and fears that he knew would be drifting from the room. He couldn't touch the earth and connect to it, feel its warnings and sense it moods as other Breeds. He was in the dark where the gifts and talents of his race were concerned. He hadn't even been able to mate the woman he'd loved to save her from the illness that decimated her body.

As a Breed, he was a failure. Recessed where the Breeds inner gifts were concerned.

He was as strong as any Breed, as intelligent, though in different areas, as Gideon, or Graeme, he reminded himself. Dr. Foster hadn't expected twins from the embryo he'd mutated with animal genetics and select human DNA. He'd definitely not expected a defective Breed. He was probably lucky they hadn't killed him at birth as they did others.

He was still alive though, and still defective despite Graeme's mocking references to his stubbornness in keeping the Tiger restrained. His genetics weren't restrained. They were simply too weak to do him much good. Definitely too weak to have done his wife much good.

"You're pensive again," Graeme murmured as he stepped from the room, no doubt to give his mate a few moments alone with her parents. "Blaming yourself again, Cullen?"

The somber question had his head lifting. For one, Graeme wasn't being mocking where his brother's recessed abilities were concerned.

Cullen simply stared back at him, refusing to answer.

"You won't believe me." Graeme sighed then. "But she wasn't your mate. When you find your mate the stranglehold you have on your abilities won't be able to hold them in check any longer."

Cullen stared back at his brother as he let a mocking smile tilt his lips. "Want to know how I know you're wrong?" he asked Graeme.

"How?" his brother asked softly.

"Because when she died, I would have died with her if I could. If I hadn't sworn to watch after Cat and Honor, if you had done your fucking part and stepped up instead of spilling blood across a dozen nations, I would have joined her. That, brother," he sneered, "is how I know you're wrong. She was my mate, and I couldn't save her. There's no stubbornness on the face of this earth that would have kept me from doing that if it were possible."

Rather than arguing with his far too superior, arrogant brother, he straightened and stalked through the rows of desks and Breeds manning them to the elevator that led to the main floor and the exit he sought. He had work to do, cases to finish. Just because he had no life outside his work didn't mean others didn't.

Watching him leave, Graeme let a satisfied smile curl his lips.

"Why do you think I didn't let you know I was near, brother?" he murmured beneath his breath, regret and knowledge filling the heavy sigh he let free. "Stubborn fucking Breed. Looks like big brother's going to have to fix it for you."

That was okay though, he thought in satisfaction. Big brother was going to like interfering in the little brother's life. He all but rubbed his hands together in glee. This was going to be fun. Then an odd thought crossed his mind, bringing a frown instead as he turned and shot his mate a curious look. He couldn't hide his machinations from her, she'd really kick his ass if he did. But he wasn't one hundred percent certain she would go along with it.

He grinned and turned from her quickly. He'd convince her. She was convincible. He just had to explain it the right way, use the right words, so to speak.

Oh yeah, this was going to be fun.

✦ B R E E D T E R Ⅲ S ✦

Breeds: Creatures of genetic engineering both before and after conception, with the genetics of the predators of the Earth such as the lion, tiger, wolf, coyote and even the eagle added to the human sperm and ova. They were created to become a super army and the new lab rats for scientific experimentation.

The Genetics Council: A group of twelve shadowy figures who funded the labs and research into bioengineering and genetic mutation to create a living being of both human and animal DNA, though references to the Genetics Council also refer to affiliated political, military and Breed individuals and groups.

Rogue Breeds: Breeds who have declared no known loyalties and exist as mercenaries following the highest bidder.

Council Breeds: Breeds whose loyalties are still with the scientists and soldiers who created and trained them. Unwilling or unable for whatever reason to break the conditioning instilled in them from birth. Mostly Coyote Breeds whose human genetics are far more dominant than in most Breeds.

Council Soldiers: Mostly human, though sometimes Breeds, soldiers who willingly give their loyalty to the Council because of their ideals or belief in the project and their belief that Breeds lack true humanity.

Bureau of Breed Affairs: Created to oversee the growing Breed population and to ensure that the mandates of Breed Law are fully upheld by law enforcement agencies, the courts and the Breed communities. The Bureau oversees all funds that are paid by the United States as well as other countries whose political leaders were involved with the Genetics Council or any labs in their countries. They also investigate species discrimination and hate crimes against Breeds and track down scientists, trainers and lab directors who have escaped Breed justice.

Director of the Bureau of Breed Affairs: The position has been held for the past ten years by Jonas Wyatt, a conniving, calculating and manipulating Lion Breed who ensures that Breed Law is upheld and all Breeds given a chance to be free to find mates who will ensure future generations of the Breed species.

Breed Ruling Cabinet: Composed of an equal number of feline, Wolf and Coyote Breeds as well as human political leaders. It governs and enforces the mandates of Breed Law and oversees Breed Law where the separate Breed communities are concerned.

Purists and Supremacists and Their Various Groups: Groups of individuals who for reasons of religion, fear or just personal feelings believe that the Breeds are not human, but no more than puppets created in man's image. They're determined to destroy first the Breeds' public standing, then their lives. They dream of a world where Breed genetics have no hope, no chance and no threat of ever infecting the human population.

Their species discrimination against the Breeds includes but is not confined to the following: capturing Breeds and Breed-mated couples for further scientific study of how to weaken them or create a drug that will prevent the conception of hybrid children; guerrilla attacks against Breeds and Breed facilities; public outcries and protests against Breeds, Breed-funded and -hosted events and/or charities; bombings of Breed offices, attempts to kill key Breed political figures and general harassment whenever possible.

Nano-nit: A tiny microscopic robotic device that can be attached to a video or audio bug. Once in the proper location, it can be activated remotely, when it then detaches and finds the closest electrical source, where it will burrow inside and then follow the current to a designated electrical impulse for cameras, computers, televisions or any audio/video or computerized component, and then begins uploading specifically programmed information. Once the internal hard drive is filled, the nit then detaches and follows the electrical currents once again, to a point away from the original location, where it then finds a device, any device capable of Internet or uploading capabilities, and then transmits the information to a location that cannot be determined unless the nit is found during the upload process, after initial activation.

Named a nano-nit because of its size and similarity to the parasitic louse egg, or nit.

There is no known security to detect a nit specifically, and once activated, it's impossible to find, detect or exterminate. To find out, the host device must first be detected, then placed in a static-free, airtight shell, where a nit reader is plugged into the host device. The nit is then activated and makes its way from the host to search for an electrical source. It moves then to the nit reader's signature using the attached nit cord, which is an open-ended electrical cord that simulates the source the nit requires. Once there, a tiny probe locks the nit in place, allowing the reader to decode the programming and determine its original commands.

Nits have very little encryption. Because of their size and the requirements for upload space, programming is confined to what to upload and where to dump.

Because of their specific technology, a host device can be only an audio or video transmitter or bug. The nit is unable to function independently when attached to any other device.

Mating Heat: A chemical, biological, pheromonal reaction between a Breed and the male or female Breed or human that nature and emotion have selected as their one mate. Believed to be able to only mate once—though as Breed scientists have noted concerning other anomalies within the Breeds, nature is playing with the rules of the Breed species. To this point, general information on Mating Heat has been contained. Tabloids and gossip columns write about it, but no proof has been found to verify the rumor of it. Yet.

Mating Heat Symptoms: (Breed) A swelling of the small glands beneath the tongue and a taste, often different from Breed to Breed, that could be spicy, sweet or a combination of both. Heightened arousal. The need to touch and be touched by the mate often. A heightened need for sex that results in a sensitivity to each touch and release that heightens the pleasure as well.

(Mate) An almost addictive need for the taste of the mating hormone secreted from the glands beneath the Breed's tongue. A sensitivity along the body and heightened need for sex that can become extremely painful for the female, whether human or Breed. Heightened emotions, an inability to refrain from touching or needing to be touched by the other.

Desert Dragoon: A vehicle built with independent suspension to traverse the rough, rocky and often uneven terrains of the desert. Built wide, for power rather than speed, blocky and capable of ramming through obstacles and carrying mounted weapons. Equipped with stealth technology, real-time GPS, satellite communications and laser- and bullet-resistant force fields that operate for short periods of time and act as theft deterrents.

Breed Ruling Cabinet: A cabinet of six high-ranking Breeds of each species and six humans of prominence and/or power that makes decisions for the Breed community as a whole.

Breed Law: The laws that govern every legal, contractual, criminal or enterprise endeavor involving any Breed or Breed affiliate, including but not limited to wives, children, siblings, parents, lovers, intended spouses or the same of mates involved, and how the various governments of participating countries must deal with them.

Law of Self-Warrant: Any Breed can, one time only, accept punishment or death for any criminal act that would cause their mate, child, parent or other associated relative to face a punishment the Breed believes would cause his mate or child more harm than the loss of the Breed would cause.

Hybrid/Breed Hybrid: A child concieved naturally of a mated couple or of a Breed-human couple, whether mated or through artificial insemination.